Cheers f

American Idle

"Laugh-out-loud funny with characters that will win your heart!"
—*New York Times* bestselling author Suzanne Brockmann

"Even more fun and much smarter than reality TV . . . A hilarious, heartbreaking, and ultimately uplifting modern romance."
—*New York Times* bestselling author Susan Wiggs

"Turn off your TV and read this book! I laughed my way through *American Idle*—much more entertaining than any reality TV show."
—*Writers Unlimited*

"Well written, fast paced, hilarious . . . I was hooked from page one and couldn't get enough of the antics of Jules Vernon (oh, yes, she's heard all the jokes about this name) and the behind-the-scenes look into reality TV talent searches."
—*The Best Reviews*

"*American Idle* [is] simply fantastic . . . Alesia Holliday has my vote for Chick Lit Queen of the Year."
—*Affaire de Coeur*

"Humorous . . . It's hard not to feel a sense of kinship as [Jules] marvels at the confidence of inept contestants or shares her insights on the reality TV phenomenon . . . A zany debut."
—*Publishers Weekly*

Nice Girls Finish First

Alesia Holliday

B

BERKLEY SENSATION, NEW YORK

THE BERKLEY PUBLISHING GROUP
Published by the Penguin Group
Penguin Group (USA) Inc.
375 Hudson Street, New York, New York 10014, USA
Penguin Group (Canada), 90 Eglinton Avenue East, Suite 700, Toronto, Ontario M4P 2Y3, Canada
(a division of Pearson Penguin Canada Inc.)
Penguin Books Ltd., 80 Strand, London WC2R 0RL, England
Penguin Group Ireland, 25 St. Stephen's Green, Dublin 2, Ireland (a division of Penguin Books Ltd.)
Penguin Group (Australia), 250 Camberwell Road, Camberwell, Victoria 3124, Australia
(a division of Pearson Australia Group Pty. Ltd.)
Penguin Books India Pvt. Ltd., 11 Community Centre, Panchsheel Park, New Delhi—110 017, India
Penguin Group (NZ), Cnr. Airborne and Rosedale Roads, Albany, Auckland 1310, New Zealand
(a division of Pearson New Zealand Ltd.)
Penguin Books (South Africa) (Pty.) Ltd., 24 Sturdee Avenue, Rosebank, Johannesburg 2196, South Africa

Penguin Books Ltd., Registered Offices: 80 Strand, London WC2R 0RL, England

This book is an original publication of The Berkley Publishing Group.

NICE GIRLS FINISH FIRST

First edition: July 2005

Berkley Sensation trade paperback ISBN: 0-425-20405-7

This title has been registered with the Library of Congress.

PRINTED IN THE UNITED STATES OF AMERICA

10 9 8 7 6 5 4 3 2 1

As always, this book is for Judd, who loves me even when I'm not nice.

And for my readers, who send me lovely notes that keep me going through the "my brain is melting" moments. Please visit me at www.alesiaholliday.com and sign up for my private, members-only mailing list, and to find out the top 10 ways you know you're NOT a nice girl. Happy reading!

Acknowledgments

To the "nicest girl" in all of publishing, Cindy Hwang—*huge* thanks for believing in me and for your gracious understanding when children's illnesses and four hurricanes put me behind schedule. I'm so lucky to be working with you!

To my fabulous agent, Steve Axelrod, who took me to the real Mountain o' Meat restaurant, but I adore him anyway. (He's just that good!) Thank you for your calm in the face of my neuroses and for your wonderful sense of humor. Wolf in the box, Dude.

Enormous thanks to Leslie Gelbman; and also to Paola Soto and everyone on the Berkley sales, marketing, and publicity teams for their talent and enthusiasm.

Heather Higginbotham, wonderful friend and talented singer. Thank you for sharing the rich and fascinating world of opera with me. Any mistakes I've made (or creative license I've taken) in the translations are entirely my own.

Kate White, for her talk at RWA National, confirming my suspicions about nice girls.

Michelle Cunnah, thank you for critiquing in a whirlwind and for your gracious insights. My book is so much better for them.

Thanks to Lani Diane Rich for literarychicks.com and for your friendship and sanity; Beverly Brandt for support always, no matter what; Suzanne Brockmann and Ed Gaffney for being my wise mentors and reality checks; the Chick Lit Writers of the World for way too much to list here; Elizabeth Jennings for taking time to check my Italian (any mistakes are mine); Barbara Ferrer, for coffee dates and laughter; Marianne Mancusi, for friendship and enthusiasm; Gerald Smith for insights into the very funny world of monster trucks (pardon the exaggerations, Big Country); and Mary Brazeau, for answering my questions about the real Seattle Opera.

To Connor and Lauren—thanks for being proud of Mommy. I love you a thousand hundred percent.

And, always, to Judd. For everything.

1

Kirby

Posso presentarmi? (May I introduce myself?)

It's hard to meet nice guys when you sell sex toys for a living. Not that I actually sell them personally. I mean, I work for a company that sells them. I'm a vice president, even. But, still, guys are intimidated by this. They think I'm secretly comparing them to our product line: *Well, he's got better girth than the* Alexander the Great *model, but nothing beats the* StudMuffin SuperTurbo *for sheer staying power.*

Like I'd compare an actual guy to something that takes four triple-A batteries to operate.

Still, if they can get beyond the comparison problem, there's the Mother Factor. In other words, am I somebody they'd take home to meet their mother? So far, it's never happened.

Not even once.

It's not so much that I'd want to meet some guy's mother. I'm not sitting around wistfully perusing the pages of *Bride* magazine and taping episodes of *A Wedding Story* on TLC, then daydreaming about the Kirby Green and Insert-Groom's-Name-Here's wedding. I'm not interested in being stuffed into some man's definition of what a wife should be. I know all about the wife-as-doormat transformation. Hell, I *grew up* with a doormat.

Still, it would be nice to be asked. Not to get married. Just home to somebody's mom's for Sunday dinner.

Even once.

* * *

"Hey, Kirby, what's going on? Still practicing those Italian tapes? When's your vacation? Going to Rome? I always wanted to go to Italy. It's so romantic. Did you have a good New Year's?" Brianna the chatterbox, my new secretary, steps on the treadmill next to mine and shatters my reverie. Plus, does anybody have the right to be that gorgeous at seven a.m.? Brown eyes shining, glossy auburn curls bouncing. It's hard not to hate her. Or at least wish she'd joined a different gym.

I sigh. Loudly. And, no, she had *not* talked so much during her interview, or I never would have hired her. I needed somebody pretty quickly, though, after I fired the iron-jawed female warden type that I inherited when I took the job at Whips & Lace Manufacturing (new corporate motto: *Enhanced Pleasures with the One You Love*; the old one—*Your Pain Is Our Pleasure*—was way too S&M and one of the first things I changed when they hired me as marketing VP five months ago).

Old Iron Jaw was one of those people who think they're too good to work for—the horror!—a younger woman. She lasted almost a week with her little tricks of bringing coffee to everyone else in a meeting but me, ignoring my overflowing out-box, and all of her other stupid games designed to let me know *she* was really in charge. But I hit my limit when she said "that's not my job" about something.

It was the morning I'd been in the office since four a.m. trying to get a draft shareholder report ready for the board meeting; it proclaimed the brilliant success of our recent IPO (no color photos of vibrators or nipple clamps, though—there's only so much that corporate shareholders can take). I'd run sixteen sets of copies since six a.m., working my way through about a thousand copier jams, when Iron Jaw finally arrived at eight thirty. I asked her to bind the sets of materials as I double-checked the collating. She had the nerve to look me right in the eyes and tell me I had to wait until the copy dudes arrived at nine thirty.

You can bet your ass that she was history before nine. And—speaking of firing—I have an ugly morning in front of me.

I realize that Brianna is staring at me. "Oh, right. Yeah, my best friend, Jules, and I are leaving in thirty-one days for three glorious weeks in Italy. I can't wait." I've nearly finished my daily three miles; all those endorphins bombarding my brain must be causing my uncharacteristically chatty mood.

Brianna's steps slow on her treadmill, as she looks at me in astonishment. "Three whole weeks? I've never been on a vacation longer than a week. And I've never been out of the U.S."

She grins, and her face flushes a little. "Actually, I've never been out of Washington state, except for the time my girlfriends and I went to Las Vegas after graduation."

I look at her in disbelief. I know from her application that her only graduation was from high school, so she hasn't been out of the state of Washington for almost *seven years?*

"How can you not have been out of Washington for seven years? Don't you like to travel? Don't you feel trapped just staying in Seattle all your life?" Jules accuses me of not having a tact filter for my mouth, and she may have a tiny point, because Brianna raises her chin and glares at me. Or at least it started as a glare, but then faded away to a shaky smile. Suddenly I feel like somebody who would be mean to puppies. I really didn't mean for it to come out that baldly . . .

"I'm not trapped, and I didn't say I stay in Seattle. We go up to

Whidbey Island every summer for a week, and I visit my grand-parents in Spokane all the time. I've even hiked Mt. Rainier. So I'm not *trapped*."

She turns away from me and fiddles with the program on her treadmill. She's obviously not paying attention to what she's doing, because she just set it for the approximate difficulty of running up the side of Mt. Rainier with leg weights strapped to her ankles. I don't bother to mention it, as I step off my own machine. She'll fig-ure it out.

I'm her boss, not her buddy, anyway. I'm not a big fan of so-cializing with the staff. First you go to lunch, and then you chat over lattes or something. The next thing you know, they're telling their secretary friends that you slept your way up the corporate lad-der, and then they're calling in sick four times a week and expect-ing you to understand since you're their *friend*. Not that I'm the type to cry about being used by people I thought were my friends.

Not much, anyway. Not anymore.

Who needs more friends? I'm never going to be that gawky thirteen-year-old again.

I sling my towel around my neck and head for the shower. I'm glad this gym opened up in my office building, because it saves me the three-block hike to my old gym. I never exercised a day in my life until I turned thirty and gravity began its vicious attack. Isaac Newton only had to deal with *apples* falling, not his boobs and ass. Yuck. I'm only thirty-three and don't intend to look like I'm middle-aged.

Not even when I *am* middle-aged.

The way I see it, I work hard to afford all of the plastic surgery I might need. It's the Kirby Green retirement plan. It's not like my health insurance is going to cover an eyebrow lift in twenty years or so. A girl's gotta look to the future, right?

As I step into the shower, I try really, really hard not to wonder if I've convinced people that I'm as tough as I act.

When will I convince myself?

2

Brianna

Aria: Song for a single voice.

"Where does she keep them, Bree?"

I raised my dazed eyes from the hieroglyphics my boss, Kirby, tried to pass off for handwriting. I was trying to translate chicken scratch into the proposed marketing plan for the fourth quarter, and not having a lot of luck. Although I'm sure she tried her best. She's just so busy.

I blinked again and focused in on my best buddy at work, Jamie. "What? Where does who keep what?"

He grinned that evil grin that never failed to get him out of trouble, and never failed to get all the single women in Seattle out of their panties, at least if the stories about him were even half true. "Where does Kirby keep her flying monkeys?"

I jerked my head around to stare at Kirby's door, hoping that she hadn't heard his not-so-subtle reference to the Wicked Witch of the West. I didn't know if she had jurisdiction over the accounting department or not, but I didn't want him to get fired.

"Shhh, silly! Kirby's in her office, and she's in a foul mood. Do you want her to hear you?"

"Does he want me to hear what?" Kirby asked, popping her head over the side of my cubicle with her usual impeccable timing.

I closed my eyes briefly at the sound of her voice. Mama always said I was the peacemaker of the family, but even *I* had problems with my new boss sometimes. That job offer I'd turned down for secretary at the construction firm was looking better and better. But, *oh, nooo.* I'd wanted something *different.*

"Something exotic," I mumbled.

Kirby swung into my cubicle, looking like she'd just stepped out of *Vogue,* as always. She looked a little pale, though. She was gorgeous—kind of like Jennifer Garner, with all that long, silky dark hair, and those impossibly high cheekbones. All the guys in the office usually drooled whenever she was around. I personally wasn't all that far up there on the drool scale, sadly. Not even to my boyfriend. I mean, fiancé. Still getting used to that word, and the idea, too.

She riffled through her notes that I'd been trying to translate. "Exotic, how? And is your conversation work-related, or water-cooler gossip? Although, I should point out, we don't even have a watercooler. James, don't you have some beans to count or something? Brianna is a little busy here."

Jamie stuck his tongue out at the top of her bent head and then winked at me. "Yes, O Vice President Lady. Shuffling off now to accounting world. See you at lunch, Bree."

Kirby scribbled another note on the top of page five, slashing an arrow down to a paragraph that said something about demon camels.

Or maybe demographics.

With her writing, it was always a little hard to tell.

"Okay, that should be good to go. I really need the rough draft of that report within the hour, Brianna. Is there a problem?" She looked at me with that slightly impatient, slightly annoyed look that seemed to be her normal expression. It made me want to give her some cookies and juice and send her for a nap. Guess I've been hanging out with my nieces and nephews too much.

Of course, Kirby thinks I'm *trapped* in Seattle. So maybe she can get her own juice.

"No, no problem. Er, well, your writing is a little difficult for me. I mean, I'm sure it's me, not you. I mean, that I'm the one who has a problem reading it. I'm sure once I get used to it, I'll be able to read anything, no matter how terrible . . . Oh, *no*. Not terrible! Just . . . rushed. That's it! Rushed. I'm sure you were rushed when you wrote it, and I—"

Kirby narrowed her eyes at me. *Oh, oh.* "Actually, I wasn't rushed at all. If you can't read my writing, that's going to be a problem."

"No! I mean, yes, I can read your writing. It's just that I need a few words translated . . . um, did you give any thought to dictating your work with that new equipment I had Office Services send up?"

She gave me a look, but didn't respond, and I figured I'd better quit while I was ahead. Well, while I wasn't too far behind, actually. We spent a few minutes going through her notes together. "Demon camels" turned into "demographics," as I'd suspected, and "mosquitoes mating with rattlers" became "methods of market research." Once I had the key, I actually figured out most of the rest of it myself.

Kirby dropped the pages back down on my desk. "Is that it? Do you think you can finish it, now?"

"Yes, definitely. I'll have it to you as soon as I can." I was already facing the open file on my computer, breathing a silent sigh of relief.

"Fine. Except make 'as soon as I can' thirty minutes or less. And stop sighing."

So much for silent.

I closed my eyes again, briefly, and took a deep breath, then opened them to the sight of Kirby peering in at me over the top of my cubicle. "One more thing. That was good thinking, taking the initiative on that transcription equipment. Thank you."

As she disappeared into her office and shut the door, I slumped back in my chair, mouth hanging open.

Was that an actual compliment? It was! That was an honest-to-goodness compliment. Plus a thank you. I just knew she was a nice girl at heart.

I smiled, feeling for the first time all week like I might do okay in my new job.

Then Kirby's door crashed open. "Brianna! What the *hell* is this disaster?"

Maybe she's a nice girl way, way, way deep down in her heart.

* * *

I put my head down on my desk and tried not to think about the fact that it was only lunchtime, and I felt like I'd been at work for ten years. *Oh, right. Lunch.* I had to call Jamie and cancel. For some odd reason, I had no appetite. Kirby had been meeting with all of her marketing staff for the past hour, one by one, and they'd each come out of her office looking dazed. One woman had been crying, even.

The phone rang as I reached for it. Outside line, though.

"Kirby Green's office, may I help you?"

"Bree, is that you? You sound funny. It's that psycho boss of yours, isn't it? Did she upset you? Do I need to come have a talk with her?"

I sighed. "Hi, Lyle. I'm fine. And, no. Do I ever offer to 'have a talk' with your boss? I'm a big girl, remember?"

Lyle and I had been dating for almost two years, but he still didn't quite get that I liked to solve my own problems. I'm twenty-five years old, and he gave me a teddy bear for my birthday last year. I kinda try not to worry about how mature he thinks I am.

"You don't have to get touchy. I know you're all grown up. I proved that with the little lace number from your catalog, didn't I? Page thirty-nine? Huh?"

Lyle had huge fun with the idea of me working at Whips & Lace. He somehow saw it as a move on my part to make myself into his personal love slave. Which is, you know, yucky.

"Right. Well, I have to go, Lyle. Busy here, very busy. I'll call you later."

"Wait! Are we having dinner tonight? I'm sure in the mood for some of your meatloaf. I can stop and get beers and ice cream, if you want."

Be still my heart, meatloaf and beer. I blinked. Where had that nasty little voice in my head come from? *Lyle wants to spend time with me, instead of going off drinking with the guys, like a lot of men do, and I'm being nasty about it?*

I switched the phone to my other hand. "Lyle, I'm sorry, honey, but you know it's Monday. I have practice tonight with my voice coach. I'll have to make you some meatloaf this weekend. Maybe you can pick up a nice bottle of wine to go with it, for a change?"

"Again? Didn't you just practice with her a couple of weeks ago? How much time are you going to spend with that woman? Once we get married, Bree, things are going to have to change. I know you have your little dream of being an opera singer, but you're going to get a lot more satisfaction out of singing lullabies to our babies than singing a bunch of boring old songs to a crowd of strangers."

I blinked at the phone. Did my future husband just reduce my lifelong dream to "singing a bunch of boring old songs"?

Again?

I lowered my voice, since I didn't have all that much privacy in my cube, and told a big, fat lie, after whispering a quiet apology to God. "Lyle, I haven't worked with her since before Christmas. Anyway, I can't talk about this now. My boss is coming. I'll call you tonight after practice."

Wimped out again. Why couldn't I be more like Kirby? She would have let him have it.

I picked the phone back up to sternly discuss the situation with the dial tone. "I'm tired of having this discussion. Just because we're engaged doesn't mean you get to run my life. Do you understand the concept of dreams? Of goals? Of . . . of dreams?" I tried to channel my best stern Kirby face.

Then I heard the sound of clapping, and heat shot up through my face. I fumbled the phone back in its cradle, as Jamie came around the corner to my cube, still applauding.

"You go, girl! Did you finally tell Lyle that it's not the fifties anymore? That he can return the pearls and vacuum cleaner he got you for Christmas?" He grinned from ear to earring-studded ear. Jamie didn't look much like your typical accountant, but since I was engaged, I tried not to notice the blond hair that curled around his ears.

Or the bluest eyes I'd ever seen on a man.

Or the way those eyes crinkled when he smiled.

Not much, anyway.

I lowered my head, defeated. "No, I was practicing on the dial tone. How pathetic is that? He means well, it's just that—"

"It's just that he wants to run your life, and the idea of barefoot and pregnant is less of an outmoded idea and more of a happy fantasy for old Lyle?" Jamie's grin flattened out and looked more like a grimace. I still couldn't figure out why he was always so nice to *me*, since every single woman (and some of the married ones, too) in the office—including Polly in shipping, and she had to be sixty—was after him.

Although maybe that was the whole point. I wasn't a threat or a potential date, so he could treat me like a buddy.

My life in a nutshell. Just "one of the guys" to the office hottie, but the future wife of Old Reliable.

I flinched from the second disloyal thought about Lyle that had jumped into my mind in the space of ten minutes, and twisted the heavy engagement ring around on my finger. Confusion turned to annoyance. (Nice girls don't get angry; we get annoyed.)

"Look, Jamie, I like you, but that was a very personal and uncalled-for remark. I'd appreciate it if you didn't insult the man I'm going to marry. Not everybody wants to run around being some kind of a . . . a . . . *playboy*. Lyle just has old-fashioned family values." I couldn't quite meet Jamie's eyes after calling him a playboy, but looked up when he started laughing.

"You're right. The man is a paragon of virtue. There must be something good about him, right, if you're in love with him? So come on, let's go to lunch before I starve to death. My treat, as an apology." He grinned at me again, and the refusal I'd been about to give turned into a smile.

"All right. But no more remarks about Lyle. And I'll buy my own lunch." I pulled my purse out of my desk drawer, set my phone to Away, and stood up. "Just a sec."

I walked over and peeked into Kirby's office. "I'm going to get some lunch now. Can I bring you anything?"

She looked up from the report she was reading. "What? Oh, no. Thanks. Bye."

I backed away from the door before she could change her mind and think of some work that needed my immediate attention. "Quick, Jamie. Let's go."

As we walked down the hall, I heard Kirby calling after me.

"Brianna? What in God's name is a demon camel?"

3

Kirby

La disturbo? (Am I disturbing you?)

"Green! Where the hell have you been? Why didn't you answer your cell?"

It's never a fun sight to be welcomed back from lunch by six feet and a couple of inches of torqued-off boss crossing the office lobby toward you at full stride. Especially after the most stressful morning of my life, when I'd had to fire three people. I still felt like I was going to throw up.

"Hi, Kirby. Happy New Year. Did you have a nice weekend? Why, yes, Banning, thanks for asking. And you?" A little selective mocking may not be the recommended path to career success, but nobody bellows at *me*.

"I don't give a damn about your weekend. It's not a particularly happy new year, either, for the three people you just fired. My office. Now." He turns on his heel, obviously expecting me to follow. Considering that he *is* the boss, I decide to comply. When we reach his corner office, he impatiently waves me in and shuts the door with just a teensy more force than necessary. I sit down gingerly in the visitor's chair, thinking that this explosion happened sooner than I'd expected.

"What the hell were you thinking? No, don't answer that. You clearly weren't thinking. There couldn't have been a single thought in your brainless head when you unilaterally wiped out the entire marketing staff this morning." He paces back and forth, then flings himself in the chair across from mine, glaring at me.

I start to answer, but he cuts me off.

"No. I don't care. That's four people you've fired in a little over four months here. Are you going for some kind of contest? Fire an average of one person a month and win a trip to Barbados? What brought on this latest round of hatcheting?"

I cross my arms over my chest and narrow my eyes. Any time I'm in a meeting with him, I usually spend at least five minutes considering the amazing similarities that Banning Stuart, president and CEO of W&L, has to Hugh Jackman (the lovely *Kate and Leopold* Hugh, not the hairy *X-Men* Wolverine Hugh) and wondering if I could persuade him (Banning, not Hugh) to invite me to waltz.

This isn't one of those times. Not even in his gorgeous cream fisherman's sweater and navy pants.

"Are you done yet? I'd be glad to explain my well-justified actions, if you're quite done with your tirade."

He glares at me with his—let's be honest—amazing green eyes. They're a shade that my interior designer, Tessa, would probably call Arctic Hazel at the moment. *Oops, wandering.*

"No, I'm not done. I have a good ten minutes of what you so professionally call 'my tirade' left, but, for the sake of argument, let's pretend you understand that I'm your boss, and that you actually have a legitimate reason for decimating your entire staff in one sweep of your ax. Let's hear it." He shoves his hand through his dark, wavy hair (and let me state for the record, that I've never liked dark-haired guys; blonds are definitely the way to go) and looks at me. "Well?"

"Fine. I gave Mickey and her team three extra weeks to come up with the basics of the plan for the new line. I gave them warning after warning, since way back at Thanksgiving. Today, when I called a meeting, they had nothing. Zip. Zero. Zilch. Nobody even had the grace to be ashamed of it, either. 'But, Kirby, it was Christmas. But, Kirby, my daughter was sick. But Kirby, my dog ate my homework.' Pathetic excuses; and too little, too late."

I stand up; it's my turn to pace.

"We're launching that line at the end of this month, before I leave for Italy, and I wanted everything done, double-checked, and triple-checked before I leave. I'll be gone for three weeks, and I don't want to have to deal with crisis calls on my cell phone when I'm gondoliering around Venice with some hot guy in a striped shirt." I whirl around and catch him staring at my legs, and I feel another band snapping loose on my not-so-tightly controlled temper. "About three feet higher, if you're lost."

"What?" He looks at me, his eyebrows drawing together.

"My face. Three feet higher than where you were looking."

"Oh. I wasn't—damn it, Kirby, don't change the subject. How do you think you're going to go on a three-week vacation out of the country, when you've just fired everyone who could cover your department while you're gone? Your vacation is history, unless you go apologize to those three employees and unfire them." He bounds to his feet and steps closer to me.

"And your legs aren't all that impressive, so get over yourself."

Ha! I happen to have fantastic legs. I work very, very hard on my legs. Three hours of Pilates and twenty miles of running a week can tell you just how hard I work on my legs. That's so, so . . . *so* not the point.

"I'm not unfiring them. They haven't done anything worthwhile since I got here. In fact, judging from the number of write-ups they each had in their personnel files, they haven't done much

of anything at all since W&L hired them. And it's not like they
don't all have ridiculously huge amounts of holiday bonus money
to spend while they look for new jobs."

I clench my hands together, to keep from poking him in the
chest. "Anyway, isn't this why you hired me in the first place, so
you didn't have to pay an exorbitant amount of money to my old
ad agency for work we should be doing in-house?"

Sucking in a deep breath, I continue. "I need to know the parameters of my job, Banning. You promised me total control over
my department, but now you're telling me how to manage my
staff. Don't you think the one-eighty is a little unreasonable?" I
don't want to get fired, but I can't do my job like this.

He's not buying it, though. "From where I'm standing, you
don't have a staff to manage anymore. Either you hire them back,
or your vacation is history. While I agree that those three employees were not the most efficient—"

"Ha!"

"—I'm not letting you leave the country for three weeks with
no backup." He's looming over me, now, even though I'm in my
three-inch-heeled Steve Madden boots.

I don't particularly care for being loomed over. It ticks me off.
Still, I try to sound conciliatory. "Look, Banning. I'll work triple-
time this month and get the launch ready to go with the staff I have
left. I'll also find new hires—people who actually want to *work* for
a living. My vacation is nonnegotiable. It was part of the agree-
ment when I took this job."

He grins the kind of grin that would make small children run
howling for their mothers, and sinks into a chair.

"You should know by now, Ms. Senior Vice President, that
everything in business is negotiable. If you were nicer to your staff,
they might want to work harder for you. What happened to your
secretary?"

"*Nice?* What is *nice?* An unimaginative word used by insipid
people. My secretary didn't want to work for a woman; certainly

not a younger woman. When she told me that helping me put the packages for the board meeting together wasn't her job, after I'd been up half the night making copies, she was toast. Anyway, that's ancient history. For a delightful change, my new assistant seems to have actual brains in her head."

"So, *last month* is ancient history, now?"

I'm pacing around the office again, and I can feel the Italian in me getting even more riled up. Grandma would be so proud.

"I work too hard to put up with laziness." Oh, *crap*. I can't believe I just said that. Dad's words coming out of my mouth. He's been dead for five years, and I can still hear him yelling at Mom at night after he'd had a beer or seven.

I work too hard to have to eat this slop.

I work too hard to have to listen to crap about these kids.

I work too hard to put up with your laziness.

I shake my head to clear it; Banning is still talking.

". . . being nice?"

I take a deep breath. "I'm sorry. I didn't hear that."

He looks up at me and pauses. "I—are you OK? You're really pale."

Never let 'em see your weakness. Offense as defense.

"I'm fine. Just not used to starting my week being yelled at by a micromanaging boss. What were you saying?" I'm trying my "sweeter than a triple-chocolate mocha with extra whip" voice, but he's not buying it. Figures. He's probably one of those anti-sugar freaks.

He shoots up out of his chair again. "Fine. Micromanage *this*. You think you're such a great manager? Here's the deal. We'll make a bet."

"What? A bet? A bet about what?" I think he's gone off his rocker. Maybe it's the pressure of being a CEO of a major corporation at only thirty-five. Maybe he's finally snapped.

Maybe I'll get his job.

I look around his office. With a little redecorating, I can see myself in it quite nicely. I think I'll give Tessa a call and . . .

"Kirby? Are you listening to me?"

Darn. Guess I'll have to listen to him, at least until the men with the straitjacket actually cart him off.

"Yes, of course. What kind of bet? Also, and I mean this in the nicest possible way, are you on any medication?" I smile widely, with what I hope is an "it's all going to be fine, just wait for some Xanax" kind of smile.

Banning cocks his head and looks at me like *I'm* the one having the meltdown. "What? No. Well, I'm taking some vitamins, but . . . *Aarghh*. You did it again! I'm talking about your job. Your trip to Italy. Your top-notch management skills. One little bet."

"I have no idea what you're talking about, but since it seems to make you calmer, please enlighten me." I lean against the wall with my hands behind my back, so he can't see me digging my fingernails into my palms.

Never let 'em see you sweat, punkin.

Great. I'm channeling my father, the man whose idea of management skills was to knock heads together if anybody disagreed with him.

"What bet, already?"

"If you can convince one person to call you *nice*—*any* person— in the next four weeks, you can go to Italy. If not, you stay here and work." He folds his arms over his chest and looks spectacularly, sickeningly, slimily smug.

"Are you nuts? Do you think I'd risk my long-planned trip to Italy, with nonrefundable tickets, I might add, on some juvenile bet? Are we in junior high school?" I'm so furious I feel the hair follicles in my head catching on fire.

Can you die of spontaneous head combustion?

"Hey, you're the one who thinks she's such a hotshot manager and all-around people person. I guess you admit that it would be nearly impossible to find anybody who would think you're a nice person in only four weeks. That kind of personality overhaul might take upwards of a couple of years . . ."

He's showing teeth, but I wouldn't call it a smile anymore.

At least not a very *nice* smile.

"You are certifiable. There is no way I'm betting my vacation on that or any other stupid idea you may dream up. In fact, this conversation is over."

I turn toward the door, contemplating how hard I'll have to slam it to knock some of his framed pictures off of the wall.

"I double-dog dare you." His voice is so quiet, I almost don't hear it.

Almost.

The low-life scum. Banning and I'd had a working lunch just before Christmas, and I'd mentioned how much Jules and I love that movie *The Christmas Story,* and how thrilled we were to find out, on our holiday shopping trip to New York one year, that Macy's had done its windows totally in scenes from the film. We'd both gone crazy and bought tons of ornaments. My Ralphie bobble-head doll is still on my desk.

To use the double-dog dare on me—going straight past the dare—is not only a serious breach of etiquette, it's a pretty ridiculous expression for a grown man to use at work.

Not that I can let it go.

"You've gotta be kidding. We're talking about the professional future of a new product line for this company, and you're taunting me with a childish dare?"

"You got it, Green. What's the matter? No guts? Let's sweeten the pot. Forget about Italy. You win—somebody, *anybody,* calls you nice—and you can keep your job."

All trace of smile is gone from his face, even the scary smile. I can feel my mouth dropping open. He's serious.

He just threatened my job.

"I can't—you can't—"

"I just did."

The man has no idea who he's messing with. I lift my chin. "Fine. I accept your stupid bet. We need to discuss the stakes."

He drops into the chair behind his desk and reaches for the phone. "We just did. I'm busy now, Kirby, and I'm sure you have the remnants of a marketing department to salvage. Be sure to report in on your progress."

I stand my ground. No way is he dismissing me like that.

"No, the stakes for when *you lose*. What are you offering?"

He puts the phone down and looks up at me; a long, measuring stare. "We just settled that. Your job is the stakes."

"I already have a job. I want more."

"What did you have in mind?"

I smile at him, deliberately making it my most shark-like smile. "I want a public apology. You will call a staff meeting and publicly apologize for questioning my judgment."

"Done." He picks up the phone again.

"Don't argue with me, I . . . um, what?"

"I said, done. Now, if you don't mind." He dials the phone, waving me out the door.

I forget to slam the door as I leave, because I'm blown away that he agreed so easily. I was prepared for a fight, and he . . .

Oh.

He's so confident that I'll lose the bet, he's not at all concerned that he might have to apologize.

The air sort of whooshes out of my lungs all at once, and I collapse back against the wall next to his closed door. My thoughts are racing around in my head like a hamster on crack.

He's not worried *at all*.

Am I really that awful?

As I trudge down the hall toward my office, I realize I have four weeks to find out.

4

Brianna

Baritone: Male singer with an intermediate voice range; the most common voice among adult men.

The forty-five-minute drive through gray and slushy Seattle traffic to get to Madame Gabriella's house didn't help cheer me up. First the demon camel mistake, and then Kirby had been in a foul mood all afternoon. I'd tried to ask her if I could help, but she'd pretty much just stared at me in a daze. I'd been sure she was about to snap at me, but she'd sort of stopped in the middle of opening her mouth and sighed, then muttered something about niceness being overrated.

I may never understand her.

I pulled into the driveway of my voice coach's cottage-style house, which she'd lived in since 1950. It was a charming red brick with white shutters that made me think of fairy tales and ginger-bread, and in the summer flowers of dozens of different bright hues and shapes exploded in the tiny yard. I parked and took a deep breath, trying to center myself for the grueling evening ahead.

We hadn't worked together in nearly a week, and I was sure to pay the price for what she would see as my "laziness." I knew exactly what was coming, too.

True talent never takes a holiday, Brianna.

I sighed. I'm betting that the great opera divas like Maria Callas didn't spend a lot of time deciphering marketing reports so they could pay their rent, either. Some days I just needed some time off.

Second shift. Nobody can say I didn't suffer for my art.

I knocked for politeness and then stepped into the overheated house. Warmth is good for the chords, but I always thought perhaps ninety degrees was taking it a bit far.

"Hello, Madame! Happy New Year!"

She appeared in the archway to the living room, as I removed my new London Fog coat that Lyle'd given me for Christmas. I smoothed a hand down a red wool sleeve as I hung the coat up on the hall tree. Lyle really did love me. We needed to work on finding our way together. That was all.

I hoped.

"Ha! True talent never takes a holiday, Brianna. I have not seen you for six days. Six days! I hope your voice has not fallen into rust with the disuse. You worked every day, no?" She didn't wait for an answer, but tsked-tsked me, then flounced into the living room, her long black dress streaming behind her. Madame's face still bore traces of the great beauty she'd been in her day, and she carried herself like the belle of the ball at all times. It usually made me smile; right then it just made me sigh.

"Hurry, hurry. We start the warm-up now."

I followed her into the tiny room, my mood brightening as it always did to see the well-used piano, the music stand already in place nearby. Need thrummed through my skin; my fingers literally itched to touch the pages of my sheet music. I almost didn't need to read the notes on the page. I'd memorized them months ago, after the painstaking work to translate the Italian to English. You can't feel the emotion in words you don't understand.

If you can't feel the music, the *audience* can't feel the music, *Brianna.* You are a conduit, Darling. Years and years of working with my teacher had given me a soundtrack in my head: The Wisdom of Opera as Ordained by Madame Gabriella.

I laughed a little and began my stretches. When your body is your instrument, it must be warmed up before you play. I felt the knots of stress firmly lodged in my neck and shoulders from the day's tension and tried to work them out, lifting my arms over my head and beginning slow, careful neck rolls.

Madame perched on the piano stool and peered up at me, her tiny fingers fluttering across the keys. "Did you see my cards, Darling? Renée Fleming sent me a lovely note. My precious Luciano sent this adorable red one. I may be tucked away in the wilds, no longer singing, but the great ones remember me. Have I told you of the time I worked with Maria Callas?"

I smiled, gritting my teeth just a little. "Yes, you have, actually."

I loved her almost as much as I loved my mother, but sometimes I was tempted to ask Madame who picked up all the names of opera greats she dropped. But only on days like this, when I was so very tired.

She has given me so much, and the least I can do is listen to her tell her stories and remember her glory days. I'm praying for triumphs in my future; hers have faded to memories played to the ghosts of audiences past.

I started shoulder rolls to shake off stress and my mood; too much spiked eggnog and *A Christmas Carol* over the past couple of weeks, probably. "But I'd love to hear it again, if you'll tell it. Maria Callas was guest starring at the Met, and you were—"

She sniffed and waved a hand in dismissal. "Never mind. If you've heard it, I certainly won't bore you with another telling. Are you ready to warm up? Descending scales, Darling."

She touched a key on the piano without another word, letting me know both that she was annoyed with me, and that I should begin. Shorthand communication in the key of D.

I drew a deep breath and started to warm up, making a mental note to apologize afterward. Nice girls don't hurt their voice coach's feelings.

*   *   *

"That was terrible. What did you eat today? Are you sleeping? Did you work at all over the holidays?"

I blew out the last note of my cooldown, feeling my shoulders slump. Madame wasn't much for soothing the sting of a bad review.

Great. If she points at the pillow, I'm so out of here.

She pointed to the pillow.

Sadly, I didn't have the energy to storm out. But I hated that stupid pillow. It smirked up at me, in all of its badly embroidered glory:

If You Want to Sing on a Cruise Ship, Don't Waste My Time

I closed my eyes and sighed. "I don't want to sing on a cruise ship, Madame. Enough with the cruise ship, please. After seven years of working together, you know my goals. Can we please stop with the pillow? Please? I've had a very long day."

Madame stood up from the piano and paced back and forth, flinging her arms in the air. "I don't want to hear about your long days. The Metropolitan Opera will not want to hear about your long days. The Seattle Opera will not want to hear about your long days. There is nothing that should come before your art. If you let this pathetic job stop you from pursuing your dreams, you will deserve the cruise ship. I will come to the dock and wave to you and give you the pillow as a present. You will sing glorified karaoke on the *Love Boat*, and I will die a lonely death, cloaked in shame for having wasted the best years of my life on a cruise ship singer."

She flung herself on the brocaded couch and draped her arm over her eyes.

This woman's picture was in the dictionary next to the phrase *drama queen*. I knew it, and I was used to it, but somehow familiarity hadn't bred contempt. I still flinched at the words *cruise ship*, secretly wondering if she were right. Maybe I was just kidding myself. Maybe I'd never have what it took to succeed. Maybe I should just marry Lyle and sing lullabies to our babies.

I opened my mouth to tell her all of this, but something got lost in the translation. Maybe my overworked, overtrained vocal chords weren't ready to say those words. What came out instead surprised both of us. "It's just TV."

She moved her arm away from her face and peeked out at me. "What, Darling? What's TV?"

"The *Love Boat*. It was a fictional ship on a TV show. I used to watch it when I was a little girl with my mom. She wanted me to grow up to be Julie, the cruise director. Julie was the *nice* one. It's a fictional ship, and I am *not* going to be a singer on a cruise ship. I am doing the best that I can, and I love you, but you have to stop browbeating me all the time. Please. *Please.*"

Her eyes softened for a moment, or maybe I just imagined that part. I kept believing that a kind, loving, caring woman hid behind the crotchety exterior.

At least, I kept *hoping*.

"Brianna, you miss the point. You were off. You missed notes. You are tense in your shoulders and in your back, and you missed the high F entirely. What kind of coloratura misses the high F? Would Joan Sutherland? Would Kathleen Battle?"

I tried to answer, but she raised her hand for silence. "I tell you to breathe, and you breathe through your chest. Or your throat, maybe. What is that? Breathe through your vagina, Darling. You know this. You know the air must flow through your entire body. You have no excuse—no children that you pushed out of your birth canal; yet where is your PC muscle tonight? It takes the vacation, too?"

I had no response to this. I'd once told Madame that sometimes my vagina just doesn't feel like breathing, and she threw me out of her house and refused to speak to me for a week. Not huge with the sense of humor about opera, is my beloved coach.

She didn't wait for an answer, anyway, but drove on, almost spitting out the words. "Your neck is a vessel. You know this, but tonight you sing from your neck. I can't even speak about your emotion. Emotion? *Ha!* You sang Puccini as though you were reciting a grocery list. "Chi il bel sogno di Doretto" is a passionate love song. Love and loss and realization. Not bacon and milk and laundry soap."

I decided that it wasn't a good time to remind her that she'd once forced me to sing a piece where I was supposed to break down in tears over the loss of my table.

That's right. My *table*.

(I'm *so* not kidding; this is why normal people think opera is nuts. Some of the composers were clearly drunk on cheap Italian wine when they thought up the lyrics.)

The haze of exhaustion blurred the pain from her words enough to make me thankful. I spoke up, so quietly she almost didn't hear me at first. "Maybe you're right."

"What?"

"I said, maybe you're right. Maybe I've been wasting your time all these years. Maybe I'll go online and check out cruise ships. If I hire on to one of those Disney cruises, do you think they'll let me dress up as a cartoon character when I sing?" I shook my head in defeat and headed for my coat and the door. I needed sleep. I needed fresh air. I needed a new life.

Maybe not in that order.

Is it worth it to keep chasing a dream that nobody wants me to have or thinks I can achieve? Mama is horrified by the idea of my being the center of all that attention on stage. "Nice girls don't draw attention to themselves, Brianna. We are the glue that holds the family together, not the . . . the ribbon on the package."

(Metaphors aren't really Mama's strong suit, but I didn't miss her point.)

Lyle doesn't want me to sing. "How can you be at the theater at night when I'm at the fire station? Who will be home with the kids? The mother is the backbone of the family, Bree."

I felt the tears threatening and whirled around to face Madame, clutching my coat.

"I don't want to be glue."

"What? Glue?" She looked at me with a vaguely alarmed expression.

"I don't want to be the glue. I don't want to be the backbone. I want to be a singer. An opera singer. And I'm good at it. So I'm not giving up, or becoming a giant singing mouse, and you're not dying a lonely death, cloaked in shame. I can do this. I *will* do this. I'm going to be *great*." My chin wobbled, but I didn't give in to the tears. I'd heard it all before: *Silly Bree. Emotional Bree.*

Well, not this time.

Madame Gabriella folded her arms across her chest and gave me a long, measuring stare. Then she smiled. "*Bella* Brianna. Of course you can do it. I never had any doubt. Now go home and rest. Hot tea with lemon and honey before bed. Maybe a touch of vodka. I will see you tomorrow, and we will have a fabulous hour."

She hugged me and shuffled to her door, chuckling and shaking her head. "Singing mouse. Crazy girl. Go home. Rest."

I smiled, feeling better than I had all day, and walked out of the door, shrugging into my coat, feeling the cold, damp Seattle air biting into me. Waking me up for the drive home, hopefully.

"Oh, and Bree?"

I turned around, wary. Madame always had to have the last word.

"You sing well for me tomorrow, and we burn the pillow."

Finally. Last words I could live with.

5

Kirby

Una bottiglia di vino locale, per favore.
(A bottle of the local wine, please.)

"Jules, call me. Call me NOW. Call me. Now. Call. Me. Now." As I leave my third voice mail message on Jules's cell phone in as many hours, I realize that a teensy tiny, ugly part of me is jealous of her happiness with her new guy, Sam, and resents that she's not as available to me as she always has been. I mean, who nursed her through the Mark thing? She never would have survived getting dumped right before her wedding, if I hadn't been there with copious bottles of wine, I pout, as I open my second bottle of Beringer's Private Reserve.

Great, I just need to stick my lower lip out and my transformation into sulking three-year-old will be complete. At least I'm still sober enough to laugh at myself.

Sort of.

I carefully set my wineglass on my antique mahogany coffee table and flop down on my gorgeous, butter-soft, caramel-leather couch. In a twisted way, it cheers me up that I can be utterly miserable in the luxury of my two-story condo, with all of the carefully selected possessions I've accumulated over the past few years. I'm a long way from Yakima, that's for sure. Something about spending my first twelve years in small-town Washington, in a house where we had plastic covers over the plaid couches (wouldn't want to spill grape Kool-Aid on that attractive indoor-outdoor fabric), sent me in screaming overreaction to the Dark Side. Translation: Why buy perfectly lovely drapes for a couple hundred bucks when I can buy imported Italian silk *window treatments* for just over a thousand?

There's a reason I cringe every month when I have to open the credit card bills, trust me. Since I cashed out my 401(k) from the ad agency to pay down my credit card balances, I would have been in great shape, except for the whole problem with the windshield wipers on my car.

They broke.

So, of course, I had to buy a new car. You can't drive a car in Seattle, Washington, home to All Rain All the Time weather with no windshield wipers, can you? The adorable little red convertible that I passed at Seattle Mercedes every day on my way to work had nothing to do with it.

Anyway, I was getting a thirty-thousand-dollar raise to take the new job, so I *deserved* a new car. Except, when it came down to it, the thirty grand included optional bonuses, based on performance. So my monthly take-home is only a couple hundred bucks more than it was at the agency, which isn't really helping with the car payment.

Or the Visa bill.

Or the Mastercard bill.

Or the student loan payments.

Basically, I have a beautiful home filled with beautiful things, and I drive a beautiful car, while up to my beautiful eyeballs (brow wax = thirty-two dollars every three weeks at Natasha's Boutique) in debt.

Compensating? Me? You think?

That's what my career coach says, anyway. He's kind of like a therapist, but tax-deductible as a business expense. And, as saith the IRS, thus saveth me money that I can spend on shoes. Maybe *that* should be my new motto. I could get it put on a T-shirt.

I glance down at the worn and faded blue tee that I'm wearing. It has last year's motto on it:

If you can't be a good example,
you'll just have to be a horrible warning

Personal mottoes are important for growth, according to Dr. Wallace, the overpaid coach slash therapist slash tax deduction. Although I'm not sure why growth is all that important. I'm just where I want to be, other than the teensy debt issues. Away from Yakima. Away from a home where I was ashamed to bring my friends. Away from classmates who made fun of me or, worse, felt sorry for me.

"I'm so sorry about your mom, Kirby," Hannah said, eyes flickering toward her friends, where they stood next to their lockers. None of them would look me in the eyes, so I knew she'd told.

She fake smiled at me, with her fake concern shining out from under her fake blond hair. "Is she going to be okay? Did the . . . door . . . run into her nose again?"

Bitch. I could feel my nails cutting into my palms, as I clenched my hands into fists.

"She's fine. But I'm really busy, so I'm not going to be able to go to the mall with you, after all. I'll just catch you later."

I walked away as fast as I could, trying not to run. Trying not to cry. I'd thought we were alone in the house the night before. My parents were supposed to be out playing cards with the Myersons. I never would have taken anybody home with me, otherwise. Not even Jules. But Hannah insisted she had to pee before we went to the library, and my house was on the way, and even though I knew she was just dying of nosiness to see inside my house, what could I say?

As soon as Hannah had shut the door to the bathroom, I'd heard the yelling start. They hadn't been gone at all.

They were home.

"What makes you think you can dress like a tramp to go play cards? You sweet on Myerson? Or Rudy? Which one is it?"

My mother's murmurings, placating. Trying to soothe.

"I never said I liked that dress! Get out of my sight!"

Mama crying out. Daddy thundering down the steps and slamming the door. Holding my breath, torn between wanting to check on Mama and just wanting to get Hannah out of the house. I took a step toward the stairs, and the bathroom door opened. Hannah's eyes were huge.

"Is everything okay?"

"I—"

Mama's footsteps on the stairs. Hannah's sharply indrawn breath. My head slowly turning. Not wanting to see. Needing to see. The blood dripping down from Mama's nose.

The grimace masquerading as a smile. "Why, it's so nice to see you, Hannah. Kirby never brings her friends around. Can I get you girls a snack?"

The yelling. It was coming from me. "No. No! We have to leave. We have to get out of here. Now!"

Dragging Hannah behind me. Telling the story of a warped door frame, a door that swings wildly. Wood smacking flesh. No problem here. No drunken fathers. Never any flashing lights and police radios squawking about the domestic, code what-the-hell-ever.

Just one big, happy family.

I blink and stare down at the silk-covered pillow I'm twisting in my hands. As I smooth the wrinkles out of the fabric, my hands pressing harder and harder, I laugh, trying not to hear the bitterness in it.

Just one big, happy family.

I didn't even go to his funeral. I sent flowers, but I couldn't bring myself to be such a hypocrite as to pretend to mourn him. Jules had told me I'd regret it. Maybe someday I will. But not today.

Today I'm content to sit in my home—*my* home—where I never have to worry about doors hitting faces. But the contentment fades as I realize I'm about a paycheck and a half away from being homeless.

It doesn't really add up to peace of mind, when I just risked my job over a double-dog dare.

I shove the pillow under my head and close my eyes. Time to pull a Scarlett O'Hara. I'll worry about it tomorrow.

* * *

I'm dancing across the Piazza del Duomo with a man so exquisite that he must be one of Florence's ancient statues come to life. A dark-haired, dark-eyed Roman god with cheekbones that surely sprang from sculpted marble; he holds me tightly in arms banded with muscle and breathes a question into my ear. *"Vende assorbenti igienici?"*

As I glance up at him, frantically trying simultaneously to look seductive and psychically communicate the fact that I have no panties on, while figuring out exactly what deliciously decadent sexual act he's inviting me to try, he translates his question for me, in an oddly high-pitched voice. "Do you sell sanitary napkins?"

Then his foot starts ringing.

"Oh, *crap!*" I smack my head on the coffee table as I fall off the couch. Clutching my probably concussed skull with one hand, I grope around for the CD player to turn off the (clearly outdated—who the heck asks for sanitary napkins these days?) Italian lessons. Then I realize that it's *my* foot that's ringing. I mean, the phone is on the floor near my foot, where I kicked it when the ringing woke me up out of a perfectly lovely, if somewhat bizarre, dream. I grab for it.

"*What,* already?"

"Hey, nice to talk to you, too, Kirbs. What the heck are you doing home at only seven o'clock? Losing points on your workaholic of the year award, aren't you?" Jules is laughing, and I can almost see the teasing expression on her face. I miss her.

"I've really done it this time, Jules. Screwed up in a screw-up of such mammoth proportions that I'm just . . . I'm just . . . screwed." I push up off the floor and head to the kitchen for some ice for my head, which is throbbing from the combined effects of the close encounter with the coffee table and, from the looks of the kitchen counter, almost two bottles of wine in fewer than four hours.

"Kirby, I'm not really sure, you're going all subtle and obscure on me, but I'm guessing you've screwed something up?"

"Oooohhhhh. You know that teensy little problem I have with authority figures?" I prop the phone between my ear and shoulder and rummage around in the ice bin, then slap a couple of pieces in a damp dish towel and hold it against my forehead.

"Ouch!" OK, that really hurts. I'll probably have an enormous green and black bruise on my face, to add to my general joy and bliss. Could this year start off any better?

"Ouch, what? What is going on there? Will you please quit moaning and give me some facts?" Her job of herding hormone-crazed teenagers on one of America's hottest new reality TV shows is responsible for this new Crisp Voice of Authority Jules, I'm betting.

"OK, today I managed to alienate my new assistant, fire three people, and call my boss an overbearing, micromanaging fascist pig. Oh, and I risked my job on a double-dog dare."

There was a silence.

A long silence.

"Jules? Um, are you there?"

I can hear her breathing. *Oh, oh.* I'm in trouble when Jules has to start her Lamaze breathing. (No, she's never had kids; long story.)

"Did you at least win?"

"Win what?"

"The *dare,* Kirby, did you at least win the dare such that you still have your new job?" We haven't been best friends since we were twelve without me learning her different voices. This one is the long-suffering, barely holding-on-to-her-patience voice that says I'd better give her the whole story quickly, or she's going to start getting nasty.

Not that I can't out-nasty Jules, but after more than twenty years of hanging out with me, she's pretty damn good at it, too.

"Um, no, not exactly. But it's an easy one. I just have to get somebody to call me *nice* in the next four weeks, or I can't go to Italy, that's all."

"That's ALL?" Her voice is definitely getting louder.

"Well, actually, no. I lose my job, too. But if . . . *when* I win, Banning has to apologize to me. In public. In front of the whole department. Ha!" I feel pretty smug about the terms I've negotiated. After all, Jules is my best friend. If anybody is going to be on my side in this, it's her.

There's another long silence.

"Can you get him to take it back?"

"What? I can't believe you, of all people, would say that to me, Jules. You're my best friend. Or at least you used to be, before you started your new celebrity lifestyle and forgot about those of your friends who don't regularly grace the pages of *Entertainment Weekly.*"

I hurl the ice pack in the sink, where it breaks the wineglass I'd just put in there.

"Aarrghh!"

"I'm still your best friend, you stupid, prickly, overaggressive wench. Now quit trying to pick a fight with me to avoid telling me what happened and just spill it."

So I did. I told her everything, in a flat, unvarnished recitation that didn't do much to make me look better.

Jules sighed deeply. "Kirby, Kirby, Kirby. How do you think you can talk to people like this—how do you think you can talk to *your boss* like this—and get away with it? Don't all those years of getting comments on reviews like 'too aggressive; no respect for authority; not really a team player' mean anything to you? I'm surprised he didn't fire you outright."

"The new chairman of the board loves me. Or I should say chairperson. She says I'm like she was in her old, conscience-free days." I grin at the thought of Matilda Jamieson, the old battle-ax.

"Kirbs, that doesn't really sound like a compliment, but whatever. Let's suppose that her approval kept you from getting fired outright. He stepped right around it by this stupid bet, didn't he? How did you go from Golden Girl to being on Stuart's shit list so fast?"

I realize I'm pacing a rut in my carpet and drop back down on the couch. "I fired three people today; basically the rest of my marketing department. He's a little freaked about it."

We talk for a little while longer but, other than telling me that I should never trust a man named Banning, Jules doesn't have any ideas. It helps just to talk to her, though, although I realize as I'm hanging up that she never did reassure me that it would be easy to find somebody to call me nice.

As I look around the kitchen, which still has this morning's breakfast dishes in the sink, along with two empty wine bottles and a half-eaten pizza on the counter, I sigh and debate just going to bed and dealing with it all in the morning. Sloth is winning a pitched battle over middle-class Puritan work ethic and guilt when the doorbell rings.

I groan. I'm not expecting anybody and definitely not in the mood to chat, if it's one of my overly social neighbors. Every other day somebody's inviting me to a barbecue or a block party or . . . well, I guess that was last summer. But the holiday parties and tree-trimming parties were every other day for the past month. Not that I attended any of them. It doesn't really pay to get too close to your neighbors. What if they hate you, and then it's all snarky looks as you pass them on the way to the pool? Much better to stay aloof and smile distantly, as you drive past on your way to work.

I head for the door and catch sight of myself in the mirror beside the front door. This time I groan with feeling. How can I look so bad? I have mascara-y raccoon eyes, probably from my *nappus interruptus,* my hair looks like the *before* shot on *Extreme Makeover,* and my eyes are red and bleary. Great.

At least I probably won't have to worry about any more social invitations after somebody sees me like this.

I blow out a deep breath. Bad idea—is that really my breath? I blow in my hand and sniff cautiously. Holy cow, I smell like a cheap wino. Marvelous. More fodder for the inexorable destruction of any remaining shred of self-respect. Maybe I can just sit down on Pike Street with some Boone's Farm in a brown paper bag later.

Oh, who cares? Maybe I'll get lucky, and whoever just rang the doorbell for the third time will be somebody trying to sell me something. My face has gotta trump any number of No Soliciting signs.

Smiling grimly, I yank open the door. "What?"

The woman on my doorstep steps back half a step and looks at me, eyes widening, then glances down at a clipboard clutched in her hand. "Um, are you, uh, Kirby Green?"

"Yes, what do you want?" I'm not even pretending to be gracious, now. She's either soliciting money or signatures for some petition or other—my neighborhood is liberal city—and I'm *so* not in the mood.

"Um, I'm Maria Estoban. From Special Siblings? I'm here for your final checkoff for approval."

6

Kirby

Vorrei qualcosa contro il mal di testa.
(I need something for a hangover.)

I stare in horror at the very official-looking woman standing at my door. Standing *impatiently* at my door. Checking her watch, in fact.

I do a mental dig for functioning brain cells. "But, but, that appointment was set for—"

"Seven thirty," she interrupts, looking pointedly at her watch again. "It's actually seven thirty-five, but I was held up in traffic. If this isn't a good time . . ."

Her gaze takes in my rumpled clothes, hair, and face with a hint of what might be distaste, if her curled lip and wrinkled nose are any clues. Great. I've only been on a waiting list for six months, why not screw this up, too? *Aaarrgh.*

"No, no, no. Please come in. I'm so sorry to be a little confused. I'm just, um, sick. That's it! I'm sick with a touch of the flu and came home early from work to take a nap. Guess that cough medicine just knocked me out." I fake a little cough into my hand as I usher her in, which reminds me of my just-walked-out-of-a-distillery breath.

"Please, sit down right here on the couch. I was just getting some tea. I'll bring some in for both of us."

Ms. Estoban's rigid pose softened when she heard the word *flu*. It's probably okay to be *sick* if you're going to be trusted to be a Special Sibling in Seattle's homegrown answer to the Big Brothers/Big Sisters program.

Drunk—not so much.

She puts her case down by the couch, but stays standing. "Can I help you? You should probably be resting. I can come back, Ms. Green, if this is a bad time. It's just that we wanted you to meet Lauren this Wednesday."

I'm rushing to the kitchen to hide the wine bottles before she can see them. "No, no, I've got it. Please sit down and make yourself comfortable. I'm really almost over the flu; not contagious at all."

I flick the button on the hot water pot, then stuff the bottles under the sink, behind the trash can, and shove the cabinet door shut.

Crash. Oh-*kay.* The sound of the bottles crashing against each other as they knock over my cleaning supplies does nothing for my nerves.

"What was that? Are you okay? Are you sure you don't need help?"

Oh, God, she's on her way in here. My breath is still one hundred proof. What can I—there's an onion on the counter. That's got to be better than nothing. I can . . .

"*Aaarmph.*"

"Ms. Green? Kirby? I can reschedule if . . ." She rounds the corner into the kitchen and stops dead.

"What are you doing?"

"Ert's um howm-grmphmgg curmm."

The produce guy at Albertson's is going to die a slow and painful death for false advertising. There is nothing sweet about this onion.

Peeling it probably would have been a good idea, too, in hindsight.

I spit pieces of onion and onion peel into the sink, as Ms. Fat Chance You're Ever Going to Be a Special Sibling Estoban watches, her jaw dropping down to somewhere around her clipboard. As I turn on the sink and splash water in my mouth, I mentally kick myself for having wondered how the day could get any worse. News flash: Today gives *worse* a whole new definition.

I snatch up the towel and wipe my mouth.

"It's a family secret. Um, famous in Yakima. Raw onion is supposed to be great for flu. You know, feed a fever, starve a cold, chomp a raw onion for flu? Or is it feed a cold and starve a fever? I can never keep those two straight."

As I flash my most blinding smile, trying to keep her off guard, it occurs to me I probably have pieces of onion peel stuck in my teeth. I clamp my lips together.

"Well, the water's ready. Let's just take our tea in the living room, shall we?" I quickly arrange teacups and the appropriate accompaniments on a tray, dump some leftover Christmas cookies on a plate, and follow a very bewildered social worker to my living room.

"Well, you, um, said I can meet Lauren this week?" I pour the tea and launch right into the topic, hoping to avoid any conversation about the healing properties of root vegetables or any tendencies toward mental breakdowns in my family tree.

"Yes. Yes. I know she was at her grandma's the times you met with Mrs. Dennison. This week would be a good week for you three to meet and see how this all works out."

She sips her tea and then pulls a file folder out of her briefcase. "This is a picture of Lauren. As you know, she's six and in first grade, although I understand there are some grade-level issues. She's quite a gifted child and bored in regular classes."

Although I'd seen a grainy school picture before, I reach for the photo with one hand while lifting my own teacup to my mouth with the other, then feel myself grimace.

Euwwwww, Earl Grey tea with onion. That is so nasty.

"Is there a problem with Lauren?" Ms. Estoban's voice has frosted over considerably, and she's back to looking at me like I could be a potential ax murderer.

"What? No, I just—the tea with the onion—it's, um, I . . . Oh, wow."

For the first time in my life, I think I just fell in love. That school pic didn't do her justice. This is the most beautiful child I've ever seen. It's one of those silly posed photos, where the photographer dresses the kids up in old-timey lace and hats, but Lauren has a small smile on her face, as though she's laughing at the pretentiousness of it all. She has enormous blue eyes and long hair with the hint of a curl at the ends. Blond? Brown? I can't tell from the photo, which has that sepia-toned look to simulate age. The word *PROOF* is printed in capital letters at the bottom. I guess Lauren's mom didn't buy the portrait package, but couldn't resist having her daughter immortalized. Botticelli himself wouldn't have been able to resist this face.

"She's the most beautiful little girl I've ever seen, Ms. Estoban. I mean, not that looks matter; I want to help any child, not just a pretty one; I mean . . . Oh, crap. I just keep sticking my foot in my mouth today, don't I?" I smack myself on the forehead, literally this time.

"Call me Maria." She starts laughing. "And I understand exactly what you mean. Lauren is an astonishingly beautiful child, and she's very bright. It's a huge challenge for her mother to keep up with her, but Mrs. Dennison is a terrific mom. She's a single mom who has to work two jobs to make ends meet and is determined to do whatever it takes to make sure Lauren has the best education and a better life than she ever did."

She smiled. "That's why she signed up for the Special Siblings program, but she's also worried about getting the kind of person who will convey the wrong kind of values to Lauren. You know, money is everything, that sort of thing. We were pleased in our interviews with you that you weren't like that."

I nod and nudge my five-hundred-dollar shoes under the couch with my left heel.

Maria puts her teacup down, looks at me, and laughs again. "For what it's worth, by the way, I don't make much sense when I have the flu, either. Are you sure you'll be up to meeting her Wednesday?"

I think of all the work I'm going to have to do by the end of the month to win the bet, keep my job, and go to Italy. Then I look back at the picture of Lauren and see the hint of sadness in her eyes that her smile can't hide.

"Wednesday will be great. Where should we meet?"

* * *

To my credit, I never even wonder until after she's gone, my kitchen is cleaned (guilt won out), and I'm soaking in a Vanilla Sugar and Spice bubble bath, whether it will count if a six-year-old calls me *nice*. As I slowly slide my entire head under the bubbles, I wonder if this is what they call rock bottom.

Somewhere, the fates are laughing their asses off.

7

Brianna

Coloratura: Brilliant vocal acrobatics consisting of rapid notes, runs, and trills; a fundamental element of bel canto opera.

I blinked, and suddenly I was pulling into the parking lot of my apartment building and wondering how I'd gotten there. It's really scary when you drive with your brain on automatic pilot and don't remember most of the trip. Can't be all that safe, either.

As I trudged up the stairs to my second-floor apartment (the elevator was broken, as usual), I idly wondered how much bed rest I'd get if I had a car accident and had to go to the hospital. Then I laughed, realizing that exhaustion was making me delirious. All I wanted was a cup of hot tea and a bubble bath. Then my flannel jammies and bed. Thank goodness I didn't have to see Lyle tonight.

I fitted my key into the lock, and somebody yanked the door open from inside. "It's about time you got home."

My fiancé stood in my doorway. I could feel my longed-for bubble bath slipping away into the distance and sighed. I'd agonized over giving him a key or not giving him a key, now that we were engaged.

Bad choice, Bree.

"Hello, Lyle. What are you doing here?"

He took my purse and briefcase out of my arms and stepped back to let me in, grinning that crooked grin that I loved so much. (The wavy black hair and clear blue eyes didn't hurt, either. Plus, he looks so good in jeans and that black sweater. Okay, he's yummy. I admit it.)

"Hey! Is that any way to greet your future husband? Especially when he comes bearing food?"

At the word *food,* my sense of smell kicked in, and the aroma of something tomatoey and delicious reached my nose. My stomach started singing an aria all of its own.

"What is that wonderful smell? And, sorry. Hi, honey. But what *are* you doing here? You knew I had rehearsal." I shrugged out of my coat and gave him a quick hug as he put my stuff down on the table.

"I know. But I felt bad about arguing with you on the phone earlier, especially when you were already having a crappy day. So I brought you some dinner. I figured you'd forget to eat, as usual."

I caught sight of the *Pasta Delicioso* bag on the table and smiled. *What a guy.*

* * *

The chicken marsala lulled me into a false sense of security, that's my only excuse. 'Cause I was totally unprepared for the flank attack when it came.

* * *

I snuggled up under his arm on the couch, trying really hard to keep at least one eye open. The eighteen-hour-day plus a full stomach combined to put me fairly close to comatose. Lyle stroked my hair and murmured something in my ear.

I snuggled even closer. This fiancé thing definitely had benefits to it. "Hmmm?"

"I said, we need to talk about our future."

Warning bells went off in my head. Loud, clangy ones. Our last "future" talk had been the night of his fire station's Christmas party and almost ended up in us having the shortest engagement in history. Six hours, to be exact.

I pushed away from him and said, "Huh?"

He looked pretty serious. *Oh, dear.* It was midnight, and we had to have a serious "future" talk. I almost moaned.

"Honey, we need to set a date for the wedding, so you can start planning. I know you have piles of girly wedding stuff to do, especially since we're having such a big wedding."

"Huh?" Okay, I needed to wake up a bit. *Big wedding?* "What do you mean, such a big wedding? I thought we agreed small and intimate, maybe somewhere outdoors?" I was almost all the way awake by that time and regretting my door key decision again. I had to get up and go to work in six hours, for Pete's sake.

Lyle bit his lip, and suddenly he wouldn't look me in the eye. "Well, ah. About that. I was talking about it with the guys, and Vince said I couldn't get away with a small wedding, or was I afraid I couldn't measure up to *his* wedding to Cookie and, well, before you know it, I'd invited the entire company."

He cleared his throat. "And their families."

I stared at him, mouth hanging open. "What? We talked about this, Lyle. You know my family can't afford a big huge production like Cookie—and what kind of grown woman goes by the name of Cookie, by the way? Anyway, we can't afford what Cookie and her rich parents could afford. It's just not possible, honey."

"Well, Vince said we could get a loan."

"A loan? A LOAN?? So we get to start out our married lives in debt for the privilege of paying for your buddies to get sloshed at the reception? Vince is such a . . . a . . . giant butt hole! If Vince jumped off a cliff, would you follow him down?"

He grinned at me, which didn't help me calm down. "What are you smiling at?"

"You're so cute when you're ticked off."

I jumped up off the couch and tried making a mean, scary face at him. (Sadly, I've never been good at mean, scary faces.) "I don't want to be cute. I want you to take me seriously. I want you to quit treating me like a child. I just . . . I mean, oh, I don't know what I mean."

I sighed and walked over to the door, shoulders slumped. "I can't discuss this tonight. I'm exhausted, and I know I sound unkind and unpleasant, and I'm really sorry. Can we please talk about this tomorrow or, even better, on the weekend? I'm going to have a really busy week at work, and I don't want to get in trouble so early into a new job."

I put my hand on the doorknob and turned around.

Lyle still sat on the couch, staring at me in disbelief. "You're going to throw me out? In the middle of our discussion? Because you're tired?"

I always tried so hard not to get angry. Mama says anger is unbecoming to a lady. But I could feel tendrils of just plain *mad* creeping up through the tiredness that threatened to swamp my brain. "I don't have a schedule like yours. I didn't get to sleep in until noon today. I was up at six to get ready to go to work and figure out hieroglyphics and flying monkeys and demon camels! Then I practiced for an hour and had to face the cruise ship pillow at Madame's house. I can't do this now. Please, please understand."

He looked at me like I'd completely lost what was left of my mind, then closed his mouth and shoved up off the couch and grabbed his coat. He didn't look all that happy about it, though, and I could feel my brief spurt of rebellion dying away. "Honey, wait. You're right. I'm so tired, but I shouldn't take it out on you, after you were kind enough to bring me dinner. Wait. It's okay. Let's talk about it. I'll just make some coffee." I put my hand on his arm, and he stopped, but didn't let go of his coat.

He shook his head. "This job is ruining you. You're the nicest girl I ever met. Or at least you *used* to be. Sometimes I don't know who you are anymore."

As I closed the door behind him, I felt the tears clogging my throat. *I am* the nicest girl he's ever met. *I am. I just want to have my own life, too. Is that too much to ask?*

Some days I didn't know who I was anymore, either.

Some days I was too tired to care.

8

Kirby

Mi lasci in pace. (Leave me alone.)

It's ten a.m. and I've already been at work for five hours. Launching a line all by myself is a lot harder than I expected. It's not leaving me a lot of time to practice my Italian tapes for my trip. Not that I'm superwoman or anything, but maybe I didn't appreciate how much work my staff was actually getting done in between their twelve coffee breaks a day.

Speaking of coffee . . .

One fab thing about living in Seattle—there's a coffee place every five yards. I need a latte infusion. Triple shot, even. As I start to uncreak my bones from the hunched-over position they've been in for hours, the phone rings. I see *Stuart* on the little Caller ID screen and flinch.

I can pretend I'm not here.

Nah, that would be chicken. One thing I'm totally not, is chicken.

Still, I stare at the phone while it rings again. Brianna calls in from her desk. "Do you want me to get that, Kirby?"

Tempting. Sooooo tempting. But . . .

I pick up the phone and make a face at it before putting it to my ear. "Kirby Green."

"Where are the preliminary figures on the proposed marketing plan for the fourth quarter? I thought you were going to have that to me yesterday? Or is trying to do three people's jobs, in addition to your own, a bit much?" Banning sounds just the teensiest bit sarcastic.

Prick. Banning may look hot, but I bet Hugh Jackman never talks to people like that.

"Good morning, Banning. Are you just arriving? Keeping bankers' hours now, are we? Some of us have been here since five, trying to keep the company running." I laugh my fake "just kidding" laugh, so he doesn't fire me. Yet.

"Oh, I've been here. Working hard, wondering where the marketing plan is, you know, little things like that. Any ETA?"

I twirl the phone cord in my hand and contemplate the pros and cons of telling him where to stick the marketing plan.

Must act like a vice president now. Can't afford petty retorts, no matter how satisfying they might be.

"On the way. We had a few minor edits to make."

Yeah. Like taking demon camels out. Not so sure about the new assistant. She seems distracted.

". . . progress?" *Oops. Banning is talking again. I hate when he does that. Whatever happened to the strong and silent man?*

"Um, excuse me?"

"Any progress on getting someone to call you nice? You only have three weeks and six days, and I'm thinking it's going to be a big job." He sounds smug and pretty sure of himself.

Trouble is, I'm starting to agree with him.

I force a laugh. "Oh, that little thing? No worries."

A nasty thought occurs to me, and I get a death grip on the

phone cord. "What exactly do you expect in the way of proof? A signed affidavit or something?"

He laughs. If he weren't such a jerk, I'd notice that he has a totally sexy laugh.

I don't notice it.

"Nope. Your word is good enough for me. You're so competitive that you'd never be able to live with yourself if you didn't really do it, and your integrity was never under question. Just your hair-trigger temper."

Was that a compliment, in some odd way? Hmmm.

"Great. No problem. The marketing plan will be on its way to you within the hour. Is that all?"

"Well, no. Actually, I need the projections for the . . . ah . . . the *things.*"

"The things? Okay, you may need to be just a touch more specific. What things?"

Silence. The sound of paper shuffling.

Throat clearing.

"You know, the . . . ah, *things.* The things with the stuff on them."

This is funny as hell. Did our fearless leader forget which products we're launching, or . . .

No way.

But . . .

"The things with the stuff on them? Do you mean the new lingerie line?" I deliberately guess wrong, to test the theory that's taking shape in my very amused head.

"No," he says, sounding very frustrated. "The, ah, the sex toys. With the . . . er . . . lotion."

It's getting harder and harder to keep from cracking up. I take a deep, if shaky, breath. "The four-speed, variable pressure, high-intensity dildos with clitoral stimulators plus bonus edible warming lotion?" I ask in a very innocent voice. (Or at least as innocent as you can sound saying *dildo* and *clitoral stimulator. Lotion,* I can handle.)

So, apparently, can Banning. "Right, the . . . ah, lotion and stuff."

I can't help it. I howl. "Banning, are you having a problem saying the names of our products?" I scan my memory, and it occurs to me that he always says things like "product" or "item" in meetings.

Hmmm. Interesting.

He blusters. "Of course not. I just, ah, don't feel the need to blurt out that sort of thing at work."

"This *is* our work, remember? Did anybody tell you what W&L stood for, when you applied for the job?"

An evil but very funny gremlin took over my mind; that's my only excuse for what happened next.

"Banning? If it's uncomfortable for you to talk about sex toys, because, for example, you haven't had any experience with them . . . it's fine, you know."

"I don't—"

"Oh. You *don't*. I should have known. But you shouldn't be ashamed. Even in this day and age, it's okay to be a virgin. In fact, I admire you for it. What tremendous willpower you must have."

"*WHAT?* A *vir*—, you, I'm not—" Now he's almost shouting.

I inject a wise, sort of knowing tone into my voice. "You're *not* all that big on willpower? Oh, I'm so sorry. Never having the opportunity is *so* much worse. But we're equal opportunity employers here at W&L, according to that big Human Resources lecture I had to attend. Nobody will look down on you for being . . . untouched . . . and unable to say the product names."

The way he's sputtering, I'm doubled over trying not to roar with laughter. I'm glad this conversation is over the phone.

"I am *not* a virgin! Not that it's any of your business! And I *can* say our product names! Dildo! Vibrator! Lotion! Nipple clamps! Nipple, nipple, *NIPPLE!*"

"It's okay, Banning. You doth not have to protest so much, or something like that. Your secret is safe with me." I gently hang up the phone, trying not to fall off my chair. At least if I'm going to get fired, I'm going to go out with a bang.

With a bang. God, I crack myself up.

* * *

Clutching my enormous latte, I stop at Brianna's desk on the way back from Starbucks. "Did you deliver the final copy of the marketing plan to Banning?"

She looks up from her computer, and I notice the dark circles under her eyes. She looks like she got less sleep than I did. Since it's only Tuesday, I doubt she was out on a drinking binge last night. Her red sweater would normally look great with her dark curly hair (which I secretly covet; I always wanted mounds of curls, instead of the completely straight, can't-hold-a-curl-for-five-seconds hair that I got from Mom), but the pale-faced exhaustion ruins the effect.

I hesitate, reminding myself of my Don't Ask about Personal Lives rule.

Ah, the hell with it.

"Are you okay? You look awful."

She musters up a weak smile. "Don't beat around the bush, Kirby. Just come right out and say what you mean. You don't have to sugarcoat it for me."

I'm a little embarrassed. This girl is so nice, she makes me feel like Attila the Hun sometimes. "I'm sorry. I just meant that you look tired. Are you feeling ill?"

"No, but thank you for asking. It's just that I had a late night."

She suddenly sits up straight in her chair. "But I'm getting my work done. Don't worry. I personally delivered the report to Mr. Stuart, not to his secretary."

Her voice drops to a conspiratorial whisper. "Sometimes she loses things. Just in case you ever need to get something to him urgently, and I'm not around."

"Thanks. Good to know. I—"

Then her eyes open really wide. "I mean, not that I won't be around. I'll always be here. I don't take lots of coffee breaks. I don't really even drink coffee. It's bad for my chords. Except when I have a cold. Then it dries out the sinuses, which actually helps the chords."

She smacks her forehead with her hand and mutters, "Great, Bree. Talk about TMI. Like the vice president of marketing wants to hear about your sinuses. Brilliant."

I briefly wonder why everybody seems so intimidated by me, then remember the whole "nice" thing.

Sigh.

Suddenly, I flash back a step. "Chords? What does that mean, it's bad for your chords? What chords? And it's only too much information if you start talking about your intestines. I *hate* that." I smile, so she knows I'm just kidding.

Brianna starts shuffling papers on her desk. "Oh. Ah, nothing. I mean, vocal chords. I sing."

"Really? Like in church? In a band?" A bad thought flashes into my brain. "You're not one of those wannabe pop stars, are you? My best friend works for *Pop Star Live!,* and she says they're all nuts."

Remember nice? Oops. "Not that I think you're nuts, of course. You're probably a completely sane singer, right?"

I do a mental groan. *Great save, moron.* But it must be okay, because she laughs a real laugh this time. "No, I'm not a wannabe pop star. I'm a wannabe opera singer, which is actually even crazier. So I'm not sure 'sane' applies. But thanks for asking!"

Opera?

"Opera? Really? Not to be offensive, but I thought opera singers were a bunch of three-hundred-pound women in weird outfits. How are you going to hold up one of those Brunhilde costumes? What are you, a size four?"

"Size six, actually, and I'll have to gain some weight for the audition. I'm about thirty-five pounds light. But that's not for years, probably. I'm just not ready."

Suddenly she looks anxious again. "I'm not going anywhere, if that's what you're wondering. I'm very happy with this job. I wouldn't desert you or anything."

I smile. "I'm glad you're happy here. You're doing a good job, aside from the occasional demon camel." We both laugh this time.

I'm oddly reluctant to go back to work, for some reason. This chatting thing is kind of fun. My gaze skims her cubicle, and I notice a framed photo of a beautiful dark-haired woman and lean over to pick it up. "Is this your mom?"

Brianna laughs. "No, although I wouldn't mind having *her* genes. That's Maria Callas. She's—"

"I know who Callas is. I took a couple of music history classes in with all those business courses at UW. She's perhaps the most famous diva of the twentieth century, isn't she? *Carmen, La Boheme,* yada yada?" I'm reaching down into the depths of my memories, but I remember enjoying some of the music. Not Wagner, though. Hated Wagner. I shudder at the memory of being forced to endure the entire Ring Cycle.

They could torture prisoners for national secrets with that music.

Brianna is staring at me. Probably because I haven't talked to her this much about nonwork stuff since she started. Great. Now she'll think I'm turning into a nice person or some . . .

Hmmm.

I smile huge, with teeth, even, doing my Nice Boss impersonation. I can chat. Chatting is fun, even. "You don't sing Wagner, do you? That might be a firing offense. You know Wagner? Racist dude who liked to wear pink silk underwear?" The things you remember from Music Appreciation 101.

She smiles. "No, Wagner is not my favorite. And I hadn't heard that about the pink silk underwear. I'll have to mention it to my voice coach."

I glance at my watch and realize I have six days' worth of work to get done before tomorrow afternoon, so I can meet my new

Special Sibling. "I'd better get back to work. We'll have to go to lunch sometime, though, so you can tell me how you got interested in opera. I thought it was mainly for the blue-haired crowd. I *love* the idea of a job where you need to *gain* weight, though."

I head back to my office, almost humming. It's not that hard to be nice. Talk to people. Show interest in their lives. Brianna's life is actually interesting, so I didn't even have to fake it, unlike orgasms with whatshisname last month.

Oops. Focus.

Nice. I can *do* this. I can win this bet.

I just need a plan.

9

Brianna

*Aficionado: Devoted fan or enthusiast;
often used to describe opera buffs.*

I stared after my boss in shock.

What was that? Was she really being nice? She was almost—gasp!—chatty.

I shook my head in disbelief. It had been a strange few months working for Kirby, not the least of which was trying to hide the name of the company from Mama (can you imagine her telling her friends that little Bree works for Whips & Lace Manufacturing?), but this new, chatty mood of hers was maybe the most bizarre. Something was definitely up.

My phone rang; Caller ID said *Jamie*. I debated whether or not to answer; after last night I wasn't really in the mood to hear any sniping about Lyle. Maybe spending time with people who didn't like Lyle was a form of being unfaithful. Maybe I really *wasn't* a nice person anymore. Maybe the not-quite-flirting with Jamie would bring me bad singing karma.

Maybe I needed to quit waffling and answer the dumb phone.

I picked it up and made my serious face. "Hi, Jamie. Listen, I can't talk to you anymore if you're going to make unkind remarks about Lyle. I'm going to marry him, and it's not right for me to be friends with someone who can't respect that. I really like you, and I value our friendship, but that's just the way it has to be."

Dead silence. *Oh, crap. Now I've offended my only office friend. Could this week get any worse? Maybe I should just sign up for the cruise ship now.*

"Jamie? Are you there? I'm sorry if I seemed rude. Maybe we should talk about—"

"Um, Bree? I actually called about the marketing budget projections for the new *Kama Sutra* line Kirby was working on, to find out if they're ready. I have you on speaker phone, and Banning is here with me."

Oh. My. Goodness.

As I sank down in my chair, wondering how fast I could book myself onto the USS *Going Nowhere,* I whispered something about *figures* and *budget* and *soon,* then clicked off my phone. If Kirby heard about this one, her new friendliness would be headed straight for her overflowing out-box. I vowed never, ever to answer my phone again.

Naturally, it rang faster than I could find a pen to write *What is Calma Sootra?*

I opened one eye and tried to read Caller ID while banging my head against my desktop, but it didn't really work. Plus, my head was starting to hurt.

Outside line.

I took a deep breath and answered. "W&L. Hello, this is Brianna. May I help you?"

"Darling, it is I who have helped *you.* Your life is soon to be reaching the pinnacle of success. The mountaintop. The zenith. The veritable star-drenched sky soaring over the previously desert-like wasteland of your existence. Except, of course, for the bright spot that is me, Darling. The rainbow washing colors over the gray and gloomy—"

(Madame could go on like this for ten minutes at a time. I'm *so* not kidding.)

"Stop! I mean, yes, the stars and the rainbow and the wet spot. What are you talking about, Madame?" I'm sure I sounded a teensy bit impatient, and Patience is a Virtue and all that, but, I mean, really. *Desert-like wasteland?*

I thought of Jamie and Mr. Stuart. *Actually, I wouldn't mind burying my* head *in the desert sand right about now.*

"Not wet spot, Darling! Bright spot! I don't know why I bother with you. I should share the gifts of my talent and my shining network of friends and stars in the opera firmament with someone who appreciates me. Perhaps that new student of mine, Magda, would show me the proper respect when I work myself into an early grave for her, unlike some ungrateful children."

Now the soothing portion of our day would begin.

"Madame, you know I appreciate everything you've ever done for me." *And I've paid for lessons for eight years; I'm not exactly a case of your selfless benevolence.*

"I'm sure Magda appreciates you, but she's just a beginner. She may sing like a nightingale . . ."

More like a crow with a bad case of strep throat.

". . . but she's too new. Now please, please . . ."

My limit is two "pleases" today.

". . . tell me why you're calling. I'm very busy . . ."

For these last few precious moments when I'm gainfully employed, until Mr. Stuart tells Kirby about her seriously disturbed assistant.

". . . so what is it? Is it good news?"

Because I could sure use some good news. Now, even.

"Weell, I am too excited to delay, even for ungrateful students. You got it! You got it!" She shrieked in my ear so loudly, I was sure my eardrum was ruptured.

I held the phone away from my head for a moment and tried to shake the ringing out of my skull, then transferred the phone to the other ear, a cautious inch away from my head. "I got what, Madame? The music we're bidding on from eBay?"

"No, silly girl. The audition! The audition with the Seattle Opera! I called in a few favors, and you will be auditioning before the music director himself in only seven weeks!"

I dropped the phone. Literally. I even watched it as—in slow motion—it hit the desk, bounced, then smacked down on the carpeted floor of my cube.

You'd think I would have picked it up.

You'd be wrong.

"Bree? Are you okay?" Dazed, I lifted my head to stare at Jamie, mouth still hanging open. (Mine, not his. Mouth, I mean.) I could hear the squawking coming from the phone, which crouched ominously on the floor, staring up at me with its evil little phone eyes.

I am so losing it, here. Over the edge. I thought she said I have an audition in seven weeks.

"Brianna? Why is your phone on the floor? Are you okay?" Jamie crouched down in front of me, laughing, but his eyes looked worried. When I didn't answer, he said some really bad words kind of under his breath and picked up the phone. "Hello? This is Jamie. Brianna was just called away for an office crisis. She'll have to get back to you. Thanks." He dropped the phone back on the hook, not waiting for a response.

Ha. He just hung up on Madame. She'll have him for lunch. I wonder why I can't feel my feet.

Jamie then gently picked up one of my hands and tried to unclench my fingers. "Bree? Honey? Did you get bad news? Is someone in your family hurt? Oh, God, I didn't just hang up on your family or Lyle, did I? I'm such an idiot."

He released my hand and grabbed my shoulders. "Bree! You're really worrying me, now. What's going on?"

The hysterical laughter exploded out of my chest. Heck, maybe it exploded out of my vagina. Wherever it came from, it sounded pretty scary, even to me. "I have an audition. I have an audition with the music director of the Seattle Opera in seven short weeks, after my voice coach told me last night that I belong on a cruise ship. Do you think they have a karaoke machine at the Seattle Opera?"

* * *

Somehow I talked to Madame again and calmed her down, reminded Kirby about the budget figures, and even did some actual work in the hour or so before I headed out to get some lunch. Something with lots of carbs. And olive oil. Carbs drenched in olive oil.

I somehow had to gain thirty-five pounds in seven weeks.

Lots of olive oil.

Jamie snuck up behind me while I was waiting for the elevator. No way was I ready for an audition. I'd thought maybe sometime next year. Or the year after, even.

Not next month.

"Hey, beautiful. Going out for our usual carbo-load?"

I looked up at him. Way up. *Annoying tall people.* "You have no idea," I moaned. "Where can I get a plate of bread and pasta drenched in olive oil? And meatballs. I have a burning need for meatballs. Plus steak. A big, fat steak."

He grinned. "Going carnivore on me? How about Gianni's? I'm in the mood for a meatball or two, if I'm still allowed to have lunch with you, after what you said on the phone earlier."

Oh, *no.* After freaking out about the audition, I'd forgotten about the utter humiliation of the morning's speakerphone fiasco. I dropped my head in my hands and moaned again.

Jamie patted my shoulder. "It's okay, kid. Banning was talking to his secretary, and I don't even think he heard you. I just didn't want you to get yourself in any deeper." He shook his head. "Especially after his nervous breakdown earlier. I walked in to ask him a question about his expense report, and he was shouting *nipple, nipple, nipple* at the telephone."

I stared at him, then shrugged his hand off. "You're making that up! And don't call me kid. What are you, twenty-seven? I have enough people in my life who treat me like a child. I don't need another one."

He held his hands up in mock surrender. "Whoa. Just trying to help, O Wise and Aged One. No offense meant. I promise never to take the beloved Lyle's name in vain, either. How about we go get that olive oil now?"

As the elevator door opened, I wondered why my most cherished dream suddenly felt like my scariest nightmare.

* * *

"You can really pack it in, Bree." Jamie studied the remains of my lunch and whistled.

I felt my face burning. "It wasn't as bad as it looked. I only ate half of the salad." (I didn't have *time* to eat salad. I'd had to save room for the New York strip steak, pasta, and tiramisu.) Not to sound indelicate, but I was a giant, bloated gasbag after consuming more calories at lunch than I usually did in two days. Maybe I needed to rethink the weight gain and take it in a more slow and steady way. Anyway, I wasn't sure if I should blame the nausea on the olive-oil-tossed noodles or on my impending humiliation, auditioning for one of the top opera companies in the country.

Probably both. *Urp.*

The waiter brought the check, and Jamie snagged it before I could reach over my ballooned-out belly for it. "I've got this."

I frowned. "No way. We decided we'd split checks when we go to lunch. This isn't a date, Jamie."

He laughed. "No, I'm not that lucky. The girls I date eat half a rice cake when they're really hungry, with a side of water. I figure the least I can do is pay for the privilege of having lunch with a woman with a healthy appetite who's not going to head for the john and throw up everything she just ate."

"That's disgusting. Do you really go out with women like that? We need to find you a nice girl, Jamie. Not all women want to be model thin, you know."

He slid his credit card into the little folder and looked at me, all traces of humor gone from his expressive face. "The funny thing, Bree, is that I don't even like skinny women. I like women with curves on them, who look like women and not ten-year-old boys. And I'd love to find a nice girl. But they all seem to be taken, don't they?"

He almost sounded wistful, but then the moment passed, and he grinned again. "Anyway, after three months, I've finally gotten you to laugh at my dumb jokes. How could I stand to have lunch with anyone else?"

The waiter collected the bill, and Jamie and I sat there in silence. I don't know what *he* was thinking, but I was mostly trying not to belch or do something really disgusting and ruin his opinion of me forever, when suddenly he leaned forward.

"Speaking of nice girls, I heard the funniest rumor at work this morning."

I shook my head. "Jamie, you know spreading gossip isn't—"

He interrupted me. "Isn't *nice*. I know. That's what's so funny about it. I heard that Banning bet Kirby she couldn't get anybody to call her *nice* in the next month. If she loses, she loses her vacation. And, get this: she also loses her *job*."

I sat back in my chair, stunned. "That can't possibly be true. Why would Mr. Stuart do such a thing? Kirby works harder than anybody else in the company. And she's always nice to me . . . well, mostly, anyway."

Jamie lifted an eyebrow and looked at me.

"*Sometimes* she is! Sometimes she's nice to me. Just this morning, we chatted! That was nice." I racked my brain, trying to find more examples of my boss's disputed niceness.

"Right. Whatever you say, Bree. Anyway, it was about her firing half the marketing department. Not that they didn't deserve it. What a bunch of losers. You wouldn't believe the problems those bozos caused for us in finance when they screwed up a bunch of cost estimates. We all cheered when we heard somebody had finally had the balls to get rid of them. Well, balls, figuratively speaking. But, still, I think Stuart was ticked off that she didn't at least consult him first. He is the CEO, after all."

"But she's in charge of marketing. It was her responsibility. And, anyway, a bet? Isn't that rather juvenile? Will that even hold up if she decides to contest it? What about . . . what about labor laws or something?"

Jamie signed the credit card slip our server had dropped off and put his card back in his wallet, then pushed his chair back. "Hell, I don't know. But I think it's interesting that even while you're defending her, you're assuming that she's going to lose."

I hefted my bloated self out of the chair. *That last bite of tiramisu may have been a bad idea.* "I do *not* assume she's going to lose. Kirby is very nice. She will totally win this bet."

Jamie stopped moving and smiled a slow, speculative smile. "Wanna place a side bet? If she loses, you let me take you out to a real dinner?"

I tried to ignore the way my stomach started fluttering when he said "take you out." It wasn't interest, it was the eight-ounce steak.

Really.

Besides, I'm engaged.

These lunches had to stop.

"Jamie, there's no way she's going to lose, because I'm going to help."

He laughed and started walking again. "Bree, you're so deluded. Kirby getting someone to call her nice? Face it, it's hopeless."

Kind of like me getting someone to think I belong in the Seattle Opera.

Hopeless.

10

Kirby

Mi chiamo Kirby. (My name is Kirby.)

IM from: KGreen@WLM.com
It's hopeless, Jules. I don't even have a plan. I should just quit now and get it over with. I tried to be nice to my assistant today and wound up questioning her sanity. Let's face it, I just don't do Nice. But, hey! I might win a trip to Barbados. LOL.

IM from: julesvernon@popstarlive.com
Nothing is ever hopeless. I just got Roger, Hypochondriac of the Century, to go out on a press junket without a full-time nurse on staff. If I can do that, getting someone to call you Nice is gonna be a breeze. LOL. What about Barbados? And how is demon camel girl?

IM from: KGreen@WLM.com
Brianna's good. *She's* really nice. I should ask her for pointers. Sigh. Barbados was just a stupid crack Banning made.

IM from: julesvernon@popstarlive.com

Hey, that's a good idea! Never hurts to have somebody on your side. Want me to come home, and we can double-team this Banning jerk?

IM from: KGreen@WLM.com

No, it wouldn't work. You know about the bet, so it wouldn't count. I'll figure it out. I'll figure *something* out. I still have almost a full month. How's Sam? Still having wild, crazy, carpet-burn-on-your-knees sex? Did you get my latest care package?

IM from: julesvernon@popstarlive.com

<blushing> Kirby, stop with the care packages from your product line, already. I'm just not the crotchless panty kind of girl.

IM from: KGreen@WLM.com

Bet Sam liked it. <evil grin>

IM from: julesvernon@popstarlive.com

Let's just SO not go there, Kirbs. And you wonder why nobody calls you nice??? ☺ P.S. I have some news about that story of yours . . .

IM from: KGreen@WLM.com

Yeah, yeah, rub it in. At least I'm not on the cover of *People* magazine with my vibrator. WHAT story?

IM from: julesvernon@popstarlive.com

HEY!!! That was totally your fault! And another thing—

IM from: KGreen@WLM.com

Gotta go, Jules. Busy, busy. Work, conquering the world, and stuff. Bye. Hugs and sloppy wet kisses to Sam. <snicker>

IM from: julesvernon@popstarlive.com

I got your sloppy wet kisses right here, you stinker. Hey, seriously, call me if you need me. You've got my cell number. I have to go shopping for our trip. Or maybe I'll just take 2 empty suitcases and buy all new clothes in Italy? Hmmm, loving that idea. ttyl

IM from: KGreen@WLM.com
Ciao, baby! ☺

I close out of Instant Messenger and grin, thinking of Jules and her crazy job. She'd fallen into a job as a rookie production co-ordinator on *Pop Star Live!,* a cheesy new reality TV show, and somehow both she and the show had shot to the top of the charts, success-wise. I'd always thought that Jules and job success—heck, even job *longevity*—were totally incompatible. Hopeless, even.

My door flies open. "It's not hopeless." Brianna, out of breath and looking curiously disheveled, skids to a stop in front of my desk.

"What?" Okay, that's creepy. How could she know that I was thinking about Jules and her hopeless—

Bree puts her hands on my desk and leans toward me. "You. Being nice. It's not hopeless. I mean, not that you're not nice. Or that there was a chance that you were hopeless, or that people hoped you were nicely, I mean nice to be hoping, I mean . . . okay, Bree, catch your breath here."

She closes her eyes and takes a deep breath, while I wonder why I always get the crazy assistants. Then her eyelids pop open, and she stares at me. "Never mind. I just, um, needed to get those figures for the budget. Do you have them ready for me to type?"

I show admirable restraint and don't clutch my head or even roll my eyes. "Yes, Brianna. The figures are on your desk. I dropped them off while you were at lunch. Will you please type them up first thing?"

She beams at me. "Of *course* I will. That's so thoughtful of you to say please. It was really nice of you. You're such a nice person. In fact . . . oh."

She stops mid-sentence and glances at my office door, which rebounded to about half-closed after her exuberant entrance. Then she sort of sidles over to it and nudges it open all the way with her foot and turns so she's half facing me and half facing the open doorway.

"Kirby! It's so NICE of you to give me those figures early, so I'd have plenty of time to work on the report. You are such a NICE PERSON."

Opera singers can definitely project. They must have heard that in Oregon . . . *Oh, shit.*

"Brianna, please close the door and have a seat."

"But—"

"Now. Please." I fold my arms over my chest and sigh, wondering how long it took Banning to spread the news of our bet. Thirty minutes? Bet he really laughed it up with his buddies, too.

The voice of reason speaks up in my head: *But he doesn't seem like that kind of guy. You worked with him for months and really respected him, before all of this bet crap came up.*

I tell the voice of reason to shut up.

As my assistant gingerly sits on the edge of a chair, I sigh again. "Okay, spit it out. How did you hear about it? Am I the office gossip du jour? Is Banning having a good laugh over my job being on the line? Let's have it."

"I don't know what you're—"

"*Now,* Brianna. Please."

She wilts a little bit, shoulders slumping. "I may have heard something about a bet. But not from Mr. Stuart. Evidently his nosy old bat of a secretary heard him on the phone with you, and she's spreading this ridiculous rumor about a bet, and you getting someone to call you nice and—well—your job being on the line." By the end of her speech, her chin is almost resting on her chest, as she stares at the floor.

Then her head snaps up, and she glares at me. "But I didn't believe it. And I didn't spread the rumor. Plus, even if it *is* true, you're going to win. I have total confidence in you."

"Riiiight. So much confidence, that you were telling me how nice I am in your best projects-to-the-back-of-the-theater voice, so everybody can hear? What's wrong, Brianna? *You* don't think anybody else will call me nice, either?"

"No! That's not . . . I mean, I was just trying to help. That's how I always get in trouble. I'm always trying to help people whether they want me to or not. Mama always called me her little peacemaker, and I guess I haven't grown out of it."

Her huge brown eyes look so sad that I can't be angry at her. It would be like being mad at Bambi or something. This time I do roll my eyes. "Got it. You think I can do it. Only not really. So you want to help. Only not in a way that is useful, because it won't really count if you call me nice, since you know about the bet, will it?"

She jumps up and starts pacing back and forth in my office, humming. "Mmm, thinking, mmmmm lllaaaaaaa, mmmmmmmm, nice, mmmmmmmm, thinking—"

"Um, Brianna? What are you doing? It's very musical, but it's not really helping get the budget to Banning."

She stops dead, face flushing brick red. "Oh, dear. I'm so sorry. I hum when I get nervous sometimes. I once hummed the entire national anthem when I was waiting for a job interview, and it was so . . . er, you don't really care, do you?"

"Well . . ."

"No, forget that. We'll work together on this and show that . . . that . . . that meanie Mr. Stuart who's nice around here." She plants her fists on her hips and raises her chin—five feet, four inches of sheer defiance.

I'm glad she's on my side. But how lame is it to involve my assistant in my personal problems? I've done everything on my own all my life.

Yeah, and see how far that's gotten you. No friends but Jules, no boyfriend, and no job, if you can't win this bet.

I lean back in my chair and smile at Brianna. "What did you have in mind?"

11

Kirby

Vuole andare a ballare? (Would you like to go dancing?)

It's almost five, and I've been at work for nearly twelve hours. The marketing plan for the "items" that Banning-the-virgin can't name out loud is shaping up to be pretty terrific. (Oh, and wouldn't I love to be the one to . . . *break him in* . . . if it were only true.)

The "get somebody to call Kirby nice" plan is nonexistent. "Can't win 'em all" somehow doesn't seem to help.

My door bangs open again. *I wonder if Human Resources has How to Open a Door Without Banging It classes for new employees?*

"Oops! Sorry about the door, Kirby. I'm just so excited!"

Now that's creepy. Are opera singers psychic? How did she know I was just thinking about the door banging? Or am I finally losing any semblance of sanity?

"Door number two, anybody?" I mutter.

"What? I didn't hear that. Anyway, take a look at this!" With a flourish, Brianna swoops a newspaper down on my desk and beams a delighted smile at me. "The answer to our problem!"

I tilt my head at her, trying not to hate how she still looks fresh and perky, at the end of a killer day, when I . . . *don't.* "*We* have a problem? More demon camels?"

She blushes a little, but stands her ground. This is definitely progress; when she started working here, the slightest frown sent her scurrying. Nice is one thing—*mouselike* totally something else. *Just ask my mother.*

I clench my eyes closed and shake my head. No time for that crap. I'm nothing like her. *Nothing.*

"Kirby? Um, you can't read the paper if you don't open your eyes . . ."

I open one eye. Brianna's still standing there. Points for her. She's saner than I am these days. I open the other eye and look down at the paper, wondering what she's so excited about.

"*Local Humane Society Polkas for Pooches?* Um, you want me to get a dog? Well, dogs have that unconditional love thing going, for sure, but they can't talk, so Fido couldn't exactly call me nice."

"But—"

"I wonder if tail wagging would count? Banning said I didn't need an affidavit, so maybe nonverbal expressions are good enough."

"But—"

"Tail wagging and face licking. Except, *euww* with the face licking. Don't dogs always lick their butts? I never had a dog growing up, so I'm not really sure, but I don't want dog-butt germs on my face. Do you know how much this Estée Lauder foundation costs? Anyway, not that dogs aren't cuddly, but I'm *so* not going to polka. A girl has to draw the line somewhere. What about—"

"STOP!" Brianna slams her hand down on the paper, then immediately looks horrified. "I'm so sorry. I didn't mean to yell at you. Oh, now you're really going to fire me, and you didn't even hear about me telling Mr. Stuart that I couldn't have lunch with

Jamie because he says mean things about Lyle and I can't afford to be fired right now, but I just wanted you to listen, and . . . oh, *poop*."

She sinks down in my visitor's chair, and it's my turn to look horrified. Then the silly factor hits me, and I grin. "Brianna, we sound like a couple of babbling nut jobs. Plus, for two super-talented women, we spend way, way too much time worrying about getting fired. Now, slow down, and tell me what I'm supposed to be seeing in this paper, and what problem it solves."

Leaning over my desk, she points to the column on the left of the page, next to the fold. It's the *Seattle Times* and Brianna's fingernail taps on the blurry black and white headshot of C. J. Murphy, one of the funniest columnists I've ever read. She translates Guy Talk into normal human conversation. In other words, something that a *woman* can understand.

"Oh, C. J.? What's she talking about this week? *The Naked Truth About Guys* is the funniest column in the world, since Dave Barry's tragic retirement. I *love* her."

I look up at Brianna and smile again. "Did you see the one where she translated 'I'll call you' into 'It's been fun, but I can't really remember your name, and only if killer monkeys take over the world and every other available female between the ages of sixteen and seventy vanishes will I ever pick up a phone and call you. Oh, and that's only if none of the killer monkey chicks are hot'?"

Brianna's lips don't even twitch. She's wearing her Be Serious face. "Kirby, it's about speed dating. You can 'date' ten guys in an hour and set up real dates with any of them that you like and who like you. You're so gorgeous and smart, you're bound to get tons of dates."

I narrow my eyes and look down at the paper again.

Speed dating, clearly invented by a Guy, is the Guy's dream date. Ten desperate women in a room, and a Guy only has to spend ten minutes with each one to sniff out his odds of getting lucky. In this context, "get lucky" does not mean find the girl of

his dreams, buy rings, and live happily ever after. Why would any
self-respecting woman ever buy into this crap?

"This is not exactly a ringing endorsement of speed dating. Are
you implying that I lack self-respect?"

"Not self-respect, just time. We only have three and a half
weeks left." She claps her hand to her mouth almost before the
words are out. "Oh, dear. It's not that I don't think someone will
call you nice all on your own. I'm just trying to be helpful. Too
much of Mama in my head all the time. 'Be a nice girl, Brianna.
Nice girls are helpful. Nice girls don't come home with hickeys.
Nice girls don't want to sing on stage.' "

I can feel my mouth falling open a little and snap it shut again.
Guess I'm not the only one with family issues. I try for a joking
tone. "Whose problems are we talking about here, anyway?"

She won't meet my eyes. "Sorry. Anyway, I was just trying to help.
It's after five. I have to get going now. I'll see you in the morning."

I watch her trudge to the door and debate calling her back.
Pride fiercely battles desperation for a moment. Desperation wins.

Guess C. J. was right. "Brianna."

She stops and turns to look back at me. "Yes?"

"Thank you. I think it's just crazy enough to cause me spectacular humiliation, but it might work anyway. I'll call in the morning and set it up."

She grins. "I already did. You're on for this Friday at eight
o'clock at El Gaucho, in the jazz bar downstairs. It's called the
Pampas Room."

As she gently closes my door, I'm surprised into laughter. The
Pompous Room? Boy, will *that* fit. Maybe my new assistant is
growing a backbone after all. I can teach her to quit being so
nice . . .

*Hey! If I can teach her to be less nice, maybe she can teach
me—*

The phone blares, interrupting my plotting. I glance at Caller
ID and then at the clock and wonder if I really need to answer an

outside line at five thirty. Workaholic Kirby wins this round. "Kirby Green."

"Hey, luscious. Got any of your new product line you'd like to try out on me?" Daniel's voice in my ear is silken heat. Just like the feel of his body always against mine.

Too bad he's such a rat bastard.

I'm childishly proud of myself for not dropping the phone, since my hands are shaking so hard. "What do you want, Daniel? Wait—let me guess. Your latest love slash bank account dumped your sorry ass?"

"Kirby, Kirby, Kirby. When did you turn so bitter? Do you still miss me that much? I miss you, my beautiful one. How about dinner? Or are you chained to your desk?" He laughs the smoky laugh I know he's practiced in front of many mirrors. Daniel's tools are seduction, charm, and flattery, and he's way too good at all of them.

Oh, and sex. He's *brilliant* at sex.

"Kirby? I kind of like you in chains. Remember when I had those handcuffs and you—"

"Daniel! I'm hanging up now. I told you the last time that we were over. No more money, no more drunken sex, no more *us*. Get over yourself, already. I've moved on, and my new boyfriend is extremely large and extremely jealous."

Daniel was always a wimp when it came to actual confrontation with anyone his size, so I figure a teensy white lie would get rid of him.

"Right, Kirby. Your new boyfriend. Except when would you have time to meet a new man with your eighty-hour workweeks? You forget you're talking to me, Kirbs my love. I know you. I know *all* about you. Even about your secret dream of writing a novel." He laughs. "There *is* no man. So how long has it been for you? Five, six months without sex? At least, sex when anyone else is in the room? I know you have all those lovely toys from your new job."

I'm going to throw up. I got this job after I dumped him the last time. And I knew I never should have let him see my writing. How did he know? Is he stalking me?

I draw a deep breath to try to buy time to answer, and my door bangs open again and Banning strides into the room, looking down at a sheaf of papers in his hand. "Kirby? Can we talk about—oh. Sorry. Didn't realize you were on the phone. Catch you tomorrow."

"No, wait! Now is good." I wave him in, then hold a hand up to partially shield my face and the phone. "We're over, Daniel. O. V. E. R. Don't call me again."

I put the phone down with perhaps a teensy bit of unnecessary force, because Banning sort of jumps in his seat and looks up at me full-on for the first time. Whatever he sees must be bad, because he frowns. "Are you all right? We can talk about this tomorrow. It's no more urgent than anything else."

I take another deep breath, wishing I'd learned meditation, self-hypnosis, or something *useful* in school. "No, of course not. Wrong number."

Wrong number, wrong man, wrong, wrong, wrong.

Is it too much to ask for something—anything—to go right?

He looks at me askance for a minute, then shrugs, and his face goes back to grim. "All right. We need to talk—and in NO way are we discussing anything to do with my sexual history or alleged lack thereof—about the figures for the . . ."

There's an almost imperceptible pause, then he continues. "Figures for the phasing out of the leather whips line."

Then he looks me right in the eye. "These figures are all wrong."

Yep. It was totally too much to ask.

12

Brianna

Maestro: Literally, "master." The conductor of the orchestra.

Home at last. My whole body heaved in a deep breath of relief. I carefully placed my keys in the pewter bowl on the cherrywood table by the door, then crossed to the window and pulled the awful orange and green-checked curtains closed, wondering again why I didn't take them down and buy something I liked. Curtains that would actually match my color scheme, for example.

I sighed. Aunt Laverne had sewn those curtains herself, in spite of her arthritis, as an apartment-warming gift for me. After she'd been so sweet, I couldn't throw her curtains away.

It's been three years, Bree. Donate them to Goodwill, and maybe a poor family who likes green and orange could give them a good home. The little voice in my head was sounding less and less like my conscience these days and more and more like a rebellious teenager. Since I'd never been a rebellious teenager, though, I couldn't quite be sure.

I collapsed down on the couch and contemplated my most pressing decision: extra cheese with pepperoni or veggie special? I dialed the phone and splurged on a large, hand-tossed, half each way. *Who says being decisive is all that important?*

About half an hour later, the phone blared, rousing me out of my fuzzy-blanket and CNN-induced stupor. I reached for it, then snatched my hand back, mentally listing all the people I didn't want to talk to right then. It was a fairly long list: Mama, Lyle, Madame, Lyle's mom, or anybody from the office.

Oh, no telemarketers, either. I'd put myself on that no-call list, but it *so* didn't work.

Third ring. *Oh, for Pete's sake. I have to get Caller ID. Tomorrow. Definitely.*

Fourth ring. *Aarrgh. I give up.*

"Hello?"

"Bree? It's Erika! How are you? Still letting Madame intimidate you with the pillow?"

Laughing, I sank back into my own pillows. "We just had the cruise ship talk this week."

Erika Kaufmann, talented singer and wonderful friend, howled.

"I'm not sure that mocking the less fortunate is a good start to your elegant new career with the Atlanta Opera, Erika. Is there a deportment person I can report you to? Manners police? I bet those nice southern girls don't know what to do with you."

She snickered. "The southern *boys* can't quite figure it out, either, but I'm damn sure keeping them guessing. Wait, let me guess: 'Dahling, Dahling, I have wasted the best years of my life on you, and I will go down in history—' "

I sighed. "No, 'to my grave' this time."

"—I will go to my grave—"

We finished it together, shouting, "cloaked in shame!"

It took a few minutes for us to get our breath back and quit cackling like crazy women. "I sure do miss you," I said.

"I miss you, too. These people out here are way too serious and a little snooty; all 'opera is my life.' Bo-ring."

I grinned. One thing Erika would never, ever be was boring. She dressed and acted more like a pop star than what she really was—one of the rising stars of opera. She'd only been in Atlanta for two years, and already a reviewer had called her "the next Renee Fleming." (That probably hadn't helped the other singers warm up to her.) We'd both trained with Madame, although Erika had been a few years in front of me.

Speaking of which . . .

"She's rookie-ing me. Some girl named Magda." Erika had coined the term for the little competitions and rivalries Madame tried to foster between her advanced and beginning students.

"No! Already? She must think you're ready for the big time, Bree. She didn't start to rookie me with you until she'd already set up the Atlanta audition . . . OMIGOD!!! Did you get it? An early audition? When? Tell me *now*!"

"How did you—well, anyway, yes. She set up an audition for next month! Only seven weeks away. There's no *way* I'm ready. There's no way I can be ready by then. Seven months, yeah, maybe. But seven weeks? No way. And I'm a good thirty-five pounds below weight."

A very huge silence swept down the phone line at me.

I laughed a little. "Well, don't rush in to tell me that I'm wrong, and I really am ready, or anything."

Another silence.

"Bree, it's just . . . you know I love you, honey. And you're totally ready. Completely ready—with the voice stuff. You're amazing, and you know it. I've told you many times that you have the capacity to become one of the world's foremost coloraturas. It's just . . ."

You know there's a problem anytime a conversation starts out with "you know I love you" and then ends with "it's just . . ."

The acid in my stomach started doing some sort of whirling

dervish dance. "It's just what, Erika? What is it *just*? I have the voice, but I don't have . . . *what*?"

She sighed. "I'm sorry. I didn't mean to stress you out. But after two years here with these barracudas, I wonder if you have the mental toughness. They don't use the word *diva* for no reason, you know."

It was my turn to be silent. As much as I hated it, she'd voiced my biggest fear. The irony wasn't lost on me, given my campaign for Kirby, but I was terrified that I was too *nice* to succeed in opera.

"Bree? I'm sorry. I'm sure that you're tough enough. I'm just overprotective. Ignore me, I had a bad day, which is why I called you in the first place, to get sympathy from somebody who doesn't say *bless your heart* when she means *kiss my ass*."

My "take care of the world" instincts kicked in on full alert, and I shoved my own worries to the side. "Oh, don't worry about it a minute longer. Now, what's wrong? You said you loved the people you were meeting out there. What about your neighbor who made you a pecan pie?"

Not to be unkind, but Erika could always be distracted by talking about Erika, so we managed to have a nice chat before the delivery guy rang the doorbell with my pizza. She never had a chance to circle back around to my upcoming doom.

I mean, upcoming *audition*.

"Oh, I have to go. That's the door. I'll call you soon. And just remember not to let those mean people get you down. You're going to have a brilliant career! Can't wait to see you this summer. Keep in touch!"

"But—"

The doorbell rang again. "I really have to run, or they'll take my pizza away, and if that happens you'll hear a grown woman cry. Hugs to you. Talk soon."

"Okay, hugs to Lowell." She hung up.

"It's *Lyle*," I said to the dial tone. It had been dislike at first sight for Lyle and Erika. She thought he was a "stick," and he hated her outrageous flair for fashion and drama. He wasn't crazy about her gay friends, either. Many of whom were my friends, too, leaving me wondering if old-fashioned really meant prejudiced in Lyle's case.

Gosh, I hope not. I don't know if I can . . .

The pizza guy pounded on the door, jolting me out of my trance. I clicked the phone off and rushed for the door, grabbing my purse on the way. Me—not tough enough? *Ha! The pizza is fifteen minutes late. I'll show them who's tough. I won't tip the delivery person at all.*

* * *

Too nice to be successful at opera. Too nice to stand up to pizza guy. Pitiful, pitiful.

Sitting on the couch, clutching my half-empty pizza box, I reflected glumly on my lack of toughness, ruthlessly rejecting each defense my pathetically nice self raised.

He was so young, he probably needed the money for school.

He was at least thirty.

It wasn't a very big tip.

It was twenty-five percent.

He had a cute face.

Well, okay.

Why couldn't I be more like Kirby? If only we could have some kind of magical personality transfer, like in the movies, except not the whole thing, just a bit of niceness going her way and a touch of toughness for me.

Hey! That's it! I can ask her to help me be less nice, while I help her win that silly bet. I mean, if asking my boss for something like that isn't too personal, or offensive, or would make her think that I'm a mouse.

I looked at my ugly curtains and sighed. I *was* a mouse. But people can change. January was a great time for resolutions, right?

Squaring my shoulders, I looked for a piece of paper to make a list.

WAYS TO BE LESS NICE

1. Don't be afraid to answer your own phone. Be polite, but firm when you need to hang up. People will have to understand that you have a life.
2. No more huge tips for late pizza! (Even if delivery guy is cute!)
3.

The phone rang before I could think of a three. It was an opportunity to try out the new me! Keeping item one firmly in mind, I answered the phone. "Hello."

"Hi, honey, it's Mama. How are you? We haven't talked in so long, I was worried you were sick or in trouble. Is everything all right? Do you need chicken soup? Or any cash? I'll send Daddy right over with some soup and cash."

Before I could say a word, she was yelling for Daddy. "Henry? Come wrap up this pot of soup for Brianna and stop by the ATM and take her some cash. Bree, honey, how much do you need? Will two hundred help? Henry, get her two hundred. Or make it three hundred, in case she needs some new winter underwear. Go on, get moving; well, that pot is hot, you have to use the—"

"Mama! I don't need soup or cash. Thank you, but I'm fine. I've just been very busy at work, that's all. Tell Daddy I don't need him to rush out and bring me anything, but thank you. Thanks to both of you. And Mama, I'm all grown up now. Please stop worrying about whether or not I need to buy new underwear. It's embarrassing."

I looked down at my list in despair. Could life *be* any more unfair? My first test of item one has to be my mother? Why couldn't some low-interest mortgage or vinyl siding salesperson call me? They called all week long when I didn't want to hear from them.

But, oh, *nooo*. Not tonight. Tonight I had to try out "Be polite, but firm when you need to hang up. People will have to understand that you have a life" on my mother.

I crumpled up the list and tossed it over the coffee table toward the wastebasket.

"I missed. Figures. Not even tough enough for that," I muttered.

"What, dear? What figures? Are you sure about the cash? Daddy is right here. I can make him put his coat and shoes on and dash out—"

"Mama, I'm fine, I don't need soup or money, and Daddy definitely doesn't need to 'dash' out. I really need to get to work, anyway, Mom. I haven't worked on my music yet tonight. Can I call you back—"

"Oh, honey. You work too hard. Do you really need to practice every night, now that you're going to get married? My friend Corinne's daughter, you know, the one with the unfortunate nose? The daughter, not Corinne, although come to think of it, I think Corinne's nose may be a bit different than it was before her African safari. Do you know if they have something in the water over there that shrinks noses? Anyway, her daughter just got married last June; you remember, I gave her that nice handmade pottery vase, which I'm still waiting on a thank-you note for, the manners of some young people these days. I swear, if you ever acted like that I'd feel like a failure as a mother."

She didn't pause, so much as stop to gulp in oxygen.

"Mama, really, I need—"

"Where was I? Oh, right. Corinne's daughter is already pregnant. She quit her job this week, so she can fully devote herself to experiencing her pregnancy and giving the baby the most healthy environment possible." It sounded like she was repeating, word for word, something that Corinne had shared over the bridge table. "Don't you think you might want to do the same once you and Lyle get married?"

"Mama? Not to be unkind, but I have worked for seven years toward a future as an opera singer. Corinne's daughter worked part time at Burger Barn. You're not really comparing us, are you?"

It was definitely time for the "be firm and hang up" part of the new plan. "I really do need to get going, Mama. I'll call you later this week. I love you! Hugs to you and Dad."

"But, Bree, I—"

"Really, Mama. It's getting late. I'll call you later. Take care. Bye." I scrunched my eyes closed, gritted my teeth, and pressed the *off* button on the phone. When the ceiling didn't immediately fall on me for daring to be disrespectful to my mother, I relaxed a little bit and opened one eye. No lightning, thunder, or plagues of frogs.

I opened the other eye. No disaster at all, unless you counted the mess from my pizza binge. Maybe there was something to this being firm idea? I crossed the room to retrieve my crumpled list from the floor, since my guardian angel had clearly kept it from going into the wastebasket. I smoothed out the paper and tapped my pencil on the page. *Number three, number three. Hmmm.*

The phone rang again, and I rolled my eyes, realizing that Caller ID was a necessity, not a luxury.

"Hello?"

"Honey, it's Mama again. We must have gotten cut off. Did I tell you that Aunt Laverne wants to give you her wedding dress for your 'something borrowed'? Now we have to find a way to tell her no without hurting her feelings, the dear, because of course you'll wear *my* dress. Maybe Laverne can sew something for the bridesmaids to wear. I think a nice eggplant color, maybe?"

My gaze strayed to Aunt Laverne's last sewing effort for me, the hideous orange and green-checked curtains, and I tried to think of anybody I hated enough to ask to wear a dark purple bridesmaid's dress.

I slumped back down on the couch, listening with half an ear to Mama ramble on and on about wedding preparations, while I kept folding and unfolding my sad little list.

". . . and we can get a discount on the cake . . ."

"Um, hmm."

". . . organist . . ."

Halfway through her discussion of something to do with the merits of a beach vacation versus a ski vacation, in terms of producing an early grandchild, I finally gave up. They were *all* right. Mama, Lyle, Erika, and even Madame with her stupid pillow.

I can't do it. I'm not tough enough. I'll call Madame and tell her.

For the next twenty minutes, while Mama planned out my wedding, I nodded and mmm-hmmm'd, methodically shredding my new plan into confetti on my lap and ignoring the tears streaming down my face.

No big deal. It's not like the world is desperate for another opera singer, right?

No big deal at all.

After Mama finally said good night, I made another call. There was no use putting it off any longer.

"Hello? I really, really need to sign up for Caller ID."

13

Kirby

Posso vedere il menù, per favore? (May I see the menu, please?)

Halfway through another twelve-hour day (but at least I'll finally meet little Lauren this evening; I'm first-date nervous about *that,* trust me), Banning drops by my office.

Normally, I'd be totally up for a view of his lovely self, but the bet has changed the way I look at him. For example, I never really noticed before that his eyes are too close together. Plus, all that thick hair is probably the kind that will bald prematurely. I never liked bald guys. *Euww.* Don't *even* get me started on the whole comb-over issue.

I'm fairly sure that my head may explode into tiny pieces if I have to hear one more time this week about how I'm not nice enough. I've spent the past four hours trying to figure out how my figures are wrong. Either everything I learned in school suddenly vanished from my brain cells, or those numbers are right.

"Green. Your numbers are right."

Oh-*kay*. People *so* have to quit doing that to me. Am I psychically projecting my thoughts? First Brianna, with "hopeless," and "door," and now Banning, with "numbers are right." Maybe I'm some kind of ESP mutant.

"Hello? Earth to Kirby? Did you hear me?" He smiles and props a shoulder against my doorway. "Oh, I get it. You're waiting for my formal apology. Well, you deserve it. You were right, and I was wrong. I spent all night backtracking the figures to where the discrepancy came up, and it turns out the head of the team you fired had been feeding me the wrong numbers for months."

He laughs, but it's not a happy laugh. "I was wondering why our marketing figures were approximating the national debt of a small country. I should have checked into it a long time ago. Good job."

I am, whether anybody will ever believe it of me or not, speechless. Luckily, it doesn't last long. But discretion is probably the better part of valuing my job. "Thanks for letting me know. I've been tearing my hair out trying to figure out where I went wrong."

I look down at my desk, battling the evil urge to do the happy dance all over my office, flinging budget papers wildly about. Gloating is so unprofessional.

Probably not *nice*, either.

"Is that all you're going to say?" he asks, staring at me with a look of "this is *so* not the Kirby we all know and love" on his face. (All right, all right, I may be ad-libbing the "and love" part of that.)

I smile gently. "Was there something else you needed?"

He shakes his head, still looking confused. *Am I really that prone to gloating? Um, oops.*

He turns to leave, then stops and looks back. "How about lunch?"

Whoa. Where did that come from? Are we suddenly going to go back to the "just colleagues who are starting to be friends and might, in fact, think each other is a hottie" phase of our relation-ship? As opposed to the "you're a hateful bitch who couldn't be nice to save her own ass, vacation, or—in fact—job" phase?

I must have a weird expression on my face, because he shrugs. "If you're busy, that's fine. I thought we'd discuss your plans for coverage while you're in Italy."

"Well, I have to—*wait*! You just said for while I'm in Italy. You believe I'm going to win your bet, don't you? Ah HA!" I lean back in my chair, cross my arms over my chest, and smile hugely. "I can't believe you're putting me through all this, when you know I'm—"

"I meant *if. If* you go to Italy." But his lips are twitching at the corners when he says it, so I consider it a moral victory.

As I enjoy the truly lovely sight of his firm butt walking away from me, it occurs to me that I should have agreed to lunch. Maybe we could get this colleague slash friend slash potential we're-two-consenting-adults-so-where's-the-harm thing going?

Yummy. Except . . . no. No dating the boss. Just a professional, businesslike lunch.

I glance at my watch, gauging how long it will take for him to reach his office, so I can call and accept the lunch date, then look up to see Brianna hovering at my door.

She shifts from one foot to the other, biting her lip a little. "Kirby, um, would it be possible for us, ah, I mean, are you free for lunch?"

I seriously have to look into this ESP thing. *The Psychic Hotline: Not just a hoax, but maybe a new career direction?*

* * *

As we hurry down the street to Oceanaire, hunched over against the cold drizzle, I'm struggling to think of things to talk about with Brianna. I've never been good at social chitchat. I figure it's a learned skill. In high school, when the other kids my age were learning to be social, I was learning to be antisocial.

It's better to be disliked than pitied.

Sometimes pride is the only thing you've got to wear that isn't a hand-me-down from the church charity or a thrift shop. Plus, it's one-size-fits-all and never goes out of style.

Not all that warm, though.

I push open the door to the restaurant, and we hurry into the warmth inside. The interior has a fifties kind of feel, but Oceanaire has the greatest seafood dishes around.

"Oh, it smells really great in here," Brianna says. "Now this is the kind of place I wouldn't mind gaining thirty-five pounds in."

She immediately turns a funny shade of pink, but before I can ask what's up—and *gain thirty-five pounds? Is she pregnant?*—the hostess comes to seat us. I'm glad I called to make reservations before we left; the place is full, as usual.

Seated in our booth against the window, I toy with the menu and glance at Brianna, wondering whether it's PC to ask about the "gain pounds" comment. Various HR departments have forced me to listen to so many boring lectures about legal stuff, you'd think I'd remember whether or not I can get in trouble for asking my assistant if she's pregnant.

Or even for congratulating her if she is.

Although, she's so nice, she's probably the type who will quit to stay home with the baby, so I'll have to hire somebody else who won't understand my writing, won't get my sense of humor, and definitely won't come up with speed-dating strategies to outwit the CEO.

I sigh, then a thought slams into me, and I almost knock my water glass over. *Oh, crap. I like her.* Friendship *like, not just* "somebody you work with" *like.*

This can't be good.

I must have a weird look on my face, because Brianna tilts her head and makes a "what's up?" face. "What's up?"

"Um, nothing. I just, ah, wondered if I'd have the crab cakes or the mahi mahi." I scanned the menu, pretending to read it.

*Never let them know you want to be their friend. That makes
it more fun for them to kick you to the curb.*

I tell my teenaged self to shut up. I have a platinum Visa now;
I'm not the too-tall girl in the too-short jeans huddling at the bus
stop while everyone else drove by me in their cars, laughing.

At *me*. Always laughing at me.

I shake my head to get rid of the vicious mood that somehow
snuck up on me. I must need food. Low blood sugar, that's it. I
need to order some food. And appetizers. And dessert, even.

Speaking of ordering, these prices are kind of high. I don't want
her to worry about paying. "Brianna, lunch is my treat."

"No, you don't have to do that. I invited you. We should at
least split the check." She looks flustered. Maybe seafood wasn't
a good idea. If we're talking morning sickness, maybe she's going
to take one whiff of my crab cakes and run for the bathroom to
hurl.

Oooo, seafood was a totally bad idea.

"We can go somewhere else, if you don't like fish," I say, leaning back against the leather seat, in case she's one of those projec-
tile cookie tossers.

She still looks distracted, but she laughs, then starts fiddling
with her salad fork. "What? No, I love seafood. Drenched in lots
of butter and garlic."

"I have to agree with that. But, really, what *isn't* better
drenched in butter? Sadly, my advanced age costs me an extra mile
on the treadmill for every butter pat, so I'm going to go with the
crab salad, dressing on the side. What about you?"

The server shows up and we order, and I ask for the crab cakes
appetizer, too. No need to take the healthy food thing too far,
right? Brianna orders the salmon, and we sit in silence as the guy
walks away with our menus. Then we both speak at the same time.

"Well, I—"

"I've got—"

We both do the nervous laugh thing, which is weird, because

this is Brianna, the one person I've worked with really well in years. Something must be up.

I suck in a huge breath. "Out with it, Brianna. Why are we here, why are you so nervous, and why do you have to gain thirty-five pounds? Are you—and I apologize in advance if this is none of my business—but are you pregnant? Are you quitting?"

Her eyes are huge. "Pregnant? Oh, gosh, no. That would be the last thing . . . quitting? No, no, no. I mean, if I actually got . . . but there's no chance, since I'm not going to do it, and anyway, well."

She grabs her glass and gulps down a pint of ice water. "Well. Okay. Why did you think I might be pregnant? Do I look fat? I told Lyle we needed to quit driving out to the Krispy Kreme place. Although I guess it doesn't matter now. *Aarrghh.*"

I laugh, a real laugh this time. "No, you look as tiny as ever. But you said something over by the door about gaining thirty-five pounds, and I didn't know what to think. The only reason I could come up with was—"

"That I'm pregnant," she finishes my sentence, shoulders slumping.

"Well, yeah. What were you talking about, then?"

She fidgets with her silverware some more, "It's a long story, and it doesn't really apply now, anyway. The reason I wanted to talk to you away from the office is I might have another idea about this, er, bet issue."

I'm not sure I'm up for any more of her ideas. The last one got me signed up for the tackiness of speed dating. What's next? Beauty pageants? Infomercials?

Reality TV? I shudder.

She must have seen me, because she starts talking. Fast.

"No, it's not bad or tacky. It's just that, well, everybody I've ever known thinks I'm nice. 'Nice Brianna.' 'Brianna's the nice one.' 'Aren't you nice, Brianna?' "

My voice is a tad wry. "Yeah, rub it in, why doncha?"

"But I'm not. That's just it. I *hate* it. I hate being called nice all the time. Especially when people don't look any deeper, so that's all they see in me. One bland, plain vanilla personality trait."

She grimaces. "*Nice!* What a stupid word."

I start to agree with her, but then our crab cakes arrive. I smile, say thanks, and impatiently wait for waiter guy to refill our water glasses, then lean forward. "I don't mean to be dense, but yes, I get that people think you're nice. How does that help with the bet? You want Banning to bet you, instead of me? I'm guessing he won't go for it."

She swallows her first bite of crab cake and puts her fork down. "Mmm. Bliss. Sorry, great crab cakes are such a distraction. No, no, no. I was wondering . . . I thought we might, well, here's the thing . . ."

I interrupt her before she dithers our entire lunch hour away. "Bree," I say as gently as possible. "Do I make you nervous? Because I thought we were working together pretty well. But if *you*, of all people, can't even force out a complete sentence around me, I don't have much hope of winning the bet anyway." Or of ever becoming somebody that people actually *like*, I think.

Pathetic, much?

Her mouth drops open, and she turns bright red again. I've never seen a grown woman who blushes so often. "No, I'm so stupid. I sometimes have a hard time . . . well. Okay. Just out with it, Bree."

She squares her shoulders and looks me straight in the eye. "I'll teach you to be nice, if you'll—"

"Teach you how *not* to be nice," I finish, feeling a weird chill as the woo woo factor washes over me. She's proposing exactly what crossed my mind last night.

"That's right," she says, totally excited. "Kirby, are you psychic or something?"

I fork up a huge bite of crab cake and pause before popping it in my mouth. "Actually, I'm beginning to think I am."

14

Kirby

Danno anche lezioni? (Can I take lessons here?)

Wiping my sweaty palms off on my pants, I climb the steps to the Dennisons' second-floor apartment, in a part of town I've never seen before. I suddenly wonder why I wanted to be a Special Sibling in the first place.

I'm way too busy at work to take the time, and it's not like I have any experience with kids. Definitely not like I'm good role model material.

(Good Kirby isn't buying it.) *But isn't that the point? I never had any good role models growing up; nobody to show me that women can be strong and independent. I had to figure it out, fight it out, and foul it up—a lot—before I got to where I am today. Maybe just spending time with her will be enough. That's what I thought when I signed up. It's still true now.*

My steps slowed in front of the door, and I saw the crooked figures glued under the peephole. 2B.

(Bad Kirby freaks out.) *This is it. My last chance to back out. I can turn around, run down the stairs, and call Miz Estoban from the car, claiming too much work, and back out. They'll probably never give me another chance, but do I really want one?*

I lift one foot and start to turn back the way I'd come, then put my foot down. I know why I signed up for this. I still haven't figured out why winning Banning's damn bet and proving that I'm a nice person means so much to me, but I sure as hell am not going to start my newer, nicer, kinder-and-gentler life by backing out on this little girl.

I take a deep breath and lift my hand to knock. The door is yanked open before my hand can touch the wood. The most beautiful child I've ever seen stands there, staring up at me with huge eyes and a serious expression. The picture I'd seen didn't come close to doing her justice. I expect her to burst forth with some angelic tune, or curtsy, or start speaking with an eighteenth-century British accent, for some bizarre reason.

She narrows her eyes. "Are you coming in, or what? It's about time you got here."

O-kay, there's another option. Sullen impatience. Not one I would have expected, but right up my alley.

I smile and use my "talk to children" voice. "Yes, dear. Is your mommy here?"

She does a kind of double take at me and rolls her gorgeous blue eyes, then speaks to me in an eerie mimicry of my careful voice. "Yes, my mother is here. Is that how you talk to everybody or just kids?"

Lauren shoots me another "you've got to be kidding" look from out of the corner of her eye, then holds the door open for me to enter, before I can figure out a response. I walk past her carefully, racking my brain for a way to yank my foot out of my mouth. The "nice grown-up talks to kiddies" voice has clearly got to go. This girl is pretty smart for a six-year-old.

I stop and lean over to whisper. "Look, kid, let's start over. I'm more nervous than a frog in a room full of kiss-happy princesses. And, really, how disgusting is the idea of kissing a bunch of amphibians? I mean, you get slimy frog-germ cooties all over your mouth, just for the chance to marry some royal guy who thinks the world owes him a living? *Euww!* I don't *think* so."

She's still giving me suspicious face, but breaks into a peal of giggles at the frog-germ cooties part. I try not to grin, but do a fake stern face, not wanting to lose ground by going all "let's be friends" too quickly.

Just then, her mom walks around the corner, drying her hands on a dish towel. She looks kind of flustered to see me there. "Oh! I didn't hear the door. Hello, Ms. Green. Please come in. I just made some coffee."

"Kirby, please," I say as I follow her into the kitchen, looking around me as we go. The tiny apartment is scrupulously clean, and the evidence of how much she loves her daughter is everywhere. The toys and games stacked neatly on the coffee table, the photos of Lauren ranging from chubby babyhood to her current big-girl smile scattered on all available surfaces, and the artwork that covers every inch of the refrigerator.

Mrs. Dennison turns toward me, and I see Lauren's beauty in her mom's face, overshadowed by lines of worry or exhaustion. Maybe both.

We sit down at the table, cups of coffee in hand, and Lauren moves to stand slightly behind her mother; tiny hand resting on Mom's shoulder. I smile a little, watching a reflection of my own memories.

Present a united front. Me and Mom against the world.

No matter how angry I'd been at Mom for never standing up for herself, I always stood ready to protect her when the police came.

Your neighbors reported shouting, Mrs. Green.

No, no. Just the TV.

What happened to your face?

Oh, that silly thing? I ran into the pantry door again. So careless of me.

Where is your husband, Mrs. Green?

He's at work.

Or, *He's in an important meeting.*

Or, *He's away on business.*

Which he never was, and I'd known that even then, at around Lauren's age. But what I hadn't known, until much later, was that he was probably sleeping off his drunk with one of the several women he kept handy for cheating on Mom.

"Ms. Green? Kirby? Are you all right?" Mrs. Dennison looked worried, and no wonder. Like you want to trust the most important person in your world to a woman who goes off on a brain-fade tangent right in front of you.

I try to snap to attention, pushing unwanted memories to the back of my mind again. Denial ain't just a river in Egypt, you know. "Yes, great, even. Just a little tired from work, but this coffee is perking me right up. No pun intended, ha ha. Perking? Coffee?" I hear myself babbling. "Um, okay. Never mind."

We've met twice before, but both appointments were under the supervision and guidance of one of Ms. Estoban's colleagues from the Special Siblings office. This is our first meeting on our own, and my first time meeting Lauren, and I think we're all nervous. I decide that getting moving is the way to get past it.

"All right, then. We're all set? I have your phone number at the college, and you have my cell phone number. You'll be in class until eight, and I'll bring Lauren home by eight thirty, since it's a school night. Is that right?"

We'd made these plans a while ago and have checked and double-checked the logistics, so I'm mostly just chattering to help calm us all down. Lauren's mom smiles—and it's only a bit shaky—and stands up. "That's right. I'm off to school, now, so I can be a college graduate and make you proud of me, Buglet. Have a great time with Ms. Green and you mind your manners, do you hear me?"

Lauren tries to smile back, but it's a weak effort. "I always do, Mom. And don't call me Buglet. That's a baby name. Remember, you're just as smart as anybody in that college. Don't let Professor Ruchas give you a hard time again."

They smile at each other in a shared moment of perfect understanding, and something in the vicinity of my heart clenches so tight I can't breathe.

Will anybody ever love me that much? Will I ever love anybody that much?

I remember that I'd told Jules that, since I never wanted kids, the Special Siblings thing was a chance to sidetrack any potential biological-clock ticking into constructive activity. As I watch Lauren hug her mom good-bye, I'm suddenly not so sure. We walk to the door together, grabbing her coat and backpack on the way, and I try to ignore the loud ticktock that starts up in my head.

Oh, crap. This may have been a really bad idea.

* * *

An evening at the Art Museum, by Kirby Green

Lauren: "What does abstrack mean?"

Me: "Abstrack, I mean, *abstract*, is not exactly realistic; looking at an object or the world through your other senses, but not your literal eyes."

Lauren: "What does literal mean? What's wrong with using your eyes? Don't you have to use your eyes to paint?"

Me (muttering and staring at a particularly horrendous painting): "Evidently not."

Lauren: "This one is stupid. It says, STILL LIFE WITH LOOOST. What does that mean?"

Me: "Um, that's . . . ah, nothing. I agree, that's stupid." (No way I'm either pronouncing or explaining lust to her.)

Lauren (moving on): "Why is there a picture of the donkey's butt in the flowers? Where is the rest of the donkey?"

Me: "I think we've had enough of the museum. How about we go get ice cream?"

Lauren: "Okay, but I can't wait to tell Mom about the donkey butt."

Me: "Great. Yet another promising first date blown to hell—o. *Hello,* let's get some ice cream." [Note to self: Must watch language.]

Lauren: "What's a date?"

Me: "Your mother will tell you in about ten years."

* * *

"Lauren, this is a really bad idea." We stand outside of the tiny dance studio, peering in through the glass at the dozen or so tiny ballerinas all decked out in matching black dance outfits with tiny toe shoes.

"But I want to be a ballerina," she says, pressing her nose so hard against the glass it's a wonder that it doesn't hurt.

"I know you want to be a ballerina. But is that a *real* want, or an 'I just saw paintings of ballerinas at the museum, so why not be a ballerina' want?" I cringe a little at sounding so, well, mom-like, but I'm not sure if I'm allowed to sign her up for ballet lessons.

There are all sorts of rules involved in the Special Siblings relationship, and I don't want to run afoul of Ms. Estoban on our very first outing. Especially after the donkey-butt fiasco.

I remember Maria Estoban and how her gaze could drill holes into a block of ice, and I shudder. Okay, I *never* want to run afoul of her.

Why couldn't we have walked the other way from the Seattle Art Museum to my car? We never would have seen the studio or— even worse—the NEW DANCERS WELCOME sign in the window. As I try to figure out how to get out of this gracefully, one of the dancers inside catches sight of Lauren's face pressed up against the window and grabs a friend's arm and points to us. Both of the little girls snicker, and Lauren flinches back, then presses closer to me.

Oh, that *so* is not happening to this little girl. Not on my shift. I grab her arm and march over to the door, fling it open, and walk up to the woman who seems to be in charge.

"We want to sign up for ballet."

The smile on Lauren's face lights up the entire studio, and I realize why kids get their way all the time. If they can turn on a thousand-watt smile like that at will . . .

I'm toast.

* * *

As I shift my butt around on the hard wooden bench for the fiftieth time, trying to get comfortable, I write out the check for the registration, the first month's tuition, the costume, and the recital fees. Catching sight of Lauren in her borrowed ballet slippers, earnestly practicing her newly learned plié, I smile past the weird lump in my throat.

I can't give her back the father who abandoned her and her mom when Lauren was a baby, but I can damn well give her ballet lessons. I make a mental note to buy her a much nicer ballet bag than the one owned by the ugly troll, er child, who snickered at her.

Does Prada make a dance bag?

I may suck at being nice, but I've got a fabulous credit rating.

15

Brianna

Soprano: Female singer with the highest voice range.

I was so tired by the time I got home, my thoughts were a jumble of randomness.

Exhausted. Singing bad—Madame mad at me. Love life bad—Lyle mad at me. Caller ID installed—Mama mad at me.

Refuse to think about any of it. Will do homework instead.

TOP 10 WAYS TO BE NICER—FOR KIRBY

1. Try to smile at ~~ten~~ . . . ~~five~~ . . . at least ONE person each day.
2. Remember that everybody is interested in his or her own life and not always sharing their stories simply to annoy you.
3. If somebody isn't actually working every single second of the day, it doesn't make her a slacker. Maybe she's just, you know, socializing a little.

4. Socializing is not the "herald of the imminent doom of the capitalist system."
5. Maybe don't say things like "herald of the imminent doom of the capitalist system." At least, you know, out loud.
6. Don't fire anybody unless they really, really deserve it, and then maybe run it by Mr. Stuart first?
7. Remember that Nice Girls Finish First.
8. Calling Mr. Stuart the Hellspawn of Demon Central may be counterproductive.
9. At least TRY your new dictating equipment. (OK, this one is selfish, but please?)
10. Is polkaing with pooches really completely ruled out???

The phone rang, and I looked at Caller ID. *Aunt Laverne?* "Hello?"

"Bree, honey, you're there! I found the most adorable eggplant tulle for your bridesmaids' dresses! They will work so beautifully with the puce satin ribbon I bought half-price at the fabric store last week. I can't wait to tell you all about it!"

Twenty minutes later, she finally let me off the phone, and I started on List Two with a vengeance.

TOP 10 WAYS TO BE LESS NICE—FOR ME
1. Do a mean Kirby face at anybody who says the following words to me:
    a. Big wedding
    b. Not tough enough
    c. Cruise ship
    d. Eggplant
2. Stand up for myself! Stop being a doormat in the doorway of life for everyone to wipe their pushy, um, feet . . .
3. Stop using dumb doorway analogies.
4. Remember that my career is just as important as any-

body else's, even Lyle's, except for the part where he rushes into burning buildings and saves babies and old people. Which he doesn't do all that often, but even if he did, I don't know how to save people, plus I'm too small to carry that fire hose around, even once I gain 35 more pounds.

5. Stop saying "even" so much.
6. Stop being afraid of Mr. Stuart's secretary, ~~even if~~ in spite of her scary vulture face.
7. Tell Aunt Laverne you're buying bridesmaids' dresses from the bridal boutique, so she doesn't have to make them.
8. Stand firm on number 7, even if she cries. (Think of the curtains!)
9. Try to work "herald of the imminent doom of the capitalist system" into a conversation at least once a week.
10. Have the talk with Lyle! (The sex talk.) Maybe use a book with diagrams?

Oh, who am I kidding? I'd die of embarrassment, book or no book. Although, when you're dead, lack of orgasms probably isn't that important. So, either way, I'd be better off . . . (But maybe that *Kama Sutra* thing might have possibilities. I'd asked Products to send one of the sample gift books over so I could check it out, after I'd looked up the spelling. I guess it's something about better sex.)

16

Kirby

Mi piace quello in vetrina. (I like the one in the window.)

Dear Ms. Green:

Thank you for the marketing posters and handselling items you sent with the *Winter Wonderland* lingerie promotion. Our store rocked the season, with a thirty-eight percent increase in sales over last year's holiday shopping figures.

Right now we're running a new campaign that I designed. The *Kick Him to the Curb* promotion is sort of "If your New Year's resolution is to throw that loser out with the trash, buy these hot new panty sets and make sure he knows he'll never get to see you in them" kind of thing. The response has been fantastic! So much so, in fact, that I thought I'd write to see if you'd be interested in running a similar nationwide campaign with your product line.

If you'd like to discuss this idea further, or discuss the idea of hiring a new person for your marketing department, please contact me at the address or number above.

Yours very truly,
Shane Madison
Assistant Manager, Sensuality Boutique
Jacksonville, Florida

"Now, *this* is initiative," I say, reading Shane Madison's e-mail for the third time. "Why couldn't any of my former staff people be like this?"

"Be like what?" Brianna asks, walking in with an armful of envelopes. Oh, *goody*. The morning mail is here. Another ten minutes I can spend *not* thinking about: how much work I have to do, how slowly the interviewing for new hires is going, how badly the whole *nice* thing is going, or how much trouble I'm going to get in with Special Siblings if ballet lessons aren't on the approved agenda.

Plus, as the ballet teacher casually mentioned last night while logging in the exorbitant payment I'd just made, Lauren's mini practice recital is the day before I leave for Italy. You know, the day before a big trip, otherwise known as Frantic Packing of Everything You Own Day?

I sigh. Again.

"Oh, this letter from one of the stores that carries our lingerie lines. An assistant manager took the initiative to design her own campaign—a really creative one, too—and then to write and tell me about it. It sounds like she's angling for a job here. Too bad she lives in Jacksonville."

Brianna deposits the mail in my in-box and scoops up the work from my out-box. "Where's Jacksonville? Is that over on the east side of the state? Near Spokane? That's not far. We could pay her travel for the interview."

I shake my head at Brianna's home-state-centric perception of the world. We *really* need to get this girl out of Washington. "It's in Florida. Pretty much a full day's flight from here. Why would someone from sunny Florida want to move here to the state of rain and gloom, anyway?"

Brianna pauses, indignation practically pouring off of her. "Washington is the most beautiful state in the nation. We have mountains, and the ocean, and nature, and—"

"Yeah, yeah. I don't need the commercial. We also have rain something like three hundred plus days of the year. Which is, you know, kind of depressing. Anyway, why don't you scan the current crop of résumés and see what the local talent is like before we go that far afield? Let me see any that you think have potential."

I start to flip through the mail, then realize she's still standing there. "Yes? Anything else?"

"I just, um, you mean . . . you want *me* to review the résumés and pick out the good ones? Before you even see them?" She looks a little freaked.

"Sure. Why not? You put the batch yesterday in order of the most promising on top, down through to that guy whose only marketing experience is when he helped his sister sell Girl Scout cookies in third grade. I'd say you have a great eye for this sort of thing. Thanks."

She still stands there for a moment, staring at me, making me go back to worrying that she might be a little . . . *off*. I mean, above and beyond the opera singing. But then she kind of snaps out of it and smiles. "No problem. Thanks."

"You're welcome. You can leave the door open. Thanks." As she leaves, I chew my lip a little and wonder if she likes working for me. The question naturally follows: If she didn't know about the stupid bet, would Brianna think I'm a nice person?

It hits me that, for the first time in a long while, I actually care about the answer. *Oh, oh. Must be time to see Dr. Wallace. I'm going in the "want to make friends" direction again, and we all know how badly that always turns out.*

I push the mail aside, making a mental note to call Jules after work. She's the one friend I can always count on, even a thousand miles away.

But isn't it sad that you only have one?

I clench my teeth and grab my calendar, slashing SET APPT. DR. WALLACE in big, bold letters. Enough with the self-pity party, already. I've got work to do.

* * *

Neck rolls are *so* not enough to get rid of the knots in my shoulders. I keep at it, anyway, while I rifle through my top desk drawer searching for some pain reliever. Stress and tension headaches are never fun, and I don't have time for one, now.

My phone rings. B. STUART flashes up at me from Caller ID, shooting the stress and tension levels up another fifty degrees or so. I grab the phone with the hand not currently occupied with one-handed medicine bottle opening, and try to sound upbeat.

"Hello," I say. (We all have Caller ID; no use pretending that I don't know it's him.)

"Hello," he says.

There's a small silence. Um, didn't *he* call *me*?

"You called?" I prompt.

"Right. Ah, about lunch. Do you have time to get some lunch? There are a few issues I'd like for us to discuss."

Double oh, oh. "Issues" sounds ominous.

I force myself to Stop the Tragedy Train at the Station before I start hyperventilating. "Sure. One o'clock?" I say, eyeing the clock.

"Twelve thirty would be better for me, if you can make it," he says.

My calendar is pretty clear, except for the first interviews later this afternoon, so I shrug, then realize he can't see me. "Sure. Meet you in the lobby."

"Great. See you then."

As we hang up, I do a mental regurgitation of all the work I've sent him lately. Other than the small "your figures are wrong" misunderstanding, there shouldn't be any problem with any of it. Maybe this is about the bet? He's going to come to his senses and realize that acting like an eight-year-old isn't really the CEO image he wants to project?

But if he gives you an out, will your pride let you take it?

Another unanswerable question. Two in one morning; that's two over my limit. I pick up the phone again and dial.

"Dr. Wallace's office. May I help you?"

As I pull my calendar toward me to try to find an hour-long block of free time, I mutter under my breath, "I sure hope somebody can."

* * *

"Union Square Grill? Okay, at least we don't have to get wet." As we exit the elevator to the lobby of our building, Banning puts a light hand on my back, as if to guide me through the crowds of hungry corporate lunch-goers. Let me just point out that this is a normal thing for a guy to do, and never, ever bothers me. I don't get weirded out if a man opens a door for me, either. There's being an independent career woman, and then there's just stupid, right?

But, for the first time ever, I feel uncomfortable from a colleague's totally unthreatening touch, and pull away almost immediately. It's not that it felt weird. It's more that it felt *good*. Kind of tingly, even.

Tingly is so not an adjective I even want to *think* about this man, let alone feel. The boss thing *might* not be as much of a problem as I thought, because it's not like W&L is going to be anything more than a brief stepping-stone in my career. I mean, who really wants to sell sex toys her whole life?

Or am I just back in denial? *Dating Boss Equals Bad.*

And, anyway, this is a man who once wore two different colored socks to work. Just think about *that* for a minute. *So* not happening.

As I grin, content to have found a semi-rational explanation for why I think with my nerve endings instead of my brain cells whenever I'm in the same room with him, Banning stops in front of the restaurant and quirks a brow at me. "Something funny?"

"Oh, nothing you'd be interested in," I say, flashing one of my biggest smiles his way and walking past him to the hostess stand. Let *him* watch *my* butt for a change.

Of course, I have to keep myself from looking to see if he's looking, because then he'd catch me looking at him looking, and it would be . . .

Oops. Brakes on the imminent brain failure. Perhaps we could just eat lunch, like normal business colleagues? As we sit down, the first thing I notice is how the green in his shirt matches his eyes almost perfectly. Then I notice, for about the gazillionth time, that his dark brown hair has touches of a warmer color in it, and that it's so thick I want to dig my fingers down in it and start purring.

I clutch my water glass and pound down about eight ounces, hoping that the ice water will cool off my overheated hormones. As I look up, I catch Banning's amused expression and have the itchy thought that he knows exactly what I'm thinking. Then he glances down at my finger, where a bead of condensation from the glass runs down the side of the glass to my hand, and watches me put it in my mouth, and I swear he tightens his jaw a little.

Hmmm. Now *that's* interesting. Maybe I'm not the only one whose hormones are doing the happy dance? Wouldn't that be a lovely development? No, no, no; how many times do I have to say this? *Dating Boss Equals Bad.*

The server—"Hi, my name is Beth"—arrives to discuss the specials; something about salmon or pork chops. I study Banning over the top of my menu. What is it about this man that gets to me? He's not my type at all. I don't like corporate guys—I've always been a sucker for starving artists, like the man forever hence to be known as Daniel-the-rat-bastard. Genius pulls me in every time; discussions of philosophy and the arts are an aphrodisiac. Nothing gets my panties off faster than a man who can discuss Tolstoy and Socrates in the same evening.

In my experience, your typical corporate wonk isn't apt to be up on anything that involves culture, unless you count season tickets to the Mariners. (I don't.) Of course, the sex isn't all bad with the money guys; there was that one investment banker in particular . . . *holy multiple orgasm, Batman!*

My face warms up a little as I realize that both the server and Banning are staring at me. "Um, the salmon special," I say and thrust my menu at Beth. "Thanks."

I shrug and smile an apology at Banning. "Sorry to drift off, there. Just thinking about, um, return on investments."

His smile fades, and he leans back, resting one arm along the back of the leather booth. "Right. So, I guess you want to get straight to business. I was hoping we could get to know each other a little bit better. We really haven't talked much since before the holidays, other than . . ."

His voice trails off, and he looks like his tie just got tighter. Now who's making whom uncomfortable, hmmm?

The hum of conversation at other tables and the musical clink of silverware on plates surrounds us, as I consider how to respond. Finally, I smile and shrug again. "Other than that stupid bet? Well, you started it. But, hey, let's call a truce and talk about something else. You never did tell me how you ended up working at W&L, after five years climbing the ladder at WorldBank."

He relaxes a little and laughs. "I'm not quite sure how it happened, to be honest. I was having a tough time following the rules in the gigantic corporate hierarchy, and a headhunter called me on a day that had been full of way too much pomposity and arrogance. None of it mine, before you ask."

Do eyes really twinkle in real life? Because, I swear his eyes are twinkling. Oh, man. I need to start remembering that I don't like him, or I'm toast.

"You?" I gasp in feigned dismay. "A rule breaker? I find that a little hard to believe. What, did you forget to put your soda can in the recycling bin one day?"

"Sure, laugh it up, Green," he says, smiling. "Actually, I wanted to institute performance rewards, instead of the old tenure-track system. You know, bonuses for actually doing a good job, versus just because you'd been there longer than anybody else? The Old Guard wasn't having it, though. I got dressed down pretty hard for 'stepping out of my place,' and that's when I realized I didn't want to work for a company that forced people into specific slots. So the headhunter called, and I agreed to the interview, and here I am."

"Just that simple?" I rest my chin in my hand, elbow on the table.

"Just that simple. Except . . . well, I really want to make a difference in environmental issues, at some point. Anyway, how about you? I mean, I know how you got here—I hired you. But why? The real reason, not the job interview reason. Why a company like W&L?"

I study him, wondering how much of my ten-year plan I can reveal. Anything I say may be used against me, and all that.

"Actually, it's a step. I think I want to run a company, too. I'm not all that great at following rules myself, as you may have noticed." We both laugh, and it's a real, warm laugh on his part, not the "I'm laughing at you" kind of laugh. Trust me, I've had years of experience at the second kind, so I know the difference.

"As you keep pointing out so graciously, I'm not the type that people really warm up to. Not really *nice*. Not a team player. So I figure I'll just run my own show, then I don't have to worry about it. I may even finish my novel someday and give being a writer a shot." My smile fades, as I hear myself saying something I didn't even consciously know about myself. I'd like to blame it on the vodka martinis, but I didn't have any.

Yet.

Hey, I can fix that! I look around for our server. "Beth?"

Banning had winced at the part about people not warming up to me, and he looks at me with a major serious face. "Kirby? About that . . . *nice* thing. I was just so angry that day, and I've been worrying about our projections and the board meeting. You know, how am I doing in my first year as CEO and all that. I'm sorry I blew up at you. From everything I've learned, you were perfectly justified in firing those bozos."

He takes a deep breath and goes on. "The only wonder is that nobody else did it long ago. So please let me apologize and let's just cancel the whole stupid bet."

My mouth falls open a little. This is the last thing I expected.

But it's great, right? I'm off the hook. What could be better? Now I don't have to worry about my trip to Italy or my job.

Or my self-esteem, which is apparently at an all-time low. Because if I agree to cancel this bet . . .

"If I agree to cancel, it means that not even *I* believe that somebody will call me nice even once in the space of an entire *month*! Do you really think I'm so pathetic that you have to let me out of the bet, because there's no chance I'll win? Why don't you just come right out and call me a big capital L Loser to my face? Or is it your evil plan to set me up, then make it look like you're being oh-so-generous letting me out of the hopeless bet?"

He has a weird expression on his face. Shocked, maybe? Surprised and ticked off that I'm onto him? I don't care, and I figure I just got myself fired, anyway. I toss my napkin down on the table and stand up. "Go ahead and fire me, if you want to get rid of me so badly. But if I'm not fired, then the bet is on. We'll see who's nice."

He stands up, too. "Kirby, I don't—you're not fired. I don't have any evil plan. I just wanted—"

Suddenly, I can't take any more. I've never cried in front of a colleague in my life, and I'm not about to start now, in front of Banning. "Okay. Well. Sorry about overreacting, then. I have to go. Lots of work to do. Thanks for lunch."

I whirl around and barely miss running into a bewildered Beth, carrying a tray full of our food. Somehow, I'm not hungry anymore. As I dash out of there, trying to outrace the tears, I realize that I'm safe on the mutant psychic powers thing.

I never saw this coming at all.

17

Brianna

Countertenor: Male singer who sings in a woman's voice range, usually performing roles originally written for castrati.

Every time the office phone rang, I jumped. I'm not sure what I was more afraid of—that it might be Lyle wanting to know when we could plan for beers and meatloaf, or that it would be Madame, wondering about my defection just after her news of my upcoming audition.

I still hadn't told her that I couldn't make it. *Or could I?* I had to make that phone call soon. The Caller ID had done wonders for helping me avoid any possible confrontation with anybody. I'd kept a little log next to my home phone of calls avoided:

Lyle—3
Madame—5
Erika—2
Mama—13

(Mama isn't one to be ignored; she's bound to turn up on my doorstep before long. I wonder if they have Caller ID for doorbells?)

Just as I seriously considered banging my head against my computer (again), my boss showed up. Kirby was dressed to kill and wearing an expression like the potential murder victim better show up soon, or she'd start practicing on innocent bystanders.

She swept by my desk, sort of hissing at me. "I can't believe you talked me into this. Speed dating! If anybody I know is there, I'll never be able to live it down. And I thought my first Chamber of Commerce meeting as the new VP of Whips and Lace was bad. This is social suicide of the worst kind."

She glared at me, then stalked into her office, still muttering. I let out the breath that I'd been holding since she showed up. *Whew.* But I noticed she hadn't told me to cancel, so she must still be up for it.

This is going to be a really loooong day.

I needed to be the soul of calm, so we could avoid total Kirby meltdown. All I asked for was one single, peaceful day.

Naturally, the phone rang immediately.

Outside line. I prayed briefly for the nerve to ignore it, but just then Mr. Stuart's secretary walked by me on her way back from the coffee room, where she usually spends the majority of her day. She gave me the evil eye when she noticed me not answering the phone.

I so wanted to ask her who was answering *her* phone while she spent her day reigning over the break room gossips.

But, you know, I didn't.

I just answered the phone. "W&L. Brianna speaking."

"At last, Darling! Where have you been all week? Have you been ill? On your death bed? Surely the earth itself has exploded in a natural disaster for you not to have returned my calls on such an auspicious week. I expected roses, at the very least, for using my many contacts and influence to gain you an early audition with the

Seattle Opera." Madame sighed her very well-rehearsed long-suffering sigh.

"But it is of no never mind. When will we meet? We have fewer than seven weeks now to prepare you for the most momentous day of your entire life! Besides, of course, the day you met me."

I rolled my eyes. *She really needs to work on her self-esteem problems.* "Madame, actually, about that audition. I meant to call you back, but . . ."

My other line rang. Saved by the bell, sort of. "Madame, I'm sorry, but I have to put you on hold."

"But—"

Click.

"W&L. Brianna speaking."

"Finally! Where the hell have you been?" Lyle sounded a teensy bit peeved.

"I beg your pardon?" My tone frosted up considerably. An engagement ring didn't give him the license to be rude.

"I left a half dozen messages at your house. Are you okay?"

"It was only three, actually," I muttered.

Ring.

Oh, poop!

"Lyle, I have to go; be right back."

Click.

"W&L. Brianna speaking."

"Bree? Is that you? Honey, I thought a serial killer had gotten you, for you not to call your own mother. I was just on the verge of sending Daddy down to your office. Are you all right? Where have you been? Is your telephone broken?" Mama sounded seriously upset, and I felt awful.

Beep.

Double poop!

"Mama, I have to put you on hold. I'm so sorry; I'm fine; be right back."

Click.

"Hello?"

"It's about time! And what's only three? Honey, I can't hear you very well. I've been really worried. Are you all right?" Lyle's voice did sound concerned rather than annoyed. *Oh, dear.*

I instantly felt like a total meanie. Poor Lyle had been worried sick about me, while I sulked like a sullen child. Maybe I was the wrong person to teach Kirby about being nice. I sure hadn't been much of a good example lately.

"I'm sorry, Lyle, but—"

Beep.

Oh, poop. That's Madame blinking on the other line. Or is it Mama?

"Lyle, I have to put you on hold."

"But—"

Click.

"Madame? Are you still there?"

"Yes, but I am a mere instant away from hanging up on you. How can anything possibly be more important to you than your future? Will that stupid company for which you toil at meaningless labor provide you with the means to achieve your dreams of operatic fame? Will you ever achieve the cover of *Opera News* there? Will you? WILL you?"

Beep.

"Yes, I mean, no. I mean, I have to put you on hold just for a second, it's really urgent. I promise, *promise* I'll be right back."

Click.

"I have to call you back. Madame is on the other line, and you know how she can be. I—"

"WHAT?? What do you mean, 'you know how Madame can be?' *How* can I be, Darling?" Madame's voice screeched out at me.

Oh, double poop! I'm obviously not all that good with the call waiting buttons yet.

"Madame, I'm so sorry. I—"

"To whom are you slandering my good name? Fine. *Fine.* If

you do not have time for me, perhaps the Seattle Opera does not have time for you. You may attempt to call me when you have some *free time* in your oh-so busy schedule, Miss Too Important for her voice coach."

"But—"

Click.

Oh, I'm so dead now. She'll never, ever let me live this down.

Beep.

Aarrghh.

"Hello?"

"Bree, honey, if you don't have time to talk to your own mother, that's just fine. I'm just the one who carried you in my womb for nine and a half months, but sure, no problem. You just do your important work and take your important calls."

"But—"

Click.

Aarrghh!!

Wearily, I pushed the call waiting button again, hoping this time it was Lyle and not, oh, say, Mr. Stuart, or the governor of Washington, or somebody else I could say the wrong thing to at the wrong time. "Um, Lyle?"

"Who else would it be? What's up, Brianna?"

"I, um, I've just had a lot on my mind."

Silence.

"Lyle?"

More silence.

Then he heaved a deep sigh. "Bree, honey, I know you have a lot on your mind, with the wedding and everything. But isn't that a good time to talk to your fiancé, not avoid him?" He laughed one of those deep, warm laughs that always made me go all shivery inside. (He really is a sweet and totally yummy guy. Really. And he kisses like Prince Charming himself. *Mmmmm.*)

"Yes. A good time for kisses."

He laughed even harder. "Kisses? Bree, how about I pick you

up from work and we talk about weddings and kisses and everything else over a nice dinner?"

I felt my face turn a nice lobster color. *That was out loud? The kisses thing? Triple Aarrghh.*

"Dinner. Dinner would be great." Maybe I could do this after all, with Lyle's support. I gathered up all of my courage. "I have some news, too. Madame got me an audition with Seattle, and I don't even have to wait till the regular auditions. It's in about seven weeks and . . . I think I want to do it. Isn't that great?"

Braced for anything, or so I thought, I was still unprepared for total silence. (Now I know what they mean by Deafening Silence, which I'd always thought was a rather silly saying, before. But this silence ruptured my eardrums.)

"Um . . ."

"I can't believe you! I thought you were excited about our wedding, and instead you're picking now, of all times, to go forward with the opera thing?"

"The opera thing? Lyle, the *opera thing*? Honey, I love you, and I want to marry you, but Prince Charming kisses or not, you have to respect my career or . . . or . . . well, I don't know what."

"Brianna, you know I respect your singing. You have the most beautiful voice I've ever heard; I tell you that all the time. But this is our future, baby. Can't you put off the opera th—the *audition* for a little while? Are you really ready, anyway?"

To hear Lyle put in words what I'd been circling around in my mind all week cemented my decision. Suddenly, the answer smacked me in the head like a stage-hogging countertenor.

I know what I have to do. It's time to quit hiding from my decision and be like the shoe commercial.

Brianna—Just Do It.

"You're absolutely right. I'll call you later, Lyle. Good-bye." As I gently replaced the phone in its cradle, I could hear the faint sound of Lyle squawking on the other end. I smiled a little bit. He'd hear all about it later.

I brushed imaginary specks of lint off of my sweater, smoothed back my hair, then picked up the phone again. A girl needed to look her best for the most life-changing decision of her entire . . . well, her entire life, right?

One by one, I dialed each of the seven digits of the phone number I knew so well. Madame would just *have* to understand.

One.

This is my life.

Two.

I don't have to let anybody push me into doing . . .

Three.

. . . anything I'm not ready for.

Four.

They'll just have to understand.

Five.

There's always next year, right?

Six.

"Brianna! Are you *ever* going to get off the phone? Get in here, so we can set up these interviews! And I can't wait to hear why you think an Amway salesman is a good choice for assistant director of marketing. *Amway?*"

I stopped, finger poised on the seventh and final number, my hand literally shaking. Then I put the phone down and stood up.

Saved by the boss.

* * *

It's five o'clock on Friday evening; do you know what your boss is doing?

Mine was staring at the small mirror she called the meeting-teeth-checker that hung on the wall behind her door. "It's hopeless," she moaned.

"Your teeth? You have great teeth," I said, trying for humor.

She glared at me, the great teeth in question bared in a grimace. "Not funny. *So* not funny. Look, I still have three weeks. Some poor idiot will call me nice in the next three weeks, right? I should just cancel this exercise in humiliation. Besides, I have piles of work to do, and I need to stop by the bookstore and buy a ballet book."

"Um, a ballet book? You're taking up ballet? I have a friend who is a principal dancer at the Seattle Ballet, if you want—"

She whirled around and stalked back to her desk, then threw herself in her chair. "No, I'm not taking up ballet. Can you see me in a tutu? Puh-*leeze*. It's for . . . nobody. Just forget it. So what's the four-one-one?"

I looked at her for a minute, wondering what she . . . oh, right. Four-one-one. Information. "I printed out directions, and you arrive at eight. I thought we could . . . ah, discuss . . . well. Maybe we could talk about . . ."

She sighed and shook her head. "I know I'm going to regret asking this, but discuss what? Last time you hemmed and hawed around like that, I got involved in this ridiculous scheme. What is it this time? Naked bungee jumping?"

I looked up from the papers I'd been twisting around in my hands, intrigued. "Really? They do that? Don't the ropes and harness thingy kind of . . . chafe?"

Kirby clutched her head in her hands and moaned again. "Brianna, I was kidding. There is no naked bungee jumping. Now, can we—"

I grinned. "I know. I was trying to lighten the atmosphere in here. It's speed dating, not a firing squad. And if we're going to be friends, you should call me Bree. I always look around for my mother or my third-grade teacher when somebody calls me Brianna."

She gave me the oddest look, like I'd shocked her or something. "Are we? Going to be friends, I mean?"

Oh, oh. Did I overstep? Is she one of those Don't Mix With the Help kind of people? She acts like it on the outside, but I'd thought . . . oh, this is silly.

I forced out a little laugh. "I certainly hope so. I mean, I don't make lists of Top Ten Smooth Opening Lines for just anybody."

She cracked up, but looked a little . . . relieved? *Hmmm.* "Great. This is how low I've sunk. The woman voted 'most likely to freeze your balls off' in B school is now reduced to tacky opening lines."

I bit my lip. "I'm so sorry. Did I offend you? It's not like I think you need opening lines, or *any* lines, or any help at all. In fact, forget I said anything. I'll just . . . um, B school? And, really? The thing about the, um, you know . . ."

My voice dropped to a whisper. "Um, balls?"

Kirby laughed again, and then held her hand out for the paper. "Business school. And I'll tell you about the balls later. We'd better get on with this, so I can run some errands before I crash and burn with the other desperate singles."

"Okay. Here they are. I've starred the ones I think are particularly compelling. This article says—"

She interrupted. "Article? You've been researching?"

I felt my face get hot. "Not exactly. A little lunch hour surfing, that's all. You'd be amazed how many dating articles are out there. Not that I was looking for dating advice, just icebreakers. I mean, now that I'm practically married, in a big wedding, even, I don't read stuff like this."

Kirby perked up. "Hey, here's a chance to talk about you for a change. What's this about a big wedding?"

I shook my head, all stern. "No, no, no. Wedding later. Dating pick-up lines now. In no particular order, here they are."

I placed my highlighted pages on the edge of her desk. "Compliments. It says, 'Men love compliments as much as women do. The male ego—' "

"Sucks it up like a sponge. Yeah, no kidding. Daniel couldn't hear enough about how big his . . . um, feet were." This time, *her* face got a little red. "Forget Daniel. Got it, compliments. What's number two?"

"Sports 'Talk about the latest sports news. Mention the hottest players or demonstrate your knowledge of the' . . . ah, it says 'infield fly rule.' " I looked up at her, puzzled. "Do you know what that is?"

Kirby looked baffled, too. "Not a clue. What is it, baseball season? Basketball? Isn't the Super Bowl soon? I just don't keep up. Who are the hot players for the Mariners? Since that yummy Alex Rodriguez moved, I don't know any of them. The whole 'spit and scratch your crotch' thing doesn't really work for me. Totally not sports girl. Next?"

This is going to be a loooong afternoon.

"Laugh. 'Men are attracted to a sense of humor. But make sure they know you're not laughing *at* them. Humor separates you from the crowd, and makes even a plain woman pretty.' " I looked up at my drop-dead-gorgeous boss. "Not that you really need that. But, still, humor. Can't hurt, right? Funny people are nice."

Kirby tapped a pen on her desk. "Right. Stroke the ego. Laugh with them, but not at them. Talk about bugs in the infield. Next?"

"Well, it was infield fly rule, but . . . okay. Well. 'Number four: Ask for help. Men like to show off their superiority.' But I guess that one doesn't really apply much in this speed-dating situation."

"Right. What am I going to ask for help with? The little timer? Speaking of which, can we talk about the setup for this thing again? Just how many men am I going out with?"

As I reached for my notes to look up the details, I heard the last voice I wanted to hear at that particular moment. Well, maybe not the last, but he definitely ranked in the top three.

"How many men are you going out with? Is that what you said?" It was Mr. Stuart, and he didn't sound happy. "What are you talking about?"

Kirby's face was dead calm. She lifted an eyebrow, like *Hello, You're in MY office.*

(I'd kill for that kind of composure.)

Then I stood up to leave and noticed her hands clutching the arms of her chair. *Hmmm*. Maybe she wasn't all that calm, after all. "I'll just get out of the way here."

"No, Brianna—*Bree*." She smiled at me, all Ms. Cool and Collected. "We were having a discussion. I'm sure Banning can't stay long."

He smiled, then leaned against the doorway and crossed his arms. "Actually, I've got plenty of time. I'm fascinated with the scope of this conversation. Considering the timetable of our new product release, it must be—in some very unusual way—about the marketing plan, right?"

I kind of sidled for the door. "Right. Um, I have to run. Have to practice . . . ah, you know. Practice. Good night, Kirby. And, ah, good luck. With, you know. The thing." I glanced down at the papers, still crumpled up in my hands, and rushed back to place them on her desk. "These are the, ah, notes. On the thing. The notes on the thing. Okay? So, good night."

Kirby mouthed *thanks* at me and smiled again. Her hands still clutched her chair arms, though. I guess Mr. Stuart intimidated everybody. And he had the nerve to give *her* grief about not being nice.

Ha.

I swept past him, silently communicating my disdain. (Actually I sort of crept by him, silently communicating "please don't fire me," but, you know, I thought about the disdain thing.)

Mr. Stuart said good night and then walked into Kirby's office and pulled the door shut behind him. I was torn between a) staying to give moral support, or b) getting the heck out of there before he remembered the embarrassing speakerphone conversation and brought it up.

The prospect of total humiliation beat out the surge of sisterhood. Anyway, it's not like Kirby couldn't hold her own in case of a big blowup—even with scary Mr. Stuart. I shuddered, glad I wasn't the vice president.

You're going to have to deal with scarier people than Mr. Stu-

art if you really want to be a diva, my inner reality check whispered.

I was so busy trying to figure out how to respond to my inner reality check, that I didn't see my own personal blowup until it walked right up in front of me. I mean, *he*. Until *he* walked right up in front of me and swept me up in a big hug.

"Lyle? What are you doing here?"

He laughed and put me back down on the floor. (Did I mention he's way taller than me?) "Not exactly the welcome I was hoping for from my beautiful girl, but understandable, after our phone call."

He looked so scrumptious, in his faded jeans and long-sleeved shirt, and the brown leather jacket I loved on him. For a moment, I shoved all of the conflict and problems out of my mind and just stood there, appreciating the fact that he was standing right there, he was gorgeous, and he was mine. "Lyle, I'm so glad to see you. But we really need to talk."

I heard footsteps from behind me, and Lyle looked over the top of my head at the person who was approaching. Then another voice I didn't want to hear right then spoke up. "Hey! This must be the famous Lyle. I've heard so much about you."

I felt all the blood in my head drain down to about my kneecaps. Of course. It had to be Jamie. How could my day get any better?

18

Kirby

È la prima volta che Lei è qui? (Is this your first time here?)

Calm, cool, and collected. Cool as a cucumber. Insert calmness cliché here, while trying to peel my fingers off the arms of my chair.

Oh, shit. Did he have to show up now?

I unclench my jaw enough to smile at Banning, after Bree scurries out of the room. Assistant deserting the sinking . . . speed-dater. Who could blame her?

"Can I help you? I'm really quite busy, and I need to leave soon to run some errands"—*I totally have to buy a book about ballet, so Lauren and I have something to talk about Wednesday, not that it's any of your business*—"so if whatever it is could wait . . . ?"

Focusing my attention on my desk, I play the paper-shuffle game, hoping that he'll take the hint and leave. After a few seconds, I peer up at him through my lashes.

He's not much of a hint-taker, I guess.

I try to ignore how broad his shoulders are, which is tough considering the way he's leaning against my door with his arms folded across his chest. I've never been the "Ooooh, muscles!" type of girl, so I don't know why his (totally yummy) ridiculously posed (great body; he must work out) self is giving me the shivers.

Stupid pheromones.

I give up and look at him, crossing my own arms over my chest. (Mostly in case my nipples are poking out. Hey, it's suddenly cold in here—it has nothing to do with any latent sexual attraction to Attila the CEO.)

"All righty, then. I assume it can't wait. What's up, Banning?" I'm going for the cool and nonchalant tone, even though I'm terrified he's here to discuss our lunch that wasn't.

He unfolds that ostentatiously long and lean body and strides over to my desk, then sits on the edge of a chair and leans toward me. "That's what I'd like to know. What's up? I'm assuming you don't want to talk about our disastrous lunch, but I'm fascinated with the line of conversation I overheard when I walked over here. Just how many men *are* you going out with? Let me guess: market research?"

(He's *so* right about lunch.) I scan our new line of warming oils in my head and think of all the products I wouldn't mind taking for a test drive with *him. BAM!* The temp in the room shoots up about a zillion degrees, and I shove my hair back away from my suddenly overheated face.

Page thirteen? Item four-seventeen? Somehow, I'm guessing Banning doesn't need a lot of electronic assistance in the sack, though. I wrestle my prurient mind back to the topic at hand. *But wouldn't his hands feel good all over my . . .*

"Market research? Right. Yes. That's exactly it. What better night to watch the market in action than a Friday night, correct?" I raise my chin and direct my "I'm in charge here" gaze at him.

He smiles slowly, but it doesn't quite reach his eyes. "Riiight. Market research. Well, I'm quite concerned about the future of this line, so you won't mind if I tag along, will you? Two heads are better than one, and all that. Even if one of the heads is your own admittedly brilliant one."

"I . . . well, you . . ." *Help! Not sounding at all brilliant here, admittedly or otherwise.* "Actually, this is a type of research I really need to do on my own. It will be difficult to convince men to talk to me if you're hovering around looking all hunky and everything."

This time the smile reaches his eyes. "Hunky? You think I look hunky? That's quite a compliment, coming from you." He leans back in the chair, giving me an unobstructed view of a long line of thigh muscle. Like I said, the man must work out. A lot.

I gulp for air. "Ah, compliment? No, just fact. You know you look good; it's no big deal. In fact, if I took *anyone* along with me, male or female, it would hinder my dating—er, my data collection process. So, thanks but no thanks."

I pull my bag out of my drawer and stand up, then move around my desk. "Thanks for stopping by, gotta go. See you Monday."

He tilts his head, considering me, for a long moment, and then stands up as well. Unfortunately, this puts him in a position less than two feet away from me. I can literally smell the faintly woodsy, spicy tang of his aftershave.

Is biting the boss's neck a firing offense? I must be a little delirious, because I actually sway a step closer to him before I snap out of my too-long-orgasm-free-induced trance and back away. "Right. Good night. Later. Bye."

I shoot past him so quickly he doesn't have time to say anything, and I almost make it out home free. As I grasp the doorknob, though, I hear his quiet laughter and make the mistake of turning around.

He's still standing exactly where I left him, staring at me. "Kirby? Have a . . . productive . . . evening. See you Monday."

I nod and make my escape, wondering why the great evil designs of fate had to give me such a massive case of the hots for

CEO Banning Stuart. As I dash for the elevator, I decide that a nice dose of hot monkey sex is just what I need and smile at the thought of the lucky winner of tonight's speed-dating disaster. He's going to get way, *waaaayy* more than he expected out of the evening. I may even try out item four-seventeen on him. Getting Banning off of my mind (and out of my hormones) is simply a matter of scratching the right itch.

* * *

"Then my hives got itchier and itchier and I scratched and scratched, but the more I scratched, the worse it got, until I was covered by a mass of inflamed boils."

I can feel my face scrunch up in a grimace of distaste, but don't seem to be able to stop it, as I stare at the bulbous nose of Harry T., my third speedy date of the evening. We're six minutes into the allotted ten, and he's still recounting the hideous dermatological nightmare of his last camping trip. Assuming he's leading with his best nose, er, *foot* forward, I cringe at the idea of ever spending an entire dinner date with this moron.

He leans toward me, his scrawny neck quivering up out of his truly toxic mud-brown and puke-green sweater. "And then they got infected."

I shove my chair back in a panic, before he gets to the part about inflamed pustules. "Okay, that's it."

I am *so* out of there.

Harry peers at me, in a sort of unfocused way. I'm guessing he left his glasses in the car, in a totally ineffective attempt to look less like a geek. "What? Did you say something?"

"Yes, I just . . . I need a break. The ladies' room. Now." I stand up, giving the coordinator a desperate little wave. She rushes over, nearly stumbling in her fashionable black ballet shoes. "I need a break. Ladies' room. I didn't know if you needed to know, or anything."

She studies me with an anxious face. Maybe nobody ever has

to pee during one of these? Or is she afraid I'm going to skip out by climbing out the bathroom window to escape from Harry? She looks down at her clipboard, like the secret of the universe (or at least a potty pass) is there. "Um, are you sure you can't wait? We're going to have a break at the end of this round."

I glance at Harry again. Yep, they've probably lost lots of potential speed daters out the bathroom window, if they get many guys like this one. Much more of Harry, and even *barred* windows couldn't keep me in. I shudder. "Yep. I'm sure. Sorry, Harry. Better luck next round."

I stalk off toward the bathroom, not waiting for the fluttery coordinator to decide that it's all right for me to go pee. What is this, third grade?

This is going to be a long night.

* * *

Somehow the laws of physics exploded, and the first forty-five minutes of speed dating lasted about a year and a half. I changed into my little black DKNY dress and my new spike heels for *this*? I try to relax and enjoy the sound of the wonderful jazz quartet playing in the corner, but then I remember that I don't even like jazz.

First I had Bob in Resources Management, who turned out to be Bobby Lee the garbage collector. Not that I'm a snob (Okay, generally I'm a snob, but I don't have time to be picky now), but he could have at least changed clothes. The not-so-faint aroma of rotting fish guts does nothing for me. The drooling lust when I said I worked at W&L—and he not only knew the company, but started naming items and page numbers in an "I've spent a lot of quality time alone in my room with your catalog and my very active left hand" total creep-out kind of way—put me over the edge.

Bachelor Number Two was blah. Blah, blah, blah. I forget his name already. He had blah hair, blah eyes, and a blah personality. This is the type of guy I could easily charm into calling me nice, by flashing a little cleavage and pretending to be interested in his blah life. But I just don't have the patience. An hour into our date, and I'd find myself trying to shake some life into his blah self.

We've already discussed the lovely Harry T., who is currently at the table next to mine telling a horrified woman the story of his advanced toenail fungus, from what I can hear. She keeps edging her chair farther back from the table and casting wild-eyed glances around the room. *Poor woman—don't they prequalify these guys?*

It's two minutes past break time, but my fourth date is still at the bar, getting drinks. I'd be annoyed that he's late, if I didn't need a drink now more than I've ever needed a drink in my entire life. *Ever.* Really.

Oh, *hello.* If this is him walking toward me, the first part of this hell may have been worth it. Tousled golden-brown hair, tall, nice (read: nonpolyester) suit, killer cheekbones . . . he's coming this way . . . he's stopping; he's pulling out the chair . . .

Yes!

"Hi, you must be Kirby? The coordinator said you'd like this," he said, placing a vodka martini on the table next to me. I flash my best Hello, My Legs Are So Totally Shaved smile at him and do just a teensy hair toss.

"Yes, I am. And you are?" I tilt my head down and glance up through my lashes, playing the coy/shy/not-really-an-aggressive-vice-president card. Ummm, yes. Still yummy on second glance. This may be just what I need to get Banning out of my mind.

Not that I was thinking of Banning. Seriously.

"I'm Ryan. Nice to meet you, even though I feel pretty stupid doing this." He grins and reaches out to shake my hand, which he does with the perfect grip, firm but not too tight ("I'm proving my manhood") or, worse, too limp ("I don't have any manhood to prove").

"Tell me about it," I say. "My assistant bullied me into this for . . . market research."

He looks a little put off. "Market research? I should have

guessed anybody as beautiful as you wouldn't be here for the dates, but I confess I'm disappointed."

Mmmm, I'm liking this guy. I mentally stick my tongue out at Banning, then wonder why I keep thinking about him. *Aarrghh.* Forget Banning! Get back to Brian.

I mean, Ryan.

I rush in to correct my earlier statement. "No, no, no. I'm totally here for the dates! I've been far too busy at work to have any time for a social life, and I thought maybe other people who were in the same boat might try this."

Glancing around, I lower my voice conspiratorially. "I tried to overlook the possible complete humiliation and social outcast potential of the evening."

We both laugh, in a "we're *so* above the rest of these losers" wishful thinking kind of way, and spend a few minutes chitchatting about nothing, while mutually taking stock. He's in real estate development, and I'm a marketing exec for W&L Manufacturing, no details asked for or given.

As the mini-date clock ticks toward the end of our time, he takes a sip of his drink and leans back. "I can't believe I wasted part of our time at the bar, when you're by far the most fascinating woman here. Wanna skip the rest of the evening and go get dinner?"

Wow, a smooth mover, too. Maybe *too* smooth, I think, remembering Daniel-the-rat-bastard. Plus, I never want to appear to be *too* easy.

"Very smooth and a nice compliment, but I need to at least finish out the evening for the market research part of my goals. I'd certainly be up for a real date, though, if that's what you're asking." No point in being shy; Ryan certainly fits the bill for recreational fun and frolic and maybe a quick "nice."

He smiles at me as the bell rings. "Definitely. Don't forget to put a big *Yes* next to my name on your list. And I can't wait to hear about this mysterious market research of yours." Ryan reaches out and pushes a strand of hair off of my forehead, and I feel a little something when his finger touches my face.

Unfortunately, the *little something* I feel is just the tip of his finger. No tingle, no *frisson,* no quiver of heat or excitement like the one that rocketed through me when Banning touched my back.

Damn it, will you quit thinking about that man? Who is, let me remind you, your BOSS? What about the never-play-where-you-work rule? What's next, photocopying your ass at the office holiday party?

There are times when my conscience is a giant pain in my never-to-be-photocopied ass.

19

Kirby

Può venire a cena? (Can you come to dinner?)

Dates five through eight were so dull I realize I already can't remember them, as I look across the table at date nine. "So you're in natural resource management. That doesn't mean garbage collector, does it?" I raise one eyebrow and stare at Buddy across the table. "I've heard that one before, you know."

Buddy starts laughing. I have to admit, Buddy has a nice laugh, in spite of the fact that he was evidently named after the family golden retriever. I mean, a grown man named Buddy? Puh-*leeze*.

He even looks kind of like a golden retriever, with the blond hair, kind of shaggy, and the big brown eyes. Just the kind of guy I like, a blond. I never liked guys with deep chestnut brown hair, like Banning has.

Oh, *crap*. I'm doing it again.

Buddy speaks up. "Yeah, I caught a whiff of garbage guy on the way in. You'd think he'd change clothes for this, at least."

I grinned to hear my earlier thoughts put into words. Either we're back to the psychic thing, or Buddy and I think alike. This could be fun. "So, tell me about resource management. What non-garbage-related job do you do?"

He shakes his head, still amused. He looks like he's about my age, but he has cute little laugh lines around his eyes. Gotta like a guy who laughs enough to get those—it says good things about his sense of humor, right? (Plus, I must have a man with the good sense to get wrinkles before I do.)

"No, Kirby, it's time to talk about you. What do *you* do for a living, other than stand around and look so beautiful that mere mortal men drop to their knees and beg for mercy?"

Hmmm. Definitely a line. He's probably used it before, too, but hey—I'm a sucker for outrageous flattery. Flattery aside, though, here we are at the Sixty-Four-Thousand-Dollar Question: WHAT DOES KIRBY DO FOR A LIVING?

Let's review, shall we? I told five different speedy dates about W&L. The reactions varied from nervous giggles (never a good sign in a grown man) to crude jokes (also unappealing) to lustful drooling and immediate mention of specific catalog items (Do Not Pass Go; Go Directly Home to Mommy's Basement).

There's nothing in the rules that says I have to be completely . . . non-untruthful.

Right. I'm gonna lie like a rug. Must continue chatting while I weigh my options.

"I like that—fall to their knees, hmm? Pretty smooth, aren't you? Do many women actually fall for that line?"

Teacher? Teachers are nice. But, no, that whole schoolboy fantasy. What if he's some nut who wants to dress up in short pants and get me to paddle him? Euww.

He grins again, not in the least abashed. "I don't get much of a chance to trot that one out, since there aren't a lot of goddesses hanging out in Seattle nightclubs these days. You definitely qualify."

"Right. Still smooth, but casting around for justification. I like quick thinking in a man."

Singer? Brianna is definitely nice. But what if he asks me to sing something? My singing sounds like stray cats trapped in a bag. Singer is totally out.

"I notice you're avoiding my question about what you do? Are you secretly a garbage collector? Exotic dancer? Or—even worse—an insurance salesperson? Now *that* would hurt my heart." He laughs, but leans forward. The body language definitely says he's interested.

Think, Kirby, think! Hurt his heart, illness, nice profession . . . nurse. That's it! I'm a . . .

"Nurse. I'm a nurse. I don't like to admit it, because . . . ah, because people like to tell me about their sick Aunt Bessie or their strange lumps or, um, skin conditions, but I'm definitely a nurse."

Buddy looks impressed. *Hey, I should have thought of this earlier! It would have saved me the "What's better, a live guy or a dildo?" question from date number five.*

"That's great. My sister is a nurse, too, over at Swedish Medical Center. She's going to love you."

Oh, crap. I'm already meeting the family and will be caught in the web of my evil, villainous lies.

Melodramatic, much? You're only going out with this guy to get him to call you nice.

"So, if I'm meeting your sister, I guess that means we're *both* going to list each other as a Yes?" I smile in what I hope is a nice, nurse-like way.

"Oh, *yeah*. You have saved my evening from being a total disaster. I was just wishing I'd stayed home and watched my DVD of Dale Earnhardt again, but then here you are. This is the best surprise I've had in a long time."

"Oh, I'm a very surprising kind of girl." *If he only knew. Still, before he finds out about the not-really-a-nurse thing, I'll bet I can get him to call me nice.* "Is Dale Earnhardt that jazz pianist from Chicago?"

He looks surprised and then starts laughing, but the buzzer cuts off any explanation. Two out of nine are distinct possibilities so far—that's way, way better than I'd hoped.

I stand up and stretch, then sit back down to wait for date number ten to arrive. No matter how awful he is, it's only ten more minutes, then I'm free to escape to my lovely, quiet condo and a pint of Godiva chocolate truffle ice cream.

Right on schedule, number ten shows up. He's tall and cute in a gangly, professorish kind of way, and he has a killer smile (although I'm withholding judgment on the orange shirt). Maybe they saved the best for last?

"Hi! I'm Steve, and I'm your date for the evening. Well, I'm your tenth date for the evening, which must be awful, since you're probably sick to death of making small talk. However, statistically and psychologically speaking—and did I mention that I teach statistics and social psychology at UW?—the final date of the night will have the effect called *recency*, which means that I'll stay in your mind the longest. Which is good, unless you don't like me at all, then it's bad, but what's not to like, right?" He beams an enormous smile at me and plops down in the chair. "Did I mention that I'm practicing to be a stand-up comic? Do you want to hear some of my material? A man walked into a bar; wait, no, actually it was two. Two men walked into a bar, except it could be a restaurant because the fact that the place served beer isn't intrinsically necessary to the story, but the . . . oh, sorry, let me start over. Two men walk into a—let's call it an eating establishment, and the parrot says . . ."

I sigh and lean back in my chair, resisting the urge to bury my head in my hands. *Well, two out of ten ain't bad.*

* * *

Who knew that "dating" ten men in just under two hours would be so exhausting? I'd marked my form quickly, selecting Ryan (of course), Buddy (no doubt), and, after some thought, Steve. He might just be a nervous talker, right? And he *was* awfully cute. On the flip side, if he really *is* a nonstop babbler, then he must not get many dates. So maybe he'll be really easy to impress or, for example, to think a woman is really . . . *nice* . . . for going out with him. (Imagine a huge used-car-salesman grin here, or the dum dum dum *duuummmm* sound of music from a cheesy B movie, and you'll nail my state of mind exactly.)

I snuggle deeper into my terry cloth robe and lean my head back against my couch, reflecting both on the evening's misery and on my sheer luck that nobody I knew had seen me. A reporter from the *Seattle Times* had wanted a shot of me with one of the guys; the paper was doing a follow-up article to C.J.'s column. But I'd glared so fiercely at the photographer, while trotting out expressions like *invasion of privacy,* and *not a public figure,* that they'd quickly backed off and moved on to the big-haired blond ex-cheerleader type who was only too happy to pose. Her name was probably Fifi or Binky.

Muffy, maybe.

I grin and reach for the ice cream again, enjoying being back in my own snarky skin and out of the guise of Nurse Green, Saver of Humanity and all-around Nice Girl.

I still think niceness is so overrated. Nobody goes around expecting men in business to be Nice with a capital N. It's back to the old dichotomy: Aggressive men are Hard Chargers, Go Getters, blah blah blah.

Aggressive women are bitches.

Not that I'm bitter.

I press the mute button on the remote, as the commercial for yet another Viagra-wannabe drug ends with everyone looking smug as they walk hand-in-hand into the sunset. I timed it wrong, though, so I still have to listen to the lawyers' litany of potential side effects: "Do not use if you are currently taking medication for blah blah blah. May cause hypertension, restlessness, nervousness, or your willie to stand up and do the River Dance."

Or something like that.

The second half of my prerecorded tape of *POP STAR LIVE!* begins, and two things occur to me. First, Jules will never really know if I watched the whole thing or not, so I can switch over to the Sci Fi channel. Second, I could have fast-forwarded through the commercials.

Aarrghh!

As I aim the remote at the VCR and punch the button—not without a small measure of guilt; Jules *is* my best friend, but how much of these shows can a human being be expected to endure?—the doorbell rings.

This is never, ever a good thing at eleven thirty at night.

In fact, the only person who ever showed up at my house un-invited, late at night was . . . oh, *shit*.

I jump up and run to the door to peer out the peephole, clutch-ing my pint of ice cream like a shield in front of me. But not even Godiva can protect me if it's Daniel-the-rat-bastard.

I pray for a neighbor's sudden need to borrow a cup of sugar as I peek out the tiny hole, then feel my heart sink down to my stomach when I see him.

It's Daniel, all right. And he's *smiling*.

I'm doomed.

I lean my forehead against the door, wondering why ex-boyfriends can't vanish the way guys you wish would call you after a first date do. They could all go someplace together, that wondrous land of My Dialing Finger Was Broken in a Freak Ac-cident So I Couldn't Call You for Two Solid Weeks, and life would be good. In fact, there would be a lot fewer men around to annoy me.

The door bangs under my head, and I jerk back.

"Kirby, my love, open up. I know you're there. I saw a sweet little Mercedes in your parking lot. Did you trade up, gorgeous?" He must be drunk, because that was really, *really* loud.

He bangs on the door again, then presses the doorbell button about seven times in a row, while I cower inside my door, wondering what to do. I can't leave him out there to disturb my neighbors, that's for sure. I toy with the idea of calling the police, but don't want the slightest hint of trouble to touch me, since it might cause a problem with Special Siblings.

The doorbell peals, even louder this time, if that's possible. *Shit, shit, shit. What to do?*

Then he starts banging on the door again. "Kirby, do you have some guy in there? Does he know that you really like it when I put my tongue in your—"

I slap the ice cream down on the table, then yank the door open, before the entire neighborhood hears about my preferences for his tongue. I'm *so* going to kill him.

"Get in here, you idiot. What the hell are you doing coming to my house at midnight? Or, for that matter, anytime, ever?" I grab the front of his shirt and yank him inside, hoping like hell that my elderly neighbors didn't hear him.

He stumbles across the doorway and catches himself by putting one hand on my right shoulder and the other on my left boob. With anyone else, you might think this was a drunken accident.

Not with Daniel-the-rat-bastard. Because he starts fondling.

I shove his hands away from me and shut the door. "Get your slimy hands off of me, Daniel. How many times do I have to say We. Are. Over. before you get the freaking point? Although, the part where I came home and found you banging not one but *both* of your nude models in my bed, and I tried to smash your head in with your easel might have been a clue . . ."

I wince and try to shove the memory of that lovely event farther down in my subconscious, where it can fester away quietly with the rest of my psychological traumas. Trust me, the sight of your boyfriend nearly buried in long, golden, cellulite-free, twenty-year-old legs—FOUR of them—is not a sight that's easy to forget.

Did I mention he's a Rat Bastard?

"Oh, Lovely One. Not *that* old story, again. How long until you forgive me? It wasn't what it looked like, really." He stumbles a little closer to me, and I back away again.

"Right. You are such a jerk. What the hell else could it have been, but *exactly* what it looked like? You were screwing two models—at the *same time*—in *our* bed, while I was at work trying to earn money to support your stupid artistic lifestyle."

I feel the tears welling up and viciously scrub at my face. "No, Daniel, I'm the one who's stupid. I thought you loved me. So I was the idiot all around. Fine. Great. Now get the hell out of my house, and don't come around again, or I'll call the police."

He suddenly doesn't look as drunk anymore. "Kirby, love. You don't have to call the police. Now, hush, Darlin'. No tears." His hands shoot out and grab my arms, but I don't feel afraid, because he's still smiling that warm, sympathetic smile that first charmed me out of my panties three years ago.

"You wouldn't have any tears left for me, if you didn't still care. Let's just let bygones be bygones and start over, shall we? You know it's never going to be as good for you with anybody else." He leans forward and breathes on my neck, trying to remind me of how hot he always made me when he would bite me in that exact spot.

Trust me, I remember.

The freeing thing is that, for the first time ever, I don't feel aroused by him. I just feel sad. And a little disgusted.

Not scared yet.

I lift my arms to break his hold, and turn away, back toward the door. "It's not going to work, Daniel-the-rat, er, I mean, Daniel. You don't *get* to me anymore. I forgave you twice before for your little indiscretions. 'But Kirby, we didn't say we'd be exclusive.' 'But, Kirby, I love you so much it scared me, so I had to fuck the gallery owner who just so happens to have the power to help my career.' "

Damn. I really had *been a fool.*

I shake my head in disbelief at my stupidity. All those years of fighting to be nothing like my mother, and I had to fall for an ass-hole. *Hey, Mom, guess what? We're more alike than you know.*

He moves up behind me and grabs my shoulders, fingers dig-ging into my skin through my robe. "Yes, I know all that," he says, sounding just a skinch impatient, like how *dare* I bring that up?

I try to pull away, and his fingers dig harder into my shoulders. Now I'm finally getting a little scared. He's about six inches taller and eighty pounds heavier than I am, after all. He's a big man, and it was sexy when we were riding his Harley, or when he was car-rying me up the stairs to my bedroom.

It's just scary now. I fight to relax my shoulders and pretend to be calm. "Daniel, I need you to leave now. You're starting to upset me, and I don't want to have to call the police and get a restrain-ing order. You know that I'll do it, don't you?"

He slams me around and up against the wall and *scared* turns to *terrified*. I'm not going to hyperventilate; I won't. If he tries any-thing, I'll knee his balls so far up his . . .

Daniel shoves his face right up next to me and practically snarls in my face. "I'm leaving, all right? You always were a cold-assed bitch. But don't think this is over. You were the best thing I ever had, and I'm not going to let you go. Get used to it."

Suddenly, awareness seeps back into his eyes. He lets me go and moves away. The charming-Daniel mask slips back in place, and I realize that the face of the man I'd thought I loved was just a fa-cade over a much scarier reality.

I need him out of my house. *Now.*

I channel Business Kirby, the one who has *What Would Machi-avelli Do?* prominently displayed in her office bookcase, and dis-play an insincere calm of my own. "Well, perhaps we can discuss this later. Over drinks or dinner sometime? Call me Monday, and we'll figure out our schedules."

They'll be ice skating in hell before I ever meet you again, you bastard.

I smile a little, and move toward the door. This time, he lets me reach it and pull the door open. Suspicion wars with smugness on his face. He's cunning enough to wonder at my easy capitulation, but the sheer enormity of his ego convinces him that I must have succumbed to his never-fails charm.

It's the Daniel way.

"All right, then. We'll play it your way, love. If you're sure you don't want me to stay and blow your mind tonight? About that tongue action I mentioned earlier . . . you didn't call me the Orgasm King for nothing." He leers at me, and it takes everything in me not to vomit or start laughing hysterically.

But I win. I'm stronger than that. Screw *nice*. I'm strong. Right now I need to be.

I smile and even reach out to touch his arm. "No, I didn't, but I'm too exhausted to be much good to you, and I have to get up at five to go back to work. I'll talk to you soon."

I even have the presence of mind to wait until he walks to the end of the sidewalk to close the door, smiling at him when he turns to glance back at me. Then I close the door, slam the dead bolt home, and rush to the bathroom, afraid I might throw up after all.

Terror, fury, and relief roil around in my stomach, as I fall on my knees in front of the toilet. I flush something that looks a lot like stomach acid and pull myself up to wash my hands and face and brush my teeth, and all I can think is, *Help. I need Jules.*

20

Brianna

Ensemble: Literally, "together." More than one character sings at the same time.

Thank goodness for Saturday. Sleeping in is way, *way* better than sex. Not that I've had a lot of sex to compare to sleeping in, but still, sleep wins. And chocolate. And, in fact, so *many* things that I don't know what the big deal is about sex. Unless I'm doing it wrong. (I really need to get that book with the diagrams.) But Lyle always seems happy when he stays over.

In the minute or two before he falls asleep, that is.

I'm the one who lies awake, sometimes for hours, hands clenched by my sides, wondering what part of the glory and the fireworks keeps passing me by, and why.

In fact, my own personal sex life reminds me of the joke Jamie told me at lunch one day about the two elderly women who were talking, and the first one asked the other if she and her husband had ever had Mutual Orgasm.

The second woman looked at her friend, perplexed, and said, "Why, no. I think we have State Farm."

I'm totally a State Farm girl, myself.

I glanced over at my bedside clock and realized that ten a.m. isn't really giving it the old college try. Not that I've ever been to college, either.

All right, already. Enough with the pity party. If you think you're in a dreadful mood now, wait till you get to Madame's house at one and tell her your decision.

I groaned, pulled the pillow over my head, and willed myself to fall back to sleep. If I could hit a high F, the most difficult note in all of music, I could sleep on demand.

* * *

As I finished scrubbing the bathroom (after I'd reorganized my closet, painted my fingernails, and cleaned the kitchen—twice), I considered that waking up at ten fifteen on a Saturday really wasn't so bad. It gave one time to clean one's home and reflect on one's life.

If I've turned into the kind of woman who calls herself "one," I'm in big trouble, here.

I peeled the enormous yellow rubber gloves off my hands and tossed them into the bucket, then wiped the sweat off my forehead with my sleeve. Catching sight of myself in the mirror, I cringed. It was definitely time for a shower before I ate a light lunch and headed over to Madame's.

Naturally, the doorbell rang. Sometimes I wondered if my life had been scripted by a sitcom writer. All that was missing was the laugh track.

I grabbed a towel and wiped the worst of the sweat off of my face, then headed for the door, wondering who could be showing up at noon on Saturday. Either Lyle or Mama, probably. I briefly wished that I'd jumped in the shower earlier, as I flung open the door.

Then I flung it shut again.

Oh, doo doo. I can't shut the door in his face!

I took a deep breath and opened the door again, prepared to offer up some lame explanation for my temporary insanity to a very surprised-looking Jamie.

My mouth opened, but what came out sounded a lot like: "What in goodness' name are you doing here?"

He grinned, then reached down and picked up two paint cans from the floor of the hallway. "Paint. Remember? You told me you wanted to paint your living room, and I said my mom had leftover paint from her guest room."

I stared at him, none of what he'd said registering in any way. Then a fat drop of sweat bounced off the tip of my nose and I flashed back to the vision of how disgustingly yucky I looked in my clean-the-house clothes.

I groaned a little and tried not to think about how bad I must smell, too. "You, what? Paint? What?"

He smiled again, in a completely cute, confident, *showered and clean* kind of way, and maneuvered past me into my apartment. "Paint, remember? You said you'd take it off our hands, so I thought I'd drop it by. So, here I am with Cerulean Blue. Cute place, by the way," he finished, putting the cans down and looking around. "Crazy curtains."

I still stood by the open door, dumbfounded. Finally, I snapped out of my daze and shut the door. "But how? I mean, thanks, but how did you know where I live?"

Jamie looked a touch sheepish. "Well, I am Accounting Guy. You know that roster we all have with everybody's name and address on it? I may have taken a peek last night, just in case I happened to be out your way any time this weekend."

I folded my arms across my chest. "And? You just happened to be over here by my apartment this morning?"

"Well, yeah. Or, kind of. Anyway, I'm here, and so's the paint, and I'd be glad to help you paint, after lunch. Which I'd be glad to take you out for. Lunch, I mean." His whole face lit up with a *Say Yes, please, willya, please, willya, please* kind of expression that I recognized well from my nieces and nephews.

"No," I said.

"No?"

"No. Look, Jamie, I appreciate your taking the time to track me down, which is sweet in a stalkerish kind of way, but I have to hop in the shower and rush over to my voice lesson. I just don't have time for painting and lunch."

He'd stiffened his shoulders a little when I said the word *shower,* but I didn't see how my being clean could offend him. Unless it wasn't that he was offended at all, but . . .

Nah. No way Super Gorgeous Guy was attracted to me. He was just doing his Boy Scout impersonation, and I was his pet good deed for the day.

Right?

I bit my lip, and noticed that he noticed me doing it. Okay, this was getting weird.

Plus, I'm engaged.

You only remember that now?

Jamie broke into my internal dialogue before it could turn into a shouting match between my mind and the little tickly thing in my head that was making the hairs on the back of my neck stand up.

Wonder if there would be fireworks with him? Bet Jamie wouldn't need diagrams.

"NO! I mean, no, I can't do lunch, but thank you so much, and I really appreciate it, even if you are just a Boy Scout, and I'm the pet, because projects are fine and fireworks are only important for the Fourth of July, and we can totally talk about the *Kama Sutra* at work, right?"

He looked dazed as I hustled him out of the room, thanking him profusely and murmuring something about *paint* and *later* and *nice guy.*

I shut the door behind him and leaned back against it, out of breath, closing my eyes in relief. Then my eyes snapped open, and I stared at the paint cans on the floor.

I just did a three-sixty, from thinking sex is vastly overrated to practically shoving a man out of my apartment because he makes me want my own fireworks. I'm in big trouble here.

* * *

"You're in Big Trouble, Darling," Madame Gabriella said, as she snatched my coat out of my hands and tossed it on the couch.

"How could you leave me hanging like this all week? Do you not have the Fire anymore? The Desire, the Will, the Passion?"

When Madame talks in Capital Letters, I really am in trouble.

My shoulders slumped, and I sank down on the couch next to my coat, prepared to do my penance. "Yes, Madame. I definitely have the fireworks. Er, I mean, I totally have the fire. The Fire, even, with a capital F. I had to make the decision in my own mind, for myself, without any outside influences, before I could discuss it with you."

She quivered all over like an indignant sparrow and stalked back and forth in front of the piano. "Fine. So you have had your Time Alone. Are you ready now to accept the most amazing opportunity—other than the day you met *me*—of your life? Or are we back to the first square, yet again?"

I tilted my head, thrown out of my prepared speech. "The first . . . *oh*. *Square one.* No, we're not back to square one. Sometimes, in a woman's life, one must . . ."

You're calling yourself "one" again.

Oh, poop. To heck with it.

"I'm in. I want to go for it. The audition, the career, the whole diva-chilada. I want to be an opera star of the highest caliber. I want to be on the cover of *Opera News*. I want it all, Madame."

She stood there, speechless for once. She must have expected me to say no. Everybody in my life probably expected me to say no. Even me.

Everybody in my life was going to be in for a big, *big* surprise.

I jumped up off the couch and grabbed her in a huge hug. "And you, my darling Madame, are indeed the brightest star in the opera firmament for getting me this chance. Let's make the most of it, shall we?"

As I let her go, I heard something that sounded an awful lot like a sniffle, and her eyes were bright and shiny when she peered up at me. She opened her mouth to speak, and I waited for the praise and support I so richly deserved.

"Now we work harder than ever, Brianna. Your days of leisure and bon bons are over. We have six weeks left, and I will work you until you beg for mercy, but you *will* be ready."

On some planet, somewhere in the universe, that's probably what praise and support sound like.

* * *

I watched from the table as an uncharacteristically domestic Lyle cleared the dishes from the meatloaf dinner I'd rushed home to make for him. He'd even remembered to bring wine, even if it did come in a box and was white zinfandel, the slightly more grown-up version of fruit punch.

Nice girls are never ungrateful, Brianna.

I shook Mama's voice out of my head, wondering when I'd finally quit hearing all of her cautions as the soundtrack to every decision I ever made.

Lyle walked back to the table with the carton of ice cream and two bowls. At least that was one bright spot in my evening, after Madame had worked me nearly into the ground: all the ice cream I could eat. All afternoon, I'd had to listen to her fret about my "skinniness" and the thirty pounds I needed to gain.

I could eat like a truck driver when the occasion called for it (if truck drivers are big on pasta and steak and chocolate, I'm *so* there), but thirty pounds in six weeks might be pushing it, even for me. I sighed at the thought of pulling my fat clothes out again. I hadn't worn them since my last audition, nearly two years ago, for a touring Broadway show.

(My voice had been great, but Broadway isn't so crazy about love interests who look like butterballs, in case you're ever interested in applying.)

"Why the big sigh, baby? Don't you feel like Rocky Road? I know you like the little marshmallows." Lyle ruffled my hair and then sat down at the table and started scooping ice cream into bowls.

The hair ruffling was a problem. Except for when he wanted us to go to bed, I sometimes got the uncomfortable feeling that Lyle looked at me kind of as a cross between his kid sister and his chocolate lab, Biscuit. Even when we *were* in bed, there were no fireworks, but lately, out of bed, not so much as a tremor.

Unlike the way you felt when Jamie was here today, the evil voice whispered in my head.

I ignored the evil voice and picked up my spoon. *I could tell him after dessert. Why spoil a good bowl of ice cream?*

I sighed again. It was no use. I wasn't going to have any appetite at all, until I put everything out there in the open. And—just a hunch—I probably wasn't going to have any appetite at all after I did.

I pushed the bowl away from me a little bit and gathered my courage. "Lyle, we have to talk."

He grinned. "Oh, oh. That's never a good opening line. Let's see, what did I do? Toilet seat up? Nah, I've been careful. Is it . . . ?" The smile on his face faded, and a weird expression, sort of a cross between horrified and delighted, took its place. "Jesus, Bree, are you pregnant?"

"*What?* Why would you think that? No, I'm not pregnant. We've been really careful! Well, except for that one time . . ." I felt my face heating up hugely.

"That one time we blew out the condom," he finished for me. "I just, wow. I don't know why I thought that. You've been so weird lately, and Vince told me how weird Cookie's been acting lately . . . well, it just seemed to make sense. Anyway, it's not like I'd mind. You know I want kids really soon."

"Yes, we've had that talk over and over, Lyle. You know, the one where I tell you I don't want to have children for at least ten years, while I get my career started? The one where I explain what pregnancy and childbirth would do to my voice? Why can't you ever accept that I . . . *Cookie*? Already?" I shook my head at the thought of the fifteen nannies her daddy had probably already hired. "Why am I not surprised? But that's not the point. We're getting way off track here."

Lyle shoved his bowl away, too, but I noticed he'd managed to finish his four heaping scoops of Rocky Road first. "Yeah, I know we've had that talk. But don't you think it's a little . . . selfish? *You* don't want to have kids right away. *You* don't want to be a mother yet. What about what *I* want? Don't I deserve a chance to have a say in how soon I want to be a father?"

I stared at him in shock. "Lyle, you can't—I mean, okay. You have a point. Yes, you do deserve the chance to have input into when you have a child. But not at the expense of my body, my career, and my dreams. You know I want children, too. I adore kids. I'd love to be a mom. I've even tried to talk to you about the idea of adopting one of the many, many kids who need a good home, but you won't listen."

He shoved his chair back and jumped up from the table. "Right. Adopt. Then what do I get? A kid who looks like somebody else? What about the boy who looks like me? The one I can teach to play ball and ride a horse?"

He dropped down into a crouch beside my chair and touched my hair. "What about the little girl who is as beautiful as her mommy? Who can play tea party with her daddy and wear tiny lace party dresses and ribbons in her hair? Instead, I get the choice of trying to love somebody else's kid or waiting ten or fifteen years until I'm too old to play catch with my own?"

I tried to pull away from him, but he caught my hands in his. "Is that really fair, Bree? Is that how you want to plan our married lives, throwing away or postponing our chance at parenting on a dream that will probably never come true?"

So there it was. Finally out in the open between us. His complete lack of faith in me. That he'd finally put it in words stiffened my spine more than anything else.

"We're going to get the chance to see about that, in about six weeks. I've accepted the audition with the Seattle Opera. If I'm really not good enough, then I guess we can reopen this discussion then, can't we?"

He started to speak, but I'd heard enough. "No. That's enough, Lyle. Since you don't believe my dreams have a chance, you shouldn't be worried. I really need to get some sleep, now. I'd like for you to go."

He stood up, still stunned, and shoved his hands in the pockets of his jeans. "Is that it? You're going to do this audition in the middle of planning our wedding? And I just have to wait around and see what happens? Is this some kind of an ultimatum, Bree? 'Cause I have to warn you, I'm not all that good at those."

I stood up, too, and tried to be angry. For some reason, all I could muster up was sadness. "Why does everything always have to be about you? If that's how you feel, then I guess you have to do what you have to do. But I'm going forward with the audition. And if they accept me, I'm joining the company. So we'll have to deal with that, too."

The phone rang, and we both glared at it. I walked over to the phone, though, and checked the Caller ID. "It's Mama, Lyle, and I'm going to have to talk to her before she sends the SWAT team out after me. I'll talk to you soon, okay?"

I clicked on the phone and sank down on my couch, deliberately not looking at him again. As I murmured soothing noises to my mother, I heard his footsteps and then the sound of the door opening and shutting behind him. When I finally looked up, the door that he very carefully hadn't slammed shimmered through the tears I was trying so hard to fight.

Somehow, I'd always thought being engaged would be a lot more fun than this.

"No, Mama, I'm not sick. I know my voice sounds funny; I just have a little allergy thing or something. No, you don't have to send Daddy to the drugstore for me. I'm sure it's nothing. How is your arthritis doing in this cold rain?"

Distracted by the chance to discuss her health issues, Mama forgot to interrogate me about my week. I propped the phone between my head and shoulder and pushed myself up to clear the ice cream dishes off of the table, listening while she happily chatted about everything and nothing. Staring at the melted Rocky Road in the bowl, I tried to come up with a pithy metaphor comparing marshmallows and chocolate chips to life.

Nope. I got nothing.

I flipped the switch to turn on the garbage disposal and wondered why I couldn't live a glamorous life like Kirby, who was probably right at that very moment enjoying one of the many, many dates with gorgeous, rich, and sensitive men that she'd set up last night on her speed-dating adventure.

Some women have all the luck.

21

Kirby

Sono in vacanza. (I'm on holiday.)

If my luck gets any worse, I'll be dead. I stare at my computer monitor, wondering how something I'd paid four hundred dollars for just three months earlier could have died such a violent and hideous death.

Shit. Why can't I have a glamorous life like Jules does, in Hollywood, or like Bree probably does, off doing some cool singing gig or another? Wonder if she knows Gerard Butler? There's something about Scottish accents, and he was so totally hot in Phantom of the Opera . . .

I sigh at the unfairness of it all and resign myself to hauling my butt to the office to finish work on the six projects I'd brought home to do over the weekend.

As I rummage around in my dresser for a sweatshirt to pull on (no way I'm dressing up for the office on a Saturday; it's not like anybody else will be there), the phone rings. I contemplate ignoring it, so as not to shed my cranky mood on anyone else, but walk over to glance at Caller ID just in case.

Tom Vernon? I adore Jules's dad, but I wonder why he'd be calling me, as I pick up the phone. "Tom? Is that you?"

"It's me, Kirby. How's my favorite second daughter?" I love Jules's parents and spent way more time at her house growing up than I ever did at my own. Both of her parents are famous writers, in different ways, and they always took the time to encourage my adolescent, angst-filled scribblings. I shudder to think of some of the truly vile poetry I inflicted upon them.

"I'm great! It's so wonderful to hear from you. How are you? How's your fiancée? Any news on a wedding date?" His midlife crisis girlfriend-turned-fiancée, Amber, is about twelve years old and weighs ninety pounds, according to Jules. But she's making Tom happy, so we've decided to be nice to her.

[Note to self: Maybe *Amber* will call me nice.]

His voice turns gruff. "No, no, no. We're . . . ah, thinking about things right now. Amber says hello, though. But this call is about you. I don't want to keep you, so I'll get right to the point. I loved your story, and I want to see more. My agent thinks it's the freshest thing she's seen in a while, and she wants to see a full-length novel from you."

I sort of fall down on the bed, or actually, *toward* the bed, but I miss it entirely and fall on the floor, where I lie, unmoving, staring at the phone.

"Kirby? Did you hear me?"

"Yes, no, *what*? You what? What story? What are you talking about, and why do I think killing Jules is going to be Item One on my To Do list tomorrow?"

"Your story—well, it's novella-length, really—*The Bitch Is Back*. It was hilarious! Not my kind of book, normally, but a good story is a good story. You had me hooked from the first page." He chuckles. "Who knew you'd turn out to be a great writer, after that crappy poetry you made us read all through high school?"

I groan and feel my face flaming. "Mr. Vernon, I mean, Tom, you're a *parent*. You're never supposed to admit that my poetry was crap. At the time, you told me it showed definite promise."

His voice turns more serious. "Right, Kirby. You were a teenager with a . . . shall we say, *challenging* home life, and you were a brilliant, difficult kid who was my daughter's best friend. Sylvia and I would have cut out our tongues before we told you your poetry was self-absorbed tripe. But you were a teenager! Your poetry was *supposed* to be self-absorbed tripe."

He laughs. "The problem is when writers never grow out of that stage, and their novels are thinly disguised attempts at some sort of therapeutic catharsis. That's why my agent keeps telling me she's going gray before her time whenever she reads slush."

I remember his agent well. She's the only businesswoman I've ever met who scared even me. But she's helped Tom onto the *New York Times* list, and now he has a movie deal in production and about a gazillion dollars, so the shark-like approach must work for literary agents.

"But, how? Of course, it must have been Jules-who-will-die, but when? She promised not to show that story to anybody." I can't believe she went behind my back; she is *so* in for it.

"Be glad she did. In spite of what Sylvia and I'd hoped, Jules will never be a writer. But she's a phenomenal reader, and she knew you really had something in that story. She also knew you'd never send it to me. So quit complaining, and let's talk about what else you have hiding under your bed. You've got a great voice, kiddo."

I pull myself up on the bed, still in a state of shock. Tom *New York Times*–bestseller Vernon and his major-force-in-the-industry agent think I have a great voice.

This is my lucky day.

* * *

"You're in luck, Kirby Green. I'm here and ready to do your bidding," says Banning, in the fantasy I'm evidently having even though I'm wide awake.

I shake my head and rub my eyes. Six hours at the office, trying alternately to work on marketing plans and quit obsessing over the novel I want to write to send to Tom and his agent, must have fried my brain cells. No way is that my boss, standing in my office doorway in scruffy jeans and a sweatshirt, offering to do my bidding.

I quit rubbing my eyes and take a peek. It *is* him. Okay, this is just freaking weird. "What did you say? Doing my bidding about what? Oh, are we bidding on some project?" Now *that* makes sense. Enough with the wishful thinking, Green.

He just looks at me and grins. "No, Kirby. No bidding on projects. *Your* bidding. As in, do you need help with anything? Can I invite you to share the enormous, loaded pizza I just snagged from the delivery guy down in the lobby?"

"I don't think . . . pizza? It doesn't have onions, does it? Or pineapple? Fruit is just sick and wrong on pizza."

"Yes to the onions, no to the pineapple, though I have been known to order the odd Hawaiian-style from time to time. But I'd gladly pick the onions off of yours for you, if you'll save me from eating alone." He smiles again, and I wonder for the hundredth time how it is that this guy isn't married. He's flat-out gorgeous and brimming with singe-your-fingers sex appeal.

Oh, right. The domineering, bossy personality might get in the way.

Like mine does?

"I'll pick off my own onions, thank you. There's no telling where your hands have been. I'll even spring for the sodas." *Oh, oh. No flirting, no flirting, no flirting. Remember—you still have a life-or-death bet going on with this man.*

(I'm actually very talented at ignoring my inner voices of reason, conscience, and/or any other form of boring grown-up think-ing, in case you were wondering.)

He pushes my door open farther and sweeps an arm out in front of him. "To the conference room, then. Your pizza awaits."

I smile and stand up to head for my door, but he has to ruin it all. "Why don't you bring your file along with you, and we'll talk about the marketing plans while we eat?"

Great. I should have known he was only interested in me for my spreadsheets. My expectant mood fizzles a little, but I grab the file. Better to keep focused on work, anyway. I take my revenge by motioning him to lead the way and then staring at his butt as we walk. He may be a jerk, but he has pizza and a truly fine ass. There are worse ways to spend an hour.

* * *

[Note to self: Eating four slices of loaded pizza in front of a guy is maybe not the way to appear, you know, *hot*.]

I fight the urge to unbutton the top button of my jeans and try to act casual as I lean back to give my expanded belly some room, while I survey the demolished remains of pizza.

Banning stretches and shifts around in his chair, too, so I figure the six pieces he ate are giving him similar problems. (I also figure, sadly, that he's not trying to impress me, either, except in a how-can-the-guy-not-weigh-four-hundred-pounds kind of way.)

"So." He looks at me in a considering and kinda serious way. "Tell me about this novel."

I can feel my face heating up. "Nothing. It's nothing. Well, it's sort of something, which completely freaks me out, but it's really nothing."

He laughs at me. "Well, that certainly cleared it up."

"Right," I say, grinning. "It's just an idea I had. I've been writ-ing since I was a kid—'self-absorbed crap,' I now find out—but I just heard from a pretty reputable source that I may actually have some talent. So now we'll see."

Lobbing it right back into his court is my only way to keep from dying of embarrassment, so naturally, I do. "What about you and the environment? You want to grow up to be a big tree-hugger or something?"

He grins that crooked grin that almost makes me forget what we're talking about. "Not exactly. I just want the chance to make a difference. I grew up here in the Pacific Northwest, and I'd hate to see our natural resources demolished any further. I'm involved in a group, and we're getting a huge groundswell of support. It's only a fledgling nonprofit right now, but maybe you could give us some marketing suggestions on ways to increase membership and donor awareness."

He slides his soda can back and forth on the table, then glances up at me and smiles. "I've heard you're pretty damn good at marketing."

As I pretend to myself that I didn't just go all warm and fuzzy from his compliment, I glance at the clock and realize we've blown an hour and a half talking about just about anything and everything except work. And, what's even odder, is that I really liked it.

I really like him.

Crap. When he's not doing the I Am Boss thing, he's really a lot of fun. We've already covered hot, and sexy, and did I mention hot? But now I have to add fun and interesting and easy to talk to to the mix.

I could be in trouble, here. Except for my rule about not dating the boss. Which is keeping me completely safe, even if he were the least bit interested in me.

Luckily, he is in no way jonesing for me. Which doesn't bother my ego one bit, thank you. Well, not much, anyway.

Okay, just what the hell is wrong with me? Why doesn't he like me?

Great, now I've reverted to third grade. Soon, I can ask Brianna to ask *his* secretary if he wants to trade peanut butter sandwiches with me on the playground. I roll my eyes and then sit up straight and pull the marketing file toward me on the table, shoving used napkins out of the way. "We've successfully killed a pizza and an hour and a half on a Saturday evening—and let's *so* not even talk about how pathetic that makes us—without discussing the marketing plans. I guess we can't put it off any longer. What do you need to know?"

He stares at me for a long moment, then flashes a decidedly non-boss-like grin my way. "I *need to know* what happened last night with your . . . marketing research. How many hearts did you break?"

My mouth falls open, and I gape at him like a beached salmon. "Um, what, well. Just getting ideas. Nothing special; no hearts broken."

"So, who is Ryan and why was he so sure you'd be at work on a Saturday morning?"

I try to remember if I know anybody named Ryan. No, I can't think of anybody . . . *oh. Ryan. From last night. I did tell him where I worked, didn't I?*

I focus on the least important part first, of course. "You answered my phone? Don't you have enough work to do without doing secretarial work? Or are you just nosy?" I smiled, but it wasn't all that warm of a smile.

"Just trying to be helpful. I happened to be walking past your office before you arrived when your line rang and rang and rang. Don't you have voice mail set to automatically pick up after four rings?" He leans forward. "Still not telling me who Ryan is, I see. Part of your market research? Come on, Kirby, we're all friends here. I just told you all about my bonehead frat buddies I still hang out and play softball with—the least you can do is come clean about the mysterious Ryan. Although he didn't sound right for you."

Okay. Now my mouth is opening and closing; still fish-like; definitely unprofessional. I snap it shut. "A few charming stories about Booger and Meathead aren't really opening up to me about your personal life, Banning. Not that I really want to know about your personal life, or about any woman nuts enough to be involved with you. And, what do you mean, Ryan didn't sound right for me? You can tell all that from taking a phone message?"

He reaches out and taps the top of my hand—the one that's clutching the napkin—and gently pulls the napkin away. "It was Bonehead and Mutt, not Booger and Meathead. Just goes to show how carefully you were listening to my deepest, darkest secrets."

"Right. Panty raids and keggers for dark secrets. How old are you, again? *Twelve*?" I toss the rest of the used napkins in the pizza box. "Anyway, what did Ryan have to say? And thanks for telling me about it earlier, by the way."

"You're welcome." Banning Stuart is apparently immune to sarcasm. "He sounded like a girly man to me. Prissy. Probably one of those guys who's afraid to get dirty."

I shove the pizza box down in the too-small trash can with just a teensy bit of unnecessary force. "Girly man? Are you channeling Arnold Schwarzenegger now? What does that even mean, 'afraid to get dirty'?"

He stands up with those smooth, coiled muscles unfurling like a big cat—or the gunslinger coming to save the day in one of Dad's old Western movies. *Totally* alpha male. *Totally* off-putting to an independent career woman. Worse, it puts him *way* too close to me.

Who am I kidding? I like him close. Any closer, and I'd set the sheets on fire with him in a major-league, forest-fire kind of way. Actually, right here on the conference table would work for me.

Sadly for me, there is no sweep-me-off-my-feet moment. I can see a muscle clenching in his jaw, then he backs away. "What it means, Kirby Green, is that niceness is overrated. It means that, after almost five months of working with you, I know that you need a man who's as strong as you are. And it also means that we are *not* having this conversation as long as I'm still working here."

He turns and stalks out of the conference room, never looking back, so he doesn't see the look on my face.

Yep. Definitely my lucky day.

* * *

At home later that night, after a quick stop at the computer store that put me back another four hundred bucks on the already over-stressed Visa, I hook up my new flat-screen computer monitor and open a new document. Then I type the scariest two words in the English language.

Chapter One.

22

Kirby

Dove sono i migliori locali notturni?
(Where are the best nightclubs?)

When you work all day Saturday and all day Sunday, Monday is less of a bad surprise and more of a dismal reality. If you wake up feeling even the tiniest bit of happiness, the commute through hideous Seattle rain and traffic will suck it right out of you.

As I pass the cluster of secretaries chatting in the doorway of the coffee room, I want to stop and say hi; maybe ask how everybody's weekend went. My steps actually slow a little, then Banning's secretary snaps a narrow-eyed, suspicious glare at me, and I rethink my momentary weakness. No un-bosslike behavior here—no way.

She continues to bore her beady eyes in my back as I pass by (I can just feel it), which makes me wonder if she knows about my Saturday pizza chat with her boss.

Paranoid, much?

Anyway, it's none of her damn business. It's not like I spent most of Saturday night trying to analyze what he could have meant by that last cryptic comment before he left the office. Or, at least, the part of Saturday night where I wasn't fumbling around with words on the pages of my fledgling first chapter. I'd come up with a pretty great title, Nice Girls Finish Last, but was still toying with the concept. Taking what Tom said to heart, I didn't want to make it autobiographical in any way, but the central characters seemed to have a little too much of me in them for comfort. (*My* comfort; *they* were characters and didn't do anything I didn't tell them to do. Sort of.)

Finally, I'd said to hell with an outline and just started writing, to see if I still could. If I still felt the rhythm and flow; the feel of the words crowding to get out of my mind, through my fingertips to the keyboard.

I still could. It was scary, it was exhilarating, and it was probably all crap, but I could still do it. I'd stayed up till around two in the morning and written twelve pages, which doesn't sound like a lot until you're the one bringing the characters up out of your imagination.

Twelve pages is *huge.*

So, between the twelve pages and the twenty hours of W&L work, I hadn't managed to spend much time studying up on famous ballerinas throughout history, so Lauren and I could have something to talk about. Something to break through the sadness she'd worn throughout much of last Wednesday evening like a shell over her interior of caution and reserve—way too much reserve for a little girl. She reminded me of *somebody.*

I round the corner, and the smell of coffee competes with the huge smile on Bree's face for title of Most Welcome. But she's standing there holding two Starbucks cups, so she gets the crown.

"Well?" she says, handing me the taller cup. "Gingerbread latte, no whip, by the way. *Well?*"

"Thank you so much! You are a gift from God, and it is totally my turn to buy tomorrow." I close my eyes and sip from the cup.

Instant, spiced happiness. Yep, Starbucks may have us all brain-washed into paying four bucks for a cup of coffee, but spiced latte is a happy, happy thing.

She follows me into my office, then stands there tapping her foot. *"Well?"*

I look at her, wondering if all that singing finally snapped something in her brain. "Well, what? What are you talking about?"

She closes the door and whispers something at me. *Geek bait?* Um, what . . . oh. Right. Speed date. Friday seems like a long, long time ago.

"Oh, you want to hear about the speed dating. It's not exactly national security, Bree. You can probably stop whispering."

She looks a little sheepish. "Sorry. I don't mean to be a goof. It's just that after Mr. Stuart walked in on us Friday, I'm trying to be more, you know, discreet."

"Yeah, Banning is all about discretion. Ask him about Booger and Meathead some time." I roll my eyes, but don't offer to ex-plain. "Pull up a chair. Let me tell you a story about Kirby and the Ten Dwarfs. Well, the Seven Dwarfs and Three Possibles."

I think of Steve and his orange shirt, and shake my head. "Maybe only Two Possibles."

* * *

Brianna keeps staring at me, making the beached carp face I know way too well. "But . . . you . . . I mean . . ."

"Spit it out, Bree. What?" I lean back in my chair, prepared for the worst. (Nice girls seem to be more judgmental than the rest of us, if you ask me.)

"Why did you pick the cute ones?" She looks a little freaked out, but keeps going. "I mean, the cute ones are all full of them-selves. The ones who are . . . er, less cute may be more . . . I mean, you're not going for *real* dates here, right?"

The lightbulb flashes or the light dawns (or choose any light-related euphemism you like), as logic strikes my stupid mind. Of course she's right. "Of course! I should have gone for the losers; they would have been much easier to manipulate."

Brianna shakes her head, then kind of clutches it with her hands. "No, no, no. Nice girls don't call people losers, Kirby. Remember the list?"

"What list? And I didn't just call *them* losers; I'm pretty much a loser myself to be in this predicament. So I'm an equal-opportunity loser-caller." I'm proud of myself for this—nobody can say I'm not all about equality.

"The list. Didn't I give you the list? I, ah, took the liberty of writing up a list for ways we can work on our, er, issues. The top ten ways I can be *less* nice, and you can be *more* nice sort of thing. Didn't I give it to you?" She looks flustered to a degree way out of proportion to the offense of losing a list. I wonder . . .

"Bree? What else is going on with you? Really? You put me off last week, but is there a problem at home? Anything you want to talk about?" I can hardly believe the words just came out of my mouth. Since when do I care about other people's problems?

It must be osmosis or photosynthesis or something—I think her niceness is rubbing off on me! Euww. Feels a lot like cooties.

Again with the regression to third grade. I sigh and slump down in my chair, fighting the urge to pooch out my lower lip. *Oh, what the hell.* I pooch.

Brianna crosses her arms over her chest and gives me a stern look. I'm not sure I'm all that happy that she's growing a backbone, to be honest.

"Kirby Green, you look like a sullen child," she says, then claps a hand over her mouth. "Oh, no, I can't believe I just said that to you. I'm so sorry! I think this nice-not-nice thing is making us both crazy! I feel like some kind of half-baked Frankenstein monster."

She jumps up out of her chair and starts backing toward the door. "Really, I'm sorry. I'm just going to go do some work now. It's odd that none of them called yet, though."

"Brianna, relax. I *was* acting like a sullen child. I just hate to have my own stupidity pointed out to me. You're completely right; I should have accepted matches with the los—um, the not-as-attractive men. I got carried away, okay?" I cheer up, remembering Steve. Not that he's a loser, but . . .

"I *did* say yes to a nervous-talker in an orange shirt. He told me a seven-minute-long joke that was so bad I don't even remember what it was about. A parrot in a bar, or something."

For the first time since I sat down, I glance at my phone. "Hey! The voice mail light is blinking. So maybe somebody did call." Then I remember Banning's weird revelation Saturday. "Banning said Ryan called. So we've got at least one. Not bad, huh?"

She leans against my closed door and casts a speculative glance my way. "Banning? *Banning* said Ryan called? Care to explain that one?"

I flush a little and look down at my desk, then remember who the boss is in this room. "Nope. Don't want to explain at all. But Ryan is one of the three prospects. So let's listen to the voice mail messages. Maybe he called back." I motion her back over and put the phone on speakerphone, while I dial into voice mail. Surely at least one of them called.

"You have seven new messages," the robotic voice tells me. *Seven? This could be interesting.* I take notes as we listen and try not to think of all the work we're not getting done.

"Hi, Kirby, it's Ryan. I called and got your . . . secretary? . . . Saturday morning. He sounded distracted, so I wasn't sure he'd give you the message. Anyway, here I am. I really enjoyed meeting you, and would love the chance to take you to dinner this week. Call me when you get a chance."

I jotted down his phone number, trying not to look too smug. Of course he'd called back. *Hello,* I do have cleavage and a brain in my head. I mentally stick my tongue out at Banning, then realize yet again that I spend way, way too much time thinking about him.

Messages two through four are hang-ups, which is a little weird. I flashback to Daniel's face on Friday night, and try not to freak out. Calm is good. Calm is my friend. Plus, the threat of a restraining order has always worked in the past. Daniel would never do anything that would impact his cachet with the rich, bored women in the country club set. Assault charges would fall in that category.

I delete all the hang-ups and press the button to play message five.

"Message forwarded from Speedy Dating Services: Hi, um, is this thing on? Ha, ha, get it? Is this thing on—I crack myself up. Well, hi! It's me, Steve, which you probably figured out by now since you just heard my voice Friday night, and it's only about two days later, well, not two full days because it's three in the morning Saturday, I mean, I guess that's Sunday, ha ha. You probably wonder why I'm calling in the middle of the night, but I kind of have insomnia, and I like to leave messages on people's work voice mails then, because they're not there, and I do so much better with machines than with real people. Oh—ha, ha. Not that you're not a real person, or, you know, like robots, but—"

Beep.

I press seven to save it, although I don't know why, exactly, since he didn't get around to any useful information like, for example, a *phone number*. I hear a weird snuffling noise and look up to see Bree trying unsuccessfully to hold in an enormous belly laugh.

"Oh, dear, Kirby, you w-w-weren't kidding about nervous talker. Lyle is one of those silent types, which always bugs me, but after this I think I'll have to b-b-be more understanding!" She doubles over in her chair, then gasps for breath. " 'Not that you're not a real person, or anything.' Oh, that is simply priceless!"

She launches into peals of laughter again, and I just stare at her, waiting till she calms down. "Glad you're so amused by my crisis. Must I remind you that when my job is history, you're likely to have a new boss who will probably be some old guy with bad breath and a hearing aid?"

She snorts a couple more times, then draws a last shaky breath and nods. "Go on. I'm sorry."

I stab the button to play message six. Another hang-up. *This is getting creepier and creepier. Must check Caller ID for the past seven calls.*

I delete and then listen to the final message, which Speedy Dating had also forwarded. "Hi, Gorgeous. It's Buddy. If you're still up for an evening out, I'd love to take you to dinner and maybe dancing. Call me and save me from pining away, imagining the sound of your voice."

He left his number, and I jot it down, thinking I'm three for three. That's not bad. I hang up the phone and look up at Brianna. She's done laughing, thankfully, but looks concerned. "That last one was way too smooth. 'Save me from pining away, imagining the sound of your voice?' *Bluch.* I liked robot guy better."

I have to agree with her. Buddy did sound a little too practiced. What was it he did? Something with the Nature Conservancy? *Hmmm.* Should have paid more attention. "Well, it's not as if I'm marrying the guy. How bad can one dinner be? I have a defined objective in mind, so my mission *will* be successful."

Great. Dating as strategic incursion. I need to quit watching C-SPAN so much. Next, I'll be planning to invade the Falkland Islands. What was my goal again?

Right. Somebody to call me nice. Maybe I should quit pursuing this stupid bet. Banning said he was willing to call off the whole thing.

But if he calls it off, you lose. Are you really so pathetic that you can't get even one person to call you nice in an entire month? This is only week two; you're giving up already?

"I'm not giving up," I say.

Brianna looks startled. "I never thought you would. Kick, scream, plot, and fight until the final minute of the final hour of the final day, maybe, but give up? *Never.* You don't have it in you." She stands up and gets a seriously determined look on her face, then starts walking toward the door. "And you know what? I'm starting to think I'm more like you than I'd thought."

I start laughing. "And is that a good thing?"

She stops and turns around to face me. "You bet your ass it is."

As she leaves and closes the door behind her, I can only contemplate the bizarre nature of the universe. Brianna just said *ass,* and I'm going to go out with robot guy.

It's going to be an interesting week.

23

Brianna

Opera buffa: Literally, "comic opera." Draws its comic characters from everyday life.

I was so proud of myself. For the very first time, I opened a porn Web site without yelling something much like *EEK!* and jumping up out of my chair like a little girl. But, still, I thought, peeking out of one half-closed eye at the site: BIG-BREASTED LESBIAN CHEERLEADERS GONE BAD, this was just not what I wanted to see before I'd even had my first cup of coffee in the morning.

I quickly shut down the site and erased any cookies, cleared the cache, and whatnot (it's complicated; the computer guys had showed me how to do it, and it kept me from getting thousands of e-mails on every facet of big breasts, lesbians, or cheerleaders doing the naked splits), contemplating again the bizarre-ness that is my job. Most people get in trouble for looking at porn sites on the Web at work. For me, it's part of the job.

Well, not actually to look at porn sites. It's just that lots of vendors want to carry our products, and part of my job is to screen them for Kirby. We're upscale here at W&L; we don't sell our products through sleazy porn sites. (Although, if Mama ever saw our catalog, I'm betting I wouldn't be able to explain the distinction.)

Anyway, the first time I looked up a site by its URL, I screamed so loudly that Jamie came running clear from accounting. Not to mention that everyone else in hearing distance showed up. I'd almost *died* of embarrassment.

But finding out that LOVES FARMGIRLS wasn't at all what it sounds like, and that the farmgirls in question had four legs, were covered with curly pelts, and said "Baa" gave me nightmares for a week. *Ick.*

Kirby said I didn't have to do the screening anymore after that; she didn't want me to feel grossed out or distressed in any way. But I'd thought of it as a challenge. If I'm going to work in a place like this, I can at least say the word . . . *nipple* . . . out loud, right?

I peek left and right; nobody's around. "Nipple, nipple, nipple," I whisper.

See, it wasn't that hard.

"Man, do I want to transfer to marketing," Jamie said, popping around the corner of my cubicle. "We never say nipple in accounting." He shook his head. "First Banning, and now you. Did I miss an important nipple memo?"

I so have to look for another job. Preferably one with an office with an actual door. I can't possibly look at Jamie now, or ever again. I wonder, if I wish hard enough, will the floor open up, so I can sink through to the next floor down? Maybe they even have job openings down there.

"Bree? Come on, you've gotta tell me what you were talking about. You can't torture a guy like that." He was laughing, but I didn't find it the least bit amusing. I peered down at the floor. *Nope, no hole yet.*

"Go away, Jamie. I can't possibly explain. There were lesbians and cookies and then sheep, which was back in the beginning but really made me almost quit, 'cause I had no idea what the W&L stood for when I took the job, and Mama would just have a coronary incident over the nipple clamps, let alone the naked cheerleaders, and I just can't talk about it anymore, so Go. Away. Now."

Silence. In fact, silence that lasted so long, I peeked around to see if he'd snuck away. *No such luck.*

He stood there, staring at me like I'd completely lost my mind. He was probably right. I thought back over what I'd just babbled on about in my stream-of-consciousness mortification moment and decided that moving to China was really my only option.

I've heard the Beijing Opera is nice. I'll even be tall, there.

I turned back toward my computer and clenched my eyes shut again, vowing never to open them until I heard his footsteps walking away or, at the very least, the sound of lightning striking my desk. Instead, I felt him lean in close to me, his hair brushing the side of my face, and I tried to control the involuntary little quiver that rushed through me.

"Bree? You are the most fascinating woman I have ever met in my entire life."

I still didn't open my eyes, even after he'd moved back and away from me. Finally, *finally,* he walked away. *Fascinating? Ha! Try stupid.* I pounded my head on the side of my cubicle, wishing I could replay the past five minutes in a way that made me look sleek and sophisticated, instead of like . . . like . . . well, like me.

Naturally, Kirby showed up mid-head pound. I froze, forehead on the wall, but she just raised one eyebrow at me. "So I take it my handwriting is bad again?"

Before I could formulate any kind of coherent response, my phone rang and Kirby walked off. *Great. Just great. Zero for two on the sophistication tally.*

I picked up my phone, determined to better my score, and used my best Marketing Professional voice. "W&L, Brianna speaking. How may I help you?"

"Dude, it's just me, in shipping. Can't you tell an inside line from an outside one? You've got, like, flowers or something down here, so you'd better come get them before they wilt and stuff."

"Flowers? But I—"

Click.

I stared at the phone. *Make that zero for three. The spaced-out teenager who works part time in shipping just hung up on me.*

Grimly, I start to punch in the numbers for hanger-upper-boy's boss, to complain about his rudeness, but my fingers slow, then stop. *Maybe he was having a bad day. Maybe I'm overreacting because of the nipple thing with Jamie.*

Maybe I'm just a wimp and will never be a diva.

Oh, good. My natural optimism is kicking in. The day is certain to improve now.

As I stood up to go retrieve the flowers that were probably really for somebody else, it occurred to me that I wasn't very good at sarcasm, either.

Maybe I really AM meant to be a cruise ship singer. At least there would be sunshine!

* * *

"Mmm, gorgeous flowers." Kirby leaned down to sniff the enormous bouquet of pink roses and baby's breath that spread over half my desk space.

"Thanks, I think so, too. They're from Lyle," I said, fingering the card he'd sent. All it said was *I'm sorry,* but that was enough. He *did* care about my feelings, after all. Lyle wasn't really a send flowers kind of guy, so he must have put a lot of thought into what to send me, because pink roses were my favorite.

I smiled and wondered again why he hadn't called yet. I'd tried his cell, but he was just coming off of a forty-eight-hour shift, so maybe he was asleep. He'd probably call me in the afternoon.

Kirby dropped yet another sheaf of papers in my in-box. "Here are some preliminary thoughts on the new lingerie line that I need typed up for tomorrow's meeting. Do you have time? The meeting's not till around eleven, I think."

I reached for the papers and riffled through to see how much was there, and also to scan for a rough estimate on how bad the handwriting was. "The meeting's been moved to ten thirty; Banning sent you an e-mail earlier. I changed your calendar," I said. "Plus, it's in the main conference room instead of his office, because some of the board members are going to attend. And, yes, I can finish this by the end of the day for you to review and make any edits."

She grinned at me. "Right. Wouldn't want any demon camels if the board is going to be there. That might be interesting to explain, especially in conjunction with a line of silk bustiers."

I laughed, too, shaking my head. "You're never going to let me live that down, are you?"

"Nope. I'm thinking stuffed camels for your present on Secretary's Day, definitely." She walked off, humming, and I thought again how much she'd changed recently. It wasn't just the bet, either. Kirby had relaxed her "I'm the fierce, hard-charging business woman" attitude, and she was actually fun to be around.

So if you don't succeed at the audition, you'll at least have a good job to fall back on.

I scowled. I didn't need any self-defeating comments internally; I was fielding enough of them *externally*. Mama'd had a cow at the thought that I might put the wedding off for a while, just until I got settled at the Opera. She was all about wanting more grandchildren. Lyle's mother was having some sort of rant, too; not that she'd ever thought I was good enough for him in the first place. But I guess all mothers are like that about their baby boys.

I sighed and started deciphering page one of Kirby's notes, so everyone at the meeting could be up on why silk bustiers and garters would increase our pubic martyrs.

Wha—? Oh. *Profit margins.*

I really, really needed to persuade her to use that dictating equipment.

* * *

Only four forty-eight, and I was finished with the report, which turned out to be a whole lot less interesting after the pubic martyrs scare. I stretched, trying to release the knots from my neck and shoulders, very aware of the vocal work I needed to do at Madame's later that evening. Kirby had to leave at five, too, for a mysterious recurring appointment she'd blocked out on her calendar for every Wednesday for the next year. She wouldn't talk about it, so naturally that made me more interested in what it might be. Maybe she was in therapy?

I shook my head, a little disgusted with my own nosiness. At this rate, I'd turn into one of the office gossips who hung out in the coffee room speculating on who was sleeping with whom. *Yuck.*

I grabbed the pages off of the printer and stuffed them into a file folder as Kirby dashed out of her office, shrugging into her coat. "Here it is, so you can take it with you."

"Thanks, Bree. You're the best. You should get going, too. The radio just said that traffic is a nightmare. Like, when is it ever *not?*" She took the file and rushed off. "Bye!"

I decided to take advantage of the novelty of Kirby leaving before me and straighten up her office before tomorrow's visit from the board. They had to walk right by us to get to the conference room. She was one of those "my office looks like a tornado just swept through, but I know where each piece of paper is" kind of organizers, so cleaning up was tricky, but I was getting pretty good at working around her various systems.

Just as I turned to go brave the fray, though, the phone rang. *Outside line; one minute till five. Do I have to answer it?*

Nice girl work ethic won out over phone avoidance, so I sighed and picked up the phone. "W&L—"

"Did you get my flowers?" Lyle's voice had that sexy, sleep-roughened thing going on.

I smiled. "Yes, I did, and they're gorgeous! Thank you so much! You are too sweet, and the pink roses—"

"Yeah, sorry they weren't red, but pink was on sale at the florist next to the station house. Glad you liked them. I wanted to say I was sorry for the way we left things on Saturday. Of course you should go for your dream, and of course I support you one hundred percent."

He paused, but I had no response. I was stuck back at "pink was on sale." So wonderful to be the bargain basement fiancée.

"Bree?"

"Sorry. I just . . . ah, nothing. You've really changed your mind? What about having a little boy who looks like you and ultimatums and everything else?" I heard the quiver in my voice, but I couldn't help it.

"I know, I said all those stupid things. I'm so sorry, honey. I just, hell, I don't know. I'm a guy, and I want to be the center of your universe. But we're way too young to have kids right away, and you should definitely go for your dreams. Your singing dream is one of the reasons I fell in love with you, right? Now I'm suddenly gonna act like a chick and try to change you?" He laughed, but it sounded a little funny.

Funny insincere, not funny ha-ha.

Or maybe you're just looking for an excuse to break up with him?

"I . . . I don't know what to say, honey. That's wonderful that you've decided to support my dreams. I love you for that! I'm so excited about the audition, and I've been dying to tell you all about what I'm doing to get ready, and—"

"That's great," he interrupted. "But I have some news, too, so let me get this out first, okay?"

"I . . . sure. Of course. What's your news? Did you get that promotion?" I fiddled with the pencils on my desk, trying not to think about how fast "I support you one hundred percent" had turned into "but just don't bother me with it now."

"We got the church!" He sounded thrilled, but I didn't have a clue what he was talking about.

"What church? Was a church on fire? What are you talking about?" I shut off my computer monitor, racking my brain. *Church?*

"For the wedding! Cookie pulled some strings; her dad is on the church board or something. Anyway, somebody canceled and we got the church for April—we can have a spring wedding! And it's almost two months after your audition next month, so you'll have plenty of time to rest up!"

I held the phone out at arm's length and stared at it, dumbfounded. Was he kidding? How did he think I'd have time to plan a wedding in eight weeks, especially if the opera company accepted me?

Oh. He doesn't think I have a prayer. This is "humor Bree until she fails her little audition for her little singing dream" strategy.

I didn't even realize I was crying until the tear rolled off my cheek, and plopped on my desk. I wanted to yell, or scream, or at least pound the phone against my desk. But I didn't do any of those things. Instead I said, as gently as possible, "Good-bye, Lyle."

Then I hung up the phone, put my head down on my desk, and cried.

When did this happen to us? When did the man who made me laugh, took me to hockey games, taught me how to ski, and once gave me one hundred pink balloons for no reason at all turn into a stranger? I'd never known anyone so kind and brave; I loved him for how much he cared about his family (okay, even his mother) and his friends. This tension was unwanted and unwelcome—but I couldn't bring myself to give in to his marriage-first demands.

'Cause if we start out this way, we've got nowhere to go but downhill.

* * *

As I brushed my teeth that night, I mentally listed the events of my sterling day.

1. I looked at a lesbian cheerleader site before coffee.
2. Jamie heard me saying nipple.
3. Kirby caught me banging my head against the wall.
4. The mailroom guy mocked me.
5. Pubic martyrs. 'Nuff said.
6. My fiancé bought me bargain flowers to try to cover up the fact that he thinks I'll never make it into the Seattle Opera.
7. Madame said I'd never, ever be ready for the audition, because I had all the emotion of a paper bag.
8. Nothing. There was NO eight. Nothing else happened. Not a single thing.

Honesty, Bree. At least with yourself.
All right, all right, already.

8. Jamie almost kissed me in the copy room. And I almost let him.

I put the toothbrush down and stared at myself in the mirror, almost able to see the giant scarlet A on my flannel pajamas.
Oops. Did I kind of skip over that last part?

24

Kirby

Dov' è il Signor Coniglietto? (Where is Mr. Bunny?)

"You should have asked me first, is all that I'm saying." Lauren's mother is ticked off at me, but trying to remain civil. We're sitting in her tiny kitchen, drinking coffee from I HEART MOMMY mugs, while Lauren does a final potty before we leave for the evening.

I squirm in my seat, knowing that she's right. "Mrs. Dennison . . ."

She smiles a little, but it's grim. "You may as well call me Anya, since you're spending time with my daughter, Ms. Green . . . Kirby. More coffee?"

I nod, and she walks over to the counter to retrieve the pot. "Look, I know you meant well. But ballet lessons are expensive, especially with all the gear. I'm budgeted pretty tightly as it is, with my college classes and books."

Oh. I never even thought of that. Crap.

"Anya, I'm so sorry. To be completely honest, it never occurred to me to check with you first. I'm so used to being on my own and going forward with any decision. I'm really sorry. But I'll pay for it, since it was my doing and it's on our Wednesday evenings together." I grip my coffee mug in both hands as she tops it off. I should have thought of this. I can't . . .

I don't want to have to forfeit my time with Lauren because of a stupid mistake. Damn, damn, damn.

Anya shakes her head. "First, you're not paying for it. I will. Second, what if you decide you're not really cut out to be a Special Sibling? Then somehow I have to find a babysitter who will take Lauren to ballet or ask her to give it up. Do you know how much that would break her heart? Ballet is all I've heard about all week."

She glances toward the hallway and lowers her voice to a whisper. "When you're dealing with kids, you have to always think of the consequences. Maybe you should start remembering that."

I feel thoroughly put in my place and start to bristle with resentment, then realize that she's completely right.

So I tell her so. "You're completely right. I'm not a mom, so I don't know all of the right ways to do things. But I *am* somebody who doesn't break her word. I like Lauren, and I want to spend time with her. I'm not going to quit on the Special Siblings program or on Lauren."

I look her in the eyes. "Or on you. I know how important this free time for your college classes is. If you want to pay for the ballet lessons, I completely understand. I know about pride. The lessons are six dollars each."

Okay, they're more like twenty-five bucks, but who's counting? I understand pride, and I'm not going to step on hers.

She reaches for her purse and pulls out her checkbook. "What about the shoes and costume?"

"The costume is included. I'd like it if you would at least allow me to buy her shoes, since I get the pleasure of watching her dance on Wednesdays." It's kind of scary how I can tell white lies without blinking, but that costume was a hundred dollars, including tights, and I bet there's no way Lauren's mom has that kind of money lying around.

She looks at me for a long moment, then nods and tears off a check. "That seems fair. Here's a check for the first five lessons. We'll see what happens after that, okay?"

I smile and nod, but I'm determined that Lauren will *plié* her way through as many classes as she wants, and I'm going to be there for them all. "I'm not going to be somebody who lets her down. I promise."

As we hear Lauren's steps galloping through the hall from the bathroom, Anya lays a gentle hand on my arm. "I kind of get the feeling that you won't. You're a nice person, Kirby. I won't ever forget this."

Did she . . . ?

Lauren bounces into the room. "Forget what? Are we ready? Do you like my braids? Can you do my hair in one of those ballerina buns like the girls had last week? Do you think my costume is ready? Are we still going to the ballet shoe shop? Are we? Huh? Kirby, are we?"

Still stunned by Anya's words, I wrench my gaze down to Lauren's excited face. She's jumping up and down in anticipation and grabs at my sleeve. "We've gotta go, or we'll be late. Gotta go, Mom. Good luck in class. Love you!"

As Lauren bounces over to kiss and hug her mom good-bye, I reflect on whether it should count that somebody called me nice, when it happened right after I lied to her.

Stupid moral dilemmas.

* * *

It wasn't my fault. Seriously. I've been getting fewer than five hours of sleep a night, and the ballet studio is totally overheated, and an hour of tap dancing to "Turkey in the Straw" is more than any human being should be forced to watch.

That's my story, and I'm sticking to it.

* * *

"WAAAAAHHHHH!!!"

"Wha?? I'm awake! Wha—happened?" I wake up to the cacophony of a hundred babies wailing in unison.

Or at least a dozen.

As I gaze blearily around me, I realize a couple of things, fast. I'm in the waiting room at Lauren's ballet studio, and ten angry women are glaring at me.

Oh, and one man.

Shit. What did I do now?

The mother nearest to me says, loudly, "If you don't *mind,*" as she yanks something out of my purse, which is sprawled on the floor, instead of hanging on the arm of my chair, where I'd hung it when I sat down.

She holds up a long ribbon that had been tangled in my bag. At the end of it is a slimy-looking thing that looks an awful lot like a rubber nipple stuck to plastic.

Do we carry those in our catalog?

Oh, right. It's a baby pacifier (double crap! That nasty thing was in my Kate Spade??) and gives it a quick wipe with some kind of cloth she has in a bag, then stuffs it into the wide-open mouth of the wailing baby on her lap. He, in turn, snuffles a little, then starts making the grossest slurping sounds I've heard since that horror movie about the giant killer octopus.

When octo-baby's mommy glares at me again, she pointedly says something to the rest of the room about inconsiderate parents who don't bother to even watch their children perform, and who let their purses rip the pacifiers out of the mouths of helpless children.

I lean down to retrieve my bag, blinking sleep out of my fuzzy brain long enough to sort out what must have happened. It must have fallen off the arm of my chair, caught on the ribbon holding the kid's slimy nipple, and ripped it right out of his face.

The other babies in the room kick up the howling a notch, as
if to underscore the magnitude of my transgression. Evidently baby
howling is like the fall of communism in Eastern Europe; set one
off and the rest fall like dominos. *Who knew?*

I sit back upright and glance in through the window at Lauren,
who is fiercely concentrating on a complicated series of tap dance
moves. Then I look at the bitch to my right.

"Oh, it's all right. I'm not her *parent*." I aim my most sinister
grin at her, and she huffs a little, but backs down fast. In my Anne
Klein suit and Gucci heels, I don't exactly fit in with the soccer
moms (and, presumably, dad) in the room, but I'm not about to let
their cull-the-herd mentality mess with me or with Lauren.

As class wraps up, the howling does, too, but not fast enough
to help me avoid the locomotive of a headache slamming through
my skull. Wow. This kid stuff can be painful. Again, *who knew?*

Lauren skips out of the door, eyes shining. "Did you see me,
Kirby? Did you? Did you see me? Miss Alma said I'm one of the
quickest learners she's ever had. I get to be in the recital as a real
dancer, not just one of the flowers."

She's literally jumping up and down with excitement, and the
expression on her face is the most beautiful thing I've seen in a
long, long time. I smile and grab her in a big hug. "I *did* see
you!"

Evil bitch woman snorts. I aim one of my teeth-baring "don't
fuck with me" scowls at her over the top of Lauren's head, and she
suddenly finds something fascinating in the bottom of her diaper
bag.

I hug Lauren again. "You were wonderful! You're going to be
brilliant in your recital, no matter what role you dance. Be sure to
practice at home, too, okay? I can't wait to see the pictures from
recital."

She looks up at me, eyes huge. "You're coming to my recital,
aren't you, Kirby? You have to be there! I wouldn't be a ballerina
and a tap dancer if it wasn't for you!"

Her lip starts to quiver. *Oh, no. I'm a sucker for the lip quiver.* "Kirby, that was our first hug. How can you say no right after our first hug?"

Oh, *good.* Now I feel like somebody who would pull the wings off of butterflies. I try to make her understand reason, though. "Honey, I have to leave for my trip to Italy the day after your recital. Remember, I told you last week? How I'm going to miss a few weeks of our meetings, but I'll send you lots of postcards and bring you a present?"

She folds her tiny arms over her chest. "I don't want presents. I want you. You *have* to be there."

"But I have to pack, honey. Now can you change your tap shoes back to your other shoes, so we can go get something to eat?" My reasonable voice plus a small bribe should work.

She slumps down on the chair and starts to untie her shoes, then smiles up at me. "Kirby, you can pack the day *before* my recital, silly. It's better to be prepared early, anyway, Mommy always says."

As she bends down to untie her shoes, I stare helplessly at the top of her head. I was just out-reasonabled by somebody who's only four feet tall.

Out loud, I say, "You're right. Why didn't I think of that? Of course I'll come to your recital. Now let's get going, okay?"

Just then, the teacher comes out to the waiting room and claps her hands for everyone's attention. "We have a little problem with the space for the recital, unfortunately. Our original space is being renovated. The repairs aren't going to be done in time for the recital, though. The contractors keep getting rained out."

She sighs and looks around at us. "The only space we could find on such short notice is considerably smaller. Unfortunately, only one parent per child will be able to attend. We'll have a professional videographer there, so anybody who wants a video will be able to purchase one for a very reasonable fee. We're also going to have to ask that you don't bring personal video cameras, because in the past we've had a big problem with so many parents taping that they blocked everyone's view."

Everybody in the room converges on the poor woman at that point, howling even louder than their offspring had been a few minutes earlier. I know it's terrible, but I feel a little relieved.

"You see, Lauren, they can only fit one guest per dancer. So there won't be room for me, anyway. You wouldn't want your mom to miss it, would you?"

She looks at me with enormous, sad eyes. *Great, the sad eyes. The sad eyes and the quivering lip. This kid really knows how to work it.*

"Kirby, Mama has to work on Saturdays. Grandma is going to keep me on the days you're in Italy, and she doesn't know how to drive. So I guess I won't get to go to my recital at all, if you don't want to take me."

WHAM! One, two, three, and Kirby Green, double-degreed marketing executive, is down for the count. Taken out by a knock-out punch of guilt from Strawberry Shortcake.

I have to smile. The kid's *good*. She reminds me of somebody.

* * *

After dinner at Wok and Roll, we drive back to her house, still chatting. Lauren's in a great mood (I roll my eyes; of course she's in a good mood, she got her way, didn't she?) and full of stories about her school teacher's pet rabbit. "I'd love to have a bunny. I'd take such good care of it! I'd feed it and tell it stories, and—"

"And clean up tons of poop pellets," I interrupt, trying for a little reality check, as I pull up to the fiftieth red light in a row. Seattle traffic just *sucks*.

"*Yuck!* That's disgusting! What are you talking about?"

"I had a rabbit in college. I read in a book that you could train them to use a kitty litter box. Sadly for me, the rabbit hadn't read that particular book. It pooped everywhere! Even a month after I got rid of it, I kept finding little poop pellets under my bed or behind the couch. Nasty." I shudder, remembering. *Oops! Almost missed the turn.*

I mutter a bad word under my breath, flip on the blinker, and barely make the sharp turn.

In the backseat, Lauren is losing it. Peals of giggles pour out from behind me. "Oh, Kirby, that's so yucky! Didn't you smell the poop? And . . . wait a minute."

Her voice turns really serious. "What do you mean, you got rid of it? What happened to your poor bunny? Didn't you love it anymore? Did you get tired of it?"

I draw a deep breath, trying to stall for a good answer. The truth, that I'd dumped it back at the pet store, wasn't going to sound good to a six-year-old.

A very tiny voice breaks into my frantic story-spinning. "Kirby? What if you get tired of *me*? Like Daddy got tired of me and Mommy?"

Oh, dear God. I am *so* not prepared for this. I say a silent prayer for forgiveness, then gear up for an enormous bunny-related lie. "First, I am not going to get tired of you. Who else would let me listen to 'Turkey in the Straw' for an entire hour, with the added benefit of watching that girl in the purple tutu who has two left feet?"

She giggles again. "That's Misha. She does get a little tangled up, doesn't she? But she's super nice."

"Of course she is, and it's wrong of me to make fun of anybody who tries hard, isn't it? Thanks for reminding me to be a nice person."

I finally, *finally* pull up to her apartment building parking lot. After shutting off the car, I release my seat belt and turn to look at her, feeling like a WARNING: BIG, FAT LIAR sticker is pasted on my forehead. "Second, I gave my bunny to a wonderful family who has a carrot farm in the country, so Bunny could roam free and eat all the carrots he wanted. Isn't that a better life for him than being trapped in my apartment all day while I went to school?

In fact," I continue, warming up to my fiction, "he has a bunny wife and bunny kids by now, and they're all very, very happy."

As we step out of the car, I congratulate myself for sidestepping a potential bunny fiasco. Walking toward her building, Lauren hoists her new Dooney and Bourke ballet bag onto one shoulder and slips her free hand into mine.

"Kirby? Can we go visit Mr. and Mrs. Bunny and the babies at the carrot farm on our next Wednesday?"

I'm doomed.

25

Kirby

Una confezione di aspirine, per favore.
(A packet of aspirin, please.)

"Hello?"

"Hey, Mom. It's Kirby."

"Kirby? Oh, baby, is that really you?" Her voice sounds like she's about to cry, and I shift the phone uncomfortably to my other ear, while I stare at my office door and wish fervently for someone—*anyone*—to come banging in, like they usually do.

No luck.

"Yep, it's me. Don't you recognize my voice?" I try for a light, joking tone and fail miserably. It's been a while since I called Mom. Or returned any of her calls, for that matter. Like, almost two months.

"Of course I do, honey. It's just that, well, it's been so long."

Before I can begin any of my lame excuses, she rushes in to supply them for me. "I know you've been so busy, with your important job, of course. I'm not nagging you."

For some stupid, unidentifiable reason, this makes me angry. "Why not?"

"Why not what?"

"Why *don't* you nag me? Why are you making excuses for me? I'm a terrible daughter. We both know it. Are you just so used to making excuses for people that you swept me under that umbrella, too?"

She tries to break in, but I don't let her. "I'm not him, Mom. You don't need to make excuses for *me*."

She sounds bewildered, and hurt, and I feel like the worst form of scum. "Not who? Not your father? I know you're not your father. You're so very different from him. But you—"

I can't take it. This was a huge mistake, brought on by the weird biological clock-ticking that spending time with Lauren was setting off. "Mom, I've gotta go. My other line is ringing. And I have a board meeting. But I'll call you soon, really."

"Kirby—"

"Gotta run, Mom. Really. Hugs to everybody. Bye."

I hang up the nonringing phone, twirl my chair around so that my back is to the door, and try to stuff my emotions back down where they belong.

How can it hurt so much just to talk to her? How can I hear myself saying hurtful things, but not be able to stop? What's wrong with me? If this tragedy of pain and love and hurt all tangled up with resentment is called growing up, I can see why nobody wants to do it.

* * *

Why did I ever want to be the boss of anything?

I slump in my chair after the door closes on the last of six candidates for assistant director of marketing. *"I'm a people person"?* Are they kidding? I thought that line was old and tired back in the eighties.

Oh, and the Yale guy? It was the first time I'd ever heard somebody use footnotes in *verbal* communication. Seriously. I'm *so* not making this up.

But, no worries. As if I hadn't already had enough fun for the whole week, I have interviews with six more candidates tomorrow. I grab the phone and stab the speed dial button for Brianna. "Brianna, please tell me you have better candidates for tomorrow? What were you *thinking* with these jokers today?"

"Well, er, I'll be right in."

Click.

She opens the door and walks in, not quite meeting my gaze. "Um, the best candidates are tomorrow, sort of a save the best for last kind of thing. Today's were more the, um, they were . . ."

The warning bells explode in my head. If she's stuttering, I'm usually in trouble. "More naked bungee jumping?"

She looks up at me, puzzled, then laughs. "Naked—no, no. It's just, well, some of them sounded so sad when I called them to say we wouldn't be interviewing them, so I had to change my mind."

Something about that didn't make sense. *Hmmm.* "What do you mean, sad?" Suddenly it hits me. "Wait a minute! Let's backtrack. You *called* them to tell them no interview? Why would you do that? We just send a thanks, but no thanks letter. You don't have to call people, for Pete's sake, Bree."

She wrings her hands together. "I know, but a letter just seems so impersonal, and it's hard to put yourself out there in a job search, and so I thought with a phone call, I could give a little encouragement. You know, like, 'We're sorry you don't fit our needs, but I'm sure there's a perfect job out there for you, and good luck! Just keep trying!' "

I groan and clutch the sides of my head with my hands, thinking of the coronary the suits in legal would have if they heard this. This is the kind of thing that could open us up to lawsuits, in a huge way. Like the "you asked your secretary to call and find out by our voices if we belonged to an ethnic minority, or sounded old,

or whatever other employment discrimination lawsuit is just waiting to explode on my head" issue might come up.

I open my eyes to see Brianna looking more than a bit freaked
out. Okay, there are better ways to handle this. I draw a deep,
calming breath. *Ommm.*

"Um, Bree? I think you should talk to the HR people about hiring issues, before we go any further with this. There are certain
problems with employment discrimination lawsuits we have to
consider in our hiring practices."

If I thought she looked freaked before, that was nothing com-
pared to now. "Calm down; it's no big deal. We just need to make
sure we're crossing all of our i's and dotting all of our t's, right?"

She laughs a little at my admittedly lame joke, but at least it's
something, so I smile reassuringly till she leaves my office. Then I
commence banging my head against my desk in rhythmic thumps.

Why did I *ever* want to be the boss of *anything*?

26

Brianna

Libretto: A publication with all the words in an opera.

Gosh, you try to be nice to a few job applicants, and it's a big, hairy, mandatory appointment with Human Resources.

I know Kirby was just trying to be helpful, but I did feel kind of punished when she told me to talk to HR, to find out why calling people at home was a no-no.

Words like *discrimination* and *lawsuits* didn't make me feel all that happy or secure. It had been a long, ugly day, and I still had one of the most miserably onerous tasks of my entire week facing me.

I had to call my future mother-in-law.

I sighed and toyed with the edge of my address book, flipping the page with Eleanor's number back and forth, trying to justify waiting for the best time to call her. Like another day later this week, or, say, a lunar eclipse, or blue moon, or cold day in . . . Mexico. It's not that I was afraid of the woman, exactly. It's just that she didn't like me all that much, and she wasn't exactly shy about showing it.

At all.

Ever.

Lyle didn't see it, either, which caused a teensy bit of tension between us. He was always trying to get us together to "do girly stuff," as he put it. I'd tried it, but we didn't exactly see eye to eye on many things, except that we both loved Lyle. Only, she was convinced that she loved him way more, and so she treated me like I wasn't quite good enough for her baby boy.

Who also happened to be her *only* boy.

Who also happened to be her only *child.*

I spent a lot of time worrying that none of this was a good basis for the future of in-law relations.

Sadly, none of this introspection was helping me dial her number. I sighed, picked up the phone, and dialed.

"Hello?"

"Hi, Eleanor, it's Bree. How are you? Lyle said you needed to talk with me, so I wanted to be sure and catch you before you were at dinner."

She tinkled her breathless little laugh which, to be entirely honest, sort of irritated me now. I know it's not nice to be irritated by somebody's laugh, especially my future mother-in-law. I mean, I'm sure she can't help how she laughs, but there you have it. I wasn't being very nice lately in so many ways.

Plus, I bet she'd be really interested to know I'm practically kissing men who are not her son in the copy room.

I cringed and tried to focus in on her words. ". . . after church?"

"I'm sorry, my, um, my boss was calling me, and I missed that. What about after church?"

Her voice turned chilly. (She hates to be ignored.) "I said that we're having you and your Mama for lunch after church Sunday at our house. One o'clock. Don't be late!"

"But—" I needed to rehearse Sunday, and I didn't know what plans Mama had. Mama wasn't exactly warming up to Lyle's mother, either, so an entire luncheon on Eleanor's turf could be tense.

"No, no, no; I won't hear another word. We need to do some wedding planning, with the big day coming up so soon! I'll see you there. I can show you my plans for your dresses, too. Bring paper to take notes, dear. Ta, ta!"

"But—"

Click.

Well, I really contributed to *that* conversation. So, I was doomed to endure lunch Sunday with Mama and Eleanor, who would each try to outdo the other, while Eleanor relegated me to being the secretary for planning my own wedding.

Really, what could be more fun? Maybe I'll get lucky and slip on the ice and break a hip before then. There's always hope.

* * *

The phone rang as I was packing up to go home. *The head of accounting?* Oh, it must be about the budget figures for the two-in-one vibrators or something.

"Brianna speaking."

"Don't hang up, please. Bree, we need to talk," Jamie said.

"Jamie? I thought—"

"I know, I ducked in here to use this phone because you've been screening my calls, ignoring me in the hallway, and suddenly getting really busy when I stop by your desk."

He was right. I'd taken the mature route of hiding from him, so I could escape the "let's talk about what almost happened in the copy room" talk.

"Bree? Please? I really need to talk to you; at least let me apologize. Can we go get a drink or coffee or something?" He had a pleading note in his voice that stopped the automatic "no" that had been forming on my lips.

"Okay. But no drinks. I think we're in enough trouble without adding alcohol to the mix. How about coffee downstairs in ten minutes?"

"Great. That's great, Bree. Thanks so much. Ten minutes." The relief in his voice was huge, but it only underscored my guilt. *Should* I meet him? Would it just encourage him?

Or me? It's not like he was the only one doing the almost-kissing.

* * *

I picked at my napkin, my latte untouched on the table in front of me. Jamie stared at me with those enormous eyes of his. It was completely unfair that he was so unbelievably cute. He'd probably gotten away with murder when he was a kid. What mother could resist that face?

I sighed, remembering I'd thought the exact same thing about Lyle back when things were good between us, before I found out how little he valued my dreams. Seriously, if I ever had another chance, I was only dating ugly men.

Toad ugly.

Jamie finally put his cup down and broke the awkward silence hovering between us. "Look, I've practiced this over and over in my mind, but it's tough to get the words out. I'm so sorry for taking advantage of your mood the other day when I tried to kiss you."

He shoved a hand through his hair and grimaced. "You're one of my best friends, Bree. I can talk to you about anything. I'd hate it if I thought I'd ruined our friendship."

I stared at him with just a touch of skepticism. "You kiss a lot of your buddies in copy rooms, do you?"

He laughed. "No, I don't. Especially not Judd; he'd punch me."

"Then why me? I'm not accusing you of setting anything up, Jamie. This is hard for me to admit, but I was right there with you. And I've paid the price in guilt, believe me."

He grabbed his cup and sucked down half of his coffee, then placed the cup very carefully in the center of his napkin. "All right. You deserve the truth. You may have noticed that I have . . . feelings for you. Way stronger feelings than just friendship."

Oh no oh no oh no. "But—"

He held up his hands to stop me. "I know, I know. I'm sorry. I know you're engaged, and I respect that, in spite of what I did the other day. I promise to back off completely and never talk about this again, after today. It's just that you seem so unhappy and, well, I think you deserve somebody who loves you for you. Dreams and all." He blew out a huge breath, and he wore the "oh, crud, did I really just talk about my *feelings?*" grimace so common to the male of the species.

Honestly, it's a wonder humanity survives.

WAIT A MINUTE! *Did he just say* love? I felt the blood drain out of my face.

"Oh, Jamie. I'm not mad at you. I can't say that this won't affect our friendship, 'cause I feel hugely weird around you now, to be honest. But you can't throw words like . . . *that* around with an engaged woman."

"I know, I know. I never will again. I just wanted you to know how I feel, and that it wasn't some game to me the other day. Trying to kiss you, I mean. I just . . . I suddenly felt like I couldn't breathe if I didn't know what your lips tasted like."

My mouth fell open. Who *talks* that way? That's the most romantic (and, let's face it, *totally hot*) thing any guy has ever said to me. (Also, the cheesiest. But still sweet.)

"You can't—you can't say anything like that to me ever again." I stood up and shoved my chair back. "I really have to go now. I'm marrying Lyle, Jamie. He's a wonderful man, if a little old-fashioned, and we're going to work things out. Please give me the space to do that. If you really care about me, you won't confuse me. I have enough on my plate right now."

He stood up, too, a slow smile spreading over his face. "I think the fact that you admit I confuse you is the closest I'm ever going to get to having my feelings returned here, so I'm going to bow out gracefully. I wish you and Lyle the best, forever and ever."

He touched my cheek for a bare whisper of a moment. "You *deserve* the best, Bree. Don't ever forget that."

Then he tossed his cup in the trash and stalked out of the coffee shop, never looking back, leaving me staring after him, wondering.

Wondering why I felt miserable, instead of relieved.

27

Kirby

Non ho ordinato questo. (This isn't what I ordered.)

Date One: Steve

Why, oh, why did I ever agree to this? I must have been out of my mind. Even naked bungee jumping—chafing and all—sounds a whole lot better than an entire evening with Steve the nervous talker.

I edge my car past a minivan and pull into a parking space right in front of Cheap Shoes A-Go-Go (which has its own irony). After I shift into park, I check the address again. Yep, this is where he said to meet him. In front of this cheesy little strip mall.

If he wants me to shop for cheap shoes with him, I'm so out of here.

I suck in a deep breath and remind myself to be nice. Be nice, be nice, be nice. Technically, Anya called me nice, but I decided it didn't really count since I'd been a big, fat liar about the cost of the ballet lessons. *If you can't have integrity in double-dog dares, what kind of person are you?* Nothing will feel better than winning this bet fair and square and scheduling time in my day for Banning's public apology.

Really? He said he was sorry already. Wasn't that enough? You're the only one making this into a huge trauma.

I shove the voice of reason back into its crate in the basement of my psyche, vowing to deal with the whole mixed-up mess Monday during my appointment with Dr. Wallace. He'd have some ideas for me, and maybe a comment or two on whether I should quit obsessing over this stupid *nice* thing.

Uncomfortably aware that I just used the O-word, I haul myself up out of my car and close the door, noticing that it's seriously in need of a wash to get rid of the coat of Seattle winter slush that dulls the red finish. It wasn't necessarily the brightest idea—buying a convertible—when I live in a city where it's only sunny two or three days a year.

"Hey, Kirby!" There he is, loping toward me. He's definitely a loper, with that tall, lanky frame. I have to admit, he is really cute from a distance, but he's two for two on the orange shirts. That could be a problem.

You don't want to marry the man, you just want him to think you're wonderful and call you nice, right? Quit being critical. And do a shoe check!

Right. I shoot a quick glance at his shoes, then breathe a sigh of relief. Definitely not the Cheap Shoes A-Go-Go type. So—we're here, *why?*

"Hey, Steve. Hi! I was worried I'd ended up in the wrong place. Aren't we having dinner?" I glance around and do a little fake-sounding laugh. "You don't need shoes, do you?"

He looks puzzled. "What? Shoes? Oh—the store. No, no, no. Although, whenever I come by here, they seem to have good specials. I mean, look in the window, *Buy One, Get One Half Off.* Hey, a pair of shoes half off! Wouldn't that mean you were half barefoot?" He whips a small pad of paper and a pen out of his coat pocket and jots something down. "That's a good one for my routine."

"What routine? I thought you were a professor. And, not to rush you, but could we perhaps start walking? I'm freezing out here!" My suit jacket is not nearly warm enough for standing out on the sidewalk in January's freezing damp.

"Oh, right. I'm so sorry, Kirby. Let's just—here, let me stuff this back in my pocket. Yes, I'm a professor, but remember I'm also an aspiring stand-up comic. You know, like Jay Leno and Jerry Seinfeld and Johnny Carson? Hey! Did you ever notice that all the greats have names that begin with J? Maybe I should change my name from Steve to Jay or Jerry or Jimmy. What do you think?"

By now, I'm hopping back and forth from leg to leg. "Sounds great, Jimmy. But can we go inside wherever we're going? *Now?*"

He smacks himself in the forehead with his hand, then takes my arm. "I'm so sorry. I get carried away sometimes. Let's go, yeah, right away. We're right down here on the end. I would have gotten reservations, but they're not usually packed on Thursdays. Although Fridays is a different story. And, actually, Thursdays in the summer are really packed, when all the adult softball leagues stop by for the barbecue specials. But nobody's playing softball this time of year, right?"

I'm dazed both with cold and with trying to keep up with the seemingly never-ending flow of words, so I just nod and hurry along next to him, until we reach the last door on the building and he pushes it open and pulls me inside. Immediately, the smell of burnt cow smacks me in the face.

"Um, Steve, what *is* this place?" I look around, and the tiny . . . restaurant? . . . hole in the wall? . . . is a mosaic of walls covered with metal horseshoes, murals of rodeo riders, and what appear to be real, live (well, real, *dead*) animal heads.

Okay, there's no *way that* can be hygienic.

Stop being a snob. Normal people must eat here all the time.

*Look at all the families. Plus, the Health Department would have
shut it down if you could get dead deer-head cooties, right?*

Ignoring the little voice in my head that wants to talk about
how overworked Seattle health inspectors probably are, I follow
Steve and the hostess to a little booth in the back corner. She slaps
the menus down on the table with a flourish and beams a huge,
"this is the best job I could get, so I'm pretending to be happy"
smile at us.

Or maybe I'm just projecting, again.

"This is fine. Thanks so much, Francie."

Francie? I scan for a nametag. Nope. He must come here a lot
to be on a first-name basis with the staff.

Her next words confirm my hunch. "You're welcome, Stevie.
Welcome to the Mountain o' Meat, ma'am. I'll send someone over
to take your order."

I edge gingerly onto the cracked vinyl bench of the booth, opposite *Stevie.*

"Did she say *Mountain o' Meat?* Really?" It had to be a joke.
Who would bring a first date to a place called Mountain o' Meat?
I pick up one of the greasy-looking menus with the tips of my fin-
gers. *Oh, shit. It's* not *a joke. Or if it is, the joke's on me.*

MOUNTAIN O' MEAT

HOWDY!

SPECIALS:

A. SEVEN MEATS, COLESLAW, AND FRIES

B. SIX MEATS, COLESLAW, AND FRIES

C. FIVE MEATS, COLESLAW, AND FRIES

D. FOUR MEATS, COLESLAW, AND FRIES

E. CHILD'S PLATE: THREE MEATS, FRIES AND TOY

Yep. One big, fat, cosmic joke. I sigh and drop the menu back
on the table. Steve is looking at me, anxiety all over his face (which
looks kinda green in this light).

"Is it okay? The food is really good, even if the menu is basic. And you can substitute a baked potato or a salad for the fries and coleslaw, if you like." He bites his lip. "It's just that the food is so good, and the people here are so nice, I thought I might not get so nervous if we came here. You might have noticed, ha ha, that I'm kind of a nervous talker, especially around girls, I mean, women, and I've never, ever had a date with somebody like you."

He drums his fingers on the table so hard I'm worried they'll drill a hole in the table.

"Steve, Steve. *Stevie.* Calm down. It's okay. It's fine. I'm open to new things. It's just, not to stress you out, but what if I'd been a vegetarian? All of the meat on the menu, not to mention the dead animals on the wall, might have been kind of a deal breaker." I smile the nicest smile I can muster, but he still looks like somebody rained out his tea party. (Or, you know, whatever the guy equivalent of that would be.)

"I'm so sorry! I never even thought of that. It's just that you're so pretty, and I get so nervous around women, even ugly women; not that I hang around ugly women, I mean, not that I think women are ugly, because beauty is only skin deep, but you have really great skin, and I don't get to date women with great skin, or deep beauty, or—"

"Steve!" *How does he do that? He doesn't even stop for air!* "Stop! I'm glad you think I'm pretty. Thank you for the kind compliment that was somewhere in what you just said."

I smile again and put my hand on top of his to stop the nervous finger-drumming. "I'm not a vegetarian. One of the meat specials sounds fine. Although, you're going to have to explain to me how there are seven meats. Isn't there pretty much just beef, pork, and chicken?"

He stares at my hand on his, and I notice that *his* quivers a little, so I gently withdraw mine. It's kind of like trying to tame a wild animal, which, I guess, is probably a foreign concept here at the Mountain o' Meat.

Here, they just shoot 'em and put 'em on the menu.

Steve gulps in a big breath and lets it out slowly, then seems to perk up at the chance to educate me on the mysteries of meat. "Oh, no. There's your beef round, and your flank, and your pork loin, and . . ."

As he meanders on down the entire butcher's catalog, I sigh to myself and think about why and how I put myself in the position of discussing cuts of meat with a guy who probably hasn't had a date since he was twelve. That's when a very important truth hits me: Monday's appointment with Dr. Wallace won't be a day too soon.

* * *

In case you wondered, it is possible to eat five different types of meat all in the same dinner. Steve just proved it.

"Wow. That was the most—interesting dinner I've had in a while. That third meat was definitely . . . intriguing." I'm trying hard for social chitchat here, but it's tough to talk to a guy who either babbles incessantly or falls into a choked silence. I don't feel all that great about myself right now, either, because this is really a sweet guy, and he has the most massively hopeful look in his eyes every time he looks at me.

Like now. He looks at me and smiles. "This is the best time I've had in a long, well, in pretty much the past ten years. How pathetic is that?" He laughs a little, then pops a small chunk of meat in his mouth and swallows. "Thanks for coming out with me, Kirby. You know, once you let people see behind your scary executive image, you're really pretty ni—, n—, n—*yaaagggkkk.*"

"I'm *nyagk?* Okay, this must be some kind of professorial code I don't know. Want to clue me in?" I grin at him, then realize he's not grinning back. In fact, he's staring at me, kind of bug-eyed, and making a weird choking noise.

Geez, I was just kidding about the "choked silence" thing.

"What? Are you okay?"

He starts slamming one hand on the table, and pointing to his throat with the other. Meanwhile, his face is turning an alarming shade of red that totally clashes with his shirt.

Oh! Choke! He's choking!

"You're choking?"

He nods frantically, now clutching his throat with both hands and bouncing up and down in his seat.

"Hang on!" I jump up, feeling my pantyhose catch on a tear in the vinyl bench and rip halfway down my leg, then kind of lurch around the table and jerk him up out of the seat. I yank him around so he's facing the rest of the tables, away from me, and put my arms around him from behind.

Then I grasp one hand with the other and shove them sharply upward, just underneath his sternum. There's a weird *thwocking* sound, and a woman screams. Then I feel and hear Steve suck in a huge, coughing breath, and everybody else in the restaurant starts cheering and clapping.

Well, except for the one woman who's still yelling. I peek out at the room over Steve's shoulder and see Francie jumping up and down, yelling, "My hair, my hair; get it out of my hair!"

Lovely. Half-eaten meat chunk. She is going to need a *serious* shampoo.

Steve turns around to face me, sort of, except for the part where he won't look me in the eyes. "Thanks," he mutters. His face is still flaming red, but I get the feeling that this is a whole different kind of red from before.

I touch his arm. "Steve, it's no big deal. If you knew how many times I've choked on stuff! It's why I learned the Heimlich to begin with, really."

He still won't look at me, and he doesn't sit down, either. "Um, right. Well, thanks. We should probably go. Early class, you know." He scoops up the check and heads for the cashier, leaving me staring after his rapidly retreating back.

Great. Just great. Save a guy's life, and this is how he acts.

As I grab my purse and follow him through the restaurant, murmuring my thanks to all the people who "way to go" me in the aisle, I remember what he tried to say before the Death Chunk of Meat episode.

He was going to call me nice.

Cheap Shoes A-Go-Go couldn't have been worse than this.

28

Kirby

A che ora finisce? (What time does it end?)

It's official! I hired all three staff positions, including my assistant director of marketing. I was able to extend offers on the spot, thanks to Bree's kick-ass research and background checks. She wasn't kidding when she said the six candidates today were the best; I only wish I'd had *six* jobs to fill.

I lean back in my chair and prop my shoes on my desk, feeling an enormous rush of relief. It's the first time I've felt good all day, since I've had a huge case of worrying about poor Steve after last night. He'd been nervous enough, even before the amazing flying meat chunk debacle. I tried to call him three different times today, but his voice mail clicked on immediately each time. I only left one message, and it was kind of brief, since Bree brought one of the candidates in while I was on the phone. Basically, just "hope you're okay; I really had a nice time."

Because, much to my serious and total shock, I *did* have a nice time. It was kind of fun just being relaxed and not playing the "who's hotter or richer or more driven or more of a workaholic or more connected-with-the-in-crowd" game. Once I got past the shock of the seven-meat special, I'd had fun. Not in a let's get all naked and sweaty way, but in a you're a great guy, let's be good friends way.

Guys never go for that one, much, though. *Bummer.*

And, as much as the thought sucks the happiness right out of my soul, I have to get ready for tonight's date. (Yes, I set up the dates for three days in a row; must have been eating my idiot pills that day.)

As I stand up and hike my skirt up a little, so I can check for pantyhose bagging issues, my door bangs open. *Oh, sure. Never when I'm on the phone with my mother, just when I have my skirt yanked up halfway to my crotch.*

I do a quick half-whirl around while dropping my skirt, and bark over my shoulder, "Does the concept of knocking totally escape *everybody* in this company?"

Banning's very amused voice floats back to me. "Why would I possibly knock and miss you doing the . . . ah, *twist?*"

I roll my eyes. Of course, it had to be him.

I turn back around and fold my arms, staring a challenge at him. "Is there something you needed? Or did you just hear that I've completed my hiring for all three positions and you wanted to stop by and congratulate me?"

"Really?" He looks surprised, but hides it almost immediately. "I mean, *right.* I knew that. That's great. So, you'll have two whole weeks to train them before you leave on your vacation, right?"

I nod, then slump down in my chair, muttering. "Right, except for the 'nice' that didn't count, and the 'nice' interrupted by meat expulsion."

"Meat expulsion? What are you talking about? Kirby, and I mean this in the nicest possible way, are you on any medication?"

I glance up at him, startled, then see that his lips are twitching and realize that he just threw my own words back at me. "Right. Very funny. Ha, *ha*. Well, if you're not here to congratulate me, what's up?"

It's his turn to look a little uncomfortable, except without the hand-up-his-skirt problem. "I thought that maybe you'd like to . . ."

The pause stretched out for a moment.

"Go naked bungee jumping?" I asked.

"What?"

I grin. "Nothing. Long story. If I'd like to what?"

He steps forward a pace or two from the door. "Go with me to a Northwest Nature Groups meeting tonight. That nonprofit I told you about? Not like a date or anything, really. I thought you might be able to offer us that marketing and donor-solicitation advice I'd mentioned."

He looks awfully fidgety for someone who just invited me out on a "marketing advice" evening. *Hmmm.* But it's not a date. Even though he's totally hot, and I think he feels the heat between us just as much as I do, he specifically *said* that it wasn't a date, so I wouldn't be breaking my Don't Date the Boss rule, right?

I sigh. I can't go, either way, since I've got a date with Buddy, in what feels more and more like my stupid and pointless quest to get somebody to call me nice.

Haven't I proven myself by now? Do I really need to keep this up?

Suddenly I hear Dad's voice in my head. *Sure, you were a quitter as a kid, and you're a quitter now. Who cares if you're nice or not? You'll never amount to anything.*

"Kirby?" Banning breaks into my self-flagellation moment, and he looks concerned. "Are you all right? I wasn't trying to put you on the spot or anything—just forget I asked, okay? I'll see you later."

"No, wait! It's not—"

He pauses, with his hand on the door, and looks back at me.

For a split second, his face has the same naked hopefulness I saw on Steve's face last night.

"Banning, I—"

Riiinnngg.

Banning pulls the door open. "I see that you're busy. I'll talk to you next week. Good job on the hiring, Kirby. Have a good weekend."

"But—"

And then he's gone, pulling the door gently shut behind him. Just for spite, I consider letting my phone ring to voice mail, but it occurs to me that it might be Steve.

"Kirby Green."

"Hey, gorgeous. I'm pretty close to the Convention Center right now. I know I'm a little early, but I wanted to try to beat the traffic. Are you out of your medical conference yet?"

(Long story; logistics. What was I going to do, take a cab over to the hospital and have him pick me up there? The whole secret identity thing is tougher than the movies make it seem.)

"You're in luck. We're just wrapping up our last lecture on, ah, new techniques in bedpans. I'll be down at the pull-in driveway in ten minutes. See you there."

As I hang up, I think about Buddy and his smooth lines and realize how abso-freaking-lutely dull this evening is going to turn out to be. Then, I think of Banning and Steve, and the hope-destroying effect I seem to have on any nice guy in a fifty-mile radius.

Maybe an evening with Buddy is exactly what I deserve.

* * *

Date Two: Buddy

"So, have you ever been to the Tacoma Dome?" Buddy asks as he pulls onto I-5 South out of the city.

I'm leaning back into the cushy leather seat of his ridiculous car (a grown man driving a Corvette with a giant spoiler on the back?

Puh *leeeo*.) "I'm not sure. I think I went there once as a kid for an ice skating show with my friend Jules's family, but that may have been in Seattle. Not recently, that's for sure. I'm way too busy at work to get out of the city."

He glances over at me and smiles. "You nurses work too hard. My sister does twenty-four-hour shifts twice a week. How does your schedule work?"

Oh, right. I'm a nurse. Nurse, nurse, nurse. Shit. Why did I do this, again?

"Oh, it varies," I respond airily. "You know those nursing schedules. But really, my life is so dull. Tell me about you."

He speeds up to pass a truck, then slows back down. It's a bit of a drive to the Tacoma Dome, so we may as well get to know each other. Or, at least, Nurse Kirby will get to know Buddy.

"You said you were in natural resource management, right? Shouldn't you be at the Nature Groups meeting tonight?" I'm impressed I remembered what he does for a living. I *did* meet ten different guys that night.

Speaking of which . . . I pull my cell phone out of my purse and set it to vibrate. I'd really like to talk to Steve if he calls, Buddy or no Buddy.

"Hey, I'm impressed that you remember what I do! I only remembered about the nurse thing because of my sister. I spent most of my time staring at your legs." He grins and winks at me, like being a caveman is a *good* thing.

"So? You neatly avoided my question again, I notice. What organization are you with? Or are you a corporate Greenie?" He must work somewhere to earn the money for the racing stripe paint job on this ludicrous car. (Talk about compensating; I'm already wondering just how tiny his winker is. If I see gold chains when he takes his jacket off, I'm going to guess . . . *petite*.)

He takes a deep breath. "Okay, here's the thing. I'm kind of a . . . salesperson for garden products."

"Hmmm. This is confusing. Either 'salesperson for garden

products' means you're growing pot in your backyard, or you're acting all hinky over rakes and fertilizer?"

He sneaks a glance at me, then starts drumming his fingers on the steering wheel. *Not with the drumming fingers again. What is this weird effect I have on men?*

He whips around a Mini Cooper, then swerves around a Beemer, doing about sixty. This would be fine, if the rest of the traffic weren't doing about twenty. I grab my seat belt with both hands. "Hey, slow down, speedy. Where's the fire?"

I hate show-off drivers. You know, his good looks aside, there isn't a single reason I can think of why I accepted this date.

Nurse. Nice. Stupid obsession with stupid bet.

Oh, yeah. Stupid. And there's that O-word again.

Crap.

Buddy at least takes my not-so-subtle hint and slows down. "Sorry. I just get anxious when I have to tell a new chick about my job. They never seem to get it, ya know?"

A new CHICK? What happened to Mr. Smooth from Speedy Dating?

"I'll try not to be one of that kind of . . . *chick*." My tone is seriously acerbic, but Buddy's not one to let a little sarcasm stand in his way.

Actually, Buddy doesn't seem to be one to *get* sarcasm. I'm suddenly suspicious. "Buddy, not to interrupt this fascinating garden tool discussion, but how many times have you done the Speedy Dating thing?"

He laughs. "Oh, like ten or twelve. The first six or eight times I struck out, ya know? But then my friends told me that I needed to be smoother. So we researched great opening lines. They work great! I usually score five or six dates a night." He's so proud of his opening line acumen, he doesn't realize that he just told me I'm one of a half-dozen women he asked out just this week.

Don't I feel special?

Plus, he's a big, fat liar. Let's face it, using canned opening lines so you can look like a sophisticated guy is perpetrating a fraud on your prospective date. It's a charade of the worst sort. It's . . .

It's sounding familiar, Nurse Green. Code Blue, stat.

I sigh again. "Goody. Glad you're so successful. Now about those garden hoses?"

He laughs again, but it sounds kind of nervous. My theory about him growing illegal drugs in his backyard might not have been too far off. Now *I'm* the one who's nervous.

Also impatient. "Just spit it out, Buddy. What the hell do you sell?"

I think I scared him, because he blurts out, "Coyote urine."

"*What?* Clearly I've had way too long of a week, because I thought you just said coyote urine." I stare at him in disbelief. No way he said that.

"That's what I said. See what I mean? Chicks freak. But there's a lot of money in coyote pee. Bobcat pee, too, but that's harder to collect." He nods his head sagely, probably thinking of the relative difficulty of collecting pee from large, fanged animals.

Okay, where's the Reality TV camera crew? There is no freaking way I'm sitting in a Corvette that's pimped out with a spoiler, talking to a grown man named Buddy who sells animal piss for a living. And maybe collects it, too.

Yanking my purse open, I check the tiny screen on my cell phone. Please, *please* let somebody have called me. Steve, Jules, the freaking Tooth Fairy. I need a reality check. No little envelope. No Missed Call flashing on the screen.

I look at Buddy, who is concentrating fiercely on the traffic. Right. He's *got* to be kidding.

"You're kidding, right? Let's fool gullible Kirby. Because there's no way you sell coyote pee. First off, how do you collect the stuff, and who the hell would buy it? And for *what?*" I start laughing a little wildly.

He goes all serious. "Predator pee is no laughing matter. The concept is based on duplicating the scent of urine in the wild.

Predators mark the perimeter of their territory with urine. This lets deer and other prey animals know if an area is safe or not for them."

I try to choke back the laughter and the ten thousand or so really crude jokes that bubble through my mind. "No, *really*? Isn't that counterproductive of the coyotes? Don't you think they'd get the idea to go pee somewhere where they *aren't* looking for lunch? But, I guess Wile E. Coyote never *was* the brightest dog in the pack. Still buying those Acme products after they backfired on him all those times." I can't help it. I'm laughing helplessly by now.

Buddy looks disgusted. "Yeah, laugh it up. This is serious business. There's not only the initial purchase plus the thirty-day dispensers, but then there are the refills. The urine has to be refreshed every thirty days or so. You hang it at nose level, and—"

"Is that *coyote* nose? Or *human* nose?" (I'm snorting now, speaking of noses. It's not pretty.)

"No, it's raccoon nose, of course. The whole *point* is that the predator urine keeps animals like rabbits, deer, and raccoons out of your garden, so they don't eat all of your flowers and plants. Nurseries use it a lot."

In a weird, alternate-reality-to-mine universe, this makes sense. I start to calm down, then another thought sets me off again. "Speaking of nurseries, it's too bad baby pee doesn't work. Just think how much of *that* there is and how easy it would be to collect. By the way, you still didn't answer my question about how the *heck* you collect the stuff."

To top it off, all this talk about pee makes me realize I need to find a bathroom, fast. "Buddy?"

"Yeah?" He looks at me warily, then yanks his attention back to the road in time to swerve off onto the I-705 exit toward City Center.

"Are we there yet? And, I almost forgot to ask, in the excitement of the coyote pee discussion, but what is the show?"

"What show?"

"The show at the Tacoma Dome. Is it a concert? Ice skating?"

He shakes his head, turning onto Twenty-sixth Street. "Nah. It's the Monster Jam Monster Truck Rally."

My mouth falls open, and I stare at him, all traces of laughter gone. *That's it, then. I'm officially in hell.*

* * *

I'm hiding in the ladies' room, crouching inside a stall, wondering why Jules never picks up the phone. Her voice mail message clicks on. "Jules! I'm trapped in the bathroom, hoping my date will never, ever find me. Jules, I'm at a *monster truck rally.* Or maybe I'm in hell. Either way, it smells really, really bad here."

As I step out of the stall to wash my hands, a woman with seventy or so tattoos looks at me strangely. "Honey? If you expect the bathroom at the Tacoma Dome to smell good, you ain't getting out enough."

She's totally right.

* * *

The stench clubs me in the nasal passages first. It's like being trapped inside of an exhaust pipe. Plus the sharp tang of . . . sulfur?

As we walk through the archway (well, okay, more like as Buddy drags me through the archway), fireworks explode over the center of the arena. *Ah. That explains the sulfur. Although the hell analogy still works, too.*

I look around at the stands, amazed at the capacity crowd. I can't believe people actually pay money to watch big trucks run over cars. I mean, don't men generally get that stuff out of their system when they're five years old and playing with Hot Wheels? But there are a good many women here, too; many of whom look like this was actually a voluntary outing for them.

How scary is that?

"Damn. We missed the pit party." Buddy shakes his head in disgust, not letting go of my hand.

"The what?"

"The pit party. It's one of the best parts! It's where you get to go behind the scenes into the belly of the beast, take pictures with the drivers and get autographs and stuff." He grins at me. "It's okay, though. I know one of the team for *Grave Digger*. We can hang out afterwards."

"Oh, goody," I mutter. And, *belly of the beast?* Sounds like somebody has been watching way too much TV lately.

Oblivious to my (let's face it, fairly obvious) unhappiness with the whole monster truck concept, Buddy drags me down the stairs to seats almost at floor level. In ice skating, this would be a good thing.

When an eleven-foot-tall truck is about to blow your head off with its exhaust, not so much.

I stare out at the most bizarre spectacle I've ever seen. Five or six enormous—*monstrously* huge—trucks rumble around the arena, which suddenly has a dirt floor. A dozen or so cars that look like they were hauled in from the nearest junkyard are lined up in a row. A track of sorts, with a finish line, is set up on one side, where two of the behemoths are revving up their engines.

Or, presumably, the *drivers* are revving the engines, but it's kind of hard to tell. Maybe these trucks are like the evil ones in bad movies that get so powerful they drive themselves around, forcing the weakling humans to live out their miserable existence pumping gas.

Maybe I need to get out more.

"You know what the best part is?" At least *somebody* is excited. Buddy's face is glowing like Lauren's did at ballet class. Speaking of Lauren, I need to call her this weekend just to say hi and remind her to practice. I kind of miss her during the week. I really wish I could remember who she reminds me of . . .

"Hey! Earth to Kirby! Did you hear me?" Buddy is shouting at me about six inches from my ear, and I still have a hard time hearing him. The din is unbelievable. My eardrums are going to explode and start bleeding any minute, I just know it.

I clap my hands over my ears, nod my head, and shout back at him. "Yes, I heard you, but I don't know how. Can't we move back a few rows? Or a few dozen? My ears can't take this. Plus, isn't it kind of dangerous to be this close?"

"Nah, it rocks right here where the action is. And it's not dangerous. They've cut way down on injury-accidents lately. They've got the RIIs on the trucks now—that's remote ignition interrupters—in case of an accident. Plus, there were only the two deaths that I know of, but that was back in the tractor pull days." He beams a huge grin at me, marred somewhat by the giant dirt clod that smacks him in the side of the head.

"See? Right in the action," says the idiot.

Okay. I'm so out of here. "Buddy? If we don't move back, right now, I'm calling a cab and going home. Got it?"

He pouts a little, but finally nods sullenly, and we move back about midway up the section, where at least I'm not in danger of losing an eye. I can hear a little bit, too, although the ringing in my ears from being so close to the trucks may not subside for a week or two.

Well, I'm here now; I got myself into this. May as well make the best of it. I put my hand on Buddy's arm and lean over toward him. "What's the best part?"

He's enraptured by the show in the stadium below. All the trucks have elaborate paint jobs with their names emblazoned on the doors. Evidently *Grave Digger, Maximum Destruction,* and *Predator* are facing off against *Gunslinger, Avenger,* and *Blue Thunder.*

Nice names. Speaking of compensating for tiny winkies . . .

Buddy looks at me, a little dazed from the sheer testosterone overload. "Huh? Oh, right. The best part of being here is having a hot chick like you with me. Plus, when they shined that strobe light around the stands, I could see your nipples through your shirt. Hey, look—it's *El Toro Loco*!! I love that truck!"

After I pick my jaw back up from my lap, I stand up and give

Buddy a little wave, pointing to the stairs and pantomiming something that I hope he takes for "I'm going to the little hot-chicks' room."

Then I dash up the stairs, dodging around an enormous man carrying a cardboard tray of hot dogs, nachos, and beer, and flip my cell phone open as soon as I hit the doorway to the concourse.

"Get me the number for a Tacoma taxi company. *Fast*."

I figure I'll get all the way home before Buddy ever notices I'm gone.

29

Kirby

Chiami la polizia! (Call the police!)

Home, sweet home. That's the first time I've walked out on a date since college, when that UW football player kept trying to make me bob for jock straps at his frat house. Trust me, there are some things that will never, ever go in my mouth.

I tear off another chunk of blueberry Pop Tart, enjoying the quiet sound of my own chewing. It took almost an hour for the ringing in my ears to go away, and three shampoos to get the smell of exhaust out of my hair. My clothes are in a plastic bag by the door, ready to be hauled to the dry cleaners tomorrow.

I shudder, thinking of Buddy and his "best part." Maybe I'll just burn the strobe-light-nipple-showing shirt, so I never, ever have to think of this evening again. Speaking of which, no way am I going through any more of this stupidity. I'm calling Ryan to cancel.

I *am* a nice person. I am. I don't need outside validation of my character, especially the kind I'd get from some stupid Speedy

Date. If I had nearly as much common sense as pride, I might have realized it before.

I get a sick feeling in my gut, wondering just what I'd been trying so hard to prove—and to whom I was trying to prove it. I flash on Dr. Wallace during our last session:

"Kirby, you can quit working so hard to prove things to your father any time. He's *dead*."

It had sounded really harsh at the time—harsh and insensitive. But I'm starting to realize that he's right. Daddy wouldn't still be the soundtrack to my life, if I weren't trying to prove something. Either to *him* or to *myself*.

I shake the self-analysis out of my mind and jump up to find more junk food. *Hey, my insurance and I pay Dr. Wallace a hundred and fifty bucks an hour to come up with this shit. I don't need to waste my weekend on pop psychology.*

I fling the fridge open, searching for the magical pizza and homemade chocolate chip cookies that would be there, if there were any justice at all.

Nope, still no justice. I swing the door shut and have just decided to troll for take-out menus in my junk drawer, when I realize I never checked my answering machine. I walk over to the counter near the stove, where I find the black machine lurking in wait, red light ominously flashing.

Oh, oh. Seven messages? This can't be good.

I push the *play* button, suddenly wishing I'd bypassed the kitchen and gone straight to bed. Whatever psychic instincts I seem to have lately are screaming at me not to listen. Or maybe it's just the fact that I never, ever have more than two messages at once on my home phone. Either way, I'm braced for this to totally suck.

"You have seven new messages. Message one:

" 'Kirby, it's Jules. Call me. How was monster truck hell? (Sound of much Jules laughter, here.) Hey, I still think you and Roger would really hit it off. He spends so much time at the doctor's office, you wouldn't have time to get bored. Smoochies.' "

God, I miss her. I think she's in New York this week. What time is it there? Probably too late to call. Tomorrow, for sure.

"Message two:

" 'Where are you, love?' "

Holy shit, it's Daniel. Again.

" 'I saw you walk over to the Convention Center and get in that joke of a car with that guy. I don't like the idea of him touching you. It hurts me, Kirby. And if something hurts me, I'll hurt back. Call me as soon as you get home.' "

My throat swells shut with fear, and I smack the stop button on the machine. For the first time, I truly believe that I might be in very real trouble here. The drunken episode was one thing—scary, to be sure—but I'd brushed it off as too much whiskey and too little sense. The Daniel on this phone message was stone cold sober.

A nasty realization slams into me. He saw me get in the car. *Is he stalking me?*

I start to dial nine-one-one, then realize I'd better listen to the other five messages. Maybe one is an apology from Daniel for being such an asshole, and I'll be able to relax.

"Message three:

" 'Kirby, where are you, darling?' " *It's him again.*

" 'And why is your cell phone disconnected? You'd never be without a cell phone, so you must have a new number. I want the new number, Kirbs, love. I've driven past your place twice, and you're still not home. You need to come home now.' " His voice is silken menace, and I'm growing more terrified by the minute.

Oh, crap, crap, crap. I push *stop* again and rush to the window to edge a corner of the blinds aside and peek out. I don't see his car, but he could be around the corner. He could be anywhere.

I totally need to calm down. I'm starting to hyperventilate.

"Message four:

" 'All right, I'm tired of this. I've got to leave for Portland for my show, but I'll be back in a week. Don't think this is over, Kirby. You know you were meant for me.' "

I sink into a kitchen chair, shivering. Is it a trick? Is he really parked around back, hoping I'll be lulled into a false sense of security?

Wait. A show. I know this. He told me about this.

I yank open the junk drawer and rummage around through the papers in there. There it is, at the bottom. A flyer for Daniel's show at the Portland Leventhal Galleria in January . . . *yes!*

The dates are tomorrow through next Saturday. He was telling the truth. He wouldn't miss a show for anything in the world. Luckily, he has a really short attention span, too, so he'll probably meet some new woman with long legs and deep pockets at the show, and I'll be out of sight, out of mind.

Maybe out OF your mind, if you don't report this to the police.

I shelve the decision for a moment and push the play button again.

"Message five:

" 'Kirby, it's me. Steve. I'm fine. Call me if you like.' "

Those are the fewest words he's ever used in a phone message. Ever.

"Message six:

" 'Hi. It's Banning. Just wanted you to know that we really could have used your help at that meeting tonight. Sorry if I weirded you out, though. I may, ah, I may have some news soon. News that affects you. At least, I hope it affects you, but I guess . . . well, we'll see, won't we? Okay, this message is stupid. See you Monday. Bye.' "

News that affects me? Oh, God. He's going to fire me anyway, without even waiting to see if I can win the bet. I've just gotten too psycho-woman lately.

I close my eyes and bury my head in my hands, groaning.

"Message seven:

" 'Banning, again. Sorry, I forgot Monday was MLK Day. See you Tuesday. Unless you want to work Monday. In which case, I'll buy you lunch. Not that you have to work Monday, or anything.

It's just—god. Why am I like this? I'm *never* like this. You make me crazy. Forget it. See you Tuesday.' "

I open one eye and peer at the answering machine. That was weird. He sounded awfully nervous for somebody who's getting ready to fire me. Unless firing people makes him nervous?

I think about his vulture-like secretary and realize option two must be the case. *Nobody* would keep that old witch around voluntarily.

Anyway, I need to call Jules. And Steve. I have a week's reprieve before I need to decide what to do about Daniel, so I'll do my Scarlett O'Hara again.

After all, I hired three people, dated a coyote-pee salesman, and went to a monster truck show today. I deserve to go to bed early with a bottle of wine and the Sci Fi Channel. I grab the phone, the wine, and the cheese puffs and head for my bedroom, already imagining how great cuddling up to my electric blanket is going to feel.

Man, I'm pathetic.

* * *

Date Three: Ryan

I *so* can't believe I'm doing this. Haven't I suffered enough?

Instead of running in the opposite direction, like I really, really want to, I plaster a smile on my face and extend my hand. "Hello, Ryan. It's nice to see you again."

He takes my hand and does that awkward shake/pat that some men do when they don't know how to shake a woman's hand. "Kirby, you look spectacular."

He looks pretty good, too. That suit is either Armani or a really, really good knock-off. Same golden-brown hair, same killer cheekbones. Although—are those *roots* showing? I drag my gaze down from his hair to his face.

"Thanks! I love this restaurant, too. Not a giant truck in sight." I scan the room as we follow the hostess down onto the floor of the dining room of Palisade. The view through the floor-to-ceiling glass windows is spectacular during the daytime; the boats docked at the marina and the occasional glint of sunlight (this *is* the Pacific Northwest; sunlight is not a *regular* occurrence) reflecting off the water. But, even at night, the lights on the water sparkle brilliantly and add a touch of elegance to the ambiance, which is already enhanced by the mingled aromas of extremely well-cooked food.

I may as well have been in a different universe from last night's sulfur-and-nachos specials.

I think back to the seven-meat special for a moment and sigh. I'd tried to return Steve's call, but finally had to concede that he must be avoiding me. His cell phone rang straight to voice mail all day long (okay, so I called him four times. Pathetic, much?), and although it was *possible* that he was really on the phone that much, given his conversational . . . predilections . . . I rather doubted it.

"Score another one for the ice queen of B school," I mutter.

Ryan was pulling my chair out for me. "Pardon?"

"Nothing. Just thinking out loud. So, tell me about your day." I need a moment to regroup and remember whether Ryan thinks I'm a nurse, or whether I told him the truth.

"I'm sure it wasn't busier than yours. I understand W&L's second-quarter profit projections are on track to be your best ever," he says smoothly.

Okay, then. Nurse Kirby doesn't have to make an appearance. I'm a little relieved, to be honest. I'm just too damn tired to put on an act tonight.

"That's flattering that you remembered where I work and even researched it," I say, smiling. "Not many men would have bothered."

He smiles back at me and, even though I know it must be the reflection of the marina lights, his teeth suddenly appear eerily shark-like. "Knowledge is power, and power is *everything*. Don't you agree? You didn't get to be senior vice president of marketing, as young as you are, just by being beautiful."

Hmmm. A doubleheader; he complimented me on my business acumen and my looks all in one shot. Not a word about my breasts, either.

So why is it I wish I were having dinner with Banning? Or even Steve? Thinking of Steve makes me sneak a peek at Ryan's shoes, which I hadn't noticed before. *Italian leather. No Shoes A Go Go here.*

I sigh again, wondering when I became the poster child for *Shallow.*

Let's face it, I've dated sharks before, and I'm tired of swimming in those waters. I'd just like to meet a nice guy for once.

Oh, shit. Now *I'm* doing it. A *nice* guy. *Aarrghh.*

Plus, this isn't a real date, is it?

Why not? He's just my type. Successful, clearly rich, considering the Jag I saw him drive up in, and no way this guy would ever embarrass me with babbling or even dream of taking me to a monster truck rally. Not to mention, he can take my mind off dating my boss.

"Kirby? Are you still here with me?" He looks annoyed. Probably doesn't like it when he's not the center of attention. Bet *he's* fun to have as a boss. *Not.*

I do the nervous laugh thing. "Sorry. Just . . . thinking of those profits. Call me Profits Girl."

Oddly, he doesn't seem to find that comment the least bit stupid. "Profits Girl. I like that. Able to leap tall NASDAQ reports in a single bound?"

Oh. That must be his "look at me, I'm hot and have a great sense of humor" smile.

I look around for the server. "So, what does a girl have to do to get a drink around here?"

As he waves his arm in an imperious demand for the server, I hide my face with my menu and sigh.

Here we go again. Where's Grave Digger when I need it?

* * *

"What would *Donald* do? Please tell me you didn't just say that."
I stare at Ryan over the remains of my seared tilapia.

He wipes his mouth delicately with his napkin and then places
it on the table next to his plate. (Guess we weren't getting
dessert.) "Donald Trump is a brilliant businessman, and he's
even a real estate developer, as am I. Whenever I face a difficult
decision, in business or in life, I think WWDD? Then I proceed
accordingly."

I stare at him, fascinated by the sheer repulsiveness of it all.
"WWDD? In your *personal* life, too? What could Donald Trump
teach you in your personal life?"

He smiles at me, eyes glittering. "It's all about the prenup."

Before I can formulate a coherent response to *that,* he waves to
our server. "Dessert menu, please. And I'll need a fresh napkin."

We order dessert—hell, if he's already talking prenup, I may as
well get a giant cheesecake out of him now—and he leans forward.
I figure this is where the big "tell me about yourself" part comes
in.

I'm wrong.

"Let me tell you about my latest business deal. I'm sure you'll
be impressed." He smiles a very self-satisfied looking smile, like
the cat that ate the small businessperson.

I smile, too, as it occurs to me that I'm a writer, now. I can use
this in a book.

*Then the serial killer stabbed the megalomaniacal real estate
developer with his own dessert fork. Blood spurted everywhere!
SPURT! SPURT! The brilliant scarlet of the spray contrasted vio-
lently (hideously?) with—*

"Kirby?" His smile looks a little less smug; Must-Have-Date's-
Full-Attention-at-Every-Moment. Yep, he really does follow the
Donald Trump religion: "All Me, All the Time."

"Yes, I'm sorry. I'd love to hear all about it." I cross my fingers under the table; it's a holdover from childhood when Jules told me that crossing your fingers gave you a free pass to tell a huge whopper. I'm totally whoppering now.

I slip off a shoe and cross my toes, too.

"I knew you'd say that." He leans back; royalty holding court for his loyal subjects now. And I thought *Steve* probably didn't get many dates. Who would go out with *this* pompous bozo?

You are, loser.

Oh, right. Oh, he's still talking.

"Then we found out that the apartment building I own is riddled with mold. The really nasty stuff; black and practically indestructible. So all the tenants are complaining. We send the manager in to clean it up and paint over it, but it keeps growing back. Stubborn little fungus," he says, sounding as if he admires the mold for its intractability.

I can feel my lip curling back from my teeth and try to compose my expression. Plus, the server picks now to bring my dark chocolate cheesecake, and the black mold story is doing nothing for my appetite. I push the plate to the side, and pretend to be fascinated. (Actually, it *is* kind of fascinating, in a train-wreck kind of way. Like the train wreck of my personal and professional life, lately. I should be more like mold, clearly.)

"Get this," he says, really into the drama of it all now. "I hire a team of lawyers to battle the jerk who wants to sue on behalf of the tenants. Now it's going to be tied up in court forever."

I tilt my head, confused. "Wouldn't it be less expensive to just clean the mold out than hire a bunch of lawyers?"

He shakes his head and starts cutting his tiramisu with his knife and fork. "Nah, they're suing for damages, too. Some of them claim to be sick with some imaginary respiratory infection. Bunch of fakers and deadbeats. That baby's hospitalization alone could cost me a couple hundred thou."

"What *baby*?" This is getting worse and worse.

He waves his hand in the air. "Oh, it's nothing. Some baby is in the ICU on a lung machine or something. I don't really pay attention to every little detail."

I can hear the ice in my voice. "Which is the baby—a *faker* or a *deadbeat*?"

* * *

And so ended date three and my pathetic attempt at speedy dating. I'm spending an awful lot of money on cabs this week. I bet Bree's snuggling up with her hunky fiancé at this very minute. I wish I had *her* life.

30

Brianna

Verismo: Romantic realism; blood-and-guts opera.

Sunday lunch with the dragon lady, er, I mean, my future mother-in-law, herself. What could be more fun? Why can't I ever have exciting weekends like Kirby? Three dates in three nights with three different attractive men.

"I wish I had *her* life," I mumbled.

Mama unbuckled her seat belt, as I pulled my car into Eleanor's driveway, put it in park, and glumly watched the windshield wipers push drizzle across the glass.

"Don't mumble, dear. What are you talking about? Whose life?"

"Nothing, Mama. Let me just get my potatoes au gratin out of the backseat. You go ahead and get out of this rain."

"I'll wait for you. There's safety in numbers," she said, laughing.

"Mama! You're terrible!" I admonished her, but secretly I was glad to have my partner-in-crime Mama back. She was always on my side before my engagement to Lyle. Now she always seemed to agree with him, no matter what my feelings were in the matter.

I shut the car door and we hurried up the short sidewalk to the small brick house that Lyle's mother had lived in ever since she married Lyle's father, God rest his soul, some thirty years ago.

Lyle had grown up in that house and still (if you asked me, which he never did) spent way too much time there, especially since his dad died a few years ago. Every Sunday lunch, without fail, unless he was working, and usually one evening a week, too. Plus the odd trips when something went wrong with the water heater, or a faucet, or a painting needed hung, or any of a thousand other reasons she kept his number on speed dial.

After the first five or six uncomfortable Sunday lunches with all three of us, I'd suggested that I didn't want to intrude on their special mother-son Sunday, and I'd use the time to rehearse, instead.

I'd expected at least a *token* protest from Eleanor. Instead, she'd smiled such a triumphant smile at me, when Lyle left the room for something, that it made me a little heartsick. "What a good idea, dear," she'd said. "I didn't want to hurt your feelings, but you can see that we need our . . . *family* . . . time."

I had a feeling that my engagement to her son didn't really change her feeling of me not being family. I doubted our wedding would change things, either. Maybe if we ever had kids, she'll request that Lyle bring them over by himself, so they can have their *family* time.

Okay, you're getting a little hysterical, now, Bree. Calm down, or this lunch is going to be way worse than it has to be.

Mama started to ring the doorbell; Eleanor pulled the door open before she had a chance. She was dressed up in her Sunday finest; a track suit with gold lamé embroidery up the side and a pink flamingo on the left shoulder. Florida shuffleboard fashion at its finest, courtesy of the winter trips to Sanibel Island she and Lyle's dad used to take.

"Come in, come in, already. You performers love to make dramatic and *late* entrances, don't you?" she asked, with the little tinkling laugh she used to disguise her snide remarks. I'd tried so hard for the past two years to be the bigger person, and make allowances for her sadness from losing her husband, but she still gets to me sometimes.

Especially on rainy Sundays, when I should be working on my music.

I followed Mama in the door. "You said one o'clock, Eleanor, and it's only one ten. Traffic was horrible, as usual, although I don't know where all those people were going on a rainy Sunday afternoon."

Eleanor took the casserole dish out of my hands and sniffed. "Oh, cheesy potatoes again? Well, don't worry, dear. I'm sure once you and Lyle are married, you'll have more time to try out a few *different* dishes."

I pasted a smile on my face and prayed for patience. Just then, Lyle came banging in through the kitchen door. Eleanor dropped my dish on the table and rushed over to him to give him a big hug. "Oh, honey, you're all wet! You'll catch your death of cold if you don't wear a warmer jacket and carry your umbrella. Now come right in and let's eat. You're just on time."

(Um, *hello*? *He's* just on time, but *I* was late? Not to be whiny, but you see the double standard here.)

I sighed. "Hi, Lyle."

We'd only talked once since the "I got the church; spring wedding; bargain roses" phone call, and that conversation was mostly about "how's the weather" kinds of things. We were dancing a delicate minuet around the basic disagreement, and I didn't know how to force a discussion. It was pretty clear we needed one, though. The saddest part of all of this is that I really loved Lyle.

If I loved him so much, I wouldn't be kissing other men.

It was almost *kissing other men. I mean,* man. One *man. And I do love Lyle.*

More than opera? Because if things keep on like this, he's going to force me to make that choice.

Right then, standing in his mother's kitchen next to my unwanted potatoes, I wondered what choice I'd make.

* * *

"Lyle, why don't you help me do the dishes?" I gave him a meaningful glance across the table. We really needed to talk, and I needed to leave for Madame's soon.

Eleanor burst into her annoying, tinkly laughter. "Oh, no, dear. Lyle doesn't wash dishes in this house. He's a *man*, you see," she pointed out, in case I'd thought I was engaged to an emu, I suppose.

I tinkled a laugh right back at her. "Oh, Lyle does dishes at my place all the time, and of course he will after we're married, too. We believe in having a partnership kind of marriage."

More like a triumvirate, really. Me, Lyle, and his mother. Can I really put up with her for the next forty to fifty years?

Mama spoke up. She'd been steadily getting quieter and quieter during lunch, as Eleanor kept up her stream of tiny, subtle jabs at me. I had the feeling she was about to blow. "That's *exactly* the way a good marriage works, Bree. Good for both of you that you want to begin on an equal basis and of course, continue on one."

I appreciated the support, but I had to smother a grin at the sentiment. Poor Daddy was definitely not on an equal basis with Mama. I think they coined the phrase "high maintenance" about Mama. Daddy and I loved her, but sometimes we had to go to a quiet place and catch our breath after a long bout of *Mama's in a mood,* as he called it. He and I used to go fly-fishing.

A lot.

I'm probably one of the only opera singers in the world who can tie Slim Beauties faster than anybody else in the fishing boat.

Eleanor tinkled again. The woman really needed to get a new laugh, bless her heart. (Unless her goal was to drive me completely out of my mind. In which case, her tinkly laugh was exactly right.)

I sat there, glumly imagining an endless line of family dinners underscored by Eleanor's tinkly laughter, and shuddered.

"Oh, honey. Lyle's an important fireman. Once Bree gives up that job at W&L to stay home and keep house—oh, and Brianna, what in the world do the *W* and the *L* stand for?"

Lyle had a coughing fit that lasted so long his face turned red, and his mother started smacking him on the back. "I'm fine, I'm fine, Mom. Bree, why don't you tell Mom what the *W* and *L* stand for? I'm sure she'll be *fascinated*."

He flashed that grin at me that used to be one of my favorite things about him. I wasn't as crazy about it there at the table. Suddenly, with a bolt of clarity, I realized a terrible truth: Lyle was a lot like his mother.

Mama looked at me, distracted from the equal partnership discussion. "Yes, dear. What does it mean? You've never told me, either. Corinne asked me about it just the other day, when we went baby shopping for her daughter," she said, then turned toward Eleanor. "You would not *believe* the adorable things they have for newborns these days, Eleanor."

"Ooh, yes, I know, and I can't wait until we're buying an entire layette for Lyle's babies," Eleanor said, confirming my earlier suspicions about my place in the family tree. *Lyle's* babies?

"Of course, they will be *Bree's* babies, too," Mama pointed out, with an edge of steel in her voice.

Oh, oh. I was happy to have the discussion turned away from W&L, but not at the cost of an all-out battle between the in-laws.

Lyle cut in, perhaps sensing the same thing. "Of course they'll be *our* babies; Bree's and mine. Plenty of grandbabies to go around, and *soon*, if I get my way. But, Bree, you were just about to tell us what W&L stands for."

I'm so going to smack him for this. Also for the "plenty of babies, and soon" crack.

I glared at him, but it was too late. Mama and Eleanor were both looking at me with way too much curiosity in their eyes. "It's simple, really. *W* and *L* stand for the, ah, the products we manufacture. That's why it's W&L Manufacturing." I smiled at everyone, hoping that was enough.

It *so* wasn't.

"And?" said traitor Mama. "The products that you manufacture are?"

Oh, goody. Think, Bree. Manufacturing, manufacturing, what about that business course you took, supply-side economics and guns and butter and widgets and . . . widgets starts with W . . .

"Widgets! Um, widgets and, ah," I wiped my mouth with my napkin, stalling, and caught sight of the candy dish on the counter. "Licorice! That's it. Widgets and licorice."

I shoved my chair back and stood up to clear the table, delighted to have found words starting with the right letters.

Mama looked up at me, puzzled. "Licorice? And widgets? What is a widget?"

Eleanor, who could never stand to appear as if she didn't know something, patted Mama's hand. "Oh, of course you know. Widgets are very important manufacturing products."

As tempted as I was to ask her exactly what she thought a *widget*—a term for an imaginary product, used to illustrate business principles—really was, I resisted. "Yes, Mama, you know. A widget is the technical name for the, er, arm and claw mechanism in those machines you see in restaurants. The ones where you put in a quarter and try to aim the claw at the stuffed animal you want? You're moving the *widget* when you put your quarter in the slot. It's a very complicated mechanism, actually."

I put my hands on my hips, very pleased with myself. Neither Mama nor Eleanor were what you'd call engineering or business savvy, so my explanation should satisfy them.

Eleanor was nodding. "Of course I knew that. You really need to try to keep up with technology in today's world, as Lyle's Daddy always used to say."

Mama just stared at me. She knows me way better and has a

sixth sense for when I'm not being entirely honest. I never got away with *anything* in high school.

Not that I'd really tried. I was too busy being a nice girl.

Gosh, I'm dull. I bet Kirby had a fabulously exciting time in high school.

"Bree," Mama said with her "I know something's up" voice. "What about the licorice? Isn't it odd for a company that manufactures vending machine parts to also make candy?"

Oh, donkey poo. I should have known she'd pick up on the logic flaws there.

Lyle piped up. "Oh, Mrs. Higgins, they make all *sorts* of edible things." He winked at me, and I knew he was thinking of the edible panties he'd ordered for me out of our spring catalog. Then he launched into another coughing fit, tears leaking out of the corner of his eyes.

Ordered for himself, you mean. There's no way I'm ever, ever wearing a pair of edible panties. Even if they ARE strawberry-flavored. That is just yucky.

"I'll go get Lyle another glass of water and start the dishes, because I really need to get going soon for rehearsal," I said, and headed to the kitchen, resisting the urge to smack him in the back of the head on the way. *Boy, was he going to hear about this later.*

"I'll help," said Mama, jumping up to help clear the table, while Eleanor pounded away on Lyle's back. I hoped she made his ribs hurt, the turd.

Realizing I wasn't sure which one of them I'd been referring to with my *turd* thought, I took a deep breath and wished for more patience. Then I brought the full glass of water back to the table, where Lyle's coughing spasms were subsiding.

As a point in my favor, I didn't pour it on his head.

Eleanor stood up and gathered more of the dishes, then followed me back into the kitchen. "Don't worry about that, Bree. I'll do them myself, since I'll be puttering around all alone all afternoon. Are you sure you can't cancel your lessons with that woman just this once and spend more time with us? We have a wedding to plan, after all."

She's good. A left hook of martyrdom followed by a right cross of selflessness. Both of which leave me looking like the bad guy. Again.

"No, I'm sorry, but I can't. With the audition coming up, I have to work with Madame every chance I get." I decided to take her at her word and piled the dishes up in the sink. I wouldn't want to deprive her of her opportunity to be the Joan of Arc of dishwashing soap.

"What audition?"

"Lyle didn't tell you?" I wasn't really surprised. My audition didn't rank high enough up there on the grand scheme of things to have been a topic of conversation, I guessed.

What surprised me was how much it hurt, though.

I explained about the audition, and when it was, and how focused I'd need to be over the coming weeks. Lyle had walked in the kitchen while I was explaining, and he stood, leaning against the refrigerator, looking anything but happy.

Eleanor's expression crossed clear over to horrified. "You *what?* But, Bree, what terrible timing this is! You'll just have to cancel."

I dried off my hands, counting to ten.

To twenty.

Okay, to thirty.

Then I thought the steam coming out of my ears might have subsided enough for me to speak in a calm tone.

"Cancel? Cancel the best shot I've ever had to achieve the dream for which I've worked my entire life? Cancel the audition that Madame had to pull in any number of favors to get for me? Cancel? I'll *have to cancel??*" So much for my calm tone.

I whirled around and shot a look at Lyle. "You signed us up for a spring wedding without even consulting me. Well, since you're in such a big hurry, *you* can plan the wedding. I'll act like the groom traditionally does, and simply show up at the church that day, after relaxing over a big pancake breakfast with my friends."

Then, for the first time in my entire life, I stalked out of a house and, also for the first time in my entire life, I slammed a door behind me.

Sadly, my dramatic exit was ruined by the fact that I had to wait for Mama to come out behind me. She got in the car and looked at me. "He's really a wonderful man, Bree. It wouldn't hurt you to quit being so hard on him."

"I don't want to hear it, Mama."

As we backed out of the driveway in silence, I realized that Lyle had never even come to the door to wave good-bye.

If it comes down to marriage to Lyle versus my singing career, which will it be?

And how long will I regret the one I give up?

31

Kirby

Lei ha sbagliato numero. (You have the wrong number.)

Alarm clocks suck. Seriously.

What kind of moron sets her alarm clock on a holiday Monday for six o'clock?

The kind of moron who wants to go to Italy in two weeks.

I drag myself to an upright position and twitch my nose, hoping for the smell of brewing coffee. Instead, I smell stale tuna and mayo, which may have gone over to the dark side. *Nasty.*

This is what I get for staying up till midnight working on my new novel. *Nice Girls Finish Last* is coming along at a fast and furious pace, but I can foresee that I'm going to get stuck by chapter four if I don't turn the much-beleaguered protagonist into less of a caricature. Nobody understands her; her boss is mean to her; blah, blah, blah.

Big deal, already. I need to make her more three dimensional, or nobody—let alone Jules's dad or his supercharged agent—is going to read far enough to even *reach* chapter four.

Yawning hugely, I grab the plate with the remains of last night's snack, stuff my feet into my slippers, and head for the kitchen. Must have forgotten to program the coffeemaker last night. I *hate* when I do that.

At least I can wear old jeans and a sweatshirt into the office. Nobody else will be there . . . except Banning. I flash back to his weird phone message on my answering machine Friday night.

Yep, he'd be there. Although, why should I dress up for *him*? In fact, I'm not even going to take a shower. Or brush my hair. It's not like I have any romantic interest in the man whatsoever.

Of course, that's no reason to smell bad. Or not to brush on a little lip gloss. Plus, I have to brush my teeth carefully, because tooth decay can lead to heart disease, according to that article in the New York Times, *and . . . oh, who the hell am I kidding? Just because I can't date him doesn't mean I don't want to look hot.*

An hour and a half of showering, blow drying, and primping later, I'm on my way out the door. But I'm *totally* wearing jeans and a sweatshirt. Banning *who*?

* * *

My brain hurts.

What kind of moron tells her new hires that they don't have to start until Tuesday?

It is a national holiday, Kirbs.

Yeah, and Martin Luther King does deserve his own holiday. Now there was a nice guy; one with grace in his manner and steel in his backbone. Why aren't there more men like that around these days?

I drop my head in my hands and moan a little, both at the unfairness of life and at the sight of the fourteen piles of paperwork on the conference table in front of me. You know it's bad when you have to leave your office in search of a bigger table, and the one that seats twelve is the only one that will do.

I moan again.

"Yeah, the sight of our products makes me moan sometimes, too, but it's more of a 'how did I ever agree to work for a company that makes *ben wa* balls?' kind of moan." Banning sounds way too cheerful for being at work on a holiday.

I don't turn around. Maybe if I don't look at him, he'll go away.

He pulls out the chair next to me and drops into it. "What's the problem? Figuring out an ad strategy for lifelike blow-up dolls giving you grief?"

I lift my head out of my hands and glare at him. "I'm fine, thank you, and we don't make blow-up dolls, as you should know, Mr. CEO."

He laughs. "Right. I forgot. Only tasteful products for us, like the cotton-candy-flavored edible panties. Really, is that a taste you *want* when you're going for edible undies?" He shakes his head, as though contemplating the important edible panty question. "The philosophy of edible panty flavors is really headline-news kind of stuff, Kirby. I can't believe we haven't issued a memo about it."

I can't help it, I start laughing, too. "The philosophy of edible panty flavors? What about the Zen of vibrators—if an Alexander the Great is turned on in an empty forest, does it really vibrate?"

He cracks up. "The Tao of nipple clamps."

"The theology of warming lotion." We're both howling, now.

"The astrology of clitoral vibrators."

"The . . . the . . . wait, did *you* just say the word *clitoral*? The paleontology of S and M gear!" I'm laughing so hard, I have to clutch my side.

He turns a little red, but ignores my question. "No way. The *paleontology*?? Can you see a d-d-dinosaur dressed up in leather and chains? M-M-Mistress Stegosaurus, punish me, p-p-p-please!"

We look at each other, speechless, then we both roar with laughter, falling forward almost into each other's laps. He catches me by the shoulders and holds me up, and I look up at him, still laughing.

Suddenly, we both stop laughing. I feel like I can't catch my

breath, and the temp in the room just shot up a hundred degrees.
I never noticed before how really green his eyes are. I can't help it;
I have to touch his hair, so I reach up and do, lightly at first; then
the look in his eyes fires up my courage, and my fingers dive into
his hair, and it's as silky and soft and wonderful as I'd imagined;
not that I'd ever imagined his hair, but if I had—

And then he's kissing me.

*It's heat and tingling and tightening and loosening all at once,
and I'm scared; I'm in trouble; I'm amazed; I'm going under.*

And then I'm kissing him back.

*I can't; we can't; we shouldn't; oh, but I want to, I want to, I
want to—*

He pulls away from me and stares at me, looking like the same
truck that ran me down right here in the conference room rolled
over him too, and he says, "We can't. I want to, but we can't. Not
yet; not like this. We can't."

And then he's kissing me again, hard, and the fireworks shoot
up from my toes, and who needs nipple clamps, anyway? What a
stupid product, oh, the tingling, the tingling, and the heat, and the
cold when he pulls away again and stands up, breathing hard and
focusing on me with that laser-like intensity I've only seen him
focus on recalcitrant board members.

"We can't," he repeats. "But we will. You've made up my
mind. We *will*."

I stare at him. "We will *what?* And—whatever it is—don't I get
a say in whether or not we will?"

He smiles a slow, dangerous smile at me, then suddenly reaches
out and touches my lips with his finger. "Oh, *yes*. We *definitely* will."

And then he's gone, leaving me staring after him like an idiot,
fingers pressed against my lips, wondering what the *hell* just
happened.

Wondering when it will happen again.

* * *

"What kind of moron kisses her boss in the conference room?" (As you may have noticed, "moron" is the theme for the day. Maybe tomorrow I'll pick something nicer, like *puppy*. Or *flower*.) I stare around my therapist, er, career coach's office, without really seeing it. Since it's decorated in early *bland*, this is not a problem. I mentioned the decor once, and he told me the room needed to be neutral and calm because the emotions expressed in it so often were anything but. Made sense, in a shrinky sort of way.

Dr. Wallace stares at me over the top of the mug of steaming coffee he's clutching with both hands. I always wonder if he feels the need to clutch things when he's seeing his *other* patients. Er, I mean, clients. Or if it's just me who drives him over the edge.

"I'm speculating that this is not a rhetorical question?"

"Not exactly," I mumble.

"What happened? And why do you think you're a moron?" He puts his coffee down on the table between us and gives me his "I'm the shrink, so I'm going to ask you a bunch of questions" quizzical glance.

"You don't shit where you eat. All office romances end up badly, and it's almost always the woman who gets the short end of the stick. Especially when he's the boss, and I'm the peon."

Dr. Wallace smiles at me. "Kirby, he may be your boss, but I can never imagine a situation in which the word *peon* would apply to you. Do you have feelings for this man?"

I sigh. "I don't want to have feelings for him. I don't want to have feelings for anybody. The last guy I had feelings for crushed my heart under his rat-bastard heel."

"Ah, yes. Daniel."

"No, if you're going to say his name, you have to say it right."

Now it's his turn to sigh. "All right. Daniel-the-rat-bastard. Although, don't you think it's time to move on?"

"It's hard to do that when he won't stop stalking me," I mutter.

"What? What do you mean, stalking?" He leans forward, all traces of smile gone.

I tell him about the phone calls and the stalking me outside the Convention Center and driving past my apartment.

"Kirby, this is serious. What did the police say?"

I shift in my seat a little. "Um, yeah. Well, I didn't actually call them, yet."

"What? We talked about him before, after that episode where he wouldn't leave your house. Kirby, I think Daniel has the potential to be really dangerous." He's *so* not happy with me, but, hey— I'm not all that happy about the stalking stuff either.

"I can't call the police. Any hint of problem could affect my eligibility to be a Special Sibling. *Dangerous ex-boyfriend?* What if they thought Lauren was in danger?"

I shake my head. "I've thought about this a lot, and, trust me, if she *were* in any danger, I'd call the police in a second. But Daniel has a boatload of nieces and nephews, and he's like some sort of Santa Claus with them. He truly adores kids; it's one of the things I really liked about him when we first met."

I jump up and start pacing around the office. "It's only me that he's going psycho on, and I don't know what it's about, to be honest. He didn't really give a damn when I dumped him. Just grabbed his clothes and his two naked models and left, laughing. Bastard."

We talk about the Daniel situation a little more, but don't really resolve anything. I promise to call the police if he does one more thing, and Dr. Wallace lets it go.

Just when I sit back down, prepared to be interrogated on the Banning thing, he blasts me with a surprise flank attack. "So, did you call your mother?"

That had been my "assignment" from our last session, which was more than a month ago. I'd hoped he'd forgotten.

"Yes, in fact I did call her, just this week." Right answer for Kirby for once; I can't help but smile.

"Kirby, this isn't about right answers," he says.

"How do you *do* that? Also, do you believe in psychic phenomena? I'm getting some crazy stuff lately . . ."

He gulps down more coffee. "Kirby, stop. About your mother? How did the call go?"

Now it's my turn to gulp coffee. "Not all that well."

"What happened?"

I can't look at him. "I don't know. It's been more than two months since the last time I called her; she should have been mad at me. But she just started making excuses for me. Like she always did . . ."

"Like she always did for *him*?" he asks, voice very gentle.

A huge lump of anger and sadness and tears is making it very hard for me to talk. "What? No. Well, yeah. Like she did for him. Why can't she ever stand up for herself? Even with me? It's not like *I'm* going to knock her around. I can't stand that she's still such a doormat, even after he's dead and buried."

He hands me the ever-present box of tissues; the one I've never, ever used in one of our visits. *The box of tissues is for the weak people, you know. The ones who worry about what other people think of them.*

"Kirby? I have an important question for you that you may finally be ready to hear." He waits till I've pulled my shaky self-control around myself like a shield, and until I look up at him.

"When are you going to forgive your mother for what your father did to her?"

32

Kirby

Mi sento poco bene. (I am ill.)

"What is that tune you keep humming?" Bree walks in my office, carrying a ton of papers. This is never a good sign. At least I have—drum roll, please—*staff* now to help out!

I have to think about it, then it hits me and I roll my eyes. "It's 'Turkey in the Straw.' Don't ask." Last night's tap dance experience had been like the Cold War at first. And let's not forget the tap dancing *I'd* had to do when Lauren reminded me about going to see Mr. Bunny.) None of the other parents were going to speak to me; I could feel the ice form in the room when we'd walked in the door. But I'd practiced my "nice Kirby" on them and gone for the proactive strike. I'd stopped by the Krispy Kreme shop on the way and bought doughnuts for everybody. After the kids skipped into the studio, I opened the box and said, "I thought we could use some fresh, hot doughnuts on a night like this."

The lone dad was the first to cave. (Guys won't sacrifice doughnuts to petty feuding; it's one of the great things about them.) After that, everybody drifted over to select a doughnut and chat a bit. Even octo-baby's mom finally gave in, because her bundle of joy kept trying to snatch the food out of the mouth of the kid next to her.

Turns out she was an okay woman; she'd just been exhausted from her job and the kids last week. Of course, who wouldn't be? I only have Lauren one evening a week; I can't imagine how hard twenty-four/seven must be.

But at least we firmed up the recital date. So Lauren's mom can take the morning off work and make it, and I can spend the day packing, as planned. I told Lauren she can share it all with me by narrating the video I'd prepurchased.

But, back to the doughnuts and chatting, the interesting part about this whole "being nice" thing is how like attracts like. The Golden Rule and all those trite clichés about "doing unto others" have a point, maybe?

"The problem is when everybody is always attacking you first," I mutter.

"Who's snacking? Is there food? I heard somebody in Jamie's department has a birthday; I'll bet you can find some cake," Bree says, dumping stuff in my in-box.

"Not *snacking,* I said . . . never mind. Why don't you go snag us some cake? I'll get coffee," I say, standing up and stretching.

An odd expression crosses her face, then she looks down at my full out-box. "No, I don't really want to go over to accounting today, if you don't mind. I need to get this work done. It's five, anyway. The cake's probably gone."

She rushes out of my office, which is strange. Almost as if she's trying to avoid talking to me. Why wouldn't she want to go to accounting? Is there some problem with my expense report or something?

I shrug. No time to worry about it now. I've got to finish my outlines for my delegation/transfer to my new assistant director. Only a little over a week until I leave for Italy with Jules!

Are we just pretending the bet never happened, now?

No worries. My new staff loves me. They'll be calling me nice *right and left in the next few days. Especially when I explain about the stock options.*

Before my rational self can tell me that HR probably explained about the stock options, my phone rings.

"Kirby Green."

"Kirby? This is Anya Dennison. I hate to impose on you, but is there any chance at all that you can take Lauren tonight?" She sounds terrible; I can hardly hear her.

"Anya? What's wrong? You sound terrible. Are you sick? *Duh!* Of course you're sick. But what is it? Do you need me to take you to a doctor?" I'm shoving stuff in my briefcase as we talk, the phone propped between my ear and shoulder.

"No, no. I saw the doctor. It's the flu; there's not much they can do about it. But my mother is out of town visiting her sister and won't be back till tomorrow." She stops for a vicious fit of coughing, then comes back on the line, sounding even worse. "If you spent just a few hours with Lauren, so I could get some rest, it would help me out so much. I feel so miserable."

"Of course; I'm on my way. In fact, why don't you ask her to pack her pajamas, and she can spend the night at my place? I'll drop her at school in the morning, and you'll get some rest."

"Oh, I could never impose on you like that. This is probably already asking too much, but I just feel so miserable . . ." She breaks off into another, worse, attack of coughing.

"Seriously, Anya, it's no imposition at all. Lauren would save me from eating dinner alone. I made her promise last night that if I had to eat a Happy Meal, she had to go eat real food with me next time. We'll have a great time—and go to bed early, since it's a school night—and call you to say good night before bed."

"Well, if you're really sure . . ." I could tell she was weakening. "Do you have room?"

"Sure! I have an entire guest room that never gets used. I'll see you in about thirty minutes, okay? Don't forget her toothbrush!"

I hear the sound of prolonged nose blowing.

"Oh, Kirby, this is so nice—"

I break in, sighing. "*Don't* say it. Illness doesn't count."

At this rate, I'll be dead before somebody legitimately calls me nice, says the Kirby with high moral fiber.

Hey, you're the one with all the stupid rules, says the Kirby who's got friends in low places. *Why can't we just adopt 'What Would Donald Do?' as our motto, too?*

"Okay, I'm thinking about myself as 'we,' this is way over the top, even for me," I mutter. "And, so not gonna happen, re the WWDD."

Bree walked in my office at some point during the call, and she stands next to the door, eyebrow raised. "Problems?"

"No, not really. It's . . . ah, a friend with the flu. She wants me to take her six-year-old for the evening. So we're going to figure out something to do." I grab my coat and laugh. "Which could be interesting, since it's not like I have toys or games or even kid-friendly movies at my place. But I'll figure something out. We'll have a great time."

* * *

"I'm having a terrible time." Lauren's little bottom lip is pooched out so far I could balance my Diet Coke on it. But I secretly sympathize with her, because I'm not having a lot of fun, either.

She hated the sushi restaurant, which, in hindsight, wasn't the smartest place to take a little girl. The look on her face when she saw the raw fish was hilarious, but she thought I was laughing *at* her instead of *with* her (which makes sense, since *she* wasn't laughing), so then the tears started.

I'd comforted her, and we'd gotten the heck out of sushi land, but then she'd refused any of the fast food places that she normally loved. So we went to the video place, but she said they only had stupid movies. Then she burst into tears again.

Finally, I'd decided to head home. We could order pizza and figure something out. She could play with my jewelry or something. *All little girls love that, right?*

As we walk in the front door, she does the lip pooch and tells me she's having a terrible time. I sigh and drop my briefcase and her backpack on the floor beside the door.

"Tell me what's wrong, Lauren, and what I can do to fix it," I say, putting my hand on her shoulder.

"Nothing's wrong. I'm just not having a good time," she says, and I see tears shimmering in those huge blue eyes.

"Oh, honey, I'm sorry. But you're going to have to tell me why, so I can fix it. Can you help me think of fun things to do?" I lead her over to the couch, and we sit down. She pulls away when I try to hug her, though.

I recognize the stiffness in her pose as the fragile brittleness of a child stretched to the edge of breaking. What I don't know, though, is why.

"Lauren, honey, are you upset because your mom is sick? Or because you're spending the night with me? Would you rather go home?"

She shakes her head, but doesn't answer.

Okay. Maybe it's time to back off and let her come around to telling me in her own time. "How about pizza, then? I don't seem to eat much else these days. We may as well go for the total artery-clogging experience. How do you feel about extra cheese and pepperoni?"

She whirls around and throws herself in my lap, exploding into tears. I'm thrown way off balance by this, and it takes me a moment, but then I tentatively touch her hair, then hug her tiny, quaking little body in my arms. "Shhh, honey, shhh. If you feel *that* strongly about pepperoni, we'll get something else. Bad pepperoni to make Lauren cry. *Bad!*"

I hear a snuffle, then something that sounds a little bit like a giggle, so I play it up. "Evil, bad pepperoni! Death to pepperoni! In fact, doom to all foul sausages of any kind!"

She's giggling for real, now, but the tears are still falling, soaking through my thin sweater. "Kirby, it's not the pepperoni, silly. It's Mommy."

Finally. I hold very still, so as not to do anything to stop the words from flowing, but keep patting her tiny back. "What about Mommy, sweetheart? Are you sad because she's sick? It's just the flu, baby. She'll be better really soon."

She pulls back. "I have a loose tooth, and I need a tissue, please."

Okay, that makes no sense to me as a response, but, then again, I'm not six. She totally does need a tissue; her face is red and swollen, and her nose is running. Funny how it's making my heart ache for her, instead of making my nose curl in disgust, like seeing a drippy-nosed kid usually does.

Maybe there's hope for me and the old biological clock, yet.

Oh, no. Let's SO not even go there.

I jump up to find her some tissues, fast. After the wiping and blowing, she climbs up into my lap and trains those big blue eyes on me. "Kirby? Can you pull my tooth out?"

She points to the tooth in question, and I take a deep breath and touch it with the tip of my finger. I can feel some give, but not enough to pull it out. "Honey, it's not quite ready yet, but I'll bet it will be in a week or so. I can help you write a note to the Tooth Fairy, if you like, so you'll be all ready."

Oh, crap. I hope Anya does the Tooth Fairy thing. I need to remember to clear stuff like this with her.

Lauren grabs my hands with hers. "No, I need to get it out now, so the Tooth Fairy can come tonight."

Chuckling a little, I squeeze her hands back in commiseration. "I know it's hard to wait, honey, but why don't we order that pizza and talk about what you're going to do with your quarter from the Tooth Fairy."

As I try to pull my hands from her grasp, her grip tightens and she shakes her head. "No, you don't understand. My friend Mikayla lost *her* first tooth, and the Tooth Fairy gave her a golden dollar with the Indian princess on it."

"A golden—oh, a Sacagawea dollar? Wow, inflation has totally slammed the Tooth Fairy. I used to get a quarter." I start to smile, but my words have set off a fresh burst of tears.

I'm starting to lose it, here. I don't know how to fix this, and she's breaking my heart. "Lauren, honey, what is it? I'm sure you'll get a golden dollar, too."

Even if I have to visit every bank in town to make sure of it.

Lauren draws a deep, shaky breath. "It has to be a whole dollar, Kirby. I want to give it to Mommy, so she doesn't have to work so hard and get sick."

And, just like that, I'm done for. Tears I never cried in high school, or in college, when Jules went for her year abroad; tears I never cried when Daniel-the-rat-bastard skewered me so spectacularly; even tears I never cried when Dad died—they all rushed up to burst out of my throat all at once. I hugged Lauren close and tried not to let her see me cry.

I'm the tough one, right?

Tough, maybe. But a six-year-old just taught me something about compassion.

* * *

As Lauren, bathed, teeth brushed, and wearing her ballerina pajamas, sleeps in my arms on the couch, I reach around her for the phone. "Mom? Hi. No, everything's okay; I know it's late."

I take a deep breath and say the words that are long overdue. "I love you, Mom. If you have some time, I thought maybe we could talk."

33

Brianna

Tenor: Male singer with a high range.
(Ex.: The Three Tenors—José Carreras, Placido Domingo,
and Luciano Pavarotti)

As I drove to Madame's after breakfast Saturday, I thought about Kirby and her secrets. Maybe *secrets* wasn't the right word, but she really wasn't one to share all that much about her personal life.

It's really not my business, though, is it? Just because I'm the type to tell total strangers my life story at the drop of a hat. . . . Although, not really. It's not like I'd told Kirby that my fiancé was being an enormous butthead, or that I was terrified that he'd turn out to be exactly like his passive-aggressive mother, or even that my burst of door-slamming courage seems to have deserted me.

Well, yeah, you didn't tell your boss all that because you're not a complete and flaming nutjob.

Anyway, I wondered about those mysterious Wednesdays. Maybe she really *was* taking ballet lessons. The thought of my take-no-prisoners boss in a tutu kept me chuckling through the rest of the drive.

As always, Madame met me at the door. She practically ripped my scarf off my shoulders in her haste to push me into the tiny music room. "Oh, Brianna, Darling, it is so fabulous. We have the delightful and famous Renata Alessandro here to be your audience for today's lesson."

Fabulous was *so* not the word I would have chosen. Terrified, I scanned the room for Renata, who just at that moment ponderously rose from the piano bench.

All three hundred pounds of her. She flicked a disdainful glance down her lovely nose at me. "So *this* is your student? She is the best you have this season? I understand why you were so distraught, earlier, Gabriella."

I clenched my mouth shut, so I wouldn't say something rude in response. (Funny how that never used to be a problem for me. Maybe I *am* learning to quit being so nice all the time. Maybe Super Door Slamming Bree is back. Go, me!)

Madame fluttered into the room. "No, no, I am never distraught about my darling Bree. She is my star student and will dazzle like the nightingale she is, when she auditions in just a few short weeks."

Renata sniffed, looking me up and down. "More like a scrawny little sparrow, if you ask me. How do you expect to resonate with that skeletal body?"

Since this was one of the things I'd been most concerned about, her comment hit me hard. Opera singers use our extra weight to enhance our singing and endurance. A three-hundred-pound woman can sing me off the stage after a couple of hours. That's why I was working so hard to gain thirty pounds before the audition. Unfortunately, with all of the stress (including the wedding stress), I'd actually *lost* two pounds.

Where's a good piece of chocolate-chip fudge cake when you need it?

"Yes, she needs to gain the weight, but she sings like a dream. Darling, you begin the warm-up while Renata and I have some tea.

We'll be back in a moment to listen to your brilliant rehearsal. Renata promised to share her thoughts with us. Isn't that wonderfully gracious of her?"

"Wonderfully," I muttered, forcing my face into the best smile I could muster. Honestly, the last thing I needed was to have Madame's best student rubbed in my face right now. The *only* student to win the New York Metropolitan Opera audition on her first try. The *only* student to be allowed to call Madame by her first name.

The only one the size of a small county, sulked my inner petulant child.

Yes, and that small county can sing you off the map, so quit pouting and listen to whatever tips she gives you. If you're lucky, she'll be so glad to demonstrate her superiority that she'll be really helpful.

* * *

As the final notes of my final audition piece vibrated in the room, I slowly opened my eyes, smiling. I knew I'd knocked the Puccini out of the ballpark, as Jamie would say.

Why am I thinking about Jamie?

I folded my hands together and waited, trying hard to appear meek and grateful for any help. It was difficult, though, because I know when I sing really well, and I sang really, *spectacularly* well.

I am going to kick butt on that audition!

"You are going to fail the audition," Renata announced.

My mouth fell open, and I stared at her in disbelief. "You . . . what?"

I noticed that Madame's mouth was also hanging open, which made me feel a teensy bit better.

Renata hoisted her bulk up off of the couch and shook her head. "You were terrible. This is the best you can do, when the audition is so soon? There is no hope."

I couldn't believe what I was hearing. Was she tone deaf? Am *I* tone deaf? How could I have been so wrong about my own singing—the one area of my life in which I'm entirely, even brutally, honest with myself?

"But, Renata, I nailed those pieces. That's the best I've ever sung the Puccini. What are you—how can you—"

She snorted. "If that's the best you've ever sung, you should quit singing immediately. Trust me, I say this for your own good. You will never rise above understudy for a chorus girl in an off-Broadway show. You were pitchy and brittle, and you have an ugly tendency to flatness." Every word arrowed its way through another deflated dream on its way to my heart.

She lifted her chin and smiled a nasty little smile at me. "There is no hope. Give up now."

Madame finally found her voice, in a big way. "You . . . you . . . *imbecile*! How can you say this about my darling Brianna? That was beautiful singing; the emotion in her Puccini would move a statue to tears. You are doing so well for yourself, Renata, but inside you are still the sad, jealous little girl I trained for so long."

Madame jumped up and rushed over to hug me. "Ignore her, Darling. I'd hoped that Renata's success would have cured her of her ugly insecurities, but it seems that I am mistaken. You must leave now, Renata, and pray that your evil tirade has not undermined the confidence of my *new* favorite student."

Renata narrowed her eyes in a glare that encompassed both me and Madame, then swept out of the room, turning back at the archway. "Fine, I will leave, but know this: If my honest feedback can destroy what little confidence she may have, then she was never meant to sing in the first place. Only the strong survive in this business, and I feel sorry for the little sparrow if she thinks differently."

I finally found my own voice. "If you think being a spiteful . . . *witch* . . . is the only way to prove that you're strong, then I feel sorry for you."

She opened her mouth, but then an uncertain look crossed her expression—almost one of sadness. She huffed out a breath and then left, slamming the door behind her.

I let out the breath I'd been holding, then started shaking with delayed reaction. I'd just insulted a person who could conceivably affect my career for years to come. I'd just stood up to a person known for her gossips and intrigues.

I knew the stakes and what was at risk, and I didn't back down. I need to remember this the next time I have lunch with Lyle and Eleanor.

I took a long moment to be proud of myself.

Then I started worrying that she'd been right.

34

Kirby

Possiamo vederci di nuovo? (Can we meet again?)

What a weekend. Is this how hermits live? Closeted in my condo, afraid to look out the windows in case Daniel is cruising by; afraid to answer the phone, in case Buddy has tracked down my home phone number.

Buddy doesn't scare me, but Daniel does. And he should be back from his show by now, unless he found another victim, er, woman.

I did manage to call Mom again, and we had a great talk; much lighter than the dredge-up-the-past session we'd had Thursday. I also called Anya and Lauren to check in on them. Anya is doing much better, and Lauren is practicing like crazy. I can't wait to see her costume.

Other than that (and a little online shopping for a dozen Sacagawea dollars), I spent the whole two days glued to my computer screen. It's enough to make me coin a new phrase: *Thank God it's Monday.*

Speaking of computer screens, my eyes feel blurry. I think I need my eyes examined for new glasses.

I think I need my head examined, for trying to write a novel.

In a fit of exhaustion-induced insanity, I'd hit "send" on an e-mail to Jules's dad at around three this morning, with a little file of about the first hundred pages of my book attached. (I figure he can tell me it's crap, so then I can get the writing bug out of my system.) After that, I'd fallen into bed for the nearly three whole hours until my alarm rang at six.

The first thing I did at six was check my e-mail, proving my imminent descent into total insanity. Like he's going to have gotten my e-mail at three, read it, and responded by six? The man probably slept through my entire drama.

I've checked my personal e-mail sixty-nine times since then, at least. Still nothing. And it's almost ten thirty. How the hell does publishing survive, if people move this slowly?

Since my cranky-assed mood is the theme of the day, let's not forget that it's week four of my stupid bet, and not a *nice* in sight. (Well, not a *legitimate* one.) I've decided to quit worrying about it and pretend we never made that stupid bet. It's not like Banning is going to hold me to it; he already tried to let me out of it, right? Speaking of *holding* me to something, I'd love it if he'd hold my . . . I sigh. If I concentrate really hard, I can get that scene in the conference room out of my mind for almost . . . oh, *ten* whole minutes at a time. We will *what*?

And, can we say Major Sexual Tension?

No dating the boss, no dating the boss, no dating the boss.

Stop. It's time to grow up and face facts: I'm never going to be nice, but I'm smart and I'm tough, and that's enough.

Right?

Right on cue, my door bangs open. "Good morning, extremely nice boss," my way-too-perky-for-words assistant sings out. Why am I always wishing I had *her* weekends? She must have the best personal life in the world to always be Ms. Cheerful at work. Plus, nobody should look that gorgeous in purple, when I'm as pale and washed out as past-its-expiration-date yogurt.

So, naturally, I grouch at her. *The saying is not "misery loves perky," right?* "Bree? Can you tone down the perkiness, just until, say, lunchtime? You're raining sunshine on a perfectly good funk here. And quit calling me nice, it doesn't count, remember?"

She looks startled. "Hey, it's funny, but you know what? I'd kind of forgotten all about the bet."

We both stare at each other; me with major skepticism, her with major delight. "Hey!" she says.

"Hey!" I interrupt. "Forget it. You're a terrible actress, too. So what's up?"

"But I wasn't . . ." She shakes her head, looking dismayed, then snaps her fingers. "Right. Phone call on line two. He called when you were on the line with that corset vendor—not that we don't carry enough corsets, anyway, if you ask me. In fact, I—"

"Bree! The phone? Who is it?" I try not to be exasperated, but sometimes it seems like I'm the only one in the world with any focus.

"Oh, right. He said to tell you it's Steve from the Mountain o' Meat. If that's some perverted S&M company, I'd just like to say—"

But I'm snatching up my phone and making shooing motions with my hands to get her to leave. "Steve? Are you there? I'm so sorry I made you wait."

"Hey, Kirby. I'm here. How are you?" He sounds a little hesitant; a little different. I can't pinpoint *how,* though.

"I'm great! I'm so glad you called back. I wanted to make sure you were okay after our . . . you know, our date." I didn't want to bring up the choking incident; he'd already been so embarrassed when it happened.

He laughs. "You mean when I blew a meat chunk across the room and into the hostess's hair, after you saved my life, then I was ungrateful enough to ditch you immediately afterwards?"

Oops. Guess he didn't need reminding.

"Well, I wouldn't go as far as 'saved your life,' but, yeah. You sound . . . better," I say, trying to feel my way cautiously through the conversation. "Actually, you sound . . . different."

"It's the part where I'm not saying ninety words to every one of yours, probably," he says, with a nervous laugh.

"You . . . ah, well . . . okay, tippy-toeing around is driving me insane, so I'll just go with my usual blunt self," I say. "I'm sorry the Heimlich thing embarrassed you, and, yes, the nervous talking is *so* not there. Where's *my* Steve, and what have you done with him?" I laugh, also nervously.

"*Your* Steve? I don't think so, Kirby. Once I got over dying of embarrassment about the whole disaster of an evening, I figured out that you must have had some ulterior motive for going out with me in the first place. I mean, come on. You're you and I'm, well, I'm *me*."

Oh, crap. Talk about being transparent. "Steve, no. I mean, well, sort of. But, really, I just—"

He laughs again, but this time it sounds more like a real laugh. "Hey, Kirby, it's okay. I have a confession. I had an ulterior motive, too. Anyway, I wondered if we could have coffee after you get off work tomorrow, so I can explain it all and maybe even ask for some advice."

"Wow. Um, well . . ." I really liked Steve, but I don't want to lead him on, either. The chemistry's just not there for me. Not like with Banning, where we'd practically set the whole chemistry lab on fire.

No dating the boss. No dating the boss. No dating the boss.

"Kirby? It's not a date. Seriously. I actually have somebody else I'm really interested in and, well, I just want to meet you and talk. But if you don't have time, that's fine. I understand that you're probably really busy, and that's no problem, because busy people are busy, and . . . oh, shit. There I go again." He sighs.

"It's okay, Steve. I'd love to have coffee with you. See you at six?" We make plans to meet the next day at the bookstore coffee shop that's near my office and then hang up, and I realize I'm smiling my first real smile of the day. Steve has a confession, too. This could be interesting.

The phone rings as I stand up to go get a refill on my coffee, so I sit back down. "Kirby Green."

"Kirby? It's Anya. I wanted to know what I need to do for Lauren's recital Saturday. She's so excited about it, now that we found out I can get the morning off so I can come, too. Do you want to drive over with us or meet us there?"

Ohhh. Here's a problem.

"Anya, didn't Lauren tell you? The recital space is only large enough to accommodate one parent per child. And, since you're the actual *parent,* you should definitely be the one to go with Lauren."

"Oh, no! That's terrible! Why couldn't they get a bigger space? Well, I'll just . . . I'll have to miss it, and you two can tell me about it afterwards." She sounds like she's going to cry, and I can't stand it.

"No, no, no. I already purchased the video, so I'll get to see the whole thing when I get back from Italy. Speaking of Italy, I need to pack and get ready—preparing for a three-week trip to a foreign country is a lot different from going away for a weekend. So, really, it works out just fine." Now I feel like *I'm* the one who's going to cry, although I don't know why. It's not like watching a bunch of little girls dance in silly costumes is going to be all that exciting. I'm the woman who goes to two or three Broadway shows every year, after all.

My throat starts to close up a little. (You can't fool your own throat.) *Damn. I'm going all girly over this.*

"No, Kirby. This is *your* activity with Lauren. She's so excited that you'll be there, and I can't . . . I can't . . ." *Oh, no.* I hear little snuffling noises and then a muffled nose-blowing sound.

Like I'm going to keep a mother from seeing her daughter's first dance recital. Especially a mother as unselfish as Anya, who already shares her daughter with me.

No freaking way.

I turn on my "important businessperson" voice. "I won't hear another word about it. I'll tell you what, though. I'll meet you afterward and take you both out to lunch. That way I can see her costume and hear all about it while the excitement's still fresh."

I tap my pencil on the desk, wondering why my very efficient solution is making my chest hurt. "Plus, I can see everything on the video when I get home from Italy, and I'll bore you both with my trip pictures, too. Oh, and is it okay if I bring Lauren a few presents?"

"Well, okay, then, on the recital. We'll look forward to lunch. You're still on for Wednesday, too, right?"

"Wouldn't miss it. It's our last rehearsal before Saturday, so it'll be just like I'm seeing the recital. Plus, Lauren still owes me a 'real' food dinner."

"All right, then. Thanks. And, Kirby?"

"Yes?"

"Thank you for asking me about the presents. It means a lot to me that you've clearly thought about our conversation. Thanks for how good you are with her, too. You are an amazingly nice—"

"Don't say it," I say, wearily. "Just don't say it."

* * *

It seems like way past *my* turn to bang open somebody's door, so naturally I pick Banning's. I've avoided him pretty successfully for the past week, ever since that weird moment of intense . . . *something* . . . in the conference room. Anyway, he's been in meetings with the board a lot. Probably figuring out a way to get rid of me.

Does he want to sleep with me or fire me? Probably both.

"Hey!" I say, as I bang his door open. *That was fun; no wonder everybody does it.*

I bang his door closed again, just for the hell of it. "Do you have a minute?"

He stretches his arms up, then clasps his hands behind his head and leans back in his chair, the picture of poise and calm.

Yeah, right, buddy. I know exactly how calm you are around me. I was the one up against the roll of quarters in your pocket in the conference room, remember?

Trying to be as crude as possible in my thoughts only makes my face hot, so it's not what I'd consider a successful strategy. This ticks me off. The fact that he looks so damn delicious in his black pants and white and gray-striped shirt with the sleeves rolled up doesn't help, either.

"Look, here's the deal. I've had people—*unsolicited* and *un-knowing* people—call me *nice* several times over the past few weeks. And the lie didn't count, really, because it was just a teensy white lie for her own good, and if you save somebody's life it deserves to count, and, okay, the one was sick with the flu at the time, but she didn't sound delirious, and, finally, giving up the ballet recital is huge, so even though I'd never use my Special Sibling or her mom, that *totally* should have counted." I finish, out of breath.

Banning has unfolded himself from his chair during my rambling monologue, and walks out from behind his desk, then leans on it and folds his arms. "What, if you don't mind my asking, in the *hell* are you talking about?"

"The bet. I won. You lost. End of story." I turn around and grasp the doorknob to leave.

"Not so fast, Green," he says.

I turn back around, almost in spite of myself. "What? I'm going to Italy, and I'm keeping my job. I hired new staff who actually do their jobs and earn their salaries, W&L's marketing department has never been so profitable, and people called me *nice,* even. Not just one person, but several people. So you're not firing me, and I'm going to Italy. End of story."

"Not quite," he says, standing up and smiling at me. It's a slow, dangerous smile. The kind of smile that says, *I want you naked.*

Or, maybe I'm just projecting.

I shiver. "What else is there? Are you going to fire me? Is that what the board meetings have been about?"

He takes a step closer. "Nope. There's just the matter of your public apology. When and where?"

"What?" I have to think about it. Oh, right. The public apology I'd demanded when we first agreed to the damn bet. "Oh, that. Well, forget it. I don't care about that. I just wanted *you* to know."

I start to leave again, but he reaches out to catch my wrist with his fingertips. "Kirby, that's all I wanted, too. For *you* to know that you're a nice person. I always knew it; but you were alienating your staff and everybody you know with the giant chip on your shoulder. Do *you* know it?"

My first inclination is to argue with the "chip on your shoulder" comment, but the tingling sweeping up my body from where his hand touches my wrist is leaving me incapable of rational thought. *Almost. No dating the boss, no dating the boss . . .*

"If I say yes, do I get my vacation?" I lift my chin and stare right at him, so close I can feel his breath on my face.

"If you say yes, you get *me*," he says, and I just have time to realize that it's the most arrogant thing I've ever heard, and then he kisses me.

He kisses me, and the same heat and ice and flame I'd felt before burns through me from where his lips touch mine, and it's not enough, not nearly enough, and I reach up to dig my hands into his lovely hair and pull his head closer and deepen the kiss and seriously consider wrapping one of my legs around him, and it's so good so good so good, and then the door opens.

"Well, I *never!*" rings out the very shocked voice of his pet buzzard, er, secretary. I pull away from Banning, almost dazed, and look at her.

She stares at us, mouth pursed, eyes glittering with the excitement of all the coffee-room gossip to come, and I feel my heart sink into my shoes. All that work, for all those years, only to ruin everything by making people think I'm sleeping my way up the ladder.

"Get out," Banning says, his voice rough, but it's far too late. I watch as the door closes behind her, and my future at this company crashes down around my head, then I feel my hands clench into fists and wish I had something to hit.

"How *could* you?" I am so furious it's amazing that fire isn't coming out of my eyes. "How could you humiliate me like that at work? Do you know what happens now?"

I pace away from him, clenching and unclenching my hands, and trying not to let the angry tears get the better of me. "By now, the buzzard hotline is in place, chattering away about how Kirby Green screwed her way up the ladder at W&L. By tomorrow, I'll be the laughingstock of the company. By next week, I won't have any authority left. You have just undermined me in the worst possible way, Stuart."

He stands there, looking shocked. "Kirby, I didn't mean to— the door was closed—what do you mean, *I* undermined you? You were kissing me, too!"

I laugh bitterly. "Right. But you're the *boss*. So I'm the *joke*. Thanks a lot. Unless I sue you for sexual harassment, I'm the slut who tried to move *up* by going *down*. Get it?"

His mouth falls open. "Sue me? *Sue* me? Oh, shit." He shoves his hair back from his forehead. "Please tell me you're kidding."

I slam the door open, then stop and look back at him. "Maybe you should have thought about that sooner."

Then I stride right past his secretary's desk, painfully aware of her avid gaze and nasty laughter following me down the hall. I don't allow my steps to speed up, no matter how much I want to run.

Here we go again. Let's all laugh at Kirby.

When I reach my office and walk inside, I close the door ever-so-gently. Then I lean back against the door and slide down till I'm sitting on the floor.

All these years of hard work, and here I am thirteen years old again. I can't do it. I won't do it. I'm going to have to resign.

And the worst part of all? That kiss had felt like the beginning of something. Instead, it turned into the end.

35

Brianna

Trouser or pants role: Male character sung by a woman.

What a beeyotch of a day.

I dragged my tired butt and my bag of groceries up the stairs to my apartment, wondering how much extra an apartment with a working elevator would cost, and feeling guilty about canceling on Madame for the evening's rehearsal. She was so lovely to stand up for me with Renata, and we'd had a long talk after the mean sow, er, I mean, *soprano,* had slammed her way out. But I wasn't quite up to the drive there and back in the freezing rain tonight.

Plus, work had been weird and draining. Kirby had some odd thing going on with some S&M guy named Steve who had mountains of flesh or some creepy product, and then Evil Buzzard Woman started a rumor that Kirby and Mr. Stuart were kissing in his office.

Talk about ridiculous! I guess he was an attractive man, in an "I'm scary and important and I may squash you like a bug" kind of way, but he and Kirby? No way. I'd seen them together, and she clearly couldn't stand to be around him.

Maybe it's sexual tension, like in those books Mama reads. "I hate you; I hate you; I hate you; let's have sex." *Nah, Kirby has more sense than that. Plus, Mr. Stuart never wears a loincloth or Scottish battle gear.*

"That I know of." I giggled as I fitted the key into my lock, thinking of Mr. Stuart in a loincloth at the next board meeting. Since we were talking W&L, though, probably everybody would think he was modeling one of the new fall line. I pushed open the door, still chuckling, and, to be honest, trying not to imagine Jamie in a loincloth, when somebody pulled the door the rest of the way open.

Lyle. Again. Wearing jeans and an old Mariners T-shirt, even, and not his uniform.

So much for my planned dinner of chocolate-chip cookie dough straight out of the package.

I sighed, just a little, and then smiled up at him. "Hi, honey. Um, I thought you had to work tonight?"

"I did, but we need to talk."

I flashed an even brighter smile at him. "Oh, dear. That sounds serious. Anyway, I thought it was always the *woman* who wanted to talk? Believe me, I could pass on the talk tonight and just lounge in front of the TV with junk food." I walked past him, noticing that he didn't even try to kiss me.

This can't be good. Anyway, like he has a reason to be annoyed? Hel-lo? He's the one who put me on the spot at his mother's about W&L and babies. He's the one who never stands up to Eleanor for me.

This is a serious problem.

"Bree, this is a serious problem. Every time I try to talk to you about the wedding, you avoid the topic. Don't you want to get married?"

There it was. Out in the middle of the room and, finally, unavoidable.

I put my bags down on the table and checked for anything that needed refrigeration immediately. Cookie dough, milk, and yogurt, check. Scooping up "the essentials," as I like to call them, I headed for the kitchen, stalling.

"Bree?"

Sighing again, I shoved my poor cookie dough into my nearly empty fridge and grabbed two bottles of water. I was *so* not offering him a beer for this discussion.

Taking the chair across from him at my table, I silently offered the bottle of water, then waited until I'd uncapped my own and taken a long drink. Then we both spoke at once.

"Lyle—"

"Bree—"

"You first," I said.

"No, you," he said.

I shook my hair back from my face and took a deep breath. "Okay, here's the thing. I love you, and I want to be with you." He started to speak, but I held up my hand.

"You wanted to talk; let me finish. I even think I want to marry you, although it would help if you would take my side against your mother once in a while. You're a good man, Lyle. But ever since all this wedding stuff has come up, you've been pressuring me."

I took another long drink of water, then continued. "A *lot*. We talked about a fall wedding, remember? Or maybe waiting till next spring? Now, suddenly, the wedding has to be right now, just a few short weeks after the audition I've spent the past several years of my life preparing for. Why? Why can't we go back to our original plans?"

I paused and—even as I heard my own words—I wondered if they were still true. *Do I still want to marry him?*

He started to speak, then paused and looked at me. "Is it my turn, yet?" His voice wasn't sarcastic, exactly, but it wasn't all that friendly, either.

I just nodded, stunned by the direction of my thoughts.

He reached for my hands and squeezed them. "I love you, too, honey. That's why I want us to be together. You won't live with me before we're married, and I want more of your time than three evenings a week. I want to go to sleep next to you every night and wake up with you every morning."

My heart started melting, a little, but before I could respond, he continued. "I want to be there to comfort you when you've had a hard day, or when the opera thing doesn't work out, or when you're hormonal or PMS-y, or whatever."

He gave me his best "I'm a firefighter, ma'am, and I'm here to save you" smile, but I was immune to that particular brand of charm by then. "When 'the opera thing doesn't work out'? What does that mean? Are you telling me that *you* don't have any faith in me, either?"

I slowly pulled my hands from his. "Because I have to tell you, that would be very difficult for me, Lyle. Very, *very* difficult to hear that the man I love doesn't believe in me." I felt the tears forming, but I was determined not to let them escape and run down my face.

He shook his head. "No, honey. It's not that I don't believe in you. It's just that you're not, well, you're not really all that tough. And performing is a dog-eat-dog world. My cousin is an actor, you know, and it's so many people competing for so few spots."

Suddenly, his face brightened. "Wait! Are there a lot of people trying out for opera? Nobody really goes to the opera that much, except for old people, so maybe you won't have much competition."

I couldn't help it. I tried, but the outburst was inevitable. I sat there at my kitchen table and totally cracked up. "Lyle, darling, light of my life, you're comparing me to your cousin, the 'actor,' who has only ever been in one commercial in his entire acting career, and that was for *hemorrhoid cream*? And you're telling me that you think I might have a shot because . . . wait, what was it?" I tried to catch my breath, but I was laughing too hard.

"Oh, wait, I know. Because nobody goes but old people, so I

won't have much *competition?*" By this point, I was clutching my side, because it started to burn.

The worst part was that he was *nodding.* Smiling, even. Nodding and smiling, pleased that he'd figured out a solution to my "opera thing" dilemma.

His utter cluelessness sobered me up faster than anything else might have done. "You really don't know how hurtful that was, do you?"

From the blank look on his face, I was guessing no.

"What? I'm trying to be supportive, since it's important to you, but I have to admit that I'd like to set some parameters. Like, if you make it into the Seattle Opera, you get two years to sing, and then we start talking about getting pregnant. You're not getting any younger, you know."

He smiled at me again, and his voice dropped down to a confiding whisper. "Vince and Cookie said that you don't want to get *old eggs.*"

No way did he just say that. No way . . .

"No way were you discussing my . . . my private reproductive status with Vince and COOKIE!" I shouted at him, finally driven beyond all endurance. "Please tell me that you did not have a conversation about our future with Vince and his bimbo wife that included the word *eggs* and the word *Brianna* in the same sentence."

Shoving my chair back, I jumped up and stretched to my full five-foot, four-inch height (no shoes) and glared down at him. "Tell. Me. Right. Now. That. You. Did. Not. Talk. About. My. Eggs!"

Lyle squirmed around in his chair, but he wouldn't look at me. He didn't say a word to deny it, either. As I glared down at the top of his head, since he'd evidently found something fascinating in the wood surface of the table, the answer came through *forte* and clear.

This marriage would never work. We don't want the same things. Or, at least, we don't want the same things on the same timetable. I would either have to surrender my opera dreams, and make peace with the loss, or spend the rest of my life resenting Lyle for the career he forced me to abandon.

That's the kind of life that ends up in bitterness, divorce, and custody battles.

"I can't live that life," I said, holding my hand over the enormous, fiery ball of regret burning in my stomach.

"What?" Lyle looked up at me, confused. "You can't live a life with old eggs? What are we talking about?"

My shoulders slumping, I sat down next to him to explain why I was pulling his ring off my finger. Funny, but I'd never realized that the diamond was so heavy. It must have weighed about fifty pounds.

That's how much lighter I felt with it gone.

* * *

Hours after Lyle had gone home, worn out and angry, but finally accepting that I really, truly was breaking up with him, I still sat on the couch. I'd wrapped an old blanket around me, and I wondered if I'd cried every tear ever allotted to me in my lifetime, all in one night.

The "what-ifs" poked and prodded me with vicious accuracy, too; aimed at my deepest insecurities.

What if I failed the audition? Then I'd have no career *and* no relationship.

What if I never found another man as caring and loyal as Lyle? Then I'd end up alone and bitter.

What if I'd just made the worst mistake of my life?

Oh, cheer up, Bree. You're still young. You have time to make plenty of way worse mistakes.

This line of thinking didn't cheer me up at all, so I decided to go to bed and try to get some sleep in the few hours I had left before morning and another day at work. As I dragged my blanket behind me into my bedroom, the most horrifying thought of all struck me:

I have to tell Mama the wedding is off.

As I stopped dead in the middle of the room, cringing at the thought of what Mama would say, the teensy, undaunted spark of optimistic nature left burning somewhere way, way down in a corner of my heart piped up:

Yeah, but you totally get out of purple bridesmaids' dresses.

I started laughing hoarse barks of laughter that went on and on and on, until I proved myself wrong. I *did* have tears left in me.

Lots of them.

36

Kirby

Arrivederci. (Good-bye.)

Bree looks like hell this morning. I asked her if she was all right, but she just nodded and wouldn't look at me. Her face has that pale, scrubbed-clean appearance you get after a huge cry. Not that I've seen that kind of expression on my own face except for once, lately, but I recognize the signs.

I didn't press her for details, but it occurred to me that maybe she doesn't have the spectacular personal life I'd imagined. All of us have our own problems, I guess.

Great. Now I'm depressed. At least I have my mysterious coffee un-date with Steve to look forward to this afternoon.

Bree knocks on my half-open door. "Kirby, your mother is on line two. She rang into my line by mistake, I think."

"Thanks, Bree."

As she turns to go back to her desk, I take a deep breath and look at the phone. During our long, painful talk the other night,

we'd hashed out a few of the things that had been bothering me
the most all of these years. Somehow, it had been easier to talk to
her while I held an armful of sleeping child. We weren't "all fixed,"
by any means, but there had been progress.

For the first time in forever, there was *hope*.

"Hi, Mom. How are you?"

"Kirby, I'm so glad I caught you. I'm sorry to bother you at
work; I know you must be so busy—no." She catches herself and
laughs. "I'm *not* sorry to bother you at work. *I'm* important, too."

I grin. "Yep. So what's up?"

"Kirby, it's so wonderful! Your cousin is coming to Seattle for
the weekend, and he said I could catch a ride! So I can come stay
with you and help you pack for your trip!"

"That would be fun, Mom," I say, and realize I really believe
it. It *will* be fun.

"I made plans to have lunch when we get in Saturday with
some friends of mine, and do a little shopping, but we'll have Saturday evening and then I can see you off to the airport on Sunday."
She's practically bubbling with excitement, and I'm kind of excited, myself. I can't remember the last time anybody dropped me
off—or picked me up, for that matter—at an airport.

A hard rap on my door sounds, and I say good-bye to Mom,
telling her I'll call her later to make plans. "Come in," I call, wondering why my guest didn't just bang my door open.

It's not like everybody else doesn't.

Banning walks in my door, looking older and sadder than he
did in the very erotic dream I had about him last night. My cheeks
heat up at the memory.

I need to be the better man, er, person, here.

I stand up. "Banning, there's something I need to say."

He cuts me off. "I need to say something first. I would like to
formally apologize for my actions yesterday. If I offended you or
made you feel that you were in a powerless position in any way, I
am deeply sorry."

He's clenching his jaw by the time he finishes, but he just looks so damn *sad* . . . and I suspect it's my fault. "Look, Banning, you don't have to apologize to me. I'm the one who should apologize for the way I acted. We've been building up to this for months, because, well, I just really like you and . . ."

Okay, feel free to step in anytime, here, and bail me out of awkward moment-ville.

He says nothing, just stares at me.

Fine.

"It's just that . . . well, you scared me, and when I'm scared, I go on the offensive, and that was utter crap about suing. I would never sue you or the company over what was basically a consensual kiss, and—"

"Kirby, please stop. I'm not trying to influence your legal decisions. I wanted to apologize; that's all. To hear you say that I scared you confirms the absolute worst I've been thinking about myself. I had no right to make you feel scared or pressured or anything else."

"But—"

He holds up his hand. "I'm leaving now. We can't talk about this anymore. The lawyers would probably have a cow if they knew I came to apologize to you in the first place. Liability, or some such shit. But I don't give a damn; I need you to know that I'm sorry."

He shoves his hands in his pockets. "I thought there was something . . . well. It doesn't matter. You'll be happy to know I'm leaving."

I'm bewildered. "Leaving what? Leaving my office? Going home for the day? Going on a trip? What are you talking about?" I tap my foot and try for a smile. "Clarity should be your watchword, Banning."

A grin twitches at the corner of his lips, then fades. "I resigned, Kirby. That's what the board meetings have been about; working out the details of my leaving. So you won't have to worry about being mauled in the conference room anymore."

He turns to go, leaving me standing, shocked, in the middle of my office. "But, you can't . . . is this about *us*? You can't leave the company over a stupid kiss. You're a terrific CEO."

He smacks his hand on my door, then whips back around. "It's about us, and it's about what I want out of life. It's about working for the environment, instead of selling a bunch of silly sex toys I can hardly pronounce. I was planning to wait another year to save some more money, but after . . ."

He smiles at me, but it's a smile filled with bitterness. "Oh, and Kirby? Two things. First, I recommended you as my successor. You're a hell of a businesswoman. Second, it wasn't a *stupid* kiss, to me. It was wonderful. Good-bye."

Before I can form a single coherent thought, he's gone, leaving me in the same place I've been for most of my life.

Alone.

* * *

Somehow, I made it through the rest of the day. My new staff knows that Friday is my last day before my trip, and they're in and out of my office continually, asking questions and wanting approval on a million different projects.

Oh, and Matilda Jamieson called me. The board chairperson wanted to let me know that Banning was leaving and that, although he'd recommended me for the post, they were going with a candidate who had actual experience running a company. "But we're definitely grooming you to move up the ladder, Kirby. You keep it up, and you'll wind up being a tough old broad like me."

She said it with affection and pride, as though I should be pleased at the prospect. The funny thing is that the *old* Kirby would have been. The *new* me, who actually cares about what people think of her, cringed at the thought. Matilda had worked her way through five different husbands; never putting anything or anyone in front of her career.

Is that really how I want to live my life?

I stared at the door that Banning had walked out, just hours earlier, and wondered why the idea of being groomed to move up the ladder didn't excite me more. It's what I'd always wanted, wasn't it?

Isn't it?

* * *

Jogging around the final corner, I'm out of breath when I reach the bookstore. With everything else going on, I'd almost forgotten about meeting Steve at the coffee shop. It was the last thing I felt like doing, considering my mood, but I couldn't cancel on him after he'd been courageous enough to call me.

There he is. A real smile—perhaps the day's first—stretches my face as I see him. He's balancing two coffees and a tray of pastries and looks like he's going to drop all of it any second. But then he manages to safely deposit his precarious load on a table and looks up and sees me. He smiles, too, but his smile seems a teensy bit strained.

I walk over to him and bypass the hand he's holding out and give him a quick hug, instead. "Hi, Steve. I'm so glad to see you."

He looks uncomfortable, biting his lip. Then he helps me off with my coat, and we sit down. "I got you a latte. I hope it's okay. If you want something different, I can get it. Or you can have mine. Although mine is a latte, too, just decaf, so I'm not sure it would be better. So I can go get you—" He pauses and takes a deep breath. "I'm doing it again. Sorry."

He smiles at me again. "You make me nervous."

I pick up my coffee and take a sip. "The latte is fine; perfect. Thanks. And, believe it or not, you make me nervous, too."

He barks out a burst of surprised laughter. "Right. *I* make *you* nervous. I can see why a geeky professor would make an elegant, beautiful, super-successful businesswoman like you nervous. Happens to me all the time."

I put my hand on his. "I'm nervous because you're a very, very nice man, and I have to confess that I've done something that wasn't very nice at all." I look down at the table, wondering when my entire life turned to shit, and prepare to confess all about my reasons for the speedy date.

"Kirby, me first."

I look up, surprised. Steve picks up my hand and holds it in both of his. "I have a confession, too. I didn't go to Speedy Dating to meet a woman. I mean, I didn't go to meet a *man,* either. Not that there's anything wrong with that. I just, oh, I'm screwing this up."

He gulps some more coffee. "Okay, here's the thing. I really like this woman. That sounds dumb, but I . . . do. I have feelings for her. She's smart and funny and pretty, and we like the same stuff. She's a theoretical mathematics professor, can you believe the luck?"

His entire face is shining, which goes to prove that there's somebody for everybody. *A theoretical mathematics professor!* I'm starting to get a warm fuzzy from this story.

"Anyway, I saw that C. J. Murphy column about Speedy Dating, and I thought, maybe I could try this. I mean, you might have noticed that I'm not all that smooth with women." He laughs a little. "I thought if I could go to this thing and manage not to make a total fool out of myself, it would give me confidence to ask Mei Ling out."

"Did it work?" I ask, grinning.

He slumps. "I haven't tried. After that disaster of our first date, I kind of thought I should give up on the whole thing and become a monk."

I slide the plate of pastries a little closer to him. "First step in plotting dating strategy should always be to eat fattening food."

He flashes a tentative smile at me. "You're not mad at me? I mean, I never planned to go out on any dates. I even got matched!

I mean, two other women besides you. But I said no to them. *You,* though. You're so amazing, and I couldn't believe you'd said yes to me. I thought, if I can go out with *her* and not be an idiot, I have serious hope."

He grabs a chocolate croissant. "You see how well *that* worked out. Mei Ling *is* a vegetarian. I asked her yesterday, since she only ever eats rice and veggies, that I've seen. Can you imagine how that would have worked out? A vegetarian at Mountain o' Meat."

Shaking his head, he takes a bite of croissant, then a sip of coffee. "She probably doesn't know the Heimlich, either, so I'd be shot down and dead all at the same time."

I can't help it. I start laughing. "Oh, Steve. Thank you so much for telling me this. I thought *I* was having a sucky week, but here you are with visions of becoming a monk or being 'shot down and dead.' I *adore* you."

He smiles, but looks alarmed. "I didn't mean to lead you on, Kirby. About Mei Ling—"

I'm laughing too hard to talk, so I just shake my head and try to catch my breath. "No, you didn't lead me on. I think you and I will be great friends, and I'm going to help you knock the panties off of your Mei Ling."

Now he looks really alarmed. "Um, isn't that 'knock the *socks* off'?"

"Hey, whatever you're into. But panties would be more fun. Now, let's plot a little." I'm delighted to have somebody *else's* problems to think about, for a change. "The first part is all about marketing, Steve, and I'm a genius at that, if I do say so myself. Once she knows you, she'll love you."

I stand up, determined. "For this, we're going to need more pastries."

* * *

An hour and a half later, I've laughed more than I have in months, we've got Steve's entire dating strategy planned out (his girlfriendto-be doesn't stand a chance!), and I'm feeling a little sad that *I'm* not the object of all this devotion. I look at Steve's cute Boy Scout face and realize the problem. He's a truly nice guy.

"And we all know nice guys want nice girls, right?" I mutter.

"What? Who's a nice guy?" he asks, folding up our strategy notes (yes, he took notes; I'm telling you a theoretical mathematician is *perfect* for him).

"Nothing. Never mind," I say, suddenly swamped by the sadness I'd kept at bay for the past two hours.

Professors are pretty perceptive, I guess, because he shoots a shrewd look at me and says, quietly, "We never talked about you."

"What?" I start to pull my coat on, but he reaches out and puts a hand on my arm.

"Kirby, when you came in, you said you were having a sucky week. So, 'fess up. I bared my soul to you and let you know what a complete and hopeless nerd I am. It's only fair of you to let me know if you have even the smallest failing."

I snort. "Right. Well, first off, I snort. How unladylike is that?"

But he won't be charmed out of his persistence. I can see it in his eyes, and he's still holding my arm. "Tell me."

So, I do. The whole ugly story about the firing, the bet, and Banning. Hell, I even tell him a little about Daniel and Mom and Dad, because by then I'm on a roll. By the time I'm done, tears are rolling down my face and he's scooted his chair right up next to mine and is holding me against his chest and patting my back. "Shhh, shhhh. It's okay."

I sit up and realize I've soaked the poor man's shirt. His *orange* shirt. "Steve," I sniffle. "We really have to buy you some new shirts. *Any* color but orange."

He looks down at his shirt and laughs. "Yeah, I know. My mother sends me shirts for Christmas and my birthday, and orange is her favorite color. It seems like a waste not to wear a perfectly good shirt, plus I never have to shop, so . . ."

I push my chair back a skinch more and blow my nose on a

napkin. "Yeah. *No.* We're totally going shopping before your date. Once Mei Ling sees you in a blue shirt, she'll probably fall in your arms from sheer amazement."

He pokes me in the arm. "Very funny. You're good, too. Distract with a little gentle offensive to get people off the subject of you. Sorry, though. Ten years of college students trying to distract me out of giving exams has taught me laser-like focus."

He hands me another napkin. "You want my take on this whole thing?"

I blow my nose again. *Lovely. I must look delightful with my red swollen nose and eyes. Just delightful.* "Do I have a choice?"

"Laugh it up, funny girl. Here's my take: I don't understand the bet at all. You *are* nice. Why in the world would you need to prove it to somebody?" He's wearing an expression of confusion that is so earnest and so sincere, it momentarily strikes me speechless.

Only momentarily, though.

"Thanks, Steve. But it doesn't count that you called me nice after you already knew about the bet."

He stares at me, then reaches over and gently tugs on a strand of my hair. "Hello? Earth to Kirby? You're awfully dumb for such a smart person. I don't give a damn about your stupid bet. *You* are a nice person."

He waves an arm to gesture at our table, which is covered with the remains of our carbo-loading strategy session. "Would anybody but a nice person go to all of this trouble to help some guy who took her to the Mountain o' Meat restaurant?"

I look at him, and we both crack up. "Steve, you gotta admit, that place is horrible. I mean, puh-*leeze.* The seven-meat special??"

He stops laughing first and touches my cheek. "Kirby, it sounds like the only person who doesn't know that you're a nice person is *you.*"

Talk about déjà serious vu. Banning's words out of Steve's mouth. *Maybe—finally—the discovery I'd been reaching on my own, too?*

Whoa. Sensory overload. I cannot take all of this emotion and self-realization without some serious pharmaceutical assistance.

I wipe my face with the napkin, then bat my eyelashes at Steve. "If I agree that I'm a nice person, will you beat him up for me?"

"Definitely. But are we talking about Banning? Or Daniel? Oh, to hell with it, I'll beat 'em both up. Except we might need to call my big sister, because she had to step in and help during the last fight I started." He looks a little embarrassed, but not as much as you'd think.

"Your big sister? Well, it takes a very confident man to admit that his sister has to protect him."

"Hey! I was four years old, and the playground bully took my Hot Wheels cars. It was a question of honor!"

As we gather up our trash to toss, so we can leave, I sneak a glance at him. "Your Hot Wheels cars, huh? You don't, by any chance, go to monster truck rallies?"

"What's a monster truck rally?"

I breathe a sigh of relief. "Just checking."

37

Brianna

Diva: Literally, "goddess." Used for leading sopranos.

It was almost four thirty, and I'd waited all day for exactly the right time. Kirby always left early on Wednesdays for her mystery appointments, so I planned to catch her just before she took off, but early enough that we could talk. I gathered my courage in both hands (actually, I clutched the pages of her expense report in both hands, but courage is too intangible for satisfactory gathering) and knocked on her door.

"Wow! Twice in one week, somebody knocks?" she said, which I took to be a Kirby-esque way of saying *come in,* so I did. Go in, that is.

"Hey, Bree, what's up?" she asked, organizing the piles of paper on her desk. "Have you seen Banning today?"

I thought she knew about Mr. Stuart. "No, he, er, Mr. Stuart cleaned out his office last night. He won't be back. I guess the last thing he did was fire his buzzard, I mean, his secretary."

She quickly put her "calm, cool, and collected" Kirby mask in place, but I knew what signs to look for, so I casually walked closer to her desk. Sure enough, her hands clutched the arms of her chair so tightly her knuckles were turning white.

Maybe there was something between them? Nah. Not possible.

She still didn't say anything, and I was losing my courage. "If you're busy, I can come back later," I said, trying to weasel out of the conversation.

She looked up at me. "No, I'm good. I've still got about ten minutes before I need to get going. Big night tonight." She tilted her head and gazed at me, then seemed to come to some decision. "I'll tell you all about it sometime soon. What's up with you?"

I stood there, clutching my shield of papers. She may have been a changed woman, but she was still the woman who'd fired four people in the past five months. My knees were literally knocking together (which is as uncomfortable as it sounds).

"Well, I . . . um, you . . . er, we—"

"Oh, no. Here we go again," she said, shaking her head. "More naked bungee jumping?"

She grinned at me, and suddenly I wasn't nervous at all. "Nope, much better than naked bungee jumping. No chafing, either. I need some time off."

"Sure." She shrugged. "Take as much time as you want. Oh, wait. Does it need to be this week? I mean, I understand if there's some . . . personal crisis, but if not, I was really hoping you'd help me clear my desk this week for my trip."

"Oh, no, not this week." I hastened to reassure her. "More like mid-February. For a week, if I can."

"Sure. Just let HR know. Taking a trip?" she said, paying attention with one ear, as she stuffed files in her briefcase and pulled her purse out of a drawer.

The moment of truth. *Mine,* that is. I was determined to be completely honest, even if it cost me my job.

As it probably would.

I sat down on the very edge of her visitor's chair. "Here's the deal, then. You know how I told you about my singing? I have, well, I may be able . . . I mean—"

Kirby tapped one finger on her watch. "Time, Bree. Just spit it out."

"I haveanauditionfortheSeattleOpera, andIhavetoprepareandifIwinIwillquit."

I whooshed out a breath. *There. I got it out.*

Unfortunately, Kirby hadn't understood a word. "Um, in English, please?"

I slumped back in the chair. "I'm sorry. I'm just so nervous, and if you have to fire me, I understand, but I have an audition with the Seattle Opera, and I have to prepare for it. Also, if I win, I'll have to quit my job here to begin my career in the opera."

I couldn't look at her. I just couldn't. She'd been so great to work with, and I'd just told her I wanted time off so I could work hard to try to abandon her. I heard a strange snuffling sound and looked up, alarmed.

"Oh, no, Kirby—are you crying? I'm so sorry, I—"

"N-n-no, I'm laughing. What a screwed-up company this is. The CEO quits to go be Smokey the Bear or something, I want to write novels, and you're leaving to be the next Maria Callas. It's too perfect." She went off into gales of laughter, bent over her desk.

After a moment, I started laughing, too, even though I didn't know what the heck she was talking about. "Um, Kirby? Does this mean you're not going to fire me?"

She wiped her face with the back of her hand. "What? Oh, God, no. The trip to Barbados for my firing average is off now that Banning is gone, anyway, I imagine."

She stood up and walked around the desk and leaned down to give me a quick hug, which I think surprised both of us. "Hey, I'm happy for you. Take *two* weeks off! Take as much time as you want, and kick ass at that audition. The world needs another talented singer way more than another sex-toy company admin worker. Although I've got to admit that I'll miss you and your demon camels. A lot."

I opened my mouth to tell her I'd miss her, too, but she faked a horrified look and waved me off. "No girly emotional stuff. I don't do girly emotional stuff. Hey, look at the time! I've gotta run, Bree. Costumes to try on, and all that. But you get out of here, too. Go kiss that fiancé of yours or something. Go rehearse! I want to hear all about it tomorrow."

She rushed out the door, coat flying behind her, leaving me staring after her, stunned. I still had no idea what the heck she was talking about—Smokey the Bear? Novels? Barbados?—but it had all turned out so much better than I'd even hoped.

Except for one thing, I realized as I followed her, more slowly, out of her door. "No fiancé to kiss," I mumbled.

"Well, if kisses are all you need . . ." said a very familiar voice. I rounded the corner of my cubicle and stared down at Jamie, who was sitting in my chair. "Hey, Bree. Got a minute?"

* * *

Since Kirby was gone, I decided to make an executive decision and use her office, so the company gossips wouldn't just happen to walk by and hear us talking. Jamie followed me in, and I closed the door, then leaned back against it, while he wandered around the room, staring at the framed prints and diplomas on the walls.

"Some office, huh? Did you see this? *Summa cum laude.*" He whistled. "Pretty impressive."

"So, you just wanted to stop by and admire Kirby's academic credentials?" I asked. "Accounting pretty slow today?"

He turned around till he faced me, then shoved his hands in his pockets. "Nope. Crazy busy, in fact. But I can't get anything done. I walked by earlier and saw you looking so sad, and I haven't been able to concentrate all day. Are you okay?"

He tried a smile, but it didn't work very well. "We're friends, right? Friends are allowed to be worried about friends."

I stared at him for a long moment, then finally decided to continue with my policy of all-honesty-all-the-time. "Yes, but friends aren't allowed to make comments about whether their friends need kisses."

"Hey, I'm sorry about that. I didn't mean—it just slipped out."

I shook my head, suddenly exhausted. "It doesn't matter. Yes, I'm sad. I broke off my engagement to Lyle. That's why I'm sad. I also just told Kirby that I need time off so I can go audition, which means I may soon be leaving the best boss I've ever had, which also makes me sad."

His entire face lit up. Seriously, like a Christmas tree or something. "Hey, that's great! I mean, not the part about Lyle. I'm not totally an insensitive clod. I'm very sorry to hear about you two."

He walked toward me, smiling. "But the other part, where you're going to go for it and audition—Bree, that's awesome news! I'm so happy for you and proud of you, and, well, just glad."

Suddenly he stopped, and his smile vanished. "Oh, except for the part where it sucks that you'll be leaving W&L, so I won't get to see you every day. But I can come hear you sing and visit, right? That's what friends do, right?"

He was kind of bouncing up and down like a cocker spaniel puppy, and I was seriously amused. Then my mind caught up to what he'd said. "You . . . you said it sucks that I'll be leaving?"

"Well, yeah, but—" he began.

I interrupted him by bursting into tears.

"Oh, no. Oh, honey, whatever I said, I was wrong. I'm stupid. I'm a stupid, jerkwad of an insensitive guy." He sounded frantic and rushed over to put his arms around me, then started smoothing my hair down over and over with one hand, while he patted my back with the other. "Shh, shhh. I'm so sorry. I'm a terrible person, and I deserve to be whipped with some of our more painful products. The leather and chains number from the winter catalog, definitely."

Now he was trying to make me laugh.

It worked.

For some reason, I wasn't quite ready to pull away from him, so I talked into his shirt. "Shut up, silly man. You didn't say anything wrong. In fact, you're the first person except for Kirby to say anything *right*. You said you'd miss me. You can't miss me unless I'm gone."

Just thinking about it set the tears flowing again. He was just so gosh darned wonderful.

"Um, honey? Bree? Thank you, I think. But what exactly did I say? Take pity on a poor confused man here and explain why you're crying." He kept stroking my hair and patting my back, and the initial warmth and comfort of it turned subtly into something hotter and less comfortable. Less safe. More . . . dangerous.

I pulled out of his arms, rubbing my face. "I'm sorry. I hate crying in front of people. I must look awful." I walked over to Kirby's teeth-check mirror.

Yep. Hideous.

I sighed. "Oh, well. It's done now. Anyway, you said you'd miss me. You wouldn't have said that if you didn't really believe that I was going to succeed in my audition."

He looked at me blankly. "Of course you'll succeed. I've heard you sing, remember? At the company holiday party? You're amazing. They'd be lucky to have you."

I laughed. "You are very good for my confidence, Jamie. Thank you for being my friend."

He glanced over at Kirby's bookcase and must have spotted the tissue box, because he went to get it for me. "Yeah, that's me. Friend. Um, well. About that friend thing? How long is a considerate interval to wait until I can ask you out? Two, three weeks?" He grinned a huge, lots-of-teeth grin.

I couldn't help it; I had to laugh again. "Thank you for your consideration in asking me. No, two or three weeks is not long enough."

I wiped my face and blew my nose, then dropped the tissue in the basket by the door. "Look, Jamie," I said, serious now. "Lyle and I were together for two years. You don't get over that in a week or two. Plus, I need to focus on my singing now. No matter what happens next month, I will not be deterred from pursuing my dream ever again. No matter what any man—or even *Mama*—may think or say about babies or weddings."

Jamie held up his hands and screwed up his face in an expression of mock horror. "Weddings? *Babies?* I was just talking about asking you out on a date. I never marry or impregnate a woman on the first date, I promise."

I blushed and looked down at my shoes. "Sorry. But you know what I mean. Let me do my thing for a while. I need to find my own path, on my own agenda, in my own time."

"Bree?" he said, gently raising my chin with one finger. "That's a lot of 'my own-ing.' And I understand, I really do. I just want you to know that I'm going to be your friend through all of it. And if—no, I'm going to retain some shred of my manly dignity here and say *when—when* you're ready to let someone share your path and your agenda and your time, you'll know right where to find me."

I stared at his beautiful face and his beautiful eyes and wondered if I were being a fool. "You'll probably find somebody way better long before that," I warned.

A slow smile curved his lips. "There is nobody better." Then he leaned down and pressed the softest kiss to my lips. "Good night, friend. See you tomorrow."

I watched him walk away, and part of me was tempted to call him back. Being alone is scary and lonely, and it makes me sad.

But it's also brave and courageous, and it's the right thing for me now. It's time to be a diva, Bree, in the very best sense of the word.

I smiled and turned off the light in Kirby's office, thinking that I'd started out trying to teach *her* how to be nice and wound up learning way more than I'd taught. Funny how things work out.

* * *

As I walked in the front door of my apartment building, I saw one of the most amazing sights, ever.

The elevator door opened, and actual people stepped out.

This has never, ever happened before. Not in the entire time I'd lived there. I chose to see it as a good omen. Heck, I even summoned my newfound courage and stepped inside. Then I pressed the number *two* and waited, almost holding my breath.

Miracle of miracles, it started moving. *Up,* even.

It was slow, and it sounded kind of creaky, but I just figured we had a lot in common. I almost applauded when it stopped on my floor and the doors opened. *Definitely* a good omen.

I was humming as I fitted the key into my lock. First Kirby, then Jamie, and now even the elevator. My week was improving every minute.

Then somebody inside my apartment pulled the door open, and my spirits sank back into my shoes. *Not again.*

I closed my eyes and took a deep breath, prepared to rehash Monday's arguments with Lyle (and get my key back from him), when I heard one of my favorite voices in the world. "Bree, honey, why are you standing in the hallway with your eyes closed? Come on in, so your mother and I can fatten you up for your audition."

"Daddy? *Daddy!*" I rushed in and threw my arms around him in a huge hug. "Oh, Daddy, it's so great to see you. Mama?"

As Daddy shut the door behind me, Mama came around the corner from my kitchen, wiping her hands on a towel. The aroma of something wonderful followed her; garlicky and buttery and delicious.

"Oh, Mama, what a wonderful surprise!" I hugged her, too, then drew back to look at them. "What's the occasion, though? Is something wrong?"

"Is something wrong? With *us*? Sweetheart, Eleanor called and told us about you and Lyle. We're here to talk." Mama laid the towel across the back of a chair and led me over to the couch.

Oh, no. I should have known better. Good things come in threes, and the elevator put me over the edge. Now it's going to be An Evening of Drama: Why Bree Is Ruining Her Life by Breaking Up with the Catch of the Century.

Act I.

I clenched my hands together and tried to remember to be brave. "Mama, Daddy, I know you're disappointed, but this is my life, and I have to live it for myself. Lyle and I—"

Mama broke in, eyebrows raised almost clear up to her hairline. "Disappointed? In *you*? Bree, whatever would give you such a foolish notion? We could never be disappointed in you, isn't that right, Henry?"

Daddy looked up from the newspaper that he must have brought with him and smiled. "Well—"

"And furthermore," Mama continued, "we're just so proud of you we could bust, for getting such an important audition at such a young age. We're going to get season tickets to the opera for everybody we know, as soon as they hire you, isn't that right, Henry?"

"Well—"

Mama patted my arm. "Plus, not to say a mean word about another soul, but that Eleanor can be a bit overbearing, don't you think? She never lets a soul get a word in edgewise, does she, Henry?"

Daddy was leaning forward this time, ready to jump in. "Ah—"

"Rushing in to marriage and babies, when you've got a God-given talent. What a ridiculous idea. We're glad you came to your senses, although, naturally, if you'd married him we would have been delighted to have grandbabies, and whenever you decide to have children, we'll be very, very happy and babysit all the time, won't we, Henry?" Mama was practically bouncing up and down on the couch in indignation by then. I just stared back and forth between her and Daddy, thinking for about the thousandth time in my life that conversations like these were good practice to become a tennis groupie.

Daddy tried, though. You've gotta give him that. "*Yes.* And—"

"Well. I called Madame Gabriella and got a whole list of the best foods for you to eat between now and the audition, so your father and I went shopping and stocked up your refrigerator and cupboards. Plus I made us all some nice steaks, and you're going to come to dinner every Sunday between now and the audition, isn't she, Henry?"

"Yes, and—"

Mama gave me a quick, fierce hug and then stood up. "I need to go check on dinner. I'm glad you and your father could have this chat."

As she bustled off into the kitchen, Daddy and I stared at each other in silence, trying desperately to keep straight faces. Finally, I couldn't stand it. "Thanks, Daddy. These father-daughter talks of yours are always so special to me."

When Mama walked back in the room, she stood, hands on hips, and stared at the two of us. "I never will understand you two. Always laughing like loons whenever we have a serious discussion. It's time for dinner. Come fix your plates."

Daddy and I dragged ourselves up, weak with laughter, to follow her in the kitchen. I almost bumped into Mama's back when she stopped dead next to my table, though. "Bree, honey? Where in goodness' name did you buy those *hideous* orange and green curtains? If you were short on money, we could have asked Aunt Laverne to whip something up for you. Those are absolutely *dreadful*."

While Daddy—who knew perfectly well where I'd gotten the curtains—tried heroically to keep from howling, I followed Mama in the kitchen and smiled at her. "Mama, you know how you raised me to be a nice girl?"

She looked at me suspiciously. "Yes?"

"Thank you. Nice girls really do finish first. Oooh, yummy! Cheesy potatoes!"

* * *

As I looked across my table at Mama and Daddy, framed by a set of horrible curtains that had been sewn with love, it came to me that the fairy tales they'd read me as a child had all gotten the *ending* right, but were too rigid on the *journey*.

There's more than one way to Happily Ever After. For now, this is mine.

"Honey?" Mama's voice broke into my thoughts. "When I spoke to Madame on the phone, she was in a lesson, and she kept telling her student—somebody named Magda—to 'look at the pillow; look at the pillow.' What in the world was that about?"

I thought of the past seven years of my life and smiled. "Poetic justice, Mama. Poetic justice."

38

Kirby

Sei una brava ragazza. (You are a nice girl.)

It's seven thirty Friday night; my last day at work before I leave for three glorious weeks in Italy is finally over. Jules and I must have traded a dozen phone calls. We're going to meet in New York at the *Alitalia* counter on Sunday at noon. She's going crazy with the show and was full of apologies for not being available to help me out with the craziness lately.

God, it's going to be good to spend some time with her.

As if thinking about Jules conjured her up, my cell phone rings, and the screen says it's her. I flip the phone open, already laughing. "What is this, thirteen times? We don't want to end on unlucky thirteen."

"Call him, Kirby." It's Sam. *What the hell is Jules's fiancé doing calling me? And what's he talking about?*

"Excuse me? Sam? Is that you? What's going on? Is Jules okay?"

He laughs, and I hear Jules yelling at him in the background. "Calm down, Hurricane. I want to talk to your friend, here. Kirby, I don't know why you'd want to spend three weeks in a foreign country with this tornado, but good luck to you."

The warm amusement in his tone makes something down in my gut clench a little; I'm so happy for Jules and Sam, but sometimes it's hard to be around them without feeling a little bit envious.

Even over the phone, evidently.

I go for light and carefree. "Oh, it will be a blast. Are you still joining us for the second half of the trip? It will be good to see you again, so long as you're prepared for much walking and much wine drinking."

"No worries. I've already been told to be prepared to shop a lot, too." I hear Jules say something, but it's muffled, then they both start laughing. Sam comes back on the line. "Look, I don't want to keep you; I know you're busy, but Jules told me about Stuart."

"What? First, tell Jules she's a dead woman. Second, it's totally none of your business. Third, why should I call him?"

"Women!" He's doing "exasperated voice," but his voice is gentle. "Kirby, the man is running a publicly traded company, and yet he's so crazed for you that he takes a chance and kisses you in his office? Then, to top it off, he does the honorable thing and quits so you don't have to face any repercussions from the office gossips?"

He makes kind of a snorting noise. "Kirby, this is a good guy. And you *deserve* a good guy. Although I'm still waiting for my chance to come beat the shit out of that prick Daniel for you."

Jules had told him some of the Daniel-the-rat-bastard story, and Sam and Jules had actually been staying at my house one weekend when Daniel pulled a "get drunk and show up at three a.m." trick. Sam wasn't amused and had made me love him forever by the way he stood up for me and put a real scare into Daniel.

I think of Steve (and his big sister) and grin. "You'll have to stand in line, Sam. About Banning . . . are you *sure*? What if he never wants to see me again, after what I said?"

"Oh, for God's sake, Kirby. We're guys. We don't have weird emotional twists and turns. He cares about you, he's hot for you—and who wouldn't be? Hey! *Ouch!* Jules, you are a mean woman," he says, laughing. "I owed you for the kiss you gave Carlos yesterday when he stopped by to visit."

I start tapping my foot. "Not to interrupt your little foreplay session, Dude, but I've got a phone call to make. Somebody's life is going to get a whole lot hotter, if you're right. Bye! Talk soon!"

As I hang up my cell phone and pick up my office phone to dial out, I think of what I'd just told Sam. "Yep. Hotter. And nakeder. Definitely nakeder."

"Surprise! I'm early!" I drop the phone on my desk and look up in shock at my mother, standing in my doorway and holding a large suitcase. "We're going to have such a wonderful time!"

I fumble with the phone and finally get it back in its cradle, then stand up and paste a big smile on my face. "Yep. A wonderful time."

Then I rush out from behind my desk to hug my mom, and my smile turns from forced to genuine. "I missed you, Mom. I'm so glad you're here."

After I showed her around the offices a little, we retrieve her suitcase and head out for the evening. Before we walk out, I dash back to my desk and grab the slip of paper with Banning's phone number on it.

No hot tonight. Or naked. But I can at least call. Maybe Sam is right? Maybe?

* * *

"Are you settled in, Mom?" I look up and smile as she walks into the living room after unpacking and freshening up.

"Yes, and hungry. Should we make some dinner? I can cook

something, if you like." She looks nervous and sort of fidgety. Our tentative reconciliation is too new to feel solid, but I think we're on the right path.

I *hope* so.

"Mom, you definitely don't have to cook while you're here. Why don't I take you out to eat? It's not like there's anything in the fridge, anyway. All I ever seem to eat at home lately is pizza."

Worry creases her brow. "Kirby, you know how important it is to eat right. Do you at least take vitamins? I . . . well. I'll back off on 'doing the mother thing,' as you call it, now."

If possible, her nervousness level seems to shoot even higher.

I just laugh. "Go ahead and nudge, Mom. I probably need it. I'll go do a makeup check, and we can head out."

"All right. I'll just straighten up these magazines."

As I head for the bathroom, I feel my chest start to tighten. Every time she comes to visit, she immediately starts cleaning, and I always bristle at the implied disapproval.

Then I glance back and see the smile on her face; she's humming to herself.

Maybe it's not disapproval. Maybe it never was. Maybe you make her nervous, and tidying up calms her down.

Maybe this can work if I can let go of the patterns in my past.

I grin, then send a mental nod to Dr. Wallace for the psychobabble. I'm not sure I can handle becoming a nice girl *and* a grownup all in the same month.

The world probably isn't ready for that big of a change.

* * *

BANG! BANG! BANG!

"What the *hell*?" I shoot up out of bed like something bit me on the ass, wakened by a pounding noise.

Maybe I dreamed it?

Then the doorbell starts ringing and ringing, and I know it wasn't a dream. More like a nightmare, I'm guessing.

It's got to be Daniel.

I run down the stairs, hoping that some miracle occurred and Mom didn't hear it.

"Kirby? What the heck was that?"

Fresh out of miracles at the Green residence, I see. Nothing new there.

"Nothing, Mom. Just my drunken neighbors. Go back to bed. I'll handle it."

I hit the front door and yank it open just as the pounding starts again, and Daniel stumbles across the threshold and nearly punches me in the eye with his upraised fist.

"Whoa! Hey, Kirby, love, it's about time you opened up. Not nice to leave Daniel standing out in the rain, now, is it?" He throws an arm around me, either in an attempt to stand upright or to try to trap me next to him.

Either way, I'm not interested.

I duck out from under his arm and close the door. "Daniel, keep it down. People are sleeping. What the hell are you doing here again? I warned you what would happen if you showed up at my house in the middle of the night one more time. I'm going to call the police and get a restraining order."

He whirls around to face me and suddenly appears a lot less drunk and a lot more angry. I draw in a deep breath and keep going. "If you leave now, you can probably get off with just a warning. But if you're still here when they get here, you're gonna go to jail, Daniel. How will that look to those rich art-show patrons of yours?"

He sneers at me and stalks even closer, then slams his palms against the door on either side of my head, effectively trapping me between his body and the door. My heartbeat picks up tempo until I'm almost afraid it's going to leap out of my chest.

Not that I'm afraid, exactly.

Liar.

"Kirby," he says, in a slurry almost-whisper. "Kirby, Kirby.

What am I going to do with you? Or, should I say, *to* you? I've got my handcuffs in my pocket, and I think I should chain you to your bed for a few days, until you see things more my way."

He grasps my jaw in his hand and squeezes, first softly, then the pressure grows tighter and tighter till he's hurting me.

"Daniel, stop it! You're scaring me. What is this about, anyway?"

He eases up on the pressure, but doesn't let go. "This is about you fucking me over, Kirby. My luck has gone straight down in the shitter since you dumped me. Everything was golden when we were together, and now I can't sell a painting to save my soul."

He laughs bitterly. "Not that I have much of a soul left. But you were my lucky rabbit's foot, Kirby. I need you back. Since *you've* been gone, my *luck* is gone. I want you back."

He fists his hand in my hair and yanks my face up toward his. "I'm going to have you back. If you don't agree, that's too damn bad. I'll fuck you blind until you do."

Then he slams his mouth down on mine and grinds his body against mine, and I'm scared now, I'm terrified, I'm crying, but he won't let go, and then . . .

I see a blur rushing through the air, and hear a *thwocking* noise, but this time it isn't a flying meat chunk, it's the sound of something heavy hitting the side of his head. Daniel yanks his head away from me and yells, his hand shooting up to the side of his head.

I'm almost frozen, but not quite. I jerk away from him and stare at my mother, standing in the middle of the room, shaking, and holding something that looks like a long wooden stick in both hands.

"Don't," she says, voice shaky but very determined, "touch my *daughter*! And we do not use *language* like that in this *house*!"

He turns around and raises a hand, probably to protect himself, but Mom takes it as a threat, and smacks him another whack with the stick, across the shoulder this time. "Don't you raise a hand to me, young man. Get out! Get out! Get *OUT* right *NOW*!"

She raises the stick again, and I've finally broken out of my shock enough to yank one of my heavy marble-based lamps off of a table and the cord out of the wall. So we face him like two wild women, stick and lamp cocked and ready to fly.

Daniel looks back and forth between us, one hand clutching his head, where blood is beginning to seep down from between his fingers. "You're a pair of lunatics! A couple of freaking lunatics! I must have been insane to think you had anything to do with my luck, you stupid bitch!"

Mom advances on him, menacing with the stick. "Language, you moron. Don't you ever call my daughter names! Now get OUT!"

I step forward, too, raising my lamp to swing at his head. He stares wildly at us, then fumbles for the doorknob and yanks the door open. "I'm leaving! I'm leaving, you stupid—"

Mom slams the door shut in his face, shutting out whatever pithy and complimentary names he was prepared to shout at us. Then she shoves the dead bolt shut and leans her back against the door and slides down till she's sitting on the floor.

I put the lamp down and run to her. "Mom, are you okay? Mom?"

She looks up at me and smiles. It's wobbly, but it's definitely a smile. "Nobody fucks with my daughter."

My mouth falls open. "Mom! You just said fuck!"

She smiles again. "I almost beat a man to death with your closet rod, and that's all you have to say?"

I fall down on the floor next to her, drop my head on her shoulder, and start laughing. She joins in, and soon we're laughing so hard we're howling, right there on the floor next to my front door.

I catch my breath first and give her a fierce hug. "I love you, Mom. I can't believe you came running to my rescue."

She smiles back at me, tears welling in her eyes. "It wasn't the first time, honey. Didn't you ever wonder why your father never came after you? I'm your mother. Nobody hurts my daughter. Not even her father."

I leaned back and stared at her. "You—but—I never knew, Mom. Why? Why—"

She sighs, and there is a world of weariness in it. But then she smiles again, and I see that glimmer of hope. "There's so much we need to talk about, Kirby. I've been seeing a therapist for about a year, now, to try to work through some of this stuff. I'm even dating."

She laughs, and her cheeks go all pink. "Well, I've been on three dates. But he's a very nice man, and we enjoy each other's company. I'd love it if you'd come visit and meet him."

I look at her, unsure my ears are actually working. *Therapy? Dating? Is this my real mother?*

And if it is, isn't that freaking wonderful?

"Mom, I'd love to meet him. I want to hear all about him. What's he like? What does he do? How did you meet him?"

I stand up and hold out a hand to help Mom up, suddenly full of questions. She smiles and shakes her head. "How about we talk about all of that tomorrow? Right now, it's two in the morning, and I need some sleep. Not to mention that we have to hang all those clothes back up in the closet."

I hug her again. "Don't worry about the clothes, Mom. I'll have to search through that stuff tomorrow . . . *today?* . . . when I pack, anyway. Just get some sleep. I have to call the police and make a report."

"I love you, Kirby. We can talk about that horrible man tomorrow, okay?" She looks at me searchingly, then smiles when I nod.

"I love you, too, Mom. Good night."

As she climbs up the stairs to the guest room, I decide that I'll call Maria Estoban in the morning and tell her what's going on. Honesty should count for something, right? There's no way I'm giving Lauren up now.

I groan. Speaking of Lauren, I have to be at the recital place at lunchtime. I need to get some sleep. I'll just make that call to the police now. And maybe I'll take a page from Steve's book and call Banning's cell phone. I can leave a voice mail without having to talk to him live and getting all flustered. Then the ball will be in his court, right?

Coward!

Hey! My mother and I just faced down a six-foot, four-inch man with a closet rod and a lamp. There are no cowards in the Green family.

Maybe facing up to my childhood and working through it makes me braver than being a hard-ass ever did.

As I dial the number for the police, I have to smile. *"Nobody fucks with my daughter."*

Hearing that one sentence was more healing than a year's worth of therapy.

* * *

"I was so good, Kirby! I was really great!" An enormous bunny rabbit wearing a bow tie is jumping up and down on the steps of the recital hall. "Wasn't I great, Mommy? Wasn't I great?"

Anya laughs, her face shining almost as brightly as that of her daughter. "Yes, little bunny. You were terrific! I'll bet Kirby can't wait to hear all about it."

I bend down and grab Lauren for a big hug, then stand up again. "Okay, bouncing girl. Let's go get some lunch, and you can tell me all about it. I shudder to say this, but Happy Meals for everybody?"

It's a little tough to talk over the lump in my throat. I had no idea that something as simple as seeing the excitement in Lauren's face would affect me so much. I must be going all girly in my old age.

Of course, crises, rape threats, and other assorted upheaval at two in the morning probably hadn't helped my stability. I grin, thinking of Mom this morning. She hadn't been a bit fazed. "No, honey, I slept great. That bully won't come around again. They never do, once you stand up to them. I finally learned that with your father, far later than I should have."

We'd scrambled some eggs and toasted some toast and enjoyed our first breakfast together in a long time, before I had to leave to meet Lauren and Anya. Mom's friends were on their way over to pick her up for lunch, then we were going to meet back up at my place this afternoon.

But first, a celebration of junk food. I smile at my favorite bunny in the world. "Okay, artery clogging it is. But no poop pellets in my car!"

Lauren collapses in giggles, while Anya raises an eyebrow at me. "Long story. I'll tell you in the car. Or would you rather walk?" I waggle a finger at Lauren. "No poop pellets on the sidewalk, you!"

She giggles again, then throws herself against me and hugs me really tight. The lump in my throat grows a size or two, till I'm worried that I'm going to do something silly, like burst into tears right here on the sidewalk, so I pull back.

"Okay, short stuff. Let's get going, in case it starts raining again. Do you think they have McCarrots? McBunny nuggets? No, wait, that would be gross; you don't want to eat your own kind. What about—"

Lauren grabs my hand and looks up at me, her whole face beaming with joy and wonder. "Kirby, you are very silly. But, 'cept for Mommy, you're the nicest person I've ever known."

Before I can say a word, a warm voice I know very well speaks up behind me. "Yes, she is, isn't she?"

I turn around, slowly, wondering how my overactive imagination conjured up Banning here at the recital, of all places. As I catch sight of him, standing a couple of steps behind me, all I can think is: *Boy, my imagination did a good job, because he looks better than ever. And, you know, yummy.*

He also looks tired, but he smiles at me. That slow, sexy smile that always sends tingles up my spine. "Hi, Kirby. I got your phone message."

Lauren skips in front of me and looks up at him. "Are you Kirby's boyfriend? Did you know Mr. Bunny? Have you been to the carrot farm? Do you know that I'm a bunny? Do you want to come to lunch and eat McCarrots with us? Except, we're really having Happy Meals, not carrots, but you can come and hear all about my recital. Okay? Well, *say* something, already!"

Banning's smile widens, and he shakes Lauren's hand, solemnly. "I'm Banning. Yes, I'm Kirby's boyfriend. Or at least, I'd like to be, if she'll let me. I think carrots are gross, but I love French fries. And I'd love to hear every detail of your recital, if you think Kirby will let me come along."

Anya finally speaks up. "Well, if *she* won't, I will. Kirby, don't leave this fine-looking man just standing there. Let's get going, before we all starve to death."

As we walk along toward McDonald's, with Lauren skipping along in front of us, holding her mother's hand and chattering happily, Banning reaches out and takes my hand. "I called your house this morning, and your mother told me where you were. I hope you don't mind. She said, 'I can tell the difference between a nice man and a scum-sucking pig just by his voice, thank you very much.' Want to let me in on what the heck *that* was about?"

I laugh and squeeze his hand. "Nope. Well, maybe later. Why were you calling?"

"For lots of reasons, but here are the top three. First, since I'm not your boss anymore, will you go out with me? A lot, like maybe for the next ten or twenty years? I think it's going to take me that long to figure you out."

"Hey!" I pull my hand free and punch him in the arm. "A woman *likes* to be mysterious. And, yes, I might have an opening in my calendar. Let's try the first year or two and see how it goes, though, okay?"

We stop, waiting for the light so we can cross the street. "What are the second and third?"

"Second, my mom is in town for the week, and I was hoping you'd go to lunch with us tomorrow at the Four Seasons. She's going to love you."

The light changes, and we start across the street. "Sure. Or, I would if I weren't getting on a plane in the morning, and—" Suddenly, I stop dead, right in the middle of the street.

"Did you just invite me to Sunday lunch? With your *mother*?"

He shrugs, then looks around and starts pulling me the rest of the way across the street, to where Lauren and Anya are laughing at us from the sidewalk. "Yes. Although, I have to warn you that I almost never bring women to meet my mother, so be prepared for a little interrogation. She's one of *those* mothers. Overly protective, you know?"

I shout out a burst of laughter, thinking of Anya with Lauren, and Mom brandishing the closet rod at Daniel. "Aren't they all? And the third?"

We finally reach McDonald's, and Lauren and Anya walk in ahead of us. Banning pulls me back as I start to walk inside. "The third reason, Kirby, is that I've spent the past five months getting to know you better and better. The more I know about you, the more I like. You're hardheaded, stubborn, critical, and demanding. You're also generous to a fault—yes, I heard about your secretary taking time off for the opera audition—brilliant, funny as hell, and the most beautiful woman I've ever known."

I stand there, mouth falling open, as the sexiest, smartest, funniest man *I've* ever known makes a speech about how terrific I am.

Right there in front of McDonald's. *Yep, it's real all right.*

He gently grasps my shoulders with his hands. "So the third reason, Kirby Green, is that I happen to like the sound of your voice. And I was looking up the price of tickets to Italy for, oh, the final week of your vacation, and wondering if you would mind having some company intrude on your vacation with your friend . . ."

Then I kiss him. I can't help it; it's the least romantic place in the history of the world, but I kiss him. Even better, he kisses me back. It's a steamy kiss, way better suited for indoors than for the sidewalk outside of a hamburger joint.

I pull back and look into his eyes, and an unmistakable truth occurs to me.

It's raining on us.

As I start to laugh, the door bangs open. "Kirby! Are you coming or what? The toy in the Happy Meal is a bunny! Can you believe it? It's like you had psychic powers to bring us to this very restaurant when I'm a bunny and there's a bunny toy! Do you have EST or something? I'm totally telling Mommy that you're a psychic!" Lauren races back inside.

Banning leans down and kisses me again, then gently pulls me toward the door. "So, are you 'totally psychic,' Kirby? With EST, even?" He laughs and opens the door.

As I walk past him, inhaling the aroma of French fries and drinking in the sight of Lauren dancing along the aisle in her bunny costume, I sigh. "You know what, Banning? I'm pretty sure that I'm not. Because I never would have foreseen that I'd be this happy."

I'm Kirby Green, and I sell sex toys for a living. But, you know what? I found a nice guy. Or maybe he found me. Either way, I'm finally going to Sunday dinner—well, in three weeks, I am.

I am *una brava ragazza*. And life totally rocks.

39

Kirby

Ciao. (Hello.)

IN ITALY—Journal of Kirby Green, Novelist and Nice Girl

So, Jules's dad finally got back to me. He and his agent loved my first hundred pages and synopsis and want me to finish as quickly as I can. His agent is sure she can sell it. Not in a huge, million-dollar, *Today* show kind of way, but just to get published would be a start. Tom reminded me that he sold his first book for five grand, and look where he is now! The only change they wanted was in the title. They think *Nice Girls Finish First* would be much catchier.

The way I'm feeling these days, I had to agree.

So it's February fifth, and I'm writing this from Italy, sitting at a tiny café in Rome. I'm loving life. With a little luck (and a lot of hard work), maybe it won't be too long before I can pursue the writing dreams that Jules's parents fostered in me, their "other" daughter.

I just finished writing out postcards for Mom, Lauren, Anya, and Bree. I'm going to have to buy another suitcase to fit all the presents I've bought them! Now I'm sitting here at this tiny café, enjoying hot Italian coffee and the warmth of the hot Italian sun. (Yes, it's winter, but at least it's not raining!)

As I look up, I see Jules dancing down the street, holding Sam's hand. I'm so glad to finally be totally happy for her. It's amazing how being content in my own life helps me to be happy for everybody else. Oops, I'd better go now. Banning is here with the pastries, and I'm going to eat one. Or maybe two. And let him kiss me in public, even.

Self-discipline is so overrated.

Am I reformed? Am I "nice" now? Well, maybe. But you might want to check the local hospitals for that guy who grabbed my ass near the Trevi Fountain. His hand's probably broken. *Nice* may make the world go round, but a little toughness is always a good thing.

Ciao.

Epilogue

Seen in *Opera News* magazine:

March 1— . . . Seattle music director announces acquisition of stunning new coloratura Brianna Higgins. For the past seven years, Higgins trained with the legendary Madame Gabriella . . .

Dear Reader,

Thank you for spending some time with Kirby and Brianna. If you liked Kirby's friend Jules, you can read her story in American Idle, *available in August 2005 in mass market paperback. Also, watch for C. J. Murphy's story in* The Naked Truth, *an anthology coming from Berkley trade in October 2005! And you'll find Shane Madison's story in* The Breakup Artist, *coming from Berkley trade in 2006.*

If you like a little thriller with your humor (Hot guys! Knuckle-biting courtroom scenes! Alligators!), check out my new series of funny legal thrillers, beginning with Murder by Mass Tort, *coming soon from Berkley Prime Crime. Trial lawyer Alex Vaughn left her big-city law firm up north to open a solo practice in small-town Florida, but she never dreamed she'd get in quite so much trouble . . .*

For more exciting news and release dates, please visit me at www.alesiaholliday.com.

Happy reading!
Alesia